Till Death Us Do Part

Penn and Ink Publishing, L.L.C.
www.pennandinkpublishing.com
in collaboration with Booklocker.com
www.booklocker.com
2006

Till Death Us Do Part

Terrence O'Neill

Andy'
Many thanks '
I appreciate your spirit

Terry

For Barbara

Who makes me whole

Acknowledgements

While writing is a solitary endeavor, books do not take shape in isolation. I wish to thank those who were most helpful to my bringing this work to print. I offer my thanks to:

The Rev. Pete Hults, retired United States Navy, who shared his seafaring stories with a generous dash of salt;

Nate Leslie, Ph.D. author, professor, relentless critic and editor who offered early words of encouragement and inspired doggedness;

Allen Gee, Ph.D. author, professor and apologetic though relentless critic, who like Nate, offered encouragement and expertise;

Charles Peterson, M. D., physician and friend, who first answered my question about how to murder a cancer chemo patient undetected before asking me why I wanted to know;

Wayne Penn, who painstakingly provided copyediting;

The congregation of the McKownville United Methodist Church and the Troy Annual Conference of United Methodist Churches both of which helped underwrite the sabbatical during which the first draft of this novel came to be;

The *McKownville Readers* who dared to read unpublished fiction and bravely tell the author about two dimensional characters;

Countless friends who have patiently listened to me obsess while their eyes glazed over;

My wife, Barbara, who bloodied her fingers at the keyboard and believed in me as well as the story.

OCTOBER 30TH
THURSDAY

Naked, Sarah stood admiring herself before the mirror tiled wall in the bathroom. Not bad, she thought. In fact, pretty good. For someone in her thirties, the decade of decline according to a recent woman's magazine, she had held up well. Even after her second child her tummy had snapped back into shape. Stretch marks were nearly invisible. Her 120 pounds were only five pounds more than she had weighed after graduating from high school. Her long red hair still had bounce, shine and its own color. She still had a great figure, and turned heads in her bikini.

She thought one of her best features were her breasts; they remained round and rode high on her chest. They reminded her of the old junior high joke – 'what's the difference between a stickup and a holdup? Age!' As she combed out her hair, she draped it over the front of her shoulders like a frame - oh, if daddy could see me now, he'd send me straight to hell.

Sarah laughed under her breath. If Eddie saw me now, he'd get so turned on he'd have me on my back and send me straight on to heaven. Maybe. It had been a while. Maybe I should see.

Sarah picked up her hunter green satin robe from the black and white tile floor, slipped into it and arranged the collar and her hair again. She sprayed the air with Eddie's favorite perfume then stepped into the descending cloud. Let's see if I can get his motor running this morning.

After stepping out of the bathroom she headed downstairs and into the kitchen. Eddie sat sideways at the breakfast table reading the paper and sucking on his third cup of coffee. When he was on second shift at the mill, he tended to be pretty lazy in the mornings. She moved up behind him and began to massage his shoulders.

"Hmm. That feels good, sugar," he said but continued to look at his paper.

She moved her hands down the front of his shirt and ran them across Eddie's chest and over to his ribs and back again. She caressed the back of his head between her breasts and began to make gentle cooing sounds. Eddie relaxed the paper to the table top and she moved around in front of him and said softly, "Eddie..."

"Hmm?" he grunted from behind closed eyes.

"Eddie, the kids are at school. Let's go back upstairs." Her voice was as soft and seductive as her satin robe. She stepped over his lap, sat straddling his hips with her knees and leaned over and kissed him deeply. She could feel him rise through his Lee Riders.

When she gave him a chance to breathe, he asked, "Do you think we should try? I mean, so soon after last time?" His face had the look of a worried and reluctant little boy being dared by his classmates to jump into a river from a bridge.

"Sure, Eddie," Sarah cooed, "you're my man. You'll send me to heaven. You'll send us both to heaven. You'll see." She took to her feet, and her robe fell open enough to expose the roundness of her breasts. She took Eddie by the hand and led him upstairs.

Once upstairs, she continued to take the lead, bringing the collar of her robe down off her shoulders, fully exposing her torso. She knew what Eddie liked to fixate upon. She managed to unbutton his flannel shirt in a seamless motion, and kissing his chest while pulling his shirt over his shoulders, she felt his arousal through his tensing muscles. Then she stood back and dropped her robe to the floor. "That's my man, Eddie."

She stepped into him and reached for his belt buckle. He gently brushed her hands away, unfastened his jeans and removed them, first hopping on one leg and then the other in a vain attempt at grace. She stifled a giggle.

While he was still off balance, she shoved him backwards onto the bed. Following after him she straddled his hips with her knees and felt his excitement brush lightly along the inside of her left thigh. She took his arms and spread them eagle fashion then leaned over to massage his face with her prized breasts. "You're gonna send us both to heaven, Eddie, aren't you?"

"I hope so." He closed his eyes as Sarah caressed his face. "You know I ain't quite been up to it lately. And I got another one of those threats in my locker at work."

"Don't worry about them lover," she cooed. "They're just bullies too lazy to work for their families." Knowing she had better act fast before

Eddie worried more, she lifted herself upright, reached back to guide Eddie to the holiest of holies but found him flaccid.

"Eddie!" She sidled off, kneeled on the bed next to him wearing a new pout and swatted at his manhood as if cuffing a disobedient child.

"Damn it, woman," he said. He rolled out of bed and held his wounded pride. "You hurt me."

She grunted.

"I told you," Eddie said, "After the other night I didn't think I was ready for this." He stood naked facing her. "Besides, the mill strike, the death threat, you after me to cross the picket lines. I'm all wound up."

She stood next to the bed with her hands on her hips. "You could have been more insistent. But no, you brought me up here to tease me." She put on her robe and turned to go.

"I teased you?"

She turned to face Eddie. "You primed me, and now I'm all frustrated."

Eddie's kicked puppy look was fading, and his jaw took on an angry set. Sarah turned to leave and was surprised by a sudden grip on her right arm as she was spun back around.

"Damn it Sarah, you wanted to hurt me, didn't you?" He gripped both of her shoulders. "Why are you doing this? You know I've got a lot on my mind."

"You're hurting me." She struggled against his grip, but Eddie tightened it. "Do you have to hurt me to feel like a man? You're no man, Eddie! A real man would walk through those picket lines every day for his family."

"For godsake, Sarah," he said and gave her a shake. "Somebody's threatening to kill me!"

"Ha! Some mill town bully puts a note in your locker like a high school prankster and you want to run home to mama. Get a grip."

His eyes narrowed, and his face reddened. His breaths became deeper and heavy.

"Don't you have any ambition? She asked. "Don't you want nice things? Don't you want to see me in pretty clothes?"

She could see the muscle move beneath the skin of his cheek as his jaw clenched. Something guttural sounded from deep inside and she wondered if she'd pressed too far. She'd never seen him so angry before, but she didn't care. Her arms hurt and she wanted to hurt him back.

"And when he got home," she continued, "he'd send his wife to heaven every night!"

"You bitch!" he shouted, then lifted her off her feet and threw her on the bed where she struck the side of her face against the headboard. "You're

3

turning into a damn nympho." He picked up his jeans and shirt, and dressed himself.

She sat holding her bruised head with one hand and supporting herself with the other. "Do you want to live in this tiny dump forever? Don't you want a bigger house, a big yard?" Her voice rose with anger, "Don't you want a nice car instead of an old pickup, a little respect in this pissant town?" Her frustration welled up in tears, and she hated herself for crying.

"No, Sarah," he said and sat on the opposite side of the bed with his back to her. He slipped into his work boots and laced them. "That's what you want. I just want to get along. Do my job. See friends. I don't want to be plant manager and hobnob with the hoity-toity. That's your dream, not mine." He turned to leave, and pausing at the open bedroom door added, "Sarah, crossing the picket line is dangerous. In other towns, where the union is on strike against the company, guys who cross the line have their cars and houses fire bombed." He disappeared from view.

"Those are just rumors to scare candy-asses like you into toeing the union line, and keeping you poor so you have to lean on the union bosses!" she called out after him.

Sarah pounded her fist into the mattress, "Damn him, for being so weak." She could hear Eddie descend the stairs and listened as he rattled the coffee pot and slammed the door to the cellar. Good, let him pout in the cellar.

She sat in the bed with arms crossed, rubbing her bruised shoulders and nurturing her bruised pride. Twelve years of marriage and all I have to show for it are two brats, a hovel, and a wimp of a husband who isn't even respected by his low-life friends.

Eddie didn't know if he was more hurt or angry. He clomped down the cellar stairs and at the foot of the stairs yanked the pull cord on the overhead ceramic light fixture. The sixty watt GE soft white popped a strobe signaling the end of its short life. Son-of-a-bitch. Can't somebody invent a light bulb that'll last longer than a week? He made his way across the dim cellar towards his heavy wooden workbench with the aid of the light shining in through the foundation window behind him near the stairs. At his bench he pulled over the arm of his architect's lamp and turned it on. At least that worked. He set his coffee down.

His old Mossberg model 800A three-oh-eight deer rifle lay on the bench before him. Two nights before, Eddie had finished the last third shift rotation at the mill and spent a rainy day hunting with his friend, Bucky. After spending the morning and early afternoon in the field, the two of them had barely enough time to shower, shave, change clothes, and head back to the mill the previous day to begin their second shift rotation.

They both agreed that it was pretty stupid to return to work exhausted and blurry-eyed to manage machinery that could suck you in whole at one end and spit you out looking like thick ketchup at the other. They had both seen the occasional red stain pass before them signaling someone's lost finger or hand.

But, what-the-hey, you only live once, and hunting season was short. After the rainy hunt, there was not time for Eddie to properly clean his rifle as was his custom after each use. He managed only to run a cleaning rag soaked in Hoppe's number nine solvent through the barrel and leave it soak overnight. He had laid it on the bench for its cleaning first thing the next day.

Picking it up and removing the bolt, Eddie held it up to the light to peer through the barrel. It was dirty, but his cursory care the day before prevented any light rust from starting. He clicked his tongue and thought, you're getting lazy in your old age, Eddie. You know you should do this as soon as you come in from the field.

A chair scraped across the kitchen floor overhead and he could hear Sarah's feet pad along. The bitch had come down from the bedroom. She'd damn well better not come down here. Eddie could feel his anger well up again. No, he thought to himself, I will not let her come down here. Not even in my head. He hefted the rifle from the bench and shouldered it. He could smell last night's solvent, and the feel of the polished wood stock took him mentally back into the woods and the hunt.

Using a bore brush, more powder solvent, and following with cleaning patches made from his old BVDs, and a touch of gun oil, Eddie cleaned and readied his deer rifle for its next kill. Finishing, he leaned the gun against the end of the bench as a reminder to take it upstairs to the gun cabinet.

With practiced ritual, Eddie prepared to steep himself in the husbandry of his reloading hobby. He loaded used brass into a cleaning tumbler with crushed walnut shells and turned it on. The rhythmic sound of the rolling empty cartridges in the square tumbler was the first step towards drowning out the concerns of life pressing in. Next, he measured the grains of powder for each round. Other reloaders used a simple measuring gauge, but not Eddie. He wanted each of his rounds to be precise and accurate. The powder for each was scale measured, and carefully funneled down the neck of freshly cleaned and primered casings.

His narrow focus forced out of his consciousness the footfalls of his wife overhead.

Eddie was particularly proud of the fact that he molded his own slugs. By trial and error, he had come up with what he considered the perfect alloy combination of old printer's type and used lead wheel weights that Rene saved for him down at the Mobil station.

Out in his garage, Eddie would melt the type and weights in a small cast iron pot heated over a Coleman camp stove. Meticulously he would mold one slug after another, inspecting each with the eye of a master craftsman. After molding the semiwadcutter slugs, he brought them into his cellar to the reloading bench, placed them in a cotton lined jig on his drill press and hollowed the noses with surgical precision. He preferred the feather sharp edge left by the drill bit over the thicker hollow point formed by a different mold. Eddie then slipped the slug into the jacket press and dressed it in a half copper jacket so the slug would keep its shape through the rifle barrel and along its hot trajectory as it searched out a target.

Eddie seated slugs into casings and crimped them securely with the care and pride attributed only to sculptors, painters, and other artisans. The rhythm and concentration of his work brought him the only peace he had recently known.

With the pride of all creators, but far less imagination, he named his creation The Deer Slayer.

Eddie labored the morning and early afternoon away mindless of his dissatisfied wife, mindless of his co-workers' expectations of his joining them on the picket line, and mindless even of his grumbling stomach demanding lunch.

Having finished several boxes of The Deer Slayer, he prepared two to give away – one to his father-in-law, and one for Bucky. For his father-in-law, he jotted a note about the trajectory properties in case dad used the rounds before Eddie had a chance to see him. This done, he turned off his bench light, picked up three boxes of ammo and his rifle, and headed upstairs.

Entering the kitchen from the cellar way, he found Sarah at the table reading a romance novel. "Hmph, that's all you think about, isn't it?" Eddie said as he passed by on the way to the living room.

Sarah was silent.

Eddie put his rifle in the maple and glass display cabinet he had built six years back, and placed a box of ammo in the drawer under the cabinet. Returning to the kitchen, he stopped at the back door and slipped a box into the pocket of his coat hanging on the doorknob. He moved to the table and placed the box with the note in front of Sarah. "Will ya give these to your father?"

Without looking up from her book, Sarah said, "Why don't you do it yourself?"

"Because I won't see him for a day or two. He might want to use these."

"Hmm."

Returning to the door and putting on his coat, Eddie said, "I'm going in."

"To picket, or to work?" Sarah asked, drawing back the corner of her mouth and finally looking at him.

"I haven't decided," he said and turned for the door. He nearly shivered at the chill of her accusation.

"You haven't eaten lunch," she reminded him.

"I'll pick up a beer on the way in." He closed the door behind him as he headed for his pickup. He wasn't sure if he heard a hint of concern in her voice, or just another slur about his foolishness.

The Reverend Keegan O'Connor sat back from his desk, easing his spine into the old leather of his study chair. He removed his glasses, placing them on the denominational reports resting on his highly polished cherry desk. Working since "oh six hundred hours", he paused to push his face into the palms of his hands, first massaging his forehead with his fingertips, then rubbing his eyes and finally slipping his hands down the side of his face, contorting his cheeks. The headache he awoke with three hours earlier was not getting any better.

Leaning back, he stared at his books lining the walnut shelves along the dark mahogany paneled walls. The church study had an old, secure and permanent feel about it. There was a palpable male atmosphere that made Keegan, a veteran U.S. Navy Chief Hospital Corpsman, feel right at home. Stroking his chinstrap beard he wondered, who would have thought more than thirty years ago aboard ship off 'Nam I'd be pastoring people in the Adirondack Mountains of New York?

Twenty years in the United States Navy seemed a distant memory at times, but the years had made their indelible mark on him. Some of his Navy habits had endeared him to the parishioners of Grace United Methodist Church. They often remarked about how they liked his sermons sprinkled with sea or war stories. Stories like the one of a visit to a particular foreign port resulting in penicillin shots for all those who had gone ashore made him real to his people.

Other habits had not endeared Keegan to the church folk. Calling one of the church trustees a silly-ass-stupid-son-of-a-bitch had been a major faux pas. And the evening he angrily and publicly reprimanded the church treasurer for spending mission funds on the fuel bill had not been a good one. Her leaving the council meeting in tears had definitely not endeared him to the people. But, that was then, and this was now. His temper was under much better control. His occasional outbursts he simply considered being genuinely human. Other than that, he thought sometimes the church suffered from "terminal niceness."

Keegan sat upright, put on his glasses, and began to reach for the desk phone, then withdrew his hand. It was still a little too early to be checking in on his wife to see how she was feeling this morning. Besides, Doctor Eileen Letterman-O'Connor would only remind him that he was being over protective and interfering with her sense of independence. Sometimes his wife didn't know when to stop being a psychologist. MaryKay from next door had probably not yet finished helping Eileen with her bath and breakfast.

Eileen had grown considerably weaker over the last month with her cancer. The mastectomy had been difficult enough, but now the post surgical chemotherapy was knocking the hell out of her. She still had strength enough to walk about the house, moving her hands from walls to furniture, back to walls, while maintaining her balance. She had seen MaryKay's presence over recent weeks not so much as help, but as company. So, when MaryKay came over to keep Eileen company, they had breakfast together, and MaryKay would casually suggest she draw a bath for Eileen, or they would walk together to the back deck to enjoy some sun. Easing back into his chair, Keegan wondered at the compassion of MaryKay to be of such intimate service to Eileen which allowed Keegan to continue on with his pastoral responsibilities.

Work, a coping mechanism for Keegan developed in 'Nam aboard ship, allowed him to both face and escape Eileen's potentially terminal condition. The breast cancer had not been caught early, so her chances were less than fifty-fifty.

The image of Eileen's failing condition flooded Keegan's mind. Her five foot, six inch frame had slipped to just under one hundred pounds. She wore an assortment of colorful scarves on her head to replace the long beautiful brown hair she had lost to the chemo treatments at the Adirondack Regional Medical Center. She grew increasingly fatigued, sometimes nodding off in mid conversation. Keegan had been through this many times with parishioners, but this time the specter of death was visiting home. He sank a little deeper in his chair.

Dear Lord, he prayed within his mind, allow healing to come to Eileen. I need her so much. I cannot imagine life without her. Keegan sat in silence with his eyes closed for a moment. If healing is not your will, Lord, he thought to God, then at least let me have understanding and acceptance. Disturbing his meditation, he heard the familiar footfalls of his secretary approaching from down the hall.

"Good morning, Keegan," called Grace, as she swung open the hall door to her adjoining office. Keegan could hear the rattle of coat hangers as Grace hung her coat in the wardrobe near the door.

Keegan answered with one of his pat good natured responses to perfunctory greetings, "What's good about it?"

As Grace settled in at her desk, within sight of Keegan through the opened inner office doors, she responded, "The sun's shining, the Canada geese are honking as they head south, and I'm shuck of my ol' husband for the week while he's at camp duck hunting. That's what's good about it!" Grace continued to get ready for her day, removing the cover from her computer, turning the intercom on, and sorting the mail she had brought in with her. "What puts you in such a fine mood?" she called.

Straightening a bit in his chair, it would not do for a crew member to see the chief flagging on duty, Keegan said, "Denominational reports. Bane of the church. You'd think the church was in the paper business, not the religion business."

"Folks around the mill would be most pleased to hear that," Grace said in a jestful scold. As she turned to her computer, she offered as an afterthought, "It might be good for more of the men on the picket lines in front of the mill to think of the church as a source of their job security, instead of the meeting place for the ladies aid society."

Keegan did not answer, but returned his attention to the reports on his desk. His attention span wasn't what it used to be. He could stare at reports for long minutes, absorbing nothing, then suddenly realize he'd been mentally drifting off to Eileen or recalling bloody bouts of triage on board ship. It seemed any time he was under stress he'd find himself recalling the war years. Each time he'd come to himself, he whispered a prayer of thanks that war and bloodshed were in the past and not a part of his daily life any longer.

The headache he'd been growing through the early morning had not subsided. He reached into his desk drawer and retrieved a small bottle of Tylenol. He snapped the top and dumped out the last two caplets. He popped them in his mouth and swallowed them with a gulp of coffee. He placed the empty bottle in his jacket pocket to refill at home.

Once again, he turned his attention to the reports, resolving to finish them one way or another before heading home to make lunch for Eileen at noon.

Barbara Ross heard a knock at her back door from her living room easy chair. She put down her copy of *Ladies' Home Journal* and headed for the kitchen to answer. Upon opening the door, she saw Sarah presenting a Millie's Bakery waxed bag.

Barb was four years older than Sarah and had been in Fort George little more than two years – a result of following her husband Wayne's career through the middle management of United Paper Company. She had heard that moving into a small town of five thousand or so could be hard on an outsider, but she could not have prepared herself for the Adirondack experience of both social and geographic isolation. Just as Barbara had come to realize the seclusion of her new home, Sarah showed up. Sarah had been the first person in town to greet Barb, stopping by her home with a pound cake to welcome the family to the neighborhood. The two had been friends ever since, with a weekly offering at one or the other's kitchen table of home baked goods or muffins from Millie's.

"Hi, Barb," Sarah said, holding aloft her bag, "I brought raisin bran muffins. I'll make a regular country girl of ya yet."

The two laughed.

"Great. Come in," said Barbara. Her golden retriever, Nutmeg, roused by Sarah's voice, came flying downstairs from her nap happily bounding out the door. Ears sailing, tongue flying, the dog lunged at Sarah full force, hitting her with both front paws high on the chest in the middle of her sternum and knocking her to the ground. Sarah screamed.

Barbara yelled.

The dog licked at Sarah's face.

"Oh my God," Barbara said, kneeling at Sarah's side and fussing. "Are you all right? Nutmeg, get lost!"

The dog stepped back with tongue hanging, tail wagging and face full of anticipation.

"Did you hit your head?" Barbara fussed. "Should I call an ambulance? Are you ...good grief you're bruising already. Look at your face."

"I'm okay." Sarah said, catching her breath and slowly sitting up. "Nutmeg just knocked the wind out of me." At the sound of her name, the dog came back to Sarah licking at her face and hands.

Barbara helped Sarah to her feet and ushered her into the house. The dog happily trailed along until Barbara sent her back outside Barb helped Sarah off with her coat and draped it over the back of a kitchen chair. Then, holding Sarah gently by the hands, she asked, "Are you sure you're all right? I'll call the doctor, if you'd like."

"No, I'm fine, Barb, just relax," Sarah said.

"Well, then sit down and catch your breath," Barb said. "I'll put the water on for tea."

Sarah dusted herself off and sat down.

"With the bruise you'll get from that dog," Barb said, "people will think Eddie beats you."

Sarah glanced at Barbara but didn't respond, instead fixing her gaze out the kitchen door window towards her own house.

"So, how are things going for you and Eddie with the strike on?" Barbara asked. She busied herself with the kettle, mugs, and tea bags. "Wayne tells me it's getting pretty nasty in other states where United has mills."

"It's okay. Eddie says some of the boys are making a lot of noise, and threats." With the familiarity that comes with close friendships Sarah rose and found silverware for the table, split the muffins, and placed them in Barb's microwave to warm. "Nothing has happened around here that we know of." She folded her arms and leaned against the counter, waiting for the oven timer to buzz. "Some sleaze left a death threat for Eddie in his locker."

"Oh, Sarah!" Barb said, turning to Sarah. "Some awful things have happened to scabs up in New Hampshire." She leaned against the stove. Furrowing her brow she added, "Their houses have been burned. I can't imagine people doing that!"

"It's an awful time," Sarah said. The oven buzzer sounded, and she turned to take out the muffins. "Eddie says he's worried about what could happen in Fort George."

The wife of management and the wife of labor sat at the kitchen table over tea and shared their muffins and concerns for their community and their husbands. With the expressions of worry that wives have when their men are on opposing sides of the same issue, the two sat in long silence, comforting one another with their presence.

Barb warmed her hands around her mug. Sarah leaned back into her chair, and with folded arms rubbed at her shoulders.

"Are you cold?" Barb asked.

"Hmm?" answered Sarah. She stopped rubbing, and just held herself. "I'm fine. Why do you ask?"

"You're rubbing your arms. I thought maybe you were cold, or hurt." Barb got up to check the thermostat. "It's seventy." She headed back for the table. "You're already wearing a sweater. Are you coming down with something?" Barbara placed her wrist on Sarah's forehead.

"Good grief, what a mother hen," Sarah said as she removed Barbara's hand from her brow. "Your chicks are at school." Stroking her arms, "I'm fine. It's just that –"

"The dog! She's really hurt you! Oh, Sarah, how can I ever –"

"Barbara, stop," Sarah said. "It's not the dog's fault."

Returning to her seat, and leaning over her mug, Barbara encouraged Sarah, "Then what? Is there something you want to tell me?"

"I got a little bruised up this morning."

"I'm sure," said Barbara, "that d –"

"Will you stop with the dog," Sarah said with raised voice. Then, a bit softer, "It was Eddie. Your little joke about his beating me isn't so funny. He hit me." She put her face into her hands as if to hide her shame.

Barbara rushed to Sarah's side, and held her. "Oh Sarah, I'm so sorry. How long has this been going on?"

"It's not regular," Sarah said, turning into Barbara's embrace. "It's just that he's so worried about what's happening at the mill."

"Don't you make excuses for him," Barbara said, stroking her hair. "There's never a reason he should hit you. Never."

"I know, Barbara. He didn't mean it." Sarah straightened up in her chair.

"I hear lines like that from women when I volunteer at the church's food pantry nearly every week. I think every man who hits a woman means it. And after he apologizes, he means to do it again. You've got to get help, Sarah."

"It would only make things worse."

"You're sounding like a battered wife, Sarah," Barbara said with sternness she was unaccustomed to hearing from herself. "I won't let a friend of mine be a battered wife. There's a women's shelter in town if you need it, or you can stay here. You can see my pastor, Reverend O'Connor, for counseling. Maybe he can talk to Eddie."

"Barbara, stop!" Sarah looked near to tears. "I think I'd better go." She stood up and put her coat on.

"Sarah, please, I'm sorry for rushing on. Please stay."

"I can't talk about this any more. I've said too much already." Stopping at the door, she said, "This is something a wife should settle with her husband on her own."

The wood yard at the mill was several acres of sailing overhead cranes, stacked logs, idling tandem trailer log trucks, chain draped grunting log skidders, whining fork lifts, sucking mud, flying wood chips, and yelling men. At ten minutes before eleven that night, the yard was soaked in the sallow moonbeams of mercury vapor lights that stood sentry around the perimeter.

Eddie finished checking in a late load of wood from a logger then gave instructions to the substitute crane operator to unload the truck and put the logs on the far side of the yard. Eddie handed the logger his receipt, "Jack, you must be about ready to head home for the wife and kids."

"You bet partner!" the logger said, wiping his brow with his forearm. "It's been a hell of a day in the woods. But I got a bear while I was in there."

"You don't say!" Eddie's interest was piqued; there was always time to chat with a fellow hunter. "How big was it?"

The logger smiled through his grime, turned to climb up on the back of his truck and called back, "Come on up and take a look."

Eddie climbed up onto the forward section of the trailer near the small loading crane. There on the trailer bed, tucked in alongside the loading crane among the tie-down chains, was a large black bear. "That's a definite prize!" Eddie bent down to heft the fore paw. "Look at the size of that big boy's claws!"

"I got him while sitting on my skidder. He never knew what hit him."

"I hope I have that kind of luck this season." Eddie said while jumping off the truck.

"Good luck," the logger said.

"Thanks, Jack." Eddie turned with a wave to head into the shop. He had seen that logger for years, exchanged pleasantries with him from time to time, knew he had a wife and three sons, but had no idea where he lived or what his name was. He was just Jack, like every other lumberjack.

As Eddie walked across the yard lost in his thoughts, he heard a shout, then his name, the blast of the shift whistle, and suddenly the earth shook as a half dozen logs slammed to the ground next to him. The last log to hit bounced off the others and slid toward him, caught him behind the legs and threw him backwards over on top of the logs.

Men came running from all directions. The young crane operator climbed down from his station and ran across the yard. With the help of a couple of men, Eddie regained his footing. Rasping for breath, he asked, "What the hell happened?"

"The crane lost its load," one of the yardmen said.

The crane operator arrived, out of breath and with a worried look on his face. As he pushed through the assembling crowd he asked, "Is he all right? Seeing he was alive, the operator said, "It was an accident buddy, I'm sorry. I ain't used to this crane. They got me on it 'cause of the strike. It ain't my fault, ya see?"

Regaining his wind, and feeling his fear turn to anger, Eddie said, "You the guy that dropped this on me? One of the union bosses got you arrangin' an accidental death? Huh?"

"It ain't my fault, pal, it was an accident."

"Yeah? So's this!" Eddie brought up his fist and popped the substitute in the nose.

"Hey, Eddie, there's no call for that!" a yardman stated. "The kid's green."

Blood flowed easily and instantly from the howling operator's nose. "Ya broke my nose, ya son-of-a-bitch!"

"Be glad that's all I broke!" Eddie said, as he pushed by everyone and headed into the shop.

The crane operator called after him but made no move from the safety of the onlookers.

Inside, Eddie opened his locker to put his hard hat and work sheets away. On the shelf, propped against the side, was an envelope addressed, SCAB. He opened it and read, "If not today, then tonight. If not tonight, then soon. Death to all scabs." Eddie stuffed the note in his shirt pocket, slammed the locker door shut and headed for the time clock. Most of the shift had passed through already with only a few stragglers lined up. He heard a couple discuss the picket lines outside.

"Man, I hate this. These guys hate my guts," moaned one on line at the punch clock.

"Yeah, but they ain't paying my mortgage," another man said.

"Or feeding my kids," a third said, clutching a lunch pail with a broken handle under his arm.

"My wife wants a dishwasher," the first man said, now beyond the clock.

"Bullshit on that, man," the third said. "Let her cross the lines."

There was nervous laughter and general agreement. "Yeah, bullshit," echoed down the line.

One by one the men punched their time cards and walked out of the shop door into the night.

"Watch your asses," the man with the lunch pail called.

"Back at ya," Eddie shouted.

As Eddie got into his truck and started it, he could see the fires burning in the fifty-five gallon drums the picket line had set up for warmth. Signal fires of the enemy encampment. He cursed his bad luck at having missed the mass exodus of the shift where he could have blended in with the dozens of cars and pickups leaving the mill. Now he was just one of a dozen or so. He'd be recognized and hear about it. If not tonight, then soon.

He pulled up behind three other cars at the chain link and razor-wire gate. The company security guards opened the gate, and the cars filed out. Once they were on public property, they were on their own. The first two cars barreled on through. The guy in the ten year old Mustang in front of Eddie lost his clutch and stalled the old Ford. Pickets surrounded the car, shouted obscenities, slapped the hood, and began rocking the car. Finally, three men got behind it and lifted the rear drive wheels off the pavement. The man inside looked terrified.

A number of the men on line called out to discourage the violence and stepped in. Their attempts at reason were elbowed out of the way, and they withdrew into the night as if to hide out of disgust or fear.

Some of the harassing pickets began to turn their attention towards Eddie. One thumped his fender with a baseball bat. "Lay off!" Eddie shouted.

The Mustang was being bounced like a basketball. The guy inside blew his horn relentlessly and stopped only to beat on the inside of his own door as a striker gave him the finger through the window. The three pickets at the rear of the Mustang held it off the ground on its last bounce. The panicked driver finally restarted the car and raced the engine and spun the tires in the air. Shouts, taunts, and laughter echoed. Eddie heard someone close shout, "You're next, Conger!" Eddie turned to his left, and saw the sneering face of Daniel Callahan, union president, pressed up against his window."

Feeling trapped behind the Mustang, Eddie decided to move. He pressed his truck forward slowly, creeping in on the men in front of him who were busy tormenting the Mustang driver. Gently, he nudged the backsides of the tormentors with his bumper. The middle one shouted, "Hey, this bastard's hitting me!"

A baseball bat came down hard on Eddie's hood. He nudged forward again. The three dropped the Mustang and the car's tires squealed when they hit the pavement. The car bucked at the sudden resistance, then lurched forward and sped off.

A dozen men were rocking Eddie's truck. He saw the baseball bat swing through the beam of his head lamp, then heard the smash of

15

breaking glass, and there was darkness to the right side of the truck. Eddie raced the engine, slipped the clutch in and out and lurched the truck, warning off his tormentors. They begrudgingly gave away a little space, but enough for Eddie to wedge his truck forward, gaining speed until he was able to break away. Once on solid pavement Eddie slammed the throttle down and roared off. A final rock was hurled as he drove down the road, landing loudly in his pickup.

"Damn, they're getting mean," Eddie said aloud and let up on the gas. "Some of those guys are out for blood."

He calmed down making his way towards home. He could feel his heart inch itself back down into his chest from his throat. The flush of the adrenaline was passing. He drove past the community hospital on Amherst, turned left onto Benedict, his dead end street, then left again into his driveway.

"Damn," he said, "I'm not ready to face her nonsense." He backed out of his driveway and drove back up Amherst to Route Nine and south until the edge of town at The Stallions Bar and Grill.

The room was dimly lit, and patrons were scattered around tables and along the mahogany bar. The blue-grey haze of cigarette smoke that hung in the air was slowly drawn up to the single ceiling fan in the center of the room which twisted the smoke in ribbons before forcing it down to the floor where it disappeared. The Stallions Bar in Fort George was not a place where word about the no smoking laws was likely to be heeded. Eddie nodded to a few familiar faces as he moved through the room and greeted the bartender. "Hi ya Johnny, make mine a Sam Adams."

"Sure Eddie, how are ya?"

"Oh, fine as hell, John, fine as hell."

Pouring the beer into a glass, the bartender said, "You don't sound so fine."

Picking up his beer, then lifting it in a mocking toast to Johnny, Eddie responded, "Damn, you're perceptive, John. You should close this place down and go into the head shrinkin' business."

"In that case, "Johnny said, "that'll be fifty bucks for the consultation, and the beer's free." Eddie threw a fiver on the bar, and Johnny made change.

At that moment, Eddie felt a hand on his right shoulder.

"Eddie, glad to see you." Larry Dwyer, Eddie's long time hunting and fishing buddy, stood next to him.

"Bucky, I'm surprised to see you here," Eddie said as he gave his friend a jab.

"Geez, Eddie, stop with the Bucky, will ya, call me Larry. Everybody calls me Larry 'cept you." Larry threw his leg around the bar stool and sat.

"Okay, Lawrence," teased Eddie.

"Anyway, why are you surprised to see me?"

"I expected you'd be on the picket line makin' a pain in the ass to guys like me tryin' to make a living." Eddie drew on his beer.

"Naw, I did my bit earlier in the day," Bucky said, leaning on the bar and staring over the top of the beer he brought with him. "I didn't want to freeze my butt off tonight." Screwing up his face, Bucky asked, "You ain't on the line?"

"The wife is giving me a hard time about money," Eddie said. Looking over at his friend and feeling self conscious he added, "I crossed the line and went to work."

"Damn, Eddie, the union is gonna want to hang your hide out to dry. Don't let Callahan see you crossing." Bucky drained his beer and waved to the bartender for another.

"Too late," Eddie said. With elbows on the bar and looking at Bucky over his shoulder he continued, "We were face to face tonight. Him cussing and spitting at me and yelling my name. Me calling him all kinds of a bastard and trying to run him over to get out. Oh, it's definitely too late."

Bucky's brow furrowed. His voice got low and conspiratorial, "Callahan's been making noises all day about taking names and kicking ass. It sounds like you're at the top of his list."

"Ain't life grand?" Eddie said, and finished his beer.

"Eddie," Bucky continued in his worried voice, "this is serious. When he talks about kicking ass, he says things like fire bombing cars and trucks, and maybe a house or two ought to go up in smoke. Callahan's a crazy s.o.b."

"Just talk, Bucky, stop your worrying. It's just talk." Trying to keep his own anxiety under control, Eddie put his hand on Bucky's shoulder and said, "He's running for re-election as union president early, is all." He reached into his jacket pocket and said, "Hey, I brought you something. I was going to drop it off at your house." He placed a box of deer slayers on the bar in front of Bucky.

Bucky took the box and opened it. "Thanks, Eddie." Removing one of the cartridges and rotating it in the dim light in front of his face, admiring its glistening brass, he added, "You sure do nice work."

"These are my best ever," Eddie said smiling with pride, "I tested them on some butternut squash. The slugs mushroom wonderfully."

"I can hardly wait to use them."

"Just remember," coached Eddie, "it's a hot round and right on at a hundred yards. But it drops like a brick after that. The slug's too heavy for those two hundred yard shots you favor. And aim two to three inches low at fifty or twenty-five yards, the slug is still climbing at that distance."

"Sure, I'll remember."

"I'm on second shift tomorrow; you want to look for Bambi in the morning?"

"I can't, Eddie. I'm on picket line duty tomorrow morning. The union has made shift assignments for all of us on strike. We're supposed to make it pretty rough on you scabs."

"Yeah, well, thanks a heap." Eddie could feel his shoulders sag. He waved at Johnny, "Barkeep. Another brewski."

"You know," Bucky said speaking low and confidentially, "you probably ought to get out of here before the rest of these guys get wind that you're a scab. Feelings are running pretty high tonight."

"Yeah, you're probably right," Eddie said paying for the second beer. "I'll leave after I finish this." He took a sip.

The front door of The Stallions opened as Eddie's glass parted his lips, and he heard, "Hey, Conger! Scab! Only real men belong in here!" Eddie turned around in his seat to see that Daniel Callahan had arrived with four lackeys in tow.

Daniel Callahan, union president, bullshit artist, braggart, and general all around pain-in-the-ass bully shouted as he swaggered into the bar holding his arm out as if he were a game show host introducing a new contestant. "Hey, you men! This scab Conger tried to run me down on the picket line tonight!" His face looked as though he smelled a fresh sloppy cow flop.

Eddie turned back towards the bar, returning his attention to his beer. Maybe he'll go away if I ignore him, he thought.

"Scabs should be punished, Conger!" Callahan shouted from the middle of the room. "Who you going to try to run over tomorrow night, Conger?"

Eddie could see Callahan's reflection in the liquor-surrounded mirror behind the bar. Callahan looked like a sad imitation of a western gunslinger calling him out. "You're mistaken, Callahan," Eddie said, "I didn't try to run you over. You accidentally slipped in front of my truck as I was pulling out. It was when you were helping that stalled Mustang in front of me."

Eddie hated this kind of confrontation. Usually people left him alone because of his size.

"I don't see it that way, Conger," Callahan said taking several steps towards him. "I got a score to settle with you."

Eddie turned in his seat and looked past Callahan towards the four men that stood behind him. One hung his head and looked at Eddie under clenched brows. The shortest one, a guy named Mickey Miles, with a squirrel-like pimply face, darted his eyes about the room. The third looked over everyone's heads off into space as if the scene were not happening.

The fourth man, with feet squarely planted and fists clenching and unclenching at his sides, stared directly at Eddie along with his boss. A scar over his left eye split his eyebrow in two. He chewed on a cigar butt. A Macanudo cigar tin poked over the top of his shirt pocket. Eddie thought he could be trouble.

Controlling his fear and reining in his anger, Eddie slowly and deliberately said, "Dan, I only came in here for a brew after a hard night." He locked eyes with Callahan.

"You called trouble back at the mill and trouble's come to answer," Callahan said as he took one step closer to Eddie and stood an arm's length away.

"Good god, Dan," Eddie said shaking his head, "you sound like a bad movie." He started to turn back to his beer when Callahan reached over and pulled his shoulder around.

"Maybe the smoke detectors in your house need to go off one night," Callahan said. His eyes narrowed. "Maybe that'll get your attention."

At the mention of smoke detectors Eddie could feel the safety switch in his head go off. The chamber was loaded; the bolt was closed and ready to fire. As his anger boiled into rage, Eddie brought his steel toed boot up and buried it hard into the bully boy's crotch. Callahan's eyes bugged out, and a breath-filled cry exploded as he began to double over. Before he could fold into an anguished fetal position, Eddie's arm, already cocked, shot his fist into Callahan's nose. Everyone heard the nose break and saw the blood spurt. Eddie knew there'd be hell to pay.

Callahan dropped to the floor, one hand between his legs, and the other holding his nose. Every breath brought a new moan.

The pimply faced squirrel ran out the front door. The other two uncertain lackeys attended their fallen hero, while the fourth with three eyebrows stood maintaining his gunslinger pose.

"You want some of this?" Eddie asked as he stepped towards the man.

Three-brows backed off and to the side and said nothing. Watching the room as he walked, Eddie crossed to the door and left. Shouts of "scab" followed him into the parking lot.

As he walked to his truck he noticed the mill parking sticker on the car parked behind his. It read, "Union President. Lot A. Expires 12/31."

"That son-of-a-bitch," Eddie said aloud. He talks about paper mill jobs going to Japan, and he drives a Toyota! He got into his truck and started the engine. He reached down and moved the transfer case lever from two wheel drive high to four wheel drive. He revved the motor a couple of times, and shifted the transmission into reverse.

Eddie turned in his seat to look over his shoulder and thought, trouble will call for sure. He let the clutch loose and slammed into the Toyota. Eddie was jolted in his truck and pushed the clutch in. The truck rocked forward. He revved the engine and popped the clutch, spinning both rear and front tires. The bumper of the truck rose over the nose of the Toyota, forcing the car's front end down. The truck's rear wheels lost their grip on the pavement and spun in the air. Bar patrons began to pour out of The Stallions. They shouted but Eddie couldn't hear them over his racing engine, and raging mind.

The front wheels of Eddie's truck grabbed hold and forced the skid plates under the rear end of the truck up onto the little car. One of the front tires on the Toyota exploded, dropping the front end even lower. The truck lurched backward, and the bumper smashed through the windshield.

Eddie stepped on the clutch and the truck rested atop the Toyota. "I shouldn't a done that," he said, but with a certain satisfaction and a smirk he shifted the truck into first.

Someone threw a beer bottle at Eddie's truck, smashing it against the side of the passenger door.

Eddie drove off the Toyota, and headed for home. Oh, I'm in deep shit, he thought.

Eddie still wasn't ready to go home and see Sarah. His adrenaline was high, and he thought for sure he'd get into an argument with her. It would be best to cool off. He hadn't finished his last beer, but a stop at another bar seemed out of the question, so he pulled into the Price Chopper grocery parking lot.

Eddie often wondered why the store was open twenty-four hours in such a small burg. Then he decided it was for guys like him who decided on a midnight beer. The rescue squad raced past the parking lot with its strobes flashing as it headed in the direction of The Stallions.

He made his way towards the store, passed the usual assortment of parked cars and pickup trucks and found a nurse, still in her whites, attempting to change a flat tire. She had the jack under the car frame, but

20

resting at a slight angle. The trunk lid was open and bobbing in the night breeze with the spare still resting inside. It looked as if the rescue squad would have to return for this nurse if she continued on.

"Let me take care of that for ya," Eddie said, as he stood at the rear of the car. The nurse turned with a startled look on her face.

"Oh, I didn't hear you approach. You're a Godsend, thank you." She got up and out of the way. "This is awfully nice."

"I just figured the way you were going, you'd be the next one to get a ride in that ambulance." Eddie checked the lug nuts on the wheel, discovered they were tight and let the car down on the flat to rearrange the jack.

"I've never done this before," she said and leaned against the car.

"I could tell. Please don't do that." He said and motioned at her leaning. He hauled out the spare, loosened the lugs one half turn, and raised the car.

"I'm, sorry." She stood straight folding her arms against the night chill. "Was it that obvious I didn't know what I was doing?"

"Yup," Eddie said, then swapped wheels, spun on the nuts, snugged them up and lowered the car.

"You've been very kind, can I pay you anything?" She began to rummage in her purse.

"Think nothin' of it," he said as he got to his feet and dusted himself off. "Someday, maybe you'll do me a good turn in that hospital of yours. You take care, now."

"You, too, and thanks so much." She extended her hand and he shook it.

Eddie turned and continued on to the store. Behind him, he could hear the nurse loading her groceries. I should have loaded them for her, he thought. Oh, well.

In the beverage aisle he picked up a six-pack of Bud. He thought better of it, and picked up a second. As he walked towards the checkouts a stock boy blocked his way pushing a large flat dolly loaded with cases of Coke, Pepsi, and Adirondack Soda. The boy looked up from his cart and Eddie realized it was one of the men from the mill.

The stock worker recognized Eddie. "Hi, pal. How ya doin'?"

"Fine." Pal, Eddie thought, the universal name for all the guys you know by sight and don't know. "How 'bout yourself?"

"The same," the stock worker said slamming price stickers to the tops of cans. "Got me a job here to see me through the strike. You?"

"Yeah," said Eddie, "I got me a job." He hurried on by in an effort to cut the conversation short and avoid yet another rousing discussion on union tactics.

After paying for his beer, Eddie quickly headed out for his truck and for home.

Seven empty beer cans were scattered around and under Eddie's truck as he sat in his driveway. He stepped out, slammed the door, woke the dog next door and heard its noisy bark. He knocked back the last of his eighth brew, tossed the can across the lawn and his fuzzy mind wondered why the law had not arrived yet.

He missed the keyhole to his locked front door with his first several attempts. Cussing, steadying the key with both hands, he managed to insert the key and unlock the door.

He plowed up the stairs to his and Sarah's bedroom where his mind began to think about sex. He dropped his boots at the door, peeled off his shirt, pants, and underwear. He brushed wood chips that had worked their way into his clothing from the mill yard off his chest.

Eddie threw back the bed covers, exposing his wife to the night air, startling her awake. She wore a see-through baby-doll gown. "For a preacher's daughter, you sure do dress fine, woman." He climbed into bed and knelt beside his wife, staring at her body. He cut loose with a beer belch, grinned and said, "'cuse me."

"What do you want?" Sarah whispered in forced hushed tones. She reached for the bedclothes, but Eddie yanked them out of her hands.

"I want you, little lady," Eddie said, as he leaned in over her. "You wanted to get screwed earlier, well now you're going to get screwed." Eddie felt his heart beat faster, and the anticipation brought on an erection.

Sarah shifted to get out of bed, but Eddie grabbed her by the upper arm, grabbed her by her bruise, bringing a wince of pain across her face, and drew her back into the bed and on her back.

"No, you can't leave yet. We're not finished. We ain't even begun." He pinned her arms over her head and swung a leg over her. "It's the love doctor come home to operate," he whispered. The smell of stale beer wafted.

"Get off me!" Sarah screamed. He leaned over to kiss her. "God, you stink!" She struggled against him, but his grip tightened. "You're drunk, and you smell like diesel! Get off me!" She threw her head from side to side and tried to squirm out from under him, but he held her fast.

22

Eddie leaned in again for a kiss as Sarah turned aside, and instead licked a mouthful of hair. "Damn you, woman, hold still." Getting nowhere with the kiss, he decided time was wasting. He backed off to better position himself, and as he released pressure on Sarah's pelvis, she brought her knee up into his groin.

Eddie instantly saw red stars, white stars, yellow stars, blue stars. His lungs exploded with a convulsed cry. A deep sickness was born in the pit of his stomach. Both of his hands grabbed at his testicles as he rolled over onto his back and tried to catch his breath."

"You son-of-a-bitch!" screamed Sarah, flying out of bed. "You can't get it up when you're sober, and you think you're gonna rape me now when you're stinkin' drunk?"

She stood alongside the bed, legs apart, fists on hips, breasts high and nipples erect through the filmy gown. At the sight, Eddie could feel himself rise again but then the pain increased.

She threw on her robe. "God, you're disgusting. I should divorce you!" She stormed out of the room.

Eddie heard Sarah go down into the kitchen. He swallowed back his nausea, and as the pain between his legs dulled to a roar, he rolled out of the bed and followed after her, stumbling into the kitchen and shielding his eyes from the fluorescent lights. "What the hell's the matter with you, Sarah?" With his free hand, Eddie continued to caress, even carry, his wounded pride.

Sarah glared a life threatening stare at him. "You come home stinking drunk and try to rape me, and you want to know what's wrong with me?!" She paced back and forth between the stove and the refrigerator. "God almighty, Eddie, you're the stupidest man on earth!"

"First you want sex, and then you don't," Eddie said. He felt a little sheepish for his attempt, but he still wanted to defend himself. "How's a man supposed to know?"

She stopped pacing and stared at him. He followed her gaze down to his consoling hand. "A man would know. But I've long given up on *you* knowing."

He felt his sheepishness giving way to anger. "You got no cause to be calling me no man, Sarah. What is it with everybody attackin' my manhood? I'm a man. I'm a hard working man. I provide for you." His courage returned, and he wanted to emphasize his point, although he kept more than a leg length away. "You know I've had a lot on my mind. To keep you happy, I'm a first class scab now. The whole plant will know by morning." He retrieved a sandwich bag from the cupboard and filled it with ice from the freezer.

"So, you went to work," Sarah said. She went to a corner further away from him and leaned on the counter facing him with arms folded. "Good. I'm glad you did that much. As for that scab nonsense, so what!"

"I'll tell you so what, I get death threats at the mill. Then I damn near ran over the union president tonight getting out of the plant lot." He put the plastic bag between his legs and felt his scrotum crawl upward immediately. "That bastard's crazy enough to torch our house in revenge," he explained and sat at the kitchen table and nursed the ice into place.

"He wouldn't dare come near our house." She looked smug to Eddie.

"What's that supposed to mean?" he asked.

"Nothing," Sarah said. She turned to face the counter. "He won't touch the home of his own –"

"His own what? He's just a crazy s.o.b. He's not gonna care what's here."

"He'll care once he knows."

"Sarah, what are you talking about? You act like you know something."

Sarah spun around and went to the table and leaned into Eddie's face.

"He won't touch this house because he's the father of our son," Sarah said. Droplets of saliva sprayed onto Eddie's face as Sarah spat out her words. He could see a hurtful glare in her eyes as if she hated him with all of hell's fury.

Her rage scared him, but as the full meaning of her words sent shock waves through him, Eddie grabbed her by the arms. The ice fell to the floor, and he was startled by the swiftness of his own action.

He backed her across the kitchen floor until his body pressed her against the cabinets and counter top. He seethed, "What did you say about our son?"

"You stupid fool," Sarah said. "I made love to Dan Callahan two months before we married. Your preemie son was his full term baby."

Eddie's rage boiled and his vision began to blur; all he saw was a red blur for Sarah's face set against a red background.

Eddie's pain was so great that he didn't have the strength to hold her fast against the counter. His relaxed grip emboldened her.

"You're not man enough to father a good looking boy like our William. The only thing you can do is sire a girl."

Sarah's words were like hot pokers in Eddie's guts. He no longer felt the throb between his legs. That pain had been replaced by a mortal wound.

"Your favorite, your daughter, is yours, all yours," Sarah continued.

In a sudden surge, Eddie's rage burst anew. He put his left hand to her jaw and neck, and forced her head backwards against the wall cabinets and hammered his right fist into the cabinet next to her head. The door panel caved in, bursting in upon boxes of Raisin Bran, Cocoa Puffs, and shredded wheat. The cereal exploded off the shelves. As the door panel let go of its hinges, its corner split the skin above Sarah's left eye.

Eddie released her, and Sarah slowly melted to her haunches and drew back into the corner. Eddie turned and walked deliberately out of the kitchen and back up to the bedroom. He slept the sleep of the troubled, alone.

OCTOBER 31ST
ALL HALLOW'S E'EN

It was Friday, October thirty-first, and pastor Bill Weakley had two things on his mind – Sunday's sermon about which God had not yet directed him, and trick or treaters to whom he would give tracts about the pagan background and evil portent of their activity.

He placed his stack of pamphlets on a TV tray by the front door of his small parsonage. Over the years it seemed he needed fewer and fewer of the tracts as fewer children approached the church house for candy. He knew, however, that the school system was growing and that there were more children in the community. Apparently, his message about this godless and godforsaken tradition was spreading, and more parents were disallowing the practice.

Pastor Weakley went into his kitchen to pour himself a cup of decaffeinated Irish Cream flavored coffee. Flavored coffees had become a small pleasure he allowed himself. He had searched his soul and prayed over it, and found no sin in this appetite.

He went to his study at the front corner of the parsonage living room, nearest the sidewalk window. Pastor Weakley thought it was important for passers-by to see him hard at work struggling over the sermon, counseling some poor soul and bowing with them in prayer or reading inspirational literature. He always held the book with the jacket facing the window so those who cared to look would know he was nurturing his faith.

Placing his coffee on the imitation oak particle board desk his parish provided with a matching set of book shelves, he sat in a steel and vinyl swivel chair he had purchased through a mail order office supply catalog.

He clasped his hands tightly, held them in front of his chest, bowed his head and prayed aloud. "Dear Heavenly Father, I beseech Thee to grant

Thy servant direction this day. I struggle to discern Thy intent for Thy people, but have seen no clear message that Thou may wish me to offer on Thy behalf. I wait patiently upon my Lord."

Pastor Weakley's prayer was interrupted by a knock at his kitchen door. He tried to ignore it. "Lord God, please help block this intrusion from my mind. Allow my ears to be deaf to their noise."

The knock came again, a bit louder.

Keeping his head bowed but opening his eyes, he glanced in the direction of the kitchen, then clinched his eyes and prayed, "God of mercy, take this temptation away."

The knock changed from the thump of knuckles against wood to the clatter of keys rapping against glass.

"Lord God, if this be Thy messenger, and Thou would have me answer, have them knock one more time, and I will go."

Sounding less urgent, but still persistent, the knock came again.

Pastor Weakley got up and crossed to the back of the house to answer the kitchen door. As he opened it he saw a young woman dressed in a short skirt hemmed too many inches above the knee and a scoop neck knit top. She wore a sweater and a silk scarf around her neck. Her makeup was heavy, her lips too red and she held aloft a small rectangular box in her left hand. Her right hand held keys.

"Hi, Daddy," she said.

"Sarah," he said, and stepped back to allow her to enter. "Why did you knock? You have a key."

"Just in case you were with someone," she said and stepped into the kitchen and gave her father a peck on the cheek. "I never know when you might be in the middle of something important."

"Leave your shoes on the doormat," he said closing the door. "You've got mud on your shoes." He realized she had probably taken the dirt path through the small wood that connected the back yards of the parsonage on Roger's Road to her home on Benedict.

"What have you been up to?" she asked, removing her shoes.

"I was speaking with God," he said, and moved across the kitchen towards the living room. "Do you know how you look? Thank you for having had sense enough to come to the back door."

"I didn't come to fight," she said, following him.

"Fight or not, you dress the part of a whore. You should be ashamed looking like this." He reached his desk and sat and turned to face his approaching daughter. "You know your style of dress inhibits the work of God I do here. If your mother were alive, she'd be shamed to tears."

27

"She would not. Mommy wanted me to have fun. Remember that time when I was fifteen and you paddled me for going to the movies?" Weakley turned to his desk and began rummaging in the drawers. "Do you remember that? Mother gave me permission. She always thought you were too strict with me, and with her."

"That's because your mother had little appreciation for the scope of the Lord's work or the power of God's wrath and retribution upon the wicked. That's why the faithful must remain above reproach at all costs. Pure and without blemish."

"Daddy," she said, standing in front of him like an accused criminal, "it's just fashion, for God's sake."

"Don't invoke God into this. If you continue to follow in the ways of the devil you'll burn in hell. How will I face my Creator if my own daughter burns?"

"It's always about you, isn't it Daddy? How *you* face your maker."

Pastor Weakley turned to his desk and opened his Bible. Without looking up, he said, "What is it you want?"

"Eddie sends these for when you go hunting with him next." She placed a box of cartridges on his desk.

"Thank Eddie for me," Pastor Weakley said, still not looking up.

"There's a note inside. it's about trajectory and aiming and such. You'll need to know," Sarah said.

"Thanks, again."

"Daddy," Sarah said. Her voice sounded as it did when she was an adolescent about to ask permission.

"What?"

"I need to talk to you about something important."

"Important like how much makeup is sinful?" the pastor asked, sitting bolt upright. "Or important like how can it be sinful to go to a movie house when a movie on TV doesn't seem to count for anything? Or important like will I go to hell if I only dance one dance at The Stallions bar and grill? Oh, you've got lots of important issues. The most important one is getting right with God. You come talk to me when you're ready for that."

"Daddy!" Sarah said, stamping her foot, "I need to talk to you about divorce."

"Jesus doesn't allow it," Pastor Weakley said with certainty and authority. "There's nothing more to be said." He turned back to his Bible, and without looking up added, "Grow up. You're over thirty and stamping your feet."

He was startled when he felt his daughter grab him by the shoulder and spin him around in his chair. The Bible fell to the floor.

28

"Eddie's been beating me," Sarah said and stared into her father's eyes. She peeled off her sweater revealing the bruises on her arms, then removed the scarf and held her head high to show an older bruise high on her sternum above the neckline of her top.

Horror spread across Pastor Weakley's face. Tears welled up and he stood to hold his little girl.

"I had no idea that you were going through anything like this." He held her tightly in his arms, and found himself rocking her back and forth in the comforting rhythm of his heartbeat.

She began to cry.

They stood together for a long while, holding onto each other. Sarah's crying fell into heaving sobs, and Pastor Weakley felt his repulsion over his daughter's bruises boil into loathing for his son-in-law.

Pastor Weakley walked his little girl to the dining room table and sat her down. He went to the kitchen and retrieved a glass of water and placed it on the table at her hand. She sipped, then drank deeply. She withdrew a tissue from her skirt pocket and wiped at her eyes and nose. He brought a chair nearer to Sarah and sat facing her, picked up the hand she had resting in her lap, and held it in both of his.

"How long has this been going on?" he asked.

Staring into her lap and balling up her used tissue in her hand she said, "Not long. Only since the mill strike has gotten serious."

"Why has he hit you? What possible reason could he have?"

"Money, Daddy," Sarah said as she lifted her eyes to her father's face. "We fight about money, and his drinking too much."

"Money isn't reason enough to strike a woman." Bill slowly moved his head from side to side disbelief. "But the drink can make a man crazy. It lets the Devil get into a man."

"Maybe it's something I did, Daddy. Maybe I'm somehow to blame."

"No," said Pastor Weakley, "I won't have you blame yourself." He got up and paced the dining room as he spoke. "People fight. That's natural. The unchurched fight more. The Devil has more control over them. I've told you that you needed to work harder at saving Eddie. If he'd given his soul to Jesus he couldn't be doing this now."

"Daaaddy." Sarah's voice sounded hurt, like a child's call after falling from her bicycle.

"I'm sorry honey." Weakley stopped pacing to look at his little girl. "But things could have been so different, if only you'd brought him up to your religious level, instead of your sinking to his depths."

"Daddy, I want a divorce." Sarah clenched her fists and pounded her thighs. "I want to end this."

29

"You can't. Jesus forbids divorce." He took up her hands, but Sarah withdrew and folded her arms. "You married for better or worse, until death parts you. This is the worse. And you're not dead. You must work this out." Weakley got up and began to pace the dining room again.

"I don't want to work this out." Sarah's voice was impatient.

"This has as much to do with your soul as Eddie's. You can't divorce and expect to enter the glory of Heaven – especially if you ever married again." Weakley kept pacing. "Maybe I should go talk to him. You stay here and I'll –"

"He's not home. He left early this morning to go deer hunting with one of his buddies, before work." She held her head in her hands and wept.

"There, there, I'll speak to him tonight or first thing in the morning. He's expecting me to hunt with him tomorrow. We'll talk then." He sat by his little girl and drew her head to his shoulder and held her.

Sarah sat up. She snuffled, dried her tears and blew her nose with a fresh tissue. She took two deep breaths and straightened her spine. "Daddy, there's more I haven't told you. I don't think I want to save a marriage with a man who tried to rape me."

"What?" Pastor Weakley sprang to his feet and stood over his daughter. "He's raped you?" Pastor Weakly picked up his little girl under her arms and brought her to her feet and held her in a tight embrace. "That illegitimate child of Satan, I'll make him feel the wrath of Almighty God for this. He'll wish that the angel of death had taken him from his mother's womb."

Eddie returned home at lunch time from a futile morning. He'd missed a perfectly open shot at a fine four point buck because of thinking about his fight with Sarah, and her relation with Daniel Callahan. He was hurt, angry, and miserable company for himself.

He imagined Callahan and Sarah pawing over each other, the two writhing and tangling in sheets. He could see their tongues flicking at each other. Steamy bodies filled his mind. He imagined Callahan on top of her; then her riding him. Loving him. Wanting him.

He entered the house through the kitchen door. "Sarah!"

There was no response.

Eddie stood in the middle of the kitchen. "Sarah, where are you?"

Still no answer.

He had not fired his Mossberg, and it had been a beautiful dry bright fall morning. The rifle didn't need cleaning so he went into the living room and returned it to the gun cabinet. His mind wandered back to Sarah and he thought about the likelihood of her probably out spending money he hadn't yet earned.

He went upstairs, removed his hunting clothes and climbed into the shower hoping to wash some of his anger away. He couldn't shake the visions of his wife in the hands of Callahan and the imaginary love whisperings between the two reverberated between his ears. He guessed at knowing glances shared between them in the Wal-Mart behind his back over the years and wondered about God knew how many phone calls or meetings the two might have had.

Letting the shower water wash over him, Eddie turned the control lever for more cold water to calm him down. The water poured, and he chilled. Goose flesh developed over his body. He began to shiver, and his testicles drew up into the warmth of his groin.

As he turned off the water he decided what to do.

He dried himself, dressed in fresh work clothes then went downstairs to the gun cabinet. From the bottom drawer he removed a shoulder holster and a box of nine millimeter cartridges. He unlocked the cabinet and removed a Smith and Wesson pistol. "Hello, cousins," he said, dropping out the magazine. He loaded eight rounds, slipped a ninth round into the chamber and drove the magazine home with a slap. Jamming his cousins in the holster under his left armpit, Eddie headed for the kitchen, threw on his jacket and left for his truck and the picket lines.

Eddie cruised the picket line slowly. Callahan had to be there. The fires of the previous night had long since burned out. An occasional fifty-five gallon drum smoldered in the early afternoon sunlight. As he approached the gate, the density of men grew. Signs reading NO UNION BUSTING, UNITED PAPER UNFAIR TO LABOR, NO GIVEBACKS, were held aloft by some. Other signs were abandoned, leaning against the chain link fence that surrounded the plant.

Eddie drove past the men, and a few women, examining them as though looking for an imperfectly cast bullet – something malformed. He drove past the plant entrance where the mill manager was hanging in effigy over the gate. The pickets walked their line. Some shouted the slogans held over their heads. A woman Eddie didn't know flipped him the bird. Maybe she was at the bar last night.

Then, he spotted Daniel Callahan about twenty-five yards ahead. Callahan was at the end of the picket line conversing with two others. It looked like two of the lackeys Eddie saw at the bar.

Eddie pulled his truck over onto the shoulder. Callahan and the others took no notice. Eddie got out and approached the trio, unzipped his jacket and one of the men recognized him. Eddie held his right forefinger to his lips to shush him while opening his jacket flap to expose his holstered cousins.

Callahan jabbed at his distracted lackey and said, "Hey, pay attention, I'm talkin' to you."

Eddie spun Callahan around by the arm and said, "Not any more," and pounded his beefy fist up into Callahan's stomach. Callahan blew out his wind and doubled over. Eddie wrapped his leg behind Callahan's, and pushed his shoulders back to knock Callahan flat on the ground. With one knee, Eddie knelt on his chest. Callahan gasped for breath.

The two lackeys began to move towards Eddie, but Eddie exposed the pistol butt with a wave of his jacket flap. They ran off towards the rest of the picket line.

Eddie returned his attention to his prey. "Listen up, you son-of-a-bitch, I know you been dippin' your wick where it don't belong."

Callahan struggled and tried to protest.

"Shut up, pecker head, or I'll rearrange your nose again." Callahan grew still. Eddie spit between his teeth as he spoke. "I don't care if you screwed Sarah twelve years ago or twelve minutes ago." Callahan's eyes were wide and flew from side to side. "You need to know I'll tear you apart if I ever see you near her or my boy again. You understand?"

Callahan managed a muffled "Yeah," and tried to nod his head.

Eddie could hear the approach of a crowd from behind. He got up to leave and noticed a large dark wet spot over the inside of Callahan's left leg.

Eddie got into his truck, started it, threw it into gear and popped the clutch, spraying gravel over Callahan and the approaching strikers. He made a U-turn and sped back towards the gate.

"Go check out your fearless leader," Eddie shouted out as he drove past the crowd, "go see how he pissed himself." He turned and sped through the gate blaring his horn to warn those poised to intimidate the scabs.

Once on mill property, Eddie slowed down and made his way to his assigned parking lot. He pulled into one of the free spaces and shut down his truck. He glanced at his watch, "Shit, I'm an hour early. Oh well, I might as well enjoy myself." He reached for one of the beers left in the truck from the night before, popped the top, and chugged it down. Then he reached for another.

A crowd gathered around Callahan, watching as he caught his breath. He sat up on the ground and coughed a couple of times. He seemed not to notice that his crotch and left thigh were soaked. One of the lackeys knelt by Callahan attempting to offer some ministrations, but Callahan waved him off. He coughed a couple more times and began breathing easier.

Three-brow pushed through the crowd. Seeing Callahan on his ass, he decided this was a good time to distance himself from the incumbent union president.

"God-almighty Callahan, every time you meet up with that scab you land on your ass," Three-brow said. "And now you've gone and pissed yourself. Maybe we need a new union president."

"Who would that be, asshole? You?" screeched Callahan, scrambling to his feet.

"I think so," said Three-brow as he turned and walked away. Callahan screamed something after him, but he paid no attention. He'd gotten as much mileage out of the situation as he wanted. He was satisfied. He opened up a fresh Macanudo, nipped off its end and lit up.

Pastor Weakley sat at his desk, with head bowed, gripping his black floppy Bible. He prayed thanksgiving to his God for sending a messenger bearing the week's theme for his flock through the person of his daughter. But he was subjected to the same conundrum that faced Adam and Eve in the garden – that of choice.

"God of abundance, Thou hast provided Thy servant with at least two messages for Thy flock. Which wouldst Thou have me present?" Pastor Weakley's eyes were tightly closed, and his prayer scowl was more deeply set than usual. "Wouldst Thou have me preach against the evil desire to divorce and Thy Son's hellfire admonishment against this? Or wouldst Thou have me preach against the abuse of a man for his wife?" With head bowed, with fingers wrapped tightly about the eternal infallible Word, he waited for God's answer.

After Pastor Weakley meditated on the message God had delivered through his daughter, he discerned God's will. He was being called of God to preach on one topic, and to act upon the other.

Callahan dusted himself off. As he brushed across the wet spot on his trousers, he heard a snicker from within the crowd. He tried to ignore it but others began to laugh as well. These were his men, damn it! They shouldn't be laughing at him.

A bearded man in green buffalo plaid near the front of the crowd shook his massive head from side to side, clicked his tongue, wagged his finger at Callahan and said, "Screwing another man's wife, eh? Shame on you."

"If I didn't have a broken nose, I'd make him eat his words!" Callahan said through clenched teeth.

An anonymous voice from the rear of the crowd shouted, "It looks like Conger'd eat your lunch, pal."

"He's crazy! I don't even know Conger's wife." Callahan seethed. Shouting to the larger crowd, and raising a fist to campaign, "He's just a scab. He's stealing your job! He's a scab looking to make himself feel better about crossing your line!"

"It looks like you crossed his line once too often," the bearded man said and turned to walk into the crowd. "Go home and change your pants. You're an embarrassment."

"Maybe we do need a new president," a new voice added.

There were a couple of chuckles, considerable murmuring, and the mob dissipated to a crowd, to a gathering, to a few, to nothing.

Callahan, clad in fresh trousers and shirt, pounded on the back door of Sarah Conger's home.

Sarah answered in purple tights and pink leotard, with a towel around her neck. Her red hair, damp with sweat, was matted against her neck. She posed at the door as if selling something. Kathy Smith counted repetitions from the TV in the living room beyond the kitchen.

With his best leer, Callahan said, "Trick or treat."

"Well, well, well, Danny Callahan," Sarah said with a lifted eyebrow, "What brings you sneaking 'round my back door?"

Danny tried to take one step forward, but Sarah did not budge. "You look good in spandex," he said.

"You came here to tell me that?"

"No, not that," Danny said. "I came here to get a little of what your husband accuses me of getting."

"In your dreams, Danny boy, in your dreams." Sarah turned from the door, leaving it open, and walked into the kitchen.

"It sounds to me as though you been accusing me of givin' you a thumping now and again." Danny boy soaked up the sweaty image in front of him.

"Don't you have a wife and kids at home?" Sarah asked, leaning against the counter.

Danny's eyes settled on her breasts and watched them rise and fall as she continued to catch her breath from her workout.

"So what," he said. "The cow at home ain't been givin' much milk of late."

"You act like you've never seen a woman's breasts before," Sarah said, and folded her arms over her chest.

Danny moved closer towards Sarah. "I hear you ain't altogether *satisfied* in your marriage, if you get my drift."

"Satisfaction is a matter of degrees."

"Temperature?" Danny asked.

"What if my mercury hasn't been raised very much lately? What do you have to offer?" Sarah unfolded her arms and rested the heels of her hands on the counter top behind her.

Danny boy stepped up to Sarah and ran his finger along the neckline of her leotard.

"You know what I want."

Sarah picked off Daniel's finger and held away. "Don't touch unless I say to touch."

"You didn't mind my touching you a dozen years ago," Danny said.

"Yeah, and as soon as you learned I was pregnant, you fell off the earth." Sarah's arms folded again.

"I was young and foolish," Danny said, stroking her arms. "I won't run out on you now. I'm mature and established now. Hell, I'm union president."

"Oh, you're mature all right," Sarah said, pushing him back. She picked up some dishes from the kitchen table then mocked him and whined, "The cow at home ain't givin' milk, so you've come shopping. Give me a break. I'd just be the next dairy queen. Get lost, Danny."

"No, I think my shoppin' days'd be over." Danny followed her with his eyes.

She returned near to where he stood and placed the dirty dishes into the sink. Then she turned and with one hand on her hip said, "I'm not giving away any free samples, Danny. You want to visit this dairy bar, you have to pay the price."

Danny boy felt like he was about to run for home. He took Sarah up into his arms and whispered, "I think I'd pay any price at all." Then he drew her into himself and tried to kiss her.

A knock sounded at the door behind Danny, and a voice called, "Sarah, oh, Sar- - OH!"

Danny boy was pushed hard at both shoulders. His kiss was broken off, and suddenly his left cheek stung and his nose screamed in pain as Sarah's hand slapped across his face.

"Get off me! How dare you!" Sarah said, with a glare that could kill. She looked over Danny's shoulder and said, "Barbara, am I glad you showed up." She motioned to the woman at the door, "Come in, please. Mr. Callahan is leaving."

Danny held his nose in both hands with head lowered. He looked up at Sarah through the corner of his eye and said, "You crazy bitch."

"I'll not have you use that kind of language in this house." Sarah crossed the kitchen and stood at the door. "I'll tell my husband about this, and maybe I should contact the mill management or union officials."

Danny stepped outside and heard the door slam behind him. She really is a crazy bitch, he thought. I'll come back though. He got into his wife's Ford and drove off.

It was Barbara's turn to bring the baked goods for the afternoon coffee klatch. She had just finished a batch of brownies with a two-layer crème de menthe and semi-sweet chocolate frosting. The mid fall day was bright, clear and cool enough for a sweater. She rounded the back of Sarah's house and rapped at the door.

What filled her eyes, if only for a moment, was the sight of a man kissing Sarah. Sarah's right leg was wrapped around his left. Then Sarah pushed him away and gave him a slap across the face. Barbara thought she recognized the man as Mr. Callahan, the union president. He looked surprised, then angry. He immediately left the house, brushing by Barbara and holding his bandaged nose.

Sarah didn't seem to know where to stand or what to do with her hands. She made a couple of false starts at conversation. Kathy Smith was encouraging her class to cool down in the other room. Sarah looked flushed, and was catching her breath. Finally, she leaned on the kitchen table with one hand and held herself around the middle with the other.

"Barbara," she said, "am I ever glad to see you."

"What was that all about?" Barbara asked, now fully inside. She placed her brownies on the table. "Who was that?"

"Danny Callahan." Sarah said then wiped her face and neck with a towel. "You know, the union president."

"I thought so," Barbara said, removing her sweater and draping it over the back of a kitchen chair. She moved to the stove. "You sit for a bit, I'll make the tea. What was he doing here? Was he looking for Eddie?"

36

"It's a long story, Barb." Sarah sat. "Danny was an old flame, a dozen years ago – a lifetime ago. Apparently he and Eddie recently had words. Eddie said something about a fight last night at The Stallions. Danny decided it was time to pay me a visit while Eddie was at work. Some kind of payback, I suppose."

"This is sounding serious, Sarah," Barbara said as she leaned against the stove waiting for the kettle to boil. "Eddie's getting into barroom fights now? I really wish you'd talk to someone about this."

"I've talked to my father, for all the good it did."

"What did he have to say?" Barbara moved to sit at the table with Sarah.

"Just what I expected. You have to stick it out. You married for better or worse. If you divorce, you'll burn in hell. I've heard it all my life, Barb. I think it's true. I don't want to spend eternity in hell. Maybe it's best I stick it out." She put her face into her hands, and cried quietly.

Barbara moved to Sarah's side and held her for a long while. Sarah stopped crying, reached her arms around Barbara's waist and hugged her. Barbara stood with Sarah's head against her and stroked her hair. Barbara felt tears roll down her own cheeks.

The kettle whistled its shrill song, and Sarah lifted her head, toweled off her cheeks and dried her eyes. "I'll get the tea," she said, looking at Barbara. "God, you look a wreck. Here," she said offering the towel, "fix yourself up, will ya?"

The two gave up small nervous giggles.

"Sarah, I want you to see my pastor," Barbara said. "I know we come from different religious traditions, but I'm sure he could help. And I'm sure he wouldn't send you to hell."

"I don't know." Sarah poured hot water over tea bags. "I wouldn't want to hurt my father by going to another pastor."

"But that's just it, Sarah," said Barb, "he's your father more than your pastor. You need someone to talk to who can offer a different religious point of view so you'd feel like you can do something."

Sarah put the mugs on the table and then retrieved sandwich plates for the brownies. She put a plate in front of Barbara, and one at her own place and sat down. "I've been told that other pastors are sometimes misdirected by the Devil, and may not even know it themselves."

"Do you think I'm going to hell?"

"I hope not...I don't think so. You do the kinds of things a good Christian woman should do."

"Then," Barbara said, "if I make the appointment and take you there myself, will you go?"

37

"Maybe."

The two women sat and finished their brownies. Sarah soon brought the conversation around to the activities of her and Barbara's children. Barbara felt that Sarah tried awfully hard to steer clear of discussion about the mill, the strike, or what their respective husbands were doing.

As Barbara walked home she played back the afternoon in her mind's eye. Callahan's advances on Sarah. Sarah's leg wrapped around his. Then the slap. Something seemed out of focus. Was Sarah leading Callahan on? And then there was news of Eddie beating Sarah. Sarah blaming herself and feeling as though there was no help from her father. Was Barbara being too nosy? She didn't know, but she decided her friend was in serious trouble, probably more trouble than she knew how to handle. When she got home, Barbara phoned her pastor.

At The Stallions, Three-brow chewed on a dead cigar and drew on his Bud. He sat at a table with Mickey Mile and Callahan's other two lackeys. "So," he said in conclusion, "that's why I think it's time for a new union president. And that's why I think it's gonna be me. Are ya in?"

Mickey's eyes moved about the room as if he anticipated someone, maybe Callahan, eavesdropping on the conversation. "I don't know, Brow..."

"Don't call me that, asshole."

"What do you want me to call you? We always call you Brow, or Three-brow."

"That was before I decided to become president. Call me by my name."

Mickey's eyes darted to the others at the table. One kept his eyes fixed at the table top, being sure to make no eye contact. The tall lanky one, Stretch, just looked back at Mickey and shrugged. With a bit of a twitching jerk, Mickey looked back at Three-brow and said, "I ain't never called ya by yer name, Brow."

"Well, start now."

"Bu...but, I don't know what it is."

"Asshole," Brow shouted.

Stretch broke out laughing.

"What the hell you laughing at?" Brow stared at Stretch.

"Oh, nothing," said Stretch, "It just seems odd you want us to call you *Asshole* instead of Brow. The other two got to giggling.

"Assholes, all of ya," Brow seethed.

"Oh," said Stretch, "It's a family name and we're related." Guffaws broke out and Brow's fist slammed down on the table. Mickey's beer bottle jumped off the edge and crashed to the floor.

"Brookhough," shouted Three-brow. "Call me Mr. Erik Brookhough."

The table grew silent. Smiles vanished. Mickey said, "Yes, Mr. Brookhough."

Brookhough took a long swallow on his Bud and waited for the table to quiet down. "Okay then. The first thing we've got to do is help Callahan lose face with the union membership. Pissin' himself went a long way to do that. But over the next few days while it looks like we're helping him, we're gonna look for ways to sink him, and sink him good."

NOVEMBER 1ST
ALL SAINTS DAY

Pastor Bill Weakley was dressed in his old field clothes ready for a day's hunt with his son-in-law. At Eddie's suggestion five or six years prior, he had purchased a used Remington Three-oh-eight deer rifle for a hundred dollars through a newspaper ad, and had fitted it with an inexpensive Bushnell three power scope that he had managed to find at a neighbor's garage sale.

Weakley pocketed Eddie's most recent reloading effort with a twinge of guilt. He was not looking forward to confronting his son-in-law about abusing Sarah.

While unable to bring Eddie to the Lord, Weakley had grown genuinely fond of the lad. By and large, Eddie had been a down to earth sort. He was a bit of a redneck who liked his beer too much. Any at all was too much. He had more often than not been a generous and affable character. For instance, Bill knew Eddie occasionally dropped off game at a mountain home filled with children, but where the father was a drunk.

Pastor Weakley had mentioned his disapproval of drink to Eddie on occasion. Water off a duck's back. But he had never seen Eddie drunk or out of control. Weakley had never had to spend all night sitting up with him while Eddie threw up, as he had with some of his parishioners. Eddie's recent drunken attack on Sarah seemed out of character.

It had never occurred to Weakley prior to Sarah's visit that Eddie could have become abusive. His daughter's marriage had its ups and downs, but no more so than most, and fewer than some. His son-in-law had never caused him a sleepless night, something he couldn't say about his daughter.

He pulled on his hunter's orange knit cap and stepped out of his house into the pre-dawn chill. He and Eddie had arranged to drive separately so Pastor Weakley could leave early enough to return home to his unfinished sermon.

He headed south in his car along route 9N, playing over in his head how he would address the issue of Eddie's beating Sarah. He would give him time enough to explain, but also knew he would have to impress upon his son-in-law that the abuse would not be tolerated.

Weakley thought about the bruises he saw on his daughter. His knuckles whitened as he grasped the steering wheel. Obscenities concerning Eddie's parentage crossed his mind, but Pastor Weakley refused to entertain them and offered a quick silent confession as he drove. Even if someone had to go to jail over this, Pastor Weakley was going to take care of his little girl.

He pulled the car off the road and into the parking area for the Tongue Mountain Range trailhead. The sky was bright with the promise of a rising sun. As he got out of his car he noticed Eddie's truck parked across the lot along with a scattering of other cars and trucks presumably belonging to hunters. A preponderance of NRA bumper stickers was in evidence.

A sticker on the back of an old Chevy read in shades of blue and green, HUNT WITH YOUR KIDS, NOT FOR THEM. Weakley slung his rifle over his shoulder, locked his car, and moved across the lot towards the trailhead. As he passed Eddie's truck he read the sticker, GUN SAFETY IS NO ACCIDENT. The sticker was pretty badly gouged, and the bumper misshapen. He wondered what that was all about.

He started up the trail for the Five Mile Mountain. About two hundred yards up the trail he stopped and unslung his rifle. He drew back the bolt, withdrew five of Eddie's rounds from his pocket and loaded them in the magazine. He slid the bolt home and flicked on the safety.

Adirondack rattlesnakes crossed Weakley's mind, but he discounted them with a mental note about it being too cold. They must be hibernating or whatever it is that snakes do in the fall and winter.

About a mile ahead he would leave the trail and move off into the underbrush to where Eddie had a tree stand. Eddie would already be there on watch in the hope that Weakley's thrashing through the woods would drive a buck towards him. This day, Weakley hoped he didn't scare anything up.

The four or five hundred foot climb over the two miles to the tree stand was a moderate hike, but enough to get Weakley's fifty-six year old paunchy body huffing and puffing. He stopped to catch his breath and leaned his rifle against a massive oak tree while he yanked out his

41

handkerchief to blow his nose. Eddie had warned him never to pull out a white handkerchief in the woods during hunting season. A careless hunter could mistake it for the waving white tail of a running deer and get a shot off in your direction. Weakley kept his white kerchief folded and concealed in his hands while he blew.

As soon as he cut loose with a rattling blow, a six-point buck, startled by his honker, jumped up from a thicket thirty yards off to his right. Bill dropped his handkerchief to the ground and reached for his rifle. He snapped it to his shoulder, took quick aim and squeezed the trigger. Nothing. The safety was still on. Bill ran his thumb over the safety, heard it click off, saw the buck leap through his scope and jerked back the trigger.

A clean miss.

He bent down to retrieve his handkerchief, brushed the dirt off and stuffed it back into his pocket. He moved on towards Eddie.

As he approached the area where he expected his son-in-law to be waiting, he rapped his small wooden squirrel call against his thigh to signal his arrival. Weakley heard his call returned and knew Eddie was expecting him.

Pushing through brush, Weakley entered a stand of old hemlocks. About twenty-five feet up Eddie was perched on a metal tree stand. He had cut a few of the branches to clear a view for himself. About fifty feet in front of him was a well worn deer trail. He had placed a half dozen old Kodak film canisters along the trail filled with cotton balls and doe lure to attract any romantically inclined bucks. Eddie's bright orange coat called alert to all who could see. He was a perfect target.

The two men waved at one another without speaking. Weakley took a position on a log nestled in a thicket, and waited for the woods to settle down from his disturbing entrance. The two hunters would wait in long cold silence in the hope that a deer would wander by on its own, or be driven their way by another hunter.

Pastor Weakley had found these long, motionless periods of quiet to be most meditative and refreshing. Often, at the end of a day's hunt, without having spotted any game, he had come out of the woods renewed, and with an entire sermon worked out in his head ready to be written. He experienced no such peace this day. He made up his mind that when Eddie climbed down at lunch time, he would confront his son-in-law. He held his Remington across his chest at the ready. The warmth of the first November sun began to bleed out through the pines and oaks.

Weakley was disturbed from his ruminating by the sound of rustling fabric and snapping twigs. Eddie was climbing down from his stand. It was time.

With his rifle carried in the crook of his elbow, Eddie approached his father-in-law, and in the hushed tones reserved for the sanctuary of the woods he said, "Glad to see ya, Pop."

"Yeah, thanks."

Crouching near to Weakley, Eddie asked, "Did you bring your lunch? I got plenty if you want some."

"No thanks," said Weakley reaching into his coat, "I've got a sandwich."

Eddie brought a knapsack he had over one shoulder around to the front and began to unpack it. Two sandwiches, a bag of potato chips, a couple of brownies with what looked like green and brown layered frosting, and a huge thermos of coffee were all disgorged from the small sack. "Dig in, Pop, there's plenty." He began to unwrap his sandwich, then stopped to rummage in the sack again. "I also brought an extra cup. I know you never think to bring one." From the sack he produced an insulated plastic mug, filled it from the thermos, and handed it to Weakley.

"Thanks, Eddie." Weakley had not yet opened his sandwich. It lay in its zip-lock bag on his lap. "Eddie, Sarah tells me you and she are having trouble. I don't like what she's told me, but I'd like to hear what you've got to say for yourself."

Looking up from his food, Eddie tried swallowing hard, then through the remaining mouthful said, "Oh it's nothin' much Pop, just husband and wife stuff. It'll blow over."

"Eddie, what I saw is not about to blow over." Weakley's jaw clenched in anger over his son-in-law's glib response to Sarah's bruising. "It looks to me like you two are in serious trouble."

"Serious trouble?" Eddie stopped eating. He looked at his father-in-law and screwed his face into a puzzled look. "I don't know how serious it is. She insists I work during the strike. It was against my better judgment, but I went in. If anything, I'm the one in serious trouble. And I'm all by my lonesome, I'll tell you that. Some of those guys want a piece o' me." Eddie took another bite and washed it down with coffee.

"I'm not talking about the mill, Eddie, or even the topic of your fight with Sarah." Weakley was feeling steamed, and he set his coffee down hard on the end of his log and spilled a third of it, splashing some over his hand and wrist. "Ow! Damn."

Eddie sat up straight at his father-in-law's curse, and with a broad smile said, "Pastor, please! Your language! My virgin ears!"

"Oh, shut up, Eddie." Weakley shook off his wet hand.

43

"Wow, you are pissed." Eddie's puzzled look returned.

"You're damn right I'm upset." Pastor Weakley was now angry with his son-in-law twice over. First there was Eddie's beating of his little girl, and second, making him so mad as to drive him to profanity. "I saw the bruises all over Sarah, and I'm here to tell you, stop beating my little girl!" Pastor Weakley could feel his heart beating faster, and his breathing was heavier.

Eddie put his sandwich down and held both hands in front of him, palms out to deflect Pastor Weakley's offense. "Pop, relax. I'm sorry. I ju..."

"Sorry doesn't cut it young man, Sorry isn't enough."

"I just got carried away one day." Eddie said. "I grabbed Sarah real hard and she bruised. You know she bruises easy."

"Don't bear false witness, Eddie. There's no excuse for a man to grab a woman like that. A man is to love his wife like Christ loved the church, and..."

"For chrissake Pops, don't go preacher on me, will ya?"

"And you can stop your blaspheming around me." Pastor Weakley jammed his sandwich back into his coat pocket. He glared at Eddie and said, "I'll not have you beating my little girl, do you understand?"

"Beating? Beating Sarah?"

"That's right. Don't lay another hand on her!"

"Pop, with God as my witness, I don't beat..."

"Don't add false oaths to your list of sins," Pastor Weakley said as he rose to his feet.

"Pop, stop." Eddie almost sounded pleading.

Pastor Weakley stood looking down on his son-in-law.

"It's true, your daughter pisses me off a lot lately," Eddie said, looking up at Weakley. "She's said some pretty hateful things, things I'd rather not repeat. And it's true that I got drunk and grabbed at her, but..."

"You mean you raped her, don't you?"

"Rape?! What the hell do you mean rape? I've never come close to raping her.

"You're still lying to me, Eddie. And I won't waste my time standing here listening to it. But hear this, you leave my daughter alone." Weakley turned around and picked up his rifle and held it across his body, then stared down at Eddie. He could feel his heart race now, and he was breathing heavier than when he had climbed the mountain. "If I see her with any more bruises, it's going to be someone else who's going to get hurt. Do we understand each other?"

Eddie's face changed from shock to defense. He nodded at Weakley's Remington and said, "You going to shoot me, Bill? Is that your threat?"

Weakley narrowed his eyes, and through gritted teeth managed to say, "The Lord thy God has commanded thou shalt not kill."

The two men glared at one another for what seemed an eternal and hellish moment. Then Pastor Bill Weakley drew his rifle sling over his shoulder and headed back down the mountain.

NOVEMBER 2ND
SUNDAY

The congregation of The Good News Apostolic Lighthouse finished singing *Guide Me, O Thou Great Jehovah*, clunked their hymnals into the pew racks and sat down. Pastor Bill Weakley rose to stand at his pulpit. The flock before him squirmed in their seats, anticipating the sermon. It was good for them to squirm, thought Weakley. Wrappers from sourball hard candies and Hall's Mentho-lyptus cough drops with vapor action rattled and unfurled in the hands of congregants.

Raising his hands to the ceiling and to God above, and closing his eyes so tightly as to wrinkle his nose and furrow his brow, Pastor Weakley called, "Let us come before Almighty God in prayer. Almighty and most powerful God, I give thee thanksgiving for the message thou has given me for thy people assembled here this day. I pray, Oh God, that the words of thy servant's mouth will be pleasing to thy ears, and a blessing unto thy people. Let them with ears, hear thy word. We pray in the precious name of our Lord, and the Savior of the world, Jesus Christ. Amen."

"Amens" sounded throughout the congregation.

Where Pastor Weakley gripped the sides of his plywood pulpit the wood had been stained by the weekly massage of his hands. He looked out over his flock and said, "We live in a throw-away society, my brothers and sisters!" On cue, the congregation murmured agreement

He started out low with a sonorous rhythm to capture his congregation in an easy flow of sensation and thought that would bring them along with him step by step. With each new indictment of someone else's sin of excess he would solicit an *amen* form the congregation. As he paced the full breadth of the platform, he raised the volume of his voice a bit to match the severity of whatever was discarded. He moved the

46

congregation from fast food wrappers to discarded babies at the Planned Parenthood Clinic bringing the fold to a near frenzied peak. "Amens" had echoed throughout the congregation and not a few of the women were in tears.

Pastor Weakley returned to his pulpit. He leaned on his elbows and draped his hands over the leading edge of the podium. He waited until there was quiet. "Sisters and brothers," he said softly, "we throw away too much, and we are throwing away our souls in the process." There were murmurs now but rapt attention. He had them, and they were ready to hear his word from God.

"Today I want to talk about how we throw each other away, about how we discard each other when we tire of one another." As Pastor Weakley spoke, he slowly stood more erect. "About how when we have a disagreement with a friend or a neighbor, we're all too willing to shun that person, and count them as lost to the Devil." He stepped next to his pulpit.

"I want to talk to you today about the most grievous of these discarded relationships, the sin of even contemplating divorce. What does our Lord Jesus expect of us when we marry till death us do part?"

Pastor Weakley turned his attention to the choir. They were all robed in bright red and seated behind him. He walked towards the front row of the choir, and looked into the eyes of the sopranos. He passed over Sarah, looking instead to the altos. He then returned to his daughter. Looking straight into her eyes but addressing the congregation he said, "I want to talk to you about the certain hell that awaits those who divorce and who willfully turn away from the laws of God."

When Pastor Weakley turned to face the congregation, he heard rustling behind him and whispers in the choir loft. He turned back to the choir to see his daughter, dressed in a skirt much too short for Sunday meeting, making her way out of the loft to the side door of the church. Her choir robe and music lay in her otherwise empty seat.

A tear welled up in the pastor's eye. With voice almost meek, and with hands at his side, he turned and looked out over the faces of his flock and said, "Brothers and sisters, my little girl just left because she cannot bear to hear the word of the Lord." The tear dampened the pastor's cheek and he pulled out his handkerchief and blew his nose. "She and my son-in-law seem to be contemplating this very transgression against the will of Jesus, and they desperately need your prayers."

Pastor Weakley knelt on the floor at the head of the center aisle, and with arms outstretched, he asked, "Will you pray with me?"

Obediently, the little congregation bowed their heads.

Barbara Ross couldn't get her mind off Sarah. She finally made up her mind to speak to the Reverend O'Connor after services. With that resolved she returned to the present and heard her pastor finish, "And so, friends, it is not our place to condemn others to hell, or even, for that matter, to elevate them to some heavenly state. This is reserved for God, and I suspect he doesn't appreciate our meddling." There were a few scattered titters. "Instead, we are called to give others the opportunity to know the love of God through us, through our every action, and then allow for the Spirit of God to witness to their spirits. Let's close with our last hymn of the day, *It is Well with My Soul*." The Reverend O'Connor raised his arms motioning the congregation to rise, the organ played the refrain of the hymn, and the cavernous stone sanctuary rang with the sound of about two hundred voices.

Barbara's pastor made his way to the back of the sanctuary during the singing, and when the hymn finished he spread out his arms for the final blessing and intoned, "As you leave this place to re-enter the world of work, school and play, go with the blessings and power of God to do his will through your lives. Amen."

The congregation responded with a collective, "Amen," the organ played, and the people began to file out, greeted at the door by their spiritual leader.

As Barbara approached and grasped his hand, she asked quietly, "Keegan, may I speak briefly with you about my phone call yesterday? It won't take long."

Keegan O'Connor's easy smile dimmed then returned. "Sure, Barb. Why don't you wait for me at the coffee hour in the fellowship hall. I'll be right along."

Barb agreed and moved out of the way of those behind her who waited to participate in the weekly ritual of shaking the hand of their holy man.

Holding his familiar mug stamped with the legend, THIS IRISH HEART IS FILLED WITH THE LOVE OF GOD, Keegan approached Barbara. Steam curled from the black coffee within. "So, Barb, about yesterday's call? Should I expect to cancel with your friend?"

"Oh no, nothing like that, Keegan," said Barbara, "it's more like...well, I'm not sure. A feeling, I guess."

Finishing a sip from his mug, and with a smile, Keegan said, "Well, I'm certainly glad you cleared that up."

"Thanks, Keegan, you're making this real easy."

"Sorry. You're really troubled about something, aren't you? Please, go on."

"It's just that I feel like I'm snitching," Barbara said, looking into the swirls of cream in her own coffee.

Drawing Barbara away from the other ears gathered at the coffee and cookies, Keegan asked, "If you tell me what's on your mind, will it be helpful to your friend, or will it do her harm?"

"Telling you won't hurt her, so long as you know it's just a feeling I have." Barbara said as she looked up at Keegan. She was thankful for his perception. "And it could help you when you see her tomorrow."

"Sounds like you've solved your own dilemma, Barb."

Barbara knew that wasn't exactly true. Keegan's ability to help others see through the fog of their own confusion was exactly why she wanted Sarah to meet with him.

"Okay," she said, then took a long sip of her coffee. "Here goes. Yesterday, before I called you, I happened to break in on Sarah and another man, Daniel Callahan, the union president at the mill. Anyway, they looked to me to be locked into a pretty hot and heavy embrace. When I knocked Sarah acted startled and pushed him away."

"Are you saying you think the embrace was mutual?" Keegan asked. "Or do you think this guy Callahan was forcing himself on her?" He rolled his mug back and forth in his hands as Barbara talked.

"That's just it. I'm not sure." Barbara paused long enough to bite her lower lip then continued. "From what I saw, I suppose it could have been either way."

"From what you saw," repeated Keegan.

"Yeah."

"Yeah, but?"

"I'm not sure," Barbara said. She drew her eyebrows into a worried look and began to feel more and more like she was telling tales. She dropped her eyes to her coffee, looked at the small crowd at the refreshment table, then back to her pastor. "It was just a feeling I had as we talked together. She seemed to be hiding something from me."

"How's that?" Keegan asked.

"I guess it's because of what we didn't talk about. She seemed to want to avoid talking about trouble at the mill, her husband, or any of what we've been discussing lately. And she definitely didn't want to talk about what had just happened with Callahan. Like I said, it's not so much what I know as what I feel, and I thought it might be helpful to you before you meet with her tomorrow." Realizing how much of what she had said was purely suspicion on her part about a dear friend, she added, "You won't mention any of this to Sarah, will you?"

"I'll keep my ears open, and we'll let your friend explore her concerns over her marriage at her own pace." Keegan drained his mug and began to lead Barbara towards the exit from the hall. She allowed herself to be led. "What you've told me is entirely between you and me."

Hoping she had done right by her friend, Barbara left.

After supper, Pastor Weakley sat at his desk, opened his Bible, and leaned over it with his face in his hands. "Lead me into thy paths, oh God. Let me not stray into sin, but fulfill thy commands." He thought in silence about his daughter. "This terrible act of divorce my daughter contemplates drives me to distraction, oh Lord. I pray for her soul, and plead with thy Spirit to drive her from this sin-sick act. Call her back into thy ways, Lord, and show me how I may be her guide. Show me too, how I may be thy instrument of salvation for Eddie. Show me how I may bring Eddie into thy loving and everlasting arms."

So troubled of heart was Pastor Weakley that he repeated his prayer over and over, well past midnight, uncertain he was heard.

NOVEMBER 3RD
MONDAY

Eileen had awakened earlier than usual of late, so Keegan had spent the early morning preparing her a hot breakfast in hopes she would manage to eat a mouthful or two and keep it down. When she had finished and settled into a comfortable chair with a favorite book, he slipped out of the house and managed to be in the church office by oh nine hundred, just moments behind his secretary Grace. As was his custom, he began his Monday mornings by organizing his thoughts around the upcoming Sunday service.

"Keegan, just a reminder," called Grace, "you have a ten o'clock appointment with Sarah Conger who wants to discuss a bad marriage."

Keegan was both annoyed and thankful for the interruption. He was annoyed because Grace had become aware of his apparent distraction over Eileen's condition and sensed the need to remind him of all his appointments. He didn't like being that obvious about personal issues.

His years in the Navy had taught him how to put aside personal feelings and get to the job at hand. During triage in 'Nam, when the wounded were flooding the deck from med-evac choppers, it had torn him up to put a severely wounded soldier aside to die in order to save three or four of his buddies who had arrived in less serious condition. There had never been time enough to mourn. At times even the chaplains couldn't offer prayers fast enough for the dead and dying. You had to put the feelings aside and get on with the job. Keegan was disappointed with himself about not getting on with the job.

On the other hand, he was thankful for Grace's observation and manner because her reminders had kept him on track without ever mentioning his failings. Leaning back in his chair so he could look at

Grace who faced away from him, he asked, "How in the hell do you know that, Grace? Sarah is a referral from Barbara Ross, and I only got the call Saturday and spoke briefly with Barb about it on Sunday. You weren't there. How do you know this stuff?"

"It's my job to know," said Grace matter-of-factly. Turning from her computer to face Keegan she added, "Besides, you can't live in this town your whole life without knowing what's going on."

Keegan knew the truth of her statement. Having lived her entire sixty-seven years in Fort George, a community of 5500 souls, Grace did know nearly everyone and everything. Grace wasn't a busybody, she had a zipped lip. Keegan had learned to trust her by letting her in on small bits of confidential information, like typing notes of encouragement to a sixteen year old expectant mother, without later hearing through the grapevine about so and so's unfortunate pregnancy. Keegan surmised that he had learned what the community already knew: Grace could hold a confidence. Because of her confidentiality, people shared things with Grace they thought the pastor should know without jeopardizing their anonymity.

As Keegan returned his focus to the upcoming Sunday, Grace could be heard clicking away at the computer keyboard entering year-end reports, handling the usual assortment of scheduling calls for A.A. meetings, Diet Workshop, aerobics, the county meals program, Girl Scouts and Boy Scouts, and dealing with the interruptions of the copier service agent and a saleswoman from a distant office supplies outfit.

As Keegan worked along, he could hear Grace greeting someone in her office. It sounded as though they were catching up on old news, then he became aware of a presence in the doorway between their work areas.

"Keegan, your ten o'clock appointment is here, this is Mrs. Sarah Conger," Grace said as she ushered Sarah into Keegan's study by the elbow.

Sarah entered the study with hesitant steps, holding a small purse in both hands clutched just under her breasts. She wore a long-sleeved floral print dress that was a little too young for her, and maybe a little too short. Around her neck she tied a coordinating silk scarf. He rose from his desk, stepped toward Sarah extending his hand and greeted her. Pointing to a couple of wing-back chairs and a leather sofa arranged around a small coffee table on the far side of the study, he suggested she be seated. Sarah moved ahead of him towards a chair facing the sofa. Keegan followed behind, pressing the open key on the intercom as he passed by his desk. He could hear Grace close the door between their offices behind him.

Keegan always felt a bit deceitful with the open intercom. People sought privacy and confidentiality from their clergy. And they got that for the most part. But charges of clergy misconduct over recent years had moved the Conference of Churches to encourage clergy to counsel with open doors, or open intercoms. Keeg had decided that the open intercom was less intrusive. He had received some protestations from Grace -- she had not wanted to be a voyeur – but in the end she acquiesced. Keegan sat in the remaining wing-back. "Well, Sarah, what brings you here this morning?"

Sarah sat bolt upright, not quite on the edge of the seat, but neither was she deep enough in the chair to rest her back. Her feet were next to one another, flat on the floor. Hands and denim fabric purse rested on her lap. To Keegan, she looked and acted like a school girl on an interview for her first part time job. But the image was out of focus somehow. While she dressed and behaved quite young, she looked like a woman in her early thirties.

"I'm here because Barbara Ross, one of your flock, thought you could help me." She bit her lower lip and then added, "I don't know if anyone can help me."

"Well Sarah, let's begin with your story." Keegan crossed his legs and settled back in his chair, hoping his posture would help relax Sarah.

"I'm feeling pretty confused, pastor," said Sarah. She was fingering the tan leather strap of her purse, and Keegan noticed that her toes were clenching inside her shoes – first one set would curl and relax, then the other. "Barbara says your religion doesn't hold it against a person if they get divorced, is that so?"

"Divorce, eh?" said Keegan as he thought, right again, Grace. "It's not something we recommend, like fasting for Lent. But we won't excommunicate you or send you to hell over it. What makes you think you're ready for divorce?"

"Oh, I'm not!" said Sarah. Her reply seemed almost frantic. Her fingers twisted the purse strap around themselves, drawing the strap tight into her flesh. "I was just asking, because it's so different from how I was raised."

Not quite comfortable, Keegan shifted his weight slightly and suggested Sarah tell him what was behind her concern over divorce, and why Barbara Ross had suggested she come to see him.

"Eddie and I haven't been getting along very well over the last couple of years," she said and lowered her head. "Longer, actually. He yells a lot," then looking at Keegan and sounding a bit defensive added, "but he's got a lot on his mind lately – he's been crossing the picket lines at the mill and getting a lot of flack over that from some of the other men. Some have even threatened him."

Her comments reminded Keegan of the Fort George Area Clergy proposal he was to make later in the week to the town board for a program on non-violent strike action.

Lowering her eyes once more, Sarah continued, "We argue a lot, and the kids set him off." She was silent for a time.

Keegan let her be silent for a bit, just long enough for her to become a little uncomfortable. When she shuffled her feet he asked, "What do you argue about?"

"Nothing in particular," she said. She looked up, then back at the floor and added, "Money, bills, sometimes the kids, church, his drinking, ...money."

"You fight about church?"

"Only when I'm going to church when Eddie thinks I should be doing something for him. Like most any time I go to church."

"Hmm." This particular line of thought interested Keegan, although he didn't think it would take them anywhere productive. "Which church do you attend, Sarah?" he asked.

"I'm a member of the Good News Apostolic Lighthouse." Sarah said this with some enthusiasm, as if playing a programmed recording. As Sarah spoke of her church, Keegan half expected to be asked if he was saved. He was familiar with their pastor, William Weakley. Weakley had been a particularly caustic character whose brand of self-righteousness and charisma fostered his sheep-stealing ways – a practice of wooing parishioners from other churches into his own.

"And it is expected that you'll spend a good deal of your free time serving God through the church," Sarah continued. Then, a little pensively she said, "Maybe Eddie's right. Maybe I do spend too much time away."

"Do you?" Keegan asked in his best counselor's voice. He hated that voice when it popped up; he preferred to be a pastor, not a therapist. Oh well, he thought, counselors were fast becoming modern day cult leaders, and counseling their new religion.

"I do spend a lot of time at church," Sarah said, "what with prayer meeting, Sunday services, teaching Sunday School, serving meals once a month at the city mission all the way down in Schenectady, it can take a lot of time." Then, looking quizzically at Keegan, she added, "That's an odd question from a pastor. Don't you expect your people to spend all of their free time here at church?"

54

"No," Keegan said. Sarah's cocked eyebrow underscored her surprise over his answer. "But let's not get into my expectations. Let's stay with what brought you here. Tell me a little of what life is like for you."

Keegan heard a story that was all too familiar since his arrival in Fort George. Most men in town, and a few women, worked swing shifts at the paper mill. The swing shifts – first shift one week, second shift the week after, and third shift the week after that – left most families' schedules and lives in shreds.

"Lately, it seems, Eddie's getting meaner," Sarah said.

Keegan encouraged her to continue with her story. As she spoke of their early years together, Keegan noticed the tired circles under Sarah's eyes and a certain harried quality about her appearance. Or, was it sophomoric? Her hair was combed, but not quite finished, the eye makeup was inexpertly applied, as if by someone just learning about such things. Even her scent was young, a perfume or cologne he had come to associate with the teenage girls in the church youth group. It was as if this woman was just beginning to explore her femininity.

"When we were first married, he never hit me. "Well, almost never hit me, and even then it was just a slap. I usually deserved it. Anyway, back then . . ."

"Wait a minute, Sarah," interrupted Keegan, holding his hand up, "What makes you say you deserved to be slapped?"

"I must have talked back, or something to make him upset." Sarah was truly on the edge of her seat now, and her confessional voice was filled with shame. "I did that a lot when we were first married. My daddy always said I was rebellious against God and man. It took me a long while to submit to my husband."

Leaning forward in his chair and resting his elbows on his thighs while clasping his hands, Keegan tried to look Sarah in the eyes which she kept protected from his gaze by the long red hair which had fallen over her shoulder to hide the side of her face.

"Sarah," Keegan said, in a voice softer than he was accustomed to hearing from himself. "Why do you think you need to submit to your husband? Why do you think he has a right to slap you if you don't submit?"

"Because the Bible says so," explained Sarah, as if pointing out the obvious to a child. Brushing the hair out of her face with her left hand and inclining her head so as to fully face Keegan, she quoted, " 'Wives, submit yourselves unto your own husbands, as unto the Lord. For the husband is the head of the wife, even as Christ is the head of the church: and he is the savior of the body.' That's Ephesians, chapter five, verses twenty-two and twenty-three." Lifting herself a bit more, and sounding a little scolding, she added, "I'm surprised you didn't know that, pastor."

"Oh, I'm familiar with it," Keegan said as he rose from his seat and moved to the credenza behind him to retrieve a Bible. Returning to his seat, he handed the Bible to Sarah before seating himself. "There's more that follows the passage you quoted. Please find it and read it aloud."

Sarah quickly thumbed to the appropriate place with practiced familiarity. Running her finger down the column of scripture, she stopped at the requested verses. Lifting the bible she began reading, "Therefore as the church is subject unto Christ, so let the wives be to their own husbands in everything." Returning the bible to her lap, she looked to Keegan and said soberly, "See pastor, I told you that's how it is."

"Read one more verse," insisted Keegan, "and read verse twenty-eight after that."

Once more Sarah lifted the Bible and read, "Husbands, love your wives, even as Christ also loved the church, and gave himself up for it." Her voice trailed off as she scanned for the next verse and then resumed, "So ought men to love their wives as their own bodies. He that loveth his wife loveth himself." Returning the Bible to her lap and sitting upright looking at Keegan Sarah asked, "What are you trying to say?"

Taking a moment to formulate his response, Keegan sat back in his own chair. We're talking her language, he thought.

"I don't know who has been preaching this *wives submit to your husbands* nonsense to you," Keegan said, "but I want you to know that scripture is clear: If wives are to submit at all, it is only to a husband who loves them as much as Jesus loves the church. And unless you believe that Jesus would abuse the church, there's no reason to accept abuse from your husband. Do you understand that?"

"I, I think so, but it's contrary to what Daddy always taught. The man of the house has the last say; he is the lord of the manor. Daddy always made that clear. He was fond of reminding Mama, God rest her soul, that she was to obey him as if he were Jesus Christ himself. He wouldn't like to hear what you've got to say very much."

"Is your father also a member of your church?"

"Oh, no sir, he's the pastor, the Reverend William Weakley of the Good News Apostolic..."

"Lighthouse," Keegan said, finishing her sentence. He rolled his eyes upward and added, "I'm getting the picture now." Keegan realized that if Weakley had any idea that his daughter was seeking counsel from the Methodist Pastor in town he would be outraged.

"I understand that you're hearing from me a very different religious perspective than you're accustomed to hearing," Keegan said. "Can you accept that there may be a different and equally valid interpretation about husband and wife relations?"

There was silence as Sarah thought. "I'm not sure," she said, "you see things differently, but I've been told all my life that you people don't speak the truth, and that your ways are of the devil." Sarah shifted in her seat, and rearranged the purse in her lap as if to cover her knees. "This is very confusing. This is beginning to feel very wrong to me. Maybe I shouldn't have come." Sarah rose to her feet. "I think I should go now, I've got to go fix Eddie's lunch; it'll be noon soon." Keegan stood at his chair. Sarah made her way towards the study door into the hall, all the while talking, "Eddie's on first shift this week, and when he comes through the door at lunch time, he wants to see his lunch on the table waiting for him."

Keegan moved a few steps towards the door. He wondered what specific emotional button he had managed to push to draw the session to such a quick close.

Opening the door, Sarah briefly faced Keegan and exited with, "I'm sorry to have wasted your time, pastor. Thank you. Good-bye." The door closed and she was gone.

"Whew!" Keegan whispered to himself. "I'll probably never see her again." He returned to his desk, spoke into the intercom, "Station K-E-E-G signing off," and released the open key. He could hear Grace laugh in the other office.

After seating himself, he cleared off a working space on the desk blotter, drew a fresh piece of paper from a drawer, and began making some notes to himself about the session with Sarah. He would begin a new confidential file under her name. In the unlikely event she called to see him again he would be able to review his observations and remind himself of the conversation before their next meeting. Among the things he noted to himself was his own wonderment about what made this woman of about thirty seem to behave so much as a young girl. Had the men in her life kept her simple? Did it have something to do with her religion? Keegan didn't think so; he had known many other charismatic Christians who had not struck him as immature or unsophisticated as a result of their faith. Was her girlishness genuine? Maybe that was the real question. Was she genuine?

Eileen's kiss was soft and loving as Keegan bent over her. She remained in a chaise lounge on the back deck of the parsonage, soaking up the warmth of the early November sun. The leaves were about two weeks past their peak color. She and MaryKay from next door were chatting when Keegan arrived from the office to share lunch with her. As Keegan greeted them both, MaryKay stood to leave.

"Don't leave on my account," Keegan said. "Please, stay for lunch."

MaryKay declined, as she nearly always did. She had to run off and do something or other – Keegan didn't really listen – feed a cat, grocery shop, rob a bank, something. MaryKay said her good-byes and Keegan escorted her to the front door through the house.

Opening the front door for her he said, "You're an angel, MaryKay, for looking after Eileen each morning."

"What are good friends for?" she asked, giving Keegan's hand a squeeze. "I'm closer to her than my own sister. I'll see you tomorrow."

As Keegan followed MaryKay with his eyes from the doorway, he said a silent prayer of thanks for the bond Eileen and her good friend had made over the last few years.

Keegan closed the door and went to the downstairs bathroom to remove the hundred count bottle of acetaminophen from the medicine cabinet and replenish the vial he'd been carrying around in his jacket pocket over the last couple of days. He emptied the twenty or so tablets into the vial and made a mental note to stop by the pharmacy to pick up another hundred count. He returned to the back deck.

Eileen was stretched out in the sun, wrapped in a log cabin quilt she had made for herself only a year ago. Keegan asked, "The usual, milady?"

"Yes, milord," she said, as she looked in the direction of his voice.

Keegan stepped back into the kitchen, just inside the sliding glass door, to put the kettle on for tea and prepare lunch. They spoke cheerily between the deck and the kitchen while Keegan made sandwiches, poured tea, and brought lunch out to the deck on a large serving tray. As Keegan set Eileen's lunch on the stand next to her, they spoke of Eileen's morning with MaryKay and Keegan's routine at the church. They fell into a long comfortable silence in the afternoon sun.

Eileen broke the silence. "You seem lost in thought. What's on your mind?"

"I was just thinking about a young woman I interviewed this morning. Do you know Sarah Conger? She's Bill Weakley's daughter."

"No, I don't believe I do," said Eileen as she readjusted the quilt around herself. Lunch seemed not to interest her.

"She came in this morning about an abusive marriage." Keegan straightened some in his chair, energized by the subject of work.

"If her father's the Lighthouse pastor, why did she come to see you?"

"If you were considering divorce, would you go see your fundamentalist pastor father for advice?" asked Keegan. "Anyway, she came in quoting scripture out of context about wives being subservient to their husbands and that's why she feels obligated to stay in the relationship." Keegan got up and headed for the kitchen. "Would you like more tea?"

"No thanks." Calling after him she said, "You still haven't answered why, with that mindset, she came in to see you."

He turned on the kettle and called back to Eileen, "Apparently she's friends with Barbara Ross who convinced her that seeing me would be a good idea."

"I would have thought Barbara had more sense than to send an innocent fundamentalist to the likes of a sacrilegious Methodist like you," called Eileen. She chuckled at her own humor, but broke into a cough.

Her coughing brought Keegan to the doorway. He waited a moment and she stopped.

"You deserved that for impugning me," he said.

"Thanks a lot."

"Why is she the assumed innocent and I the heavy?" Keegan remained at the doorway waiting for the kettle to boil. "Anyway, after she told part of her story I had her read a bit of scripture beyond her limited quote to show her that subservience was a response to selfless love."

"Subservience was a what?" exploded Eileen, craning her neck around to look towards the kitchen and Keegan through the opened door. "You told this girl she should be subservient?"

"Wow, what happened to the cool keep-your-distance counselor?" He realized he had folded his arms in the typical look of self defense. "How many times have you told me to use the language of the client – your words – so that they understand what I'm saying?"

"But subservience, Keegan?" Eileen yowled.

"Jeez-Louise, give me a break, will ya Eileen?" He put his hands in his pockets and added a shrug. "I was just trying to show the kid that the very passage she was quoting to me had a decidedly different intent from what she was taught. I don't think she's ready for a discussion on Historical Biblical Criticism just yet. Besides, she's probably been told that women's liberation has been sent from the devil to corrupt the world and upset God's order." The kettle began whistling. As Keegan turned, he added under his breath, "They might even be right," and stepped back into the kitchen to pour his tea.

"They might be WHAT?" intoned Eileen, indignantly.

"I said they might try being contrite, dear," Keegan said with a smile. It seemed to him that he and Eileen had always managed to jab fun at each other, even during serious conversations. He supposed humor had been a good defense against taking on all of the world's problems as their own. But now it was time to focus a bit more. Leaving humor behind, he stepped back out onto the deck, stood by Eileen's chaise, and sipped his tea. After a moment he continued, "All I tried to do was to begin to help her see that there was a very different perspective about husband and wife relationships." He moved to the deck railing opposite Eileen, and leaned against it facing her.

"How successful do you think you were?" Eileen asked. She pulled the quilt up around her neck.

"Not very," said Keegan, sipping his tea, "It was as If once confronted by a conflicting perspective from the Bible itself, she had to run away. In fact, she did. Within seconds, she was out of my study, and I was left there with my face hanging out. I don't expect I'll see her again."

"It's a shame she left so quickly, you really set her up."

"Set her up?"

"Sure," Eileen said. She settled deeper into the quilt. "You confronted her with a perspective contrary to what she has always held as truth, not to mention holy. And, you presented that contrary perspective from the very same source she holds as sacred. In addition, you're holding the prospect of providing her permission for the thing she wants, divorce, from the very same source she has believed prohibited it."

"That's not true," Keegan said. "Her old man is the source of the erroneous assumption, and scripture is the source of the liberating truth."

"She may not yet be able to tell the difference, Keeg," said Eileen, with gentleness in her voice. "I hope you see her again, because right now she's got an internal conflict of holy war proportions that's going to have to be resolved one way or another."

Keegan took his tea back to the Adirondack chair. They sat in quiet contemplation for a while.

Eileen lowered the back of her chaise. She curled into a fetal position for her afternoon nap. Drifting off she said, "It occurs to me, Keeg, usually everyone involved in a holy war gets hurt or killed."

The ringing phone startled Keegan out of the nap he had not intended for himself. After rubbing the sleep from his eyes, he glanced at his watch. "Damn, it's three-thirty already." The phone rang again, getting through to Eileen now. Keegan moved quickly to answer the phone before its ringing could bring Eileen completely around.

Through sobs, Keegan heard a female voice ask, "Is this Pastor O'Connor? I have to speak to Pastor O'Connor." On the other end of the line was Sarah. Through her tears and catching breath she explained that she had been beaten by Eddie because his lunch was late. "I have to see you Pastor, can you please meet me?"

Not wanting to leave Eileen alone, but concerned about this young woman's obvious crisis, Keegan reluctantly agreed to meet Sarah briefly at the church. After hanging up the phone, he scribbled a note to his wife to leave on the stand by her chaise. He wouldn't be gone long, he thought, back in time to help Eileen come inside before the late afternoon grew cool.

As he slipped the note under Eileen's tea cup so it wouldn't blow away, Eileen spoke sleep laden words without turning over to face him, "Watch out for the holy wars."

When Keegan arrived at the church, Sarah was already there waiting. She was seated on the stone retaining wall near the entrance of the fellowship hall, closest to the office wing. She was hunched over, holding her face in her hands, and her body heaved with sobbing. As Keegan approached her up the walkway, he could hear her crying. When he got to her, he sat on the stone wall next to her and placed his hand on her shoulder. She responded by burying her face into his Donegal tweed jacket and sobbing with abandon. Keegan did the only thing he could think to do, hold her, stroke her hair, and let her cry.

When her sobs began to subside, her breath began to catch in child-like hiccups. Lifting Sarah to her feet, Keegan said, "Come on, we'll go inside."

Wordlessly she followed his lead. He took her down the hall to his study, unlocked the door, and led her to the wingback chair she had occupied earlier. Placing a box of Kleenex on the table before her and withdrawing one to give her, he said, "You wait here, and I'll bring you some water. Or would you prefer tea?"

"Water will be fine," she said, drying her eyes and looking up at Keegan. "Thanks."

Keegan left the room. Once out the study door he heard a trumpet blast that was Sarah blowing her nose. He smiled at the noise as he continued on toward the kitchen and water for the distressed maiden with cleared sinuses.

When he returned to the study, he found Sarah where he left her. She had removed her sweater and laid it over the arm of the chair. He handed the water to Sarah. She lifted her face towards him, and with her scarf missing, Keegan noticed for the first time the terrible bruise high on her sternum, and the bruises on her upper arms.

"My God, Sarah, did your husband do this to you?" He put the glass on the table next to the tissues and moved to Sarah's side to examine her arm.

Sarah drew back and clutched at her arm with one hand, and attempted to cover her bruised chest with the other, as if caught topless by a park ranger along an abandoned stretch of beach. "I, uh...Eddie didn't mean it. He got carried away and..."

"This is very serious, Sarah." Keegan didn't let her finish. Sarah's withdrawal made Keegan realize he'd invaded her space. He eased himself into the chair next to Sarah and continued, "Do you want me to check on available space at the women's shelter? There's no need for you to put up with this."

"No, no, please," Sarah said, almost panicked. She twisted in her seat to face Keegan. "That would only make things worse. They've settled down just now."

"Very well, for the moment. But you're going to have to do something to get yourself out of danger. You can't let this sort of thing go on." He leaned forward, and gently brushed aside some of her hair that had fallen over her arm, and scowled at the bruise.

Sarah turned from him and began to cry into a tissue. Through her tears she managed to say, "I feel so confused, so alone...it's as if God's punishing me. I feel so helpless."

Keegan let her cry, and when he could hear her catch her breath, he asked, "Do you feel as if the three most important men in your life are conspiring to hold you down...to beat you up?"

"I'm not sure I know what you mean?" Her tears had streaked her mascara, and when she wiped her eyes with a tissue, she smeared eye shadow and eye liner into indistinguishable swirls. Her bloodshot eyes blinked at Keegan as she stared at him.

"Do you feel as if your husband wants to control you, and that your father approves? And on top of that, do you feel as if Jesus has betrayed you in the bargain?"

"That almost sounds blasphemous."

"I don't mean to sound sacrilegious." He spoke in the soft voice that had earlier surprised him. He wondered why he felt so protective over this young woman. "I'm asking if you feel trapped in a bad marriage by both your husband and father; and do you feel that your faith endorses that? Supports that?" Sarah seemed to be thinking that over, and Keegan added, "Do you feel there is no place to turn?"

Sarah reached out her hand and touched the side of Keegan's face, running her fingers down the side of his beard. Looking into his eyes with what felt to him to be adoration, she said, "Until now." She stared into his eyes, forcing him to divert his look from hers. "Your flock must love and respect you a great deal."

Keegan felt a blush come on and began to wish for Grace in the adjoining office with an open intercom. He straightened up to create a bit of professional distance. Groping for something to say that would defuse the situation, he said, "Well, that depends upon the day of the week, and who I've disappointed most recently." He glanced back at her only to see that she held him in her gaze.

"No, no, you're being modest," Sarah said. "You have a very different way of seeing things, of saying just the right thing to make everything so very clear."

Keegan thought that this last comment may have meant she was indeed beginning to develop a different perspective. He decided to press, and said, "Tell me what you think I said, or what you believe you see differently."

"I suppose I do feel trapped." Turning her body to more directly face Keegan she continued, "I'm married to Eddie, and he's the head of household." She paused, then added, "The Bible says I...I have to obey him. Daddy says I'd burn in hell if I was to divorce Eddie, and Daddy says Jesus is very clear about this."

Keegan sat back into his chair and stroked his chin. After a moment he said, "Sarah, would you allow me to share a very different understanding about divorce, and what we believe Jesus expects of husbands and wives?"

"I think maybe Daddy is...wrong." She stared into Keegan's eyes and once again raised his color. "I don't think you speak for the devil. I'd like to hear what you believe."

"Please don't misunderstand, I rarely recommend separation or divorce, but neither do I wish to see people remain in a bad marriage out of their sense of fear or guilt. There's enough of that in the world without the church adding to it." Keegan leaned into the arm of the wingback chair and crossed his legs. After briefly describing biblical archaeology and the use of biblical puns that did not translate well into English he summed up by saying: "Biblical archeology has shown us that Jesus actually spoke against the popular practice of *putting a wife away* –

making a prisoner of a wife in her own home – and taking another wife. Jesus was upset with the injustice of that practice, not the equitable dissolution of a marriage through divorce. The word that we translate *put your wife away*, was a pun on the Aramaic word for divorce. So Jesus never spoke against divorce, only against imprisoning and oppressing women in their own homes so as to avoid the inconvenience and considerable expense of divorce by their husbands while taking other women as wives. Jesus stood against injustice, not for bad relationships."

Sarah sat in her chair in what seemed to Keegan to be rapt attention. He wished he could see the same level of energy and attentiveness in his weekly congregation. Her eyes never left him. He found that flattering, a bit exciting and unnerving. An image of Eileen at home on the back deck floated across his mind and stabbed at his conscience.

"That's a lot to hear all at once," Sarah said. She let out a big sigh as if she had been holding her breath the whole time Keegan spoke. "It's so contrary to what I've always been taught. What do you think I should do?"

"I can't answer that for you, Sarah. But I wanted you to hear a different perspective so that you can make your decisions based on something other than fear and guilt."

"It's all so confusing," Sarah said. She turned her eyes from Keegan for the first time in a long while, and sounded almost ashamed. "Your words sound so freeing. But I'm not sure they're God's will."

"I'm sure it is confusing," Keegan said. He uncrossed his legs and sat square in his chair. "It would be particularly confusing when you're right in the middle of a difficult time in your marriage."

Sarah remained silent, contemplative. After a few moments she spoke.

"I have to think this over," she said, and stood. Keegan followed her lead. "I want to thank you so much for seeing me. I feel better for having talked, and for your listening." She walked towards the study door. "I'm glad for your words. I'm not sure what I'll do with them." Keegan followed to escort her out.

She stopped at the door while Keegan reached in front of her to open it. Sarah turned her head over her shoulder to face Keegan and asked, "Pastor, please don't mention any of this to my father."

"Not to worry, Sarah, all such conversations are strictly confidential. You take care of yourself, and be sure to call if you need me. God bless."

"Thank you so much." Sarah leaned into Keegan and kissed him on the cheek. "You've been very kind." She walked through the doorway and down the hall.

Keegan closed the door, returned to his desk, and found the confidential file marked CONGER, SARAH and made additional notes about his meeting. His final comment read: *Young woman feels like a girl trapped in a bad marriage by husband, fundamentalist pastor/father, and her belief system (Jesus also viewed as an oppressor). How do I avoid setting her up for severe internal conflict regarding polarizing effect of different religious perspectives?*

Keegan returned the file to its cabinet and headed for his own hat and coat. As he passed by Sarah's chair, he noticed her sweater. It was getting late in the day; he decided he would drop it off at her house on his way to the office tomorrow morning. He'd have to come up with some feasible story about how he came to possess the sweater. He'd think of something. Just now, it was time to get back to Eileen.

Eddie dragged his feet towards the time clock. There was always a bit more fatigue the first day or two of a shift change, but the three hours of overtime had done him in. At least Sarah would be happy with the additional pay. As he punched out for the night the time clock flashed 18:32. He heard fire sirens outside and figured one of the fifty-five gallon fire barrels on the picket line outside the mill fence had gotten out of hand. Some ass, he thought, probably tried to start a fire with gasoline. He walked out the door.

He wandered out into the parking lot and saw a pumper fire truck, several firefighters, and foam everywhere. Some poor bastard's car had caught fire.

As Eddie got closer he noticed that an unofficial truce was apparently declared as strikers put their picket signs down, crossed over onto mill property, and intermingled with scabs who had come out of the mill to see the spectacle. Eddie could also see that the fully involved car, or truck, was somewhere near his own vehicle.

Near?

No. It was his truck, fully ablaze. He broke into a run and when he got to the crowd he began to elbow his way through. He was stopped by one of the firefighters.

"But that's my truck!" Eddie yelled.

"Take it easy pal," the firefighter said, "it's junk now. There's nothing you can do about it."

Eddie struggled against the firefighter and another who had come to assist upon seeing the commotion. Then he felt his muscles relax as he gave up on the truck.

The air filled with the smell of burning rubber mixed with the acrid steam from the fire retardant foam. The firefighters let go of Eddie and returned their attention to the fire.

The last flame flicker was extinguished with another blast of foam from the pumper. Firefighters, in full turn out gear, stood at the ready like a local militia surrounding the enemy. The old Chevy smoldered and hissed.

Eddie stood staring at his ruined truck, when from behind him he heard, "Hey Conger, this is what happens to scabs!"

At the sound of the words, Eddie felt a darkness come over him. His jaw set, and his brow felt heavy and low. He turned in the direction of the voice, but did not see anyone in particular that looked as though they were talking to him. He took a step in the direction of the crowd, which by now had begun to thin, and searched the crowd with his eyes.

The mob shuffled as all mobs do when a new and palpable tension erupts. Here was a man who looked to kick ass and collective testicles crawled up for safety's sake. Eddie's eyes settled on Daniel Callahan.

Callahan stared at Eddie and smiled the smile of the self-important.

Eddie lunged at Callahan, and caught him by the throat with his left hand. He brought his right back with the full intention of burying it deep inside Callahan's skull.

Two arms grabbed Eddie's right, two more his left. Two more men tackled him, bringing all five men to the cold wet pavement. Eddie immediately thought Callahan's lackeys had him. He landed hard on his back, knocking the wind out of him. While trying to free himself, he tightened all of his muscles expecting to be kicked and beaten.

He was held fast.

Nothing more happened.

Callahan was screaming, "Let me go, you idiots, let me go!"

Eddie raised his head and saw that Callahan was pinned under a bulky firefighter sitting on his chest.

Two mill workers, scabs, were on Eddie's arms, and a town constable was on Eddie's chest.

The fourth man had gotten off Eddie and now stood over him. It was the police chief, Arthur Erichson, looking down upon the two combatants. He removed his Smokey-the-Bear hat and ran a hand through his full head of steel grey hair. He put the hat on so it cocked on the side of his head like a 1940's police drama.

"You boys looked like you were about to get yourselves into a lot of trouble," Erichson said.

"That crazy son-of-a-bitch over there set my truck on fire!" Eddie struggled again, and felt the men tighten their grip on his arms. The constable rode out the body roll like a man on horseback.

"He's got no proof of that, Chief," Callahan sounded off. "He's just a scab lookin' for trouble. He probably set it."

"Oh, Mr. Callahan, don't get too uppity," Chief Erichson said as he moved to stand next to Callahan's ear, "I heard what you said. I suspect Mr. Conger did too. Sounded mighty implicative, don't you think?"

"I didn't say nothin'! I was just standin' there like everybody else!" Callahan claimed. It was his turn to struggle against the hold on him.

The chief knelt down next to Callahan and tisked at him. "You're lying now, Mr. Callahan. I don't like to be lied to. I was standing right behind you when you shouted something about this fire being Mr. Conger's reward for being a scab." He tisked at Callahan again.

"Arrest him, will ya?" Eddie called to the chief. He felt like he was on the winning side of this argument even if he was flat on his back. "He's got to pay for this! He's got to pay for my truck!"

"Oh, I don't think you're entitled to compensation Mr. Conger, at least not from Mr. Callahan." The chief got up and walked over to Eddie, and knelt over him this time. "It's my understanding that you may be the source of some significant repair bills for Mr. Callahan's Toyota, as well as some medical expenses. Isn't that so?"

"I, uh, I don't know what you're talking about." Eddie decided to play stupid, which he thought had not been all that difficult for him lately. Then, confirming his suspicions about his own IQ he added, "If that bastard had any balls, he would have faced me like a man, not torched my truck!"

"I'll tell you who's got gonads, Conger," Callahan called. Your boy is MY kid!" Callahan struggled against those who held him. "I'M the man in YOUR house!"

"You BASTARD!" Eddie roared. He broke his right arm free, wrapped it around the constable and pulled him off his chest, and started to roll over and up onto his left hip. But before he could get a leg under himself, the constable and mill worker both tackled Eddie from the back and rolled him over onto his belly and pushed his face into the pavement. Spitting into the blacktop, Eddie yelled, "I'll kill you, you bastard Callahan. If I ever see you again, I'll kill you!"

"Not if I see you first, Eunuch!" returned Callahan.

"Boys, boys, this is most uncivilized," the chief said from behind Eddie. "Auto wrecks, hospital bills, truck fires, and now death threats. What's a police chief to do? This is all very serious stuff."

Then the chief seemed to address others standing about, and in a business like voice said, "Get these galoots on their feet. Put one in Constable Henry's car, and the other in my Blazer." Turning his attention to the crowd he added, "The rest of you people can go about your business." All moved away but one; a man who had been near Callahan in the crowd momentarily stood firm, chewing on a cigar. A scar made it appear as though he had three eyebrows. After a moment he left.

"You boys are going down to the station for a while, the chief said, looking alternately between Callahan and Eddie. "I'm going to have you sit in opposite corners until you can make up your minds to play nice." Nodding to the constable he said, "Take them away."

The siren wailed and Eddie snapped out of sound sleep. He sat up in his bunk and slammed his head into the steel springs of the bunk above which sent him reeling back into his mattress.

"Shit!" He held the top of his head. "Damn!" The 8:05 P.M. county mutual aid siren test signaling to all on Mondays, Wednesdays and Fridays that the volunteers were at the ready and the system was A-OK wailed on atop the roof of the police station.

NOVEMBER 4TH
TUESDAY

Eddie lay in his bunk. Chief Erichson stood in front of the cell with hooked thumbs in his holster belt.

"Well Conger," the chief said, "you seem to be a lucky man. Callahan says you didn't ram his car with your truck. It seems your vehicle was parked on a hill and the brakes gave way. It just rolled into his. Just dumb bad luck, according to Callahan. He likens it to your probably leaving a butane lighter in the windshield of your truck, igniting the blaze last night. I didn't know you smoked, Eddie. You smoke?"

"Uh, yeah...a little," Eddie said. He sat up on the bunk. He was having a hard time keeping up with the meaning of the chief's words.

"Callahan also says he doesn't know who hit him in The Stallions the other night." The chief unhooked his thumbs and unlocked the cell door. "It seems that in the thick of a barroom brawl, it's difficult to tell who's hitting who." He swung wide the cell door.

"He's a mighty angry man, though," Erichson continued. "If I were the man responsible for breaking his nose, I'd steer clear of him." Standing in the open doorway he added, "All things being equal," and he stared at Eddie right in the eye, "and they *are* equal, I can't seem to find any evidence that your truck fire was anything but an accident." The chief stepped into the cell and stood over Eddie's bunk.

"Furthermore, I've impressed upon Mr. Callahan, and I wish to impress upon you, that there will be no more *accidents* in town. Should there be any more accidents during these tense times, I will call upon you gentlemen first. I expect I will not have to call upon any others. Am I making myself perfectly clear, Mr. Conger?"

Eddie nodded.

69

"Fine. Now get up, collect your belongings at the desk, and get your sorry ass out of here."

Wordlessly and quickly, Eddie rolled out of the cell bunk, slipped his feet into his laceless shoes, and shuffled past the chief, down the hall to the counter in the waiting area. After collecting his shoelaces, belt, watch, pocket change, jacket, and now useless truck keys, he left the police station and walked home. Maybe things were equal.

Eddie entered his house through the back door into the kitchen. It was a little past six thirty. Sarah and the kids were at the table eating breakfast. They stopped in mid conversation and stared at him. The rug rats looked fearful. He wondered what she had been telling them?

"Nice of you to come home," Sarah said. She half glanced up at him and instantly returned her stare to her cornflakes.

"Don't start," Eddie said. He draped his jacket over an empty kitchen chair. "I'm only home to clean up and get ready for work."

"You could have at least called," Sarah said, not letting up. "I was worried sick."

"Yeah, right," Eddie said. "Since when?" He was sure her last comment was for the benefit of little William's and Becky's ears. He stood at the sink washing his hands. "You afraid your meal ticket wouldn't come home?"

"Damn you!" Sarah said. She slammed her napkin on the table then folded her arms and faced the empty seat across from her at the table.

"That's enough Sarah," Eddie said. He got the hand towel that hung over the sink and dried his hands. He faced the table and noticed the children sitting at their places watching between their parents; their eyes were wide and afraid. "Let the kids finish their breakfast in peace."

"It's a little late for that, isn't it?" He couldn't see Sarah's face, but her muffled voice signaled a clenched jaw.

Eddie grabbed a bagel out of the bakery bag on the counter and poured himself a cup of coffee. Leaning against the counter, he ate. The children played with their cereal, warily glancing first at one parent and then the other. After a long while, Eddie realized that the kids were not so much eating as dribbling milk on their chins with their spoons. "If you kids are done, you can go get ready for school."

William and Becky broke out of their chairs and ran up the stairs like horses out of the gates at Saratoga.

"Hey, you kids..." Sarah called after them.

"Ah, leave them alone; can't you see they're scared to death?"

"And who do you think they're afraid of?"

Eddie drained the rest of his coffee down the sink and followed the kids upstairs. He showered, shaved, and dressed. He heard the kids ramming around their bedrooms getting their school clothes on, assembling books and whispering in raspy-kid-tones about their parents. Pounding footfalls descended the stairs with shouts of "goodbye" followed by the slam of the back door. The kids were off.

Once Eddie was dressed, he came down the stairs and back into the kitchen with leaden feet. Sarah was still seated at her place with folded arms. She glared straight ahead at the empty seat that served as Eddie's coat rack.

"We're gonna have a knock-down-drag-out when I get home." Eddie stepped behind the empty chair, leaned over it with his hands on the table and stared into Sarah's blank green eyes. Her face had gone to stone, and her stare did not return his, but looked through him to some distant place. "Have the kids take their supper with your father."

The front doorbell rang.

"For godsakes," Eddie said, as he turned to head for the door. "It's 7:30 in the morning. Who in hell could that be?" He swung open the door and saw a man in a chin strap beard standing on the porch. "Yeah?"

"Hi, I'm Keegan O'Connor, the Methodist pastor in town. Are you Mr. Conger?"

"Yeah, but we already got a religion," Eddie said and began to close the door.

"Oh, yes, I only stopped by to return Mrs. Conger's sweater. She left it at the church office yesterday.

"Why was she there?" asked Eddie. He opened the door a bit more and stared at Keegan.

"Seems Grace, my secretary, is the mother of childhood friends of Mrs. Conger, and they were visiting. Anyway, I felt sure she would need her sweater and I offered to save Grace the trip since this is on my way. I do apologize for the early hour, it's..."

"Yeah, okay," Eddie said. "Come on in, I'll call her." O'Connor stepped into the living room and seemed to nose around, while Eddie moved closer to the kitchen before calling, "Sarah, there's a preacher here to see you."

"Just a second," Sarah called.

"See anything you like?" Eddie said, and wished he hadn't. He wasn't aware of any argument he had with this man.

"I'm sorry," O'Connor said. "I was simply admiring your gun cabinet. It's a nice collection."

"Thanks. You know anything about firearms?" Eddie felt a little more at ease with this guy.

"Some," said the preacher. "I was in Uncle Sam's employ for a little more than twenty years. He taught me a little."

"Do you hunt?" Eddie asked as he headed for the cabinet.

"I used to," O'Connor said and followed along. "But I haven't taken the time in years."

Eddie unlocked the cabinet and pulled out his deer rifle. "This is my favorite. It's not worth anything. But she shoots true. She and I bring home a deer every season." He handed it to O'Connor.

The preacher accepted it, checked the chamber, then shouldered it. "It's got nice balance. Is it an easy carry through the woods?"

"Oh, she's not too heavy"

"Good morning, Pastor O'Connor."

Eddie turned to see his wife enter the living room. She had combed her hair since he last saw her in the kitchen.

O'Connor returned the rifle to Eddie. As Eddie put it back into the cabinet, the preacher retrieved a sweater he had laid on the arm of the sofa.

"You left this at the church yesterday when you were visiting Grace." O'Connor handed the sweater to Sarah. "I thought I'd return it before you missed it."

"Thank you," Sarah said. "It's very kind of you to drop this off."

"Not at all," O'Connor said. "It gave me an opportunity to meet your husband." He gestured towards Eddie and then to the cabinet and added, "He's got a fine collection here."

"He's very proud of his guns, all right," Sarah said.

Eddie saw what he thought was a sneer with that remark.

"Would you like a cup of coffee?" she asked.

"No, thanks," the preacher said. "I don't mean to be an imposition. You folks need to get on with your morning routine." He made his way towards the door. "I saw your lights on from outside and took a chance that my stopping by wouldn't be too inconvenient. I really only wanted to drop off the sweater. Thanks very much for the offer, but I should get under way." He opened the door and finished with, "Goodbye." The door closed behind him.

"Who is this Grace you went to see at the Methodist Church? Eddie asked as he turned toward Sarah. "Why are you visiting her?"

"He's just being polite. I went to the church to see him." She snapped.

"Why did you see him?"

"It's confidential," Sarah said, and folded her arms. "I don't have to tell you." She turned and headed into the kitchen.

"What do you mean, you don't have to tell me?" Eddie asked, and followed Sarah. "You screwin' the Methodist preacher, now? First Callahan, now the preacher?"

"Pastor O'Connor says that the conversations between a clergyman and a parishioner are private and personal." Sarah took her place at the table and sipped from her coffee cup. "That's just how I plan to keep it. Personal."

"We'll finish this when I get home tonight," Eddie said and grabbed his jacket from the kitchen chair. "Tonight," he repeated, and pointed his finger at Sarah. "You and me."

Keegan, the Reverend Brigham of the American Baptist Church, Father Joe and Sister Margaret Mary of Saint Anne's Roman Catholic Church, Father Rutherford of All Souls Episcopal Church, and Brother Tom of the Mennonite Fellowship just outside of town, were all meeting in the lounge at Grace United Methodist. All of the men nursed cups of coffee with the exception of Father Rutherford, who sipped tea. Sister Margaret Mary favored water in her quart bottle and straw. She carried it everywhere; Keegan had once seen her in the Grand Union pulling on her straw while reading cat food labels. With a tinge of guilty suspicion, he couldn't help but wonder if it was really water. He had once remarked to Eileen that he found it hard to believe that the woman could be as giddy as she was naturally.

Margaret Mary was not giddy this morning. She wore the same serious face all of the men wore this day.

"So we're agreed," Keegan said. "As the Fort George Area Clergy Association, we will seek the town board's endorsement of our community wide study called, NON-VIOLENT CONFLICT RESOLUTION."

"We'll have to make it clear that this is not a crossing of church and state lines," Father Rutherford said, stirring his tea. "We're simply looking for the town board to encourage the public to study ways to resolve conflict in non-violent, non-hurtful ways."

"It's too bad we weren't thinking along these lines two months ago when we met," Father Joe said, shaking his head back and forth. "If we'd gotten something like this off the ground then, maybe we could have helped avoid that truck fire at the mill."

"Or that poor s.o.b. from getting his nose broken at The Stallions the other night," Keegan said.

Brother Tom looked to Keegan and lifted his palm up as if to stop traffic and displayed a wince of pain.

"Sorry, Tom, just a little Navy slipping out there."

Sister Margaret Mary, not at all her usual ebullient self, played with the straw in her quart mug and asked quietly, "Who will make this presentation tomorrow night at the board?"

"Count me out," Reverend Brigham said and waved both hands in front of himself. "Wednesday evening is prayer meeting. I'll be at church."

"I've got my confirmation class Wednesdays," Father Joe said. He was comfortably settled into his chair, with his hands clasped across his belly.

"I think Keegan should do it," said Rutherford. "It was, after all, his brainstorm." Flashing a smile at Keegan he added, "Besides, who would argue with the Navy at a town board meeting?"

The gathering politely smiled church smiles at Father Rutherford's attempt at humor.

The door off the parking lot leading to the fellowship hall just down the corridor from the lounge slammed. A moment later, into this polite, mostly content and self-assured though concerned circle, Pastor William Weakley stormed.

Heads turned, brows furrowed, Father Rutherford stopped stirring his tea. Pastor Weakley had been extended numerous invitations to participate in the clergy association. He had made it clear to the association that he would not allow himself to be *adulterated*, in his own words, *by mixing with the emissaries of the Whore of Babylon and other cohorts of Satan.*

He stood at the outside of the ring of clergy and pointed his finger at Keegan. "You, sir, are a sheep stealer!"

Keegan, in mid coffee sip, nearly gagged at the accusation. He controlled his impulse to laugh, not wishing to embarrass Weakley any more than he was embarrassing himself. After swallowing the coffee he managed, "Excuse me, I, uh...what?"

Stepping into the middle of the room, and with arm and finger still extended, Weakley accused, "You are attempting to steal my daughter away from my fold and into the ways of darkness. Sheep stealer!"

The other clergy and Sister Margaret Mary watched the drama unfold in their midst with seeming relish. Father Rutherford, now fully behind Weakley, grinned broadly and mocked Weakley's accusatory finger by extending his own index finger and pointing it at Keegan.

"Pastor Weakley," Keegan said; he was now fully recovered from the intrusion. "I prefer not to think of the people of God called Methodists as sheep. And I do not wish to think of myself as leading a bunch of stupid animals."

"Our Lord and Savior Jesus Christ is called the Good Shepherd," said Weakley with his fists clenched at his sides. And with the haughty tones of those who know they have a special truth he said, "Do you call the role of Jesus beneath you?"

"Ow," Father Joe feigned pain across his face. His gesture was immediately followed by two others sounding "Ooo."

"Not at all," said Keegan from his seat, "It is simply that I do not presume to fill the role of our Lord as shepherd. I leave such divine drama for a leading man such as yourself."

"Oh, bravo," said Father Joe, obviously enjoying himself.

"As for your daughter," Keegan continued, trying to ignore Joe, "she has sought out my counsel and I have met with her as I would meet with anyone."

Keegan got to his feet and stepped out into the circle of clergy to meet Pastor Weakley head on. He felt he had tolerated Weakley's intrusion well enough, but was feeling his old Navy temper rise.

"Furthermore, if she seeks additional advice I will afford that, or direct her to appropriate services." Extending his hand towards the lounge exit, Keegan ended with, "Now you will excuse us. You know the way out."

"You keep away from my little girl." Weakley glared at Keegan for a silent moment, then added through gritted teeth and almost with a growl, "I'll see to it the wrath of God comes down on anyone who hurts my little girl, or jeopardizes her soul. I'll see to it they burn in hell."

Pastor Weakley spun on his heels and started for the door.

Keegan called after him, and Weakley stopped to face him. "You'd go a long way towards helping your daughter and her soul," Keegan said, "if you'd stop treating her as a little girl, and started thinking of her as a full grown woman."

Weakley grunted, turned and left.

"My, my, Brother Keegan," intoned Tom, "What *Young and the Restless* episode do we have here?"

"Here, here," added Father Rutherford. Joe applauded and said, "Most entertaining, most entertaining. When is the next show? I'd like to bring friends."

The room broke out in laughter which helped relieve the tension.

Keegan returned to his seat. "Let me put it to you this way," he said, "who among you would go to him for marriage counseling?"

"Not likely," said Joe, and the married men in the room laughed. Sister Margaret Mary caught on a little later and tittered.

"Well, I've had all the excitement for one day I can handle," Brother Tom said as he stood up. "We've agreed, right? Keegan does our dirty work at the board meeting tomorrow night."

The noon whistle blew, and Eddie stopped work to head back to his locker and retrieve his lunch. He made his way to the employee cafeteria, sat at one of the long tables and began to eat. As the morning had worn on, he had started to feel badly about what he had done to Callahan's car and nose.

After he finished the sandwich, he reached in for the banana. Under the fruit was a slip of paper. Maybe it was a note from Sarah. Maybe she was sorry. He brought the note out and unfolded it. In scrawled letters it read, "CHECK THE BATTERIES IN YOUR SMOKE DETECTORS."

NOVEMBER 5TH
WEDNESDAY

By six twenty-five the union hall was shrouded in the blue haze of Marlboros and Lucky Strikes. Empty plastic cups emblazoned with *Saranac Amber Ale* lay on their sides on the floor near the garbage cans they had been haphazardly tossed towards. The spilled contents dried on the floor in a sticky residue and the aroma of stale beer and flat Coke wafted through the hall and mixed with the smoke. The meeting had been filled with union representatives advising members on New York State unemployment benefits, union supplemental benefits and available part-time jobs. When Sam LaFontain, the union trustee in charge of aid, finished describing the procedures for applying for help at the union pantry should a member have a food emergency, a man with a mass of bushy hair and full beard looking like a huge talking hairball set upon a rotund body clad in green buffalo plaid carrying a full plastic cup called out, "What about when I have a beer emergency?"

The crowd laughed more than the quip deserved. Daniel Callahan took the podium. He stood close to the mike and it squealed like a pinched girl who wanted more of the same. He moved his head back and forth, trying to decide how close he could get without her squeal rising. Satisfied with his position, he raised his hands to command attention.

"Attention, you guys, and gals," Callahan said. The system squealed a pained delight and the crowd quieted. "You all know what's available to see you through the long haul. We gotta bring United Paper to its knees, or our union label butts are gonna be kicked outta here." Remembering his old high school days and the pep rallies where the cheerleaders would get the crowd to shout, he decided to add, "Do ya hear me?"

The assembly responded with a disappointing scattering of "Yeah, yeah," and one enthusiastic "We can do it?" that generated more laughter than the beer emergency.

The union's taste for the strike was already souring. Callahan decided to go ahead with something that he had been plotting out in his head for a couple of days.

"Before I let you people go," Callahan shouted over the voices of a hall now near totally disinterested in him or the proceedings, "I have a special job for about six or eight hardy men." The PA let loose with an ear splitting howl that silenced the crowd into attention. "I'd like some volunteers to meet me up here by the stage after we end the meeting. Any other business?" He waited about two seconds. "We're adjourned."

Several cheered and others whistled as the mass moved for the various exits and flooded out into the parking lot of waiting four-by-fours, assorted big three pickups, Cavaliers, Escorts, Neons and the rare Honda or Toyota.

Callahan stepped away from the podium and sat on the edge of the stage, waiting for some volunteers to come forward. He had all but given up as the hall emptied when finally Three-brow showed up. Callahan felt sure this cigar chewing character wanted his job as union president. He wanted Brookhough on his side, but he didn't trust him. Mickey Miles came over by them, then three more drifted over.

Mickey Miles, a jittery pimply faced little squirrel, was the first to ask, "What's it about, Dan?" The others mimicked with "Yeah" or "What's up?" Brookhough hung back but within earshot.

Callahan waved them closer and in conspiratorial tones said, "We've gotta make sure the scabs get the message that they're gonna get no peace during this strike, and that we ain't gonna forget who they are."

"Yeah, we'll show them," Mickey said, looking to the others for supportive nods. He caught Brookhough's eye then grew silent.

"A fat lot you know about showing anybody anything," Callahan said. "You sure as hell showed Eddie Conger what you're made of."

"Hey, hey, hey," Mickey protested. His eyes darted about the others, measuring their reaction. "I didn't sign up to get the hell beat outta me by some scab gorilla." He took about a half step back from the huddle.

"I guess none of us have to worry about you hangin' tough with the rest of us, then do we?" Callahan sneered. He turned his attention to the others and said, "Look, by the time we get done tonight, there won't be any scabs. They won't dare."

"Good," Mickey said. "I'm getting grief from my wife already about not working and no money. She's allatime telling me '*the other men are working, the other men are working.'"* He pouted his lower lip as he imitated his wife. He tried to step back into the huddle but didn't manage to get through the shoulders and elbows.

"Ya see," said Callahan, "we gotta put a stop to this. We gotta scare 'em a little."

A collective and hushed "Yeah" came from the huddle.

"Tonight," Callahan said, drawing the boys closer, "we're going to Eddie Conger's house and picket his street. By tomorrow morning everybody in town will know he got no rest."

"You don't think he'll come out after us, do you?" Mickey asked.

"He's not that crazy," Callahan snapped. "Besides, we ain't gonna trespass or nothin', just make a bunch of noise in the street. By tomorrow afternoon, evening at the latest, the number of scabs will be down to zip." Callahan felt bolstered by the small group's acceptance of his plan. "Hell," he said, "they'll be joinin' us on the line! Let's go."

As the others packed up and made their way out, Mickey and Stretch started to edge over towards Brookhough. Brookhough gestured for them to 'get on along' so they filed out with the others. Within ten minutes Callahan and all of his volunteers save one left the building and headed for Conger's on Benedict Street. They soon arrived at Eddie's and began to shout their epithets. Brookhough hung back to consider his options.

Pastor Weakley paced back and forth in the sanctuary of The Good News Apostolic Lighthouse waiting for the pianist, Leona Thomas, to arrive. His steps were fast and heavy. His right hand massaged his left fist. Then the left hand worked over the right fist.

Leona arrived her usual quarter hour before practice. She came in through the front doors and waddled down the center aisle removing her overcoat.

"Good evening Past—"

"Where the devil have you been, Leona?" interrupted Weakley.

"Aren't you in a mood," Leona said, a little defensively. She draped her coat over the modesty panel in front of the first pew.

"Sorry," Weakley snapped, "I'm a little preoccupied."

"Hmph. I suppose you want me to do something," Leona said. She flopped herself down on the swivel stool at the piano.

"No. Nothing. Thanks." Pastor Weakley started up his pacing and without looking at Leona said, "I won't be staying for choir practice tonight. I have a personal matter that needs attending. I'll be next door at the parsonage for a while if you need me, then I'll be gone for a good bit. I'm sorry for the inconvenience." On his last turn of pace, Pastor Weakley kept on walking out the side door, across the lawn between the church and the parsonage, and into the house straight to his study corner.

He sat at his desk with head in hands praying "Father God, give unto thy servant the strength necessary to do what must be done that the souls of daughter and son-in-law may be released from the grip of Satan." He lifted his face to the ceiling of his living room and raised his hands toward the God that he believed drove him so. Filled with fear, and with cheeks wet with tears, he ended his prayer, "Thy will be done. Amen."

He decided to hold his position for a moment should anyone arriving for choir practice benefit from seeing him at prayer, then dried his eyes with a handkerchief, opened his Bible to the Prophet Daniel's confession, and began to read. He would wait until the time was right.

Eddie punched out at 18:42. As he left the shop he scanned the mill perimeter and noticed only a handful of drum fires. Then he recalled that the union members were having a meeting over at the union hall to discuss strike benefits to sustain the striking workers while they brought United Paper to its corporate knees.

He found Sarah's car, unlocked it and climbed in. Getting into Sarah's small car always felt like what he imagined a woman climbing into a girdle felt like. He fastened the seat belt, started the car, and headed across the half empty parking lot towards the gate and home. At the gate he heard assorted jeers and shouts; he stared straight ahead trying to ignore the taunts and sped off.

Eddie considered stopping by The Stallions for a sandwich and a beer, then decided better of it. Without detours he drove for home. Eddie pulled onto his street and headed for the dead end and his home. As he approached he noticed a number of cars and trucks parked in front of his house. He slowed and stopped at the curb about seventy-five yards away from the closest pickup. Eight or ten men were picketing his home with signs that read simply SCAB.

"Sons-a-bitches!" Eddie shouted into the silent interior of Sarah's car. He dropped the transmission into reverse, backed into a neighbor's driveway and turned around to head back down Benedict Street to Amherst. He turned right, went one block, turned right again onto Rogers Rock Road, drove up to the Apostolic Lighthouse and parked.

Sarah walked down the unlit Rogers Rock Road towards her father's church for choir practice. She had taken the children to dinner at Barbara Ross' home. William and Becky would play the evening away with Barb's boys and their dog before spending the night. It was like a pajama party – or whatever boys might call it. A knock-down-drag-out was what Eddie said he wanted tonight when he got home, and by God she was going to give it to him.

From Barbara's house near the end of Benedict, it was a pleasant walk around the block and down Rogers Rock Road to get to her father's church. Stretching her legs felt good. The cold evening air was refreshing, and the sound of crunching dry leaves under her feet reassured her that the cycles of life and death were unending and reliable.

Sarah had managed to remain cool and collected for most of the day, especially around young Billy and Becky. But now, as she walked closer to her church and the argument she anticipated after choir practice she grew more apprehensive. Her palms began to sweat, and she felt her mouth grow dry. She wondered if she would be able to concentrate on the music. Most of the day she had imagined different fights with Eddie, one scenario after another, with him seeming to win some and she others. She would avoid the losing tactics of her ruminations.

While still about three hundred yards from the church, Eddie drove past in her car. She felt a surge of anger rise within herself that surprised her at the sight of the car. He could have left me a way to get around for the day. She clenched her jaws so tightly her teeth hurt. He came to a sudden stop in front of the church. Sarah expected the backup lights on her old Cavalier to flash and the car to speed towards her. She clenched her fists at her sides. Nothing.

The brake light blinked out, then the running lights died, and the exhaust ceased. As she approached, still two hundred yards away, she watched as Eddie got out of the car, slipped the key into the door, locked it and walked off across the lawn between the church and the parsonage, presumably towards home. He didn't seem to notice her.

Her pace slowed a bit. She wondered why he would leave the car there. Is this an attempt at courtesy? That would be stupid; the church is in our own back yard. Even he isn't so stupid as to think that would matter.

As she approached the car, she ran her hand along its fender as she peered in the window. Everything looked as usual. "At least it's not littered with beer cans," she whispered to herself.

"What'd you say?"

Sarah let out a startled cry and spun around.

"Oh my goodness, I didn't mean to startle you so, dear."

"Oh, it's you, Miss Berkley." Sarah recognized the old maiden lady who had sung in the choir for over fifty years. Her voice cracked and frequently slipped to discordant notes, but the choir simply tried to sing over her in the hopes that the congregation would not notice. Sarah knew, from occasionally sitting in the pews, that was a vain hope.

"Oh, I wasn't saying anything important," Sarah said, still recovering her breath and feeling her heart rate settle down. She put her arm under Miss Berkley's, helping the old lady up the church steps, and both entered the building exchanging "hellos" and "how ya beens." The choir was already singing *Rock of Ages*. It occurred to Sarah that for all of the years she had known Miss Berkley, the woman's first name had always been *Miss*.

The two women took their places in the assembled and singing choir as the director flashed disapproving glares at them over their tardiness.

Eddie decided that Sarah was probably at choir practice, and when she came out she would see her car parked in front of the church and bring it home. Meanwhile, he would head home through the adjoining back yards and slip into his house through the back door.

Eddie locked the car door and started across the parsonage lawn. He saw his father-in-law perched in his study window poised over his Bible like a store mannequin on display for all who cared to see. Eddie didn't think many cared to see, at least he'd never seen a crowd gather to watch Pastor Weakley wrinkle up his face and look pious. Bill Weakley, in the woods with a rifle in his hands, could be an okay kind of guy. But Pastor Weakley was a royal pain in the neck. As he crossed the lawn towards the back, between the church building and the parsonage, he could hear strains of *Rock of Ages* drift out. My God, they really do sing that, he thought.

The music also made him wonder why Pastor Weakley was not in the church. Sarah had said that her father was nearly always at practice. Well, he thought, at least with her at practice I won't have to look at her sour puss for a while. As he walked away from the church, the singing behind him began to mingle with the shouts and taunts from the strikers in front of his house mixing into a demented hymn.

When he got to the house, he edged himself to the back corner of the garage to see out into the street. Maybe he knew some of the guys. There seemed to be no organization to it. The men were not picketing his house so much as milling around, bouncing homemade signs up and down, and tipping back an occasional beer.   Eddie noticed at least a dozen empties scattered across his side lawn.   He couldn't decide if the cans were theirs or the empties he'd left there the other night.

When he spotted Daniel Callahan he noticed that Callahan wasn't shouting or carrying a sign.   Callahan paced back and forth behind the men, stopping occasionally to speak to first one man and then another.   Then back to his pacing.   The guy from The Stallions with three eyebrows was chewing on a cigar.   He stood to the side like he was some kind of observer.

Eddie moved to the back of his house, unlocked the door, stepped into the kitchen, then closed and locked the door behind him.   Leaving the lights off so as not to alert the jerks outside that someone was home, he groped his way through the kitchen to close the swinging door between the kitchen and the dining and living rooms beyond.   With that done, he opened the refrigerator door.   He made and ate a sandwich by the appliance light.   The red light was still burning on the coffee maker, so Eddie poured himself a cup of tar and headed for the cellar door, closing the fridge on his way.

At the top of the cellar stairs, Eddie turned on the lights, and for a moment panicked that someone might see the light escape through the foundation windows.   But the burned out light at the foot of the stairs did not come on, and Eddie breathed a sigh of relief.

Eddie felt his way down the stairs, running his hand down the cinder block foundation on his left and trying not to spill his coffee.

At the foot of the stairs, he turned to the right and walked slowly straight ahead.   He swapped hands with his coffee, managing to slop some on his left wrist.   "Ow." He knew the back foundation wall should be about five or six feet to his right – beyond a clutter of summer yard toys from the kids.   Ahead, about fifteen, maybe twenty feet, would be his work bench.   With his right hand waving far out in front of him, and stepping ever so carefully, Eddie picked his way through the thick darkness.

The closer he got to his work bench, the closer he got to the strikers outside in front of his house.   The shouts of SCAB and TRAITOR and remarks about his parentage and legitimacy filtered through the cellar wall and windows.

Eddie finally kicked the leg of his workbench and signed, "Home free." He set his coffee on the bench and groped his way to the window just beyond.   He felt his way up the cinder block wall, found the ledge, and drew closed the curtains Sarah had made from towels a couple of years back. Eddie remembered telling her he thought it was a silly idea to make curtains for the cellar. He decided he'd have to tell her thanks, when she got home.

He knew it was a clear shot to the other front window. Tracing his fingers along the block seams, he felt his way across to the window ledge. He drew that curtain closed, then returned to the bench.

Once at the bench, he turned on the architect's lamp over his work area. He grabbed an old flannel shirt he had by his bench for chilly nights and draped it over the lamp to further block the light from the windows. He reached for his coffee and took a long sip. The warmth of the coffee ran a shiver up his spine, so he decided to light up the kerosene heater.

He went back to the stairway near the back of the house and reached over his head to open the foundation window located there to allow air to get in and fumes to escape. For a moment, he thought he caught a whiff of cigar smoke. But it passed. He knelt by the heater located under the window and lit it. It spewed black soot for a few seconds then settled into an even burn.

Back at the bench, Eddie poured forty empty brass shell casings into the square plastic tumbler drum, snapped on the top, slipped it into the drive bracket and started the electric motor. The tumbler slowly rotated, scattering the casings and crushed walnut shells across the drum walls, creating a din of motor, brass, shells and drum that all but drowned out the beer soaked shouts from outside Eddie's foundation window. For a moment he wondered if the tumbler would draw attention to his being home but then decided that it wouldn't likely be heard over the crowd's own racket.

Eddie's tumbler droned on, and it seemed like music to his ears. Just now it was the only music he cared to hear, now or ever again.

A few minutes before the seven o'clock town board meeting, Keegan climbed the steps of the town hall. The municipal building was on a knoll with expansive lawns rolling away from it down to Amherst Avenue on its north side and Lake George Avenue on its east. Across Lake George Avenue was the town park and public beach – two hundred yards of white sea sand making one of the most beautiful beaches on the lake. During the summer people drove all the way up from Albany and Schenectady to enjoy the beach.

Keegan found his way into the room designated BOARD ROOM and took a seat near the back. In his ten years in Fort George he had never had much reason to attend town board meetings. Since he owned no property in the community, and since neither he nor the church paid property taxes, he felt it was more important for those who paid the bills to make the decisions about how much to spend on a new snow plow for the town dump truck and who to hire to manage the town sewage treatment plant. By and large, he'd not seen a lot of social justice issues come to a head in town until now.

He had managed to convince Father Joe to join him at the meeting and to entrust the confirmation class to Sister Margaret Mary. Joe had considerable influence over the town supervisor, a devout Roman Catholic of the old school, and Keegan hoped that Father Joe's support of Keegan's presentation would help sway the supervisor's favor.

Keegan breathed a sigh of relief when Joe entered the board room. He flagged Joe over to the empty seat next to him. The two men greeted each other with hand shakes.

"Thanks for coming, Joe," Keegan said. "I appreciate the support."

"Not at all, Keegan," Father Joe said as he sat down. "It's actually a relief not to have to spend the evening with a room full of kids who'd rather be anywhere but with me in religious instruction."

The supervisor entered the room from an adjoining office and took her place at the center of the board table, flanked on either side by eight board members. She whispered to the board member on her left and shuffled some papers.

Keegan leaned over and whispered to Joe, "When I first moved here I thought it was quite progressive of a mountain town to have elected a woman supervisor."

"Buuut?" Joe asked as if expecting a punch line.

"But," said Keegan, "I knew the community was in trouble when I learned that the town supervisor went by the name *Dearie*. Imagine. *Dearie* Dirkson."

Joe began to snicker.

"Governor Pataki refers to her as his quaint mountain-woman supervisor," Keegan added. "For God's sake we have a *quaint* supervisor – just what every town needs. Quaint."

Father Joe's face flushed, and his chest heaved as he stifled his laughter.

The supervisor's gavel rapped once, and Dearie Dirkson called, "The Fort George town board meeting will now come to order."

Keegan and Joe sat patiently as the order of Roberts Rules was carefully observed and a variety of tedious reports were inexpertly read aloud. Each was accepted with only the occasional question or correction. To Keegan's surprise, Dearie ran a pretty tight ship, and she sailed through the preliminaries at best speed.

85

In as little as twenty minutes Dearie was calling upon Keegan to make his presentation. "As you all know," she said, "we are living through very tense times with the strike at the mill, and the Reverend O'Connor has asked to make a presentation on behalf of the area clergy association. The chair recognizes Reverend O'Connor."

Keegan went to the front of the room and distributed copies of the proposal to each of the board members and the supervisor, then stood off to one side to better see the faces of those he was addressing in the assembly as well as the town board. "Madam supervisor, board members, ladies and gentlemen..."

Keegan made his case for the clergy, seeking town board endorsement of a multi-part educational series on conflict resolution, and suggestions for families about coping with trying times.

"As you can see," Keegan summed up, "we are not asking you to endorse any particular church, we are not seeking funding or space or personnel. We simply wish your sanction, and your encouragement of the public to participate in the series. Indeed, it would speak well of the program and of the supervisor and the board members if they participated in the series as a means of encouraging the public to do so."

"Rev, are you sure this here ain't against the constitution of these New Knitted States?" Coot Barstow asked. There were scattered chuckles throughout the room.

Coot had been a board member for over thirty years and tended to tug at his chin whiskers through the board meetings. Keegan had been told that Coot had been saying *New Knitted States* echoing the L'il Abner comic strip ever since he had been elected. The strip had been out of print so long that young adults in town thought that the phrase was a Coot original.

Keegan assured Coot that all was legal. With only light questioning from the audience and the board, the endorsement was given, and the next bit of new business was taken up.

Keegan returned to his seat, leaned over to Father Joe and said, "I'll stay a bit longer to be polite – no sense eating and running – then I'm outta here."

"Good notion," Joe said. "I'll follow along."

After a motion to replace the sidewalk snowplow tractor passed, both Joe and Keegan left the room and stepped out into the evening air.

"You want to stop off at the village diner for coffee?" Joe asked at the top of the steps. "My treat."

"Thanks, but no thanks, Joe," Keegan said, "I think I'll..."

The Wednesday night test of the county mutual aid sirens shrieked. Keegan and Joe fell silent until the test subsided.

"I'll run over to the church study and file away these left over proposals, and get back home to see how Eileen is doing."

"How is Eileen these days?" Joe closed the collar of his suit coat around his neck. "Is her treatment going well?"

"The surgery was bad," Keegan said. He jammed his hands into his pockets and hunched his shoulders against the cold. "She's had to go through all the self-image stuff that comes with a mastectomy. But I'll tell you, this chemotherapy is just plain hell on her. And she's still experiencing pain that we haven't quite figured out. Other than that, she's keeping her spirits up."

"Give Eileen my best. "I won't hold you up. I keep you both in prayer." "Thanks, Joe."

The two men parted company, with Keegan heading south along Lake George Avenue towards Grace Methodist, and Joe moving west on Amherst towards his rectory.

Mickey Miles was stamping his feet and throwing his arms around himself. His Carhart jacket simply was not cutting muster on this cold November night. He needed to piss – BAD. He'd been yelling his lungs out in front of Conger's house for three quarters of an hour or more, chugged four beers, and now he needed to take a picked wiss. He decided he would water Conger's spirea bushes along their property border and wandered away from the others to tend to that little chore. Nestled in the shadows, his fly down, and his pride and joy in hand, he opened the sluice gates and knew FAST FAST RELIEF as the old *Alka-Seltzer* commercial used to say.

As the second or third beer passed through – Ya never drink beer, ya only borrow it for a while – he heard leaves on the lawn crunching. His sphincter slammed shut and Mickey turned quickly, expecting to see Eddie Conger sneaking up on him in the dark.

"Aim that thing somewhere else, will ya?" said Callahan, pointing at Mickey's member.

"Oh, yeah, yeah, sorry about that," Mickey said, turning back to the bushes and cutting loose again. "Ya scared me is all, sneaking up on me like that."

"Will you shut up!" Dan hissed in a harsh whisper, "I'm trying to *quietly* check around back."

"Oh," Mickey said as he zipped up and turned back to Callahan, only to find he had moved further towards the back of the house. "What for?" he called in a whisper that nearly broke onto speaking fully aloud.

Callahan turned towards Mickey, glared at him and waved him off, then disappeared into the back yard shadows.

Mickey returned to the others, picked up his protest sign with SCAB hastily scrawled across it, and went over to Callahan's truck where he opened another can of beer that was so thoughtfully provided by the truck's owner.

Erik Brookhough went over to where Mickey was standing and gave him a cuff up the side of the head as Mickey was taking a long swallow. Mickey's head came forward and he coughed beer out of his nose.

"Hey, what's the idea?" Mickey managed between coughs and chokes.

"I thought you were on my team now," Brookhough said.

"Yeah, well, there's no point pissin' off the guy that brings the beer."

"Make sure that's all it is." Brookhough moved around to face Mickey. "What's Callahan up to?"

"I dunno, he didn't tell me nothin'. He wandered off towards the back of the house. Nosing around, I guess."

"Listen up," said Brookhough. "I want you to get Stretch and hang out by the side of the house Callahan went down. When he comes back out make sure everybody notices."

"Whatya mean?"

"Just shout something like, 'Here comes Callahan now!' Then point, like you and the others were looking for him."

"What for? Why do ya want me and Stretch to do that?"

"Never mind. That's my business. Let's just say Daniel Callahan won't be running for union president long after tonight." After saying this, Erik made his way down the side of Conger's house opposite from Callahan and disappeared into the darkness.

Sarah must have looked at her watch a dozen times, crossed and uncrossed her legs another dozen, and cut loose with long, anguished sighs five or six times. Miss Berkley couldn't imagine what was troubling the girl so. She leaned over to Sarah's ear.

"Gracious, Sarah," Miss Berkley whispered, "you are so fidgety tonight. Whatever is the matter?"

"Oh, I'm just a little distracted is all, Miss Berkley," Sarah said with a wan smile.

The front door of the church swung open and Jean Fremont came walking down the center aisle at a near trot.

"You can't imagine what I've seen," she called to the choir as she came. When she got to the choir loft she plunked down her purse. Leona tried her disapproving stare to no avail.

"They're picketing," Jean continued. "There must be twenty of them at least." She struggled out of her coat and flung it to the floor. "They're shoutin', and carryin' signs, and drinkin' beer, and cussin', and carryin' on."

"We've all seen the men striking," Leona intoned. "Now if you'd like to join us, we're..."

"You ain't seen them strikin' a scab's house before." Jean posed with hands on hips and leaning forward as if scolding a child. "And that's what they're doin'," she took her seat in front and twisted to face the others. "They're picketin' over at Sarah's. Quite a sight."

The choir members fell into an instant buzz. Leona's disapproving look changed to a furious glower. She pounded on the piano four times, literally rocking the old upright and shouted, "ARE YOU READY?"

Silence.

"Very well," Leona said in her best choir mistress voice, "let us begin."

Sarah looked back to her music – turned it over, flipped through the pages, then looked through the music in her file – as the rest of the choir started to sing. She pulled a piece of music out and put it on her lap and studied it. She did not sing.

Miss Berkley watched, looked over Sarah's shoulder to read the music title, then leaned to whisper, "It's the wrong anthem dear, we're singing *The Apple Tree*."

"Oh, thanks." Sarah looked up at Miss Berkley. She seemed to stare through her, or past her. She fumbled with the anthem music in her folder and spilled some of it on the floor. As she bent over to retrieve the music, the rest of the folder on her lap emptied on the floor.

"Goddamn!" Sarah said.

The room hushed with horrified silence at the blasphemy.

Sarah sat up slowly, raising her head cautiously as if worried she might lose it. She looked around, and all twenty-four eyes of the choir and director were on her.

Leona Thomas peered over the top of the piano directly at Sarah with the disapproving scowl of a choir director with nearly thirty years experience of disapproving of a large variety of things, including Miss

Berkley's occasional outburst of laughter at song lyrics she thought particularly foolish – like her first reaction to comparing Jesus to an apple tree. Leona said, "If you are quite finished taking the Lord's name in vain, Mrs. Conger, we shall continue. Measure thirty-six, sopranos..."

Testing Leona's patience, Miss Berkley leaned over to Sarah one more time and whispered, "If I can help, please tell me."

"Thanks," Sarah said as she turned to Miss Berkley, smiled her small smile, and patted her hand, "but I think I know what I have to do. I have to go see Pastor." With that Sarah folded her music, slipped out of the choir loft and headed for the front door of the church.

When Sarah opened the door of the church, Miss Berkley noticed her brother Clarence sitting on the stoop with his customary bottle wrapped in a brown paper bag.

She had been looking after her younger brother, ten years her junior, for the last two decades – ever since he had his accident in the wood yard at the mill. The company put him on disability until he could collect his pension. That started five years ago. The fire siren whistled and Clarence raised his bottle in salute and howled, "Whoooop!" She thought, the drunken old fool has come to embarrass me to death.

A quarter mile south of the town hall on Lake George Avenue, Keegan unlocked the Fellowship Hall door to his church, stepped in and locked the door behind him. Down the corridor he let himself into his study, flicked on the lights and went to his desk.

He stuffed the left over proposals into the file drawer of the desk and when he lifted his eyes, he was staring at some incomplete denominational forms that Grace must have placed on his desk after he had gone. A blue sticky note read: I CAN MAIL THESE ONLY WHEN YOU'VE FINISHED. G. She had circled in red a number of blanks begging for answers and a signature line.

I'll take fifteen or twenty minutes and knock these off, he thought, then I can spend the rest of the evening with Eileen with a clear conscience. With an audible sigh, Keegan turned on a small desk top radio, tuned into all talk WGY out of Schenectady, and dove into the reports.

The statistical report on top required information that was most easily gathered from Grace's computer. He mentally cussed her out for not having done this herself. He got up and went through to Grace's adjoining office and sat at her desk. He turned on her computer and waited for the screen to warm into focus. He moved through the files and found the weekly data he needed and jotted it down on a slip of scrap paper.

Keegan killed the IBM, returned its dust cover, and left Grace's office for his own where WGY was finishing the half hour news report.

A loud rap sounded at the fellowship hall door. He looked out his window, but through the overgrown shrubbery by his windows he could only see a smallish silhouette, probably a female, standing at the door.

Keegan got up, left his study, went down the corridor and turned left into Fellowship Hall. At the door, he turned on the outside lights, opened the door, and saw...no one. He called, "Hello?"

There was no answer.

The brass tumbler growled with mind-numbing cadence. The shouts from outside had been reduced by cold and beer to "Come out, you shunabish!" and "Lesh torsh the plash!" Eddie listened to the rhythm of the tumbler and put the final crimp around the final slug of his final deer slayer. He held the finished product up to the light to admire it before putting it in the cartridge box.

Eddie did not hear the footfalls to his right. He did not hear the barrel of a rifle tangle in the lamp cord of the burned out light hanging by the stairs. Eddie never heard the thud of a three-oh-eight explode into a foam rubber pillow. Eddie never heard anything...ever again.

A slug pierced Eddie's skin just behind his right temple and smashed through his skull, splintering it like the balsa wood of a model plane under the foot of a clumsy fat kid. Eddie's arm was still aloft, with hand and cartridge in the bench light.

The resistance of the bone matter started the hollow point of the slug peeling back, increasing the diameter of the projectile. As the slug entered Eddie's brain, his eyes stopped seeing as the lead alloy formed a mushroom, forcing a shock wave ahead and around the slug liquefying his brain.

A portion of skull, about the size of Eddie's palm, blew out the left side of his head, exploding pressurized gray matter. Eddie's arm dropped to the bench. A portion of Eddie's childhood memories splattered onto the cinder block wall to his left, while that part of his brain governing his sex drive, such as it was, dribbled down the inside of his shirt collar.

Eddie's two hundred fifty pounds of dead weight kept him firmly seated at his bench, with half of his head still attached, face down on twenty bright and shiny newly loaded deer slayers.

A few bits of foam rubber filtered through the air and settled on the floor. A small throw pillow – the kind tossed onto couches or over-stuffed chairs for God only knows what effect, the kind of pillow that actually interferes with the intended purpose of furniture, that of sitting – that kind of pillow lay at the foot of the cellar stairs, beneath the open foundation window with a small scorched hole on one side and a blowout on the other.

Mickey was leaning on Callahan's truck finishing his fifth beer and yearning to urinate again when he noticed Callahan coming around from the side of Conger's house. He ran toward Callahan and grabbed Stretch as he had pre-arranged on his way. He called out "Here's Callahan now!" A few heads turned and saw Callahan come out of the shadows to be greeted by Mickey and Stretch.

"Hey, Dan, what's up?" Mickey asked as Callahan approached. "Whatcha doin' around there? You been gone a long time." He threw his empty beer can in the direction from which Callahan had come.

"I'm just settling a little personal business." Callahan's voice and sneer forced Mickey's scrotum to crawl up. They walked back to Callahan's truck and Callahan reached into the cooler in the bed of the truck and pulled out a beer. He popped the top and said, "Get over there and yell at the house. And stop suckin' down my beer."

Mickey walked over with the other men and resumed his hoarse protest. He looked back to see Callahan tip his head back, drain his can, and toss the empty onto the Conger lawn. Mickey looked around for Brookhough but didn't see him. Mickey decided he'd probably gotten into an argument with Callahan out back and just left.

Choir practice finished as per usual, and Miss Berkley gathered herself up and, along with nine other women and one man, exited out the front door of The Good News Apostolic Lighthouse. She hung back, not wanting to see the pitying faces of the others when they tripped over her drunken brother. When she got to the door she was both surprised and relieved to find the stoop barren. No brother, and no empty bottle.

She descended the church steps – first step, right foot left foot; second step, right foot left foot; third step, right foot left foot – until she climbed down to the sidewalk. The others got into their cars and drove off, leaving Miss Berkley on the empty street facing the long walk home down Rogers Rock Road along Lake George towards Roger's Rock of French and Indian War fame.

As she passed the parsonage, she looked to where Pastor Weakley customarily sat in the window of his living room. The lights were out and no one seemed to be at home. Miss Berkley shuffled on down to where the sidewalk ended and continued on her way home down the darkened road.

Keegan rounded the corner onto Flintlock Avenue and passed quickly over the hundred yards or so to his front porch. The community street names had always struck Keegan as funny.

Generals and explorers were named on one side of town, while the closer you got to the pre-revolutionary fort you drove over Flintlock, or Cannon Run, or Fortress Road. When he had asked the church's lay leader how the names had come to pass, he was told that the town renamed all of the streets during the nation's bicentennial, hoping to capitalize on their revolutionary heritage with increased tourist trade. Keegan understood that the effort had been a general bust.

Keegan heard police sirens off in the distance and supposed that one of the constables was in hot pursuit of an out-of-state tourist who managed to miss the forty mile an hour speed limit out on Route 9N.

He unlocked his front door and let himself in. The entrance hall was dark, and so was the formal parlor beyond it. He could hear the TV playing in the living room further back. By the time he made the parlor, MaryKay met him midpoint.

"Glad you're home, Keeg," she said, "I've gotta run." Keegan followed her back into the entrance hall and helped her with her jacket from the hall closet. "Eileen was counting on watching *Mystery* at nine o'clock on PBS," she said, adjusting her jacket sleeves and collar. "It's just coming on now." She zipped the jacket. "But she dozed off in her chair. I'll leave it up to you whether or not to wake her. Bye." She gave Keegan a peck on the cheek, he managed a "Thanks, MaryK..." and she disappeared out the door.

"Whew." Keegan shrugged off the whirlwind exchange, headed to the living room through the parlor and found Eileen soundly sleeping in her recliner. *Mystery* was being announced, so Keegan quickly popped a video tape into the VCR and began taping the program.

He went out into the kitchen, mixed himself a bourbon Manhattan, returned to the living room and his own recliner, took a long sip, cranked the footrest up into position, settled in to watch the show, and promptly dropped off to sleep.

Arthur Erichson was not altogether surprised to get the emergency call for the Congers' place. Mrs. Conger was pretty hysterical over the phone, trying to cram in every detail – husband's shot, broken glass everywhere, send ambulance, crazy strikers out front – all in a ten to fifteen second call.

He logged the call, 20:57 SHOOTING AT CONGERS' ON BENEDICT, dispatched the rescue squad, and paged two constables to meet him at the scene. Grabbing his hat and jacket, he locked up the police station and got into the town's one police cruiser, a Chevy Blazer.

It took Chief Erichson less than two minutes to get from the station on Lake George Avenue, on the opposing corner from the town hall, to the Congers' place. As he pulled into the driveway behind an old Cavalier, he found Sarah Conger standing on her front door stoop holding the sides of her head screaming at a bunch of guys with picket signs who all looked like whipped puppies after messing the living room carpet. Constable Dirkson, Dearie's nephew, pulled up behind him. The fire company's sirens were still blowing in the background calling volunteers to the rescue squad. The Chief got out of his truck and crossed the lawn towards Mrs. Conger.

"You DEMONS!" she was screaming, "You KILLED him! You'll burn in HELL for this!"

The men were all looking at one another and then all eyes focused on the Chief.

"All right, Mrs. Conger," he said as he climbed the front stairs and held out his arms to comfort her if she accepted, "show me what's happened."

Mrs. Conger immediately buried her face into his nylon police jacket and wrapped her arms around him, cutting loose with great sobs. Her grasp was so firm it squeezed some breath out of his lungs.

Constable Dirkson stood at the bottom of the stairs, looking up to the Chief waiting for instructions. Constable Smith arrived in his old Subaru and ran towards Dirkson and the Chief.

"Get the names, addresses, and phone numbers of each of these men," Chief Erichson said, looking at Dirkson. "And get a statement from them about when they arrived and everything they saw. Got that?"

Dirkson nodded and pulled a pad from his hip pocket.

The Chief looked out over the small crowd of men, and the gathering of neighborhood people drawn by sirens and the presence of police.

"ATTENTION EVERYONE!" Erichson yelled, "All of you men line up over by the cruiser and give Constable Dirkson your statements. No one leaves until that's done!"

Mrs. Conger was beginning to calm down. The sobs let up and her breath was catching. A new set of sirens turned onto Benedict and the rescue squad pulled up in front of the Congers' residence.

"You come along with us," Chief Erichson called to Constable Smith, who had sat upon Eddie in the mill parking lot, "you can direct the rescue boys."

"You bet, Art," Smith said.

Art glared at him.

"Uh, Chief. Yessir." Smith tucked in his uniform shirt as he climbed the stairs to the porch.

Chief Erichson peeled Mrs. Conger away from his chest, looked into her tearful, red and puffy eyes, and said, "Take me to your husband, Mrs. Conger."

She sniffed, nodded, and started for the back of the house.

In the kitchen there was the faint aroma of kerosene and an open door leading to the cellar.

"Geeze!" said the Chief, "the place is littered with broken glass!"

Mrs. Conger crunched glass underfoot and seemed not to hear the chief. She pointed at the open cellar door and with shaking voice said, "He's ... he's down there."

The Chief looked over at Smith who had been following along and said, "Have the rescue squad wait here in the kitchen. And see that they don't touch anything." He then stepped to the top of the stairs and peered down the dark stairwell. A small glow of light stretched from somewhere to the right of the stairs, but the stairs themselves were quite dark. A deep and fairly loud growl sounded from the same direction as the light. A kerosene heater sat at the bottom of the stairs, glowing warmly. "You stay here with her," the Chief said to Constable Smith. He then drew a Mag-lite from his belt, turned it on and descended the stairs. He flashed his light about to acquaint himself with the surroundings. A throw pillow was on the floor with its stuffing strewn about. The Chief yanked the light cord at the bottom of the stairs a couple of times, but only the distant glow of a bench light remained, accompanied by the sonorous growl of...whatever.

He moved across the cellar towards Eddie, who was seated on a stool and slumped over onto his workbench with his face kissing a spilled box of rifle cartridges. Powder scales and reloading press stood silent sentry on either side of his head, while a brass cleaner sitting on the bench tumbled and growled its bereavement over mortality past. Erichson reached over and silenced the tumbler.

The bench light was more than enough to allow him to see that half of Eddie's head was missing and that there was no one left to rescue. He called upstairs, "Hey Smith!"

"Yeah, Chief?"

"Get the camera out of the cruiser and bring it to me, will ya?"

"You bet, Art, uh, Chief."

Above him he heard the clatter of the rescue squad and Smith say, "Wait here in the kitchen. Watch what you touch. Art's downstairs." A muffled voice spoke and Smith responded, "Ya, sure, you can go down." Heavy footfalls thumped on the cellar stairs, and the Chief was relieved to see the face of Dr. Eli Shapiro.

"Glad to see ya, Doc. This your night on the squad?"

"Nope," Eli said, approaching. "It was my night to look for a little excitement. Besides, I heard the call go out on my scanner about a possible gun shot victim, and decided you needed a county coroner to come over before the rescue boys had a chance to do more harm than good." He jammed his hands into latex gloves and carefully looked over the body without moving much. "Someone has already done all the harm they could here. He's as dead as they come."

"Hell, Doc, half his head is missing; I could have told you he was dead."

"Yeah, yeah, I know," said Eli as he lifted Eddie's right arm, moved it back and forth, then returned it to its resting position. "He hasn't been dead long. No rigor mortis. Still warm."

"How long?" Erichson asked. He leaned on the workbench and watched the doctor.

"Less than an hour." Eli snapped off his gloves and tossed them into a paper sack in his doctor's bag. He removed a Kodak digital and snapped a number of photos of the body. He returned the camera to the bag. He returned to the bench, and with hands clasped behind his back he scanned over the bench.

"What are you looking for, Doc?"

"Reviewing his hobby. A lot of reloading goes on in the Adirondacks, but Mr. Conger seems to have been particularly meticulous." Eli reached over Eddie's head and picked up one deer slayer. He stooped to drop it in the medical bag and closed it with a snap. When he stood upright he had bag in hand, ready to leave.

"That's it?" shrugged Erichson.

"For now. When you're finished here, bring him up to the hospital and I'll perform an autopsy. I should have the preliminary results by tomorrow afternoon, maybe earlier." Eli headed for the stairs. At the foot he stopped, turned towards the chief and said, "I can tell you one thing right off the bat, Art, the only other time I've seen a wound like this around here has been on a deer or bear during hunting season. This is not a small bore rifle or handgun wound. Somebody's deer rifle did this." Eli started up the stairs, and near the top offered what sounded like an afterthought, "Good night."

"Yeah. Same to ya," Erichson called. He looked over the scene one more time and heaved a great sigh. He moved to the stairs and ascended to the kitchen.

Constable Dirkson entered the kitchen, crunching glass under foot and said, "I've got all their statements, Chief. Should I let them go home now?"

"Did any of them say anything about this broken glass?" Erichson asked. He pulled out one of the kitchen chairs and rested his foot on its seat. "It would have made a considerable racket."

"No, Chief," said Dirkson. Then, looking around as if seeing the room for the first time he added, "Wow, what a mess."

"Get back out there, and one at a time, not all bunched up, ask them if they heard any unusual noises. And if you get no response, ask if they heard breaking glass or a gun shot."

"Okay Chief," Dirkson said, and was gone.

"Smith!" the Chief called, "Where the devil are you?"

"In here Art," Smith's voice sounded from the living room.

"Get out here!"

Smith appeared at the swinging door to the kitchen. "What's up?"

"Where's Mrs. Conger got off to?"

"I've got her in the living room, Chief," Smith said, nodding his head behind him to indicate direction. "The doc took a look at her and gave her something to help settle her down. She's kinda catchin' her breath in there. You want me to bring her out here?"

"No, no. I'll be there in a minute," said the Chief. "Thanks. You can go back."

He took in a long deep breath, let it out slowly. He removed his foot from the chair, dusted the seat off with his hand and replaced the chair under the table. He left the kitchen and entered the living room through the dining room. Mrs. Conger was seated in an easy chair with Constable Smith attentively at her side. Erichson sat on the hassock at her knees. She held tissues at her nose. Her face was ashen, and looked as if she had spent the whole of last summer in a cellar. Her hair along the side of her face was matted with the moisture of her tears.

"I know this has been a very difficult night for you, Mrs. Conger. But would you try to answer a few questions?"

She nodded, sniffed, and blew her nose.

"When did you get home?" Erichson pulled out his notebook and pen from his breast pocket and flipped it open.

"It was about nine o'clock," she managed through tears and sniffles. "Maybe a little before."

"Where had you been before coming home?"

"Choir practice," she said, "then . . ."

"Go on," said the Chief, "then what?"

Mrs. Conger dropped her hands to her lap and gazed into Erichson's eyes. "Then I went over to see Pastor Keegan."

"So you were with the Reverend O'Connor?" He penned a question to himself: Thought Conger was Weakley's daughter. Why did she want to see O'Connor?

"Not exactly," Mrs. Conger said, "I went to see him, but he didn't seem to be at the church, and I didn't want to disturb him at his home." Her eyes welled up and she said, "His wife's very ill, you know." The tear breached the dam of her lower lids and came flowing over onto her cheeks. Hands and tissues returned to the eyes and nose.

"Why did you go to see the reverend?"

"Pastor Keegan was trying to help me." She brought the tissues away from her eyes. "Eddie and I have been arguing some lately. You know, the strike and all." Her features hardened and a darkness came over her face. "Then those children of Satan came tonight to kill my Eddie." And the tears started to flow freely again.

Chief Erichson reached into his pocket and pulled out a nearly clean handkerchief, unfolded it and gave it to Mrs. Conger.

As she cried, the Chief motioned to Smith to come closer and he whispered, "Have you got that camera yet?"

"Yeah, sure."

"While I'm here, run downstairs and photog the place good. Photograph everything, got it?"

"Sure, Chief. Right away." Smith turned to leave and Erichson grabbed his arm.

"When you're sure you've got everything, send the squad downstairs to collect Mr. Conger and take him to the hospital."

"You bet." Smith left, and Art could hear the camera's high-pitched whine signaling the flash was charging up.

He reached over and touched Mrs. Conger on the shoulder and said, "I'm sorry for this, but just a couple of more questions. When does choir practice end?"

"Eight-thirty."

"And you left then and headed for the Methodist church?"

Mrs. Conger returned the Chief's handkerchief with a brief smile of thanks and said, "No. I left a little early because one of the choir members who came in late said that she noticed pickets outside my house. And I couldn't get that off my mind, so I decided to leave a few minutes early to see."

Erichson sat up straight on the hassock, and with both hands on the small of his back he tried to stretch out a kink. He asked, "So you went home before you went to see Reverend O'Connor?"

"Well, yes and no," Mrs. Conger said. "Really, I'm getting awfully tired."

"I'm sure, but yes *and* no?"

"You see, I went home, but when I saw all those men outside I was afraid. I knew all the racket would have put Eddie in a terrible mood and I didn't want an argument." She was beginning to shred the used tissues in her lap, and her eyes were welling up again. "So I went to see Pastor Keegan hoping he could maybe tell me how to calm Eddie down. You know, smooth things over for the night. I had no idea that Eddie was..."

The water works cut loose. The Chief offered his wet hanky and she accepted.

"Please, Chief Erichson," Mrs. Conger pleaded with her eyes as much as her voice, "I'm exhausted. And I'm afraid what the doctor gave me is making me very fuzzy. I can't think straight."

"You're right, Mrs. Conger, of course," said the chief. "Is there someone I can phone for you? You should stay with family tonight, and I'll have the constables watch over your house tonight while we check for fingerprints, look for any other evidence, and tidy up."

"My father, Pastor Weakley, lives right in back of us," she said. "I'm sure I can stay there."

The chief looked over to Smith, who had returned from the cellar, and said, "You call the Reverend Weakley, and ask him to come over."

Constable Smith left the room, and Chief Erichson got up from the hassock to stretch his legs and move the crick out of his back. As he moved across the living, he stopped at the gun cabinet in the corner.

"Your husband has a nice collection of firearms, Mrs. Conger." Gesturing at the cabinet door he asked, "May I?"

"Yes," she said, "but I, I think it's locked."

The chief gave a tug on the door and it snapped open. The smell of powder solvent and gun oil, the smells of well-cared-for pieces, filled his nose. The stocks were all polished and the barrels had the rich, deep look of oiled blued metal. Side by side stood a Springfield pump shotgun, an old L.C. Smith field grade double barrel, a Ruger twenty-two semi-automatic, a Chinese SKS with a sport-orized stock and scope, and a Mossberg three-oh-eight. A couple of handguns lay on the bottom of the cabinet: a nine millimeter and a three-fifty-seven.

The chief closed the cabinet door and turned to Mrs. Conger and said, "We'll be borrowing these for examination."

Smith returned and announced, "Nobody answers at the Weakleys' number."

Still standing in front of the gun cabinet and looking across to Mrs. Conger, Erichson asked, "Is there someone else we can contact for you, Mrs. Conger? A relative or a neighbor?"

"Yes," Mrs. Conger seemed to brighten and sat up. "Barbara Ross, down near the corner, she has my children for the night. Take me there. Barbara will take care of us, I'm sure."

Looking at Smith, the chief said, "Help Mrs. Conger collect whatever she'll need for the night and escort her to the Ross'."

"You bet, Chief." Smith helped Mrs. Conger to her feet, and she went directly for the closet, got her jacket, and the two exited out the front door.

Dirkson came in with his patrolman's cap pushed back on his head and with pad in hand to say, "Well, Chief, I've got everything you told me to get. Should I let them go?"

"Did you find out anything interesting?"

"Yeah, a little," said Dirkson, stepping into the living room about half way. "A guy by the name of Callahan was seen nosing around the back of the house by a number of guys. And one mentioned that an Erik Brookhough was doing the same." Dirkson looked at his notes. "His name's Miles. Seems there was a little score to settle between Callahan and Conger. And it seems, according to Miles, that Brookhough wants Callahan's job. Callahan's outside, but this guy Brookhough is nowhere to be found." With a little too much eagerness in his voice, Dirkson added, "Do you want me to cuff Callahan?"

"No thanks, Dirkson," Erichson said. "There's plenty of time for that. You can let them go. Give 'em the old don't-leave-town-and-be-available-for-questioning routine."

"Yessir!" Dirkson said. He looked pleased over his assignment and was soon heard on the front stoop making his announcement with a near perfect imitation of Barney Fife.

100

Constable Smith rapped on the front door of the Ross residence. It was a nicely cared for old mill house one lot in from the corner of Benedict and Amherst. The care and attention to the place could be seen even in the low light escaping through the sparkling front windows. The lawn was raked, shrubs already had their winter covering of burlap, the driveway had the look and smell of having recently been coated with coal tar.

The porch light flashed on, and soon a trim woman in her late thirties appeared in a sweat suit at the front door beyond the enclosed porch. At the sight of Smith and Conger, her face furrowed with concern. She crossed the porch, and as she opened the porch door she opened her arms and Mrs. Conger threw herself into them with renewed sobs.

Mrs. Ross, embracing Mrs. Conger on the porch, looked down at Smith who remained on the first step.

"What's this all about?" Mrs. Ross asked. "What's happened? Has he been beating Sarah again?" She stroked Mrs. Conger's hair.

"I'm afraid there's been a terrible tragedy," Smith said. Mrs. Conger's husband has been killed."

"Oh, my God, Sarah," Mrs. Ross tightened her embrace and began a shared communion of tears.

Constable Smith stepped up onto the porch closer to the women. "May Mrs. Conger spend the night with you while we search for evidence and remove the...uh...tidy up?"

"Of course, Constable, we'll take care of her." Then turning her full attention and embracing Mrs. Conger as only women can seem to do for each other, she whispered, "I'm so sorry, Sarah, I'm so sorry."

NOVEMBER 6TH
THURSDAY

The chief pulled alongside the first shift picket line and stopped at Mickey Miles. He lowered the power window and called out, "Mr. Miles, please get in."

Mickey stopped, lowered his sign and peered into the cruiser. "Hi, Chief. What do you want me for?"

"Questioning. Please get in."

Mickey leaned his UNITED PAPER UNFAIR TO LABOR sign against the chain link fence and climbed into the Blazer.

"Wh—What's up?" Mickey's eyes darted about the truck's interior and settled on Erichson momentarily before moving on to the dash, the mounted shotgun, through the windshield, the roof and back again.

Erichson pulled away from the picket line and drove several hundred yards past the mill's entrance gate, then pulled off the side of the road. He put the transmission in park and left the engine idling and the heater fan blowing. He shifted in his seat to face Mickey.

"I would like you to tell me everything you know about last night at Conger's."

"Not much to tell, Chief," Mickey said. His eyes lit on Erichson and off again. "I think I told the constable everything."

The chief wondered if Mickey's uneasiness was due to guilt, withholding evidence, or simplemindedness.

"Tell me again, anyway," Erichson said. He hated it when he sounded like a detective novel. "I like to hear things for myself." He offered Mickey a cigarette, but Mickey waved it off. The Chief lighted up and popped the window down a crack to ventilate the smoke.

"Well, we went to Conger's to make an example of a scab," Mickey said. "Dan Callahan, our union prez, says we gotta keep all the guys in line, or the company will bust up the union, and we'll all be workin' twelve hour shifts for minimum wage." Mickey looked out the passenger window towards the mill and continued, "You know, Danny says this mill wants us to give back..."

"Let's get back to last night," the Chief said, "then I'll let you get back to bringing United Paper to its knees."

"Yeah, sure." Mickey faced Erichson. "Sorry Chief." Mickey held his gaze on Erichson for a longer moment. "We got to Conger's and the place was pretty dark. But Callahan said we'd picket anyway 'cause the neighbors would see and the whole town would know by daybreak that we wasn't gonna let no scabs off scot-free, ya know?"

"Eddie Conger didn't get off scot-free, would you say?"

"Uh...no, Chief. Nothin' like that was s'posed to happen."

"I understand you boys get pretty excited at your union rallies. Lots of talk about breaking arms, torching people's cars or homes. Is that right?"

Mickey's face screwed up and he drew one corner of his mouth back. "Aw, that's just bullshit talk, man. Guys soundin' tough. Nobody means that crap."

"Somebody meant that crap." Erichson pressed a little harder. So far he believed Mickey, and thought he might prove to be helpful if encouraged. "What about Conger's truck the other night?"

"I wasn't there for that, man!" Mickey started to frisk himself. "Ya gotta butt? I'll take that butt now."

"Sure Mickey, here." Erichson passed a pack of Camels to him. He thought to himself that he'd found Mickey's exposed nerve. "Nobody says you were at the fire, Mickey. It was a bad bit of business, though. What have you heard about it?"

"Nothing." Mickey sat looking straight out the cruiser window working his lips around the cigarette like a squirrel worrying over a peanut shell.

Erichson let him sit there in silence for a while, maybe thirty whole seconds. Maybe a minute.

"I don't believe you."

More silence.

"Maybe I should investigate your whereabouts that evening," the Chief pressed. "You seem pretty upset about this."

"I told you I wasn't there that night." Mickey glared at Erichson, then back out the window. "I was home."

"You don't have to be somewhere to know what happened there," Erichson pressed. "And I think you've heard something you should tell me."

"It's just rumors, Chief." Mickey looked at Erichson. "Just rumors."

"Sometimes rumors have a basis in fact. Out with it."

Mickey looked back out the cruiser windshield. He took a deep drag on his cigarette and exhaled. The smoke billowed across the windshield. "I hear Callahan wanted to get even with Conger for something. The fight at The Stallions maybe. Anyhow, rumor has it that maybe he torched his truck. Some of the guys there said they seen him do it."

"Is that what last night was all about at Conger's? Picketing to get even?"

"Maybe. I don't know," Mickey said. "It wasn't why I went there. But afterwards Callahan told me..." Mickey glanced at the Chief, then stared back out the windshield.

"Go on," Erichson gently encouraged.

"Callahan told me he had a score to settle last night."

"When did you hear that?"

"When I was taking a piss."

"Excuse me?"

"I just went there to picket, and drink a few free beers with the guys." Mickey flicked some ash in the cruiser's ash tray. "When I was off to the side lettin' go of a couple of those beers, Callahan scared the bejeebers outta me sneaking around to the back of the house. I asked him what he was doing. That's when he said he was settling a score. Then he told me to shut up and get out. So I did."

"Then what?" asked the Chief.

"I went back out front. Then Brow collars me and he says..."

"Brow? Who's Brow?"

"Brow. That's Erik Brookhough. He's got a scar through one eyebrow so he kinda looks like he's got three eyebrows. We call him Three-Brow or Brow for short."

"Okay. Go on. What about Brow?"

"He wants to know what Callahan's up to. He wants Callahan's job as union president. Anyway he wants me to make a big deal when Callahan shows up again. You know, draw attention to his comin' round the house. Then Brow goes out back on the other side."

"What for?"

"He didn't tell me. Nobody tells me nothin'. I don't think they like me. Anyway, maybe fifteen minutes later Callahan comes 'round front. I make a commotion and get a few guys to notice him like Brow wanted. That kind of pissed Danny off. But I go up to him and ask what he was up to. Ya know? Makin' conversation. He just cussed me out and told me to get lost. So I joined the rest of the guys picketing the house."

"What about Brow?"

"I never seen him again. I figured him and Danny got into it around back and Brow musta left."

"What happened then?"

"Nothin' much. It was about a half hour later, maybe three quarters, when all hell broke loose and Mrs. Conger came out screamin' at us and then you guys showed up."

"Did you see anyone else?"

"Nope."

"Hear a gun shot?"

"No sir," Mickey said, shaking his head. He was looking visibly calmer. "You guys took our statements and sent us home. And that was it until you showed up this morning." He took a last drag from his cigarette, powered down the window and flicked the butt outside.

"That's a fifty dollar littering fine, Mickey, the Chief said as he faced forward in his seat. He put the cruiser in drive, made a U-turn and drove back to where he had picked up Mickey. He extended his hand to Mickey, whose face had drawn into a pinched brow worried look.

"Uh, should I go back and get the butt?" Mickey asked.

"Not this time, "Erichson said. "I'll let you off for being cooperative. I'll be in touch."

Mickey took Erichson's hand with the cautious approach of a squirrel sniffing around a have-a-heart trap, shook it one time, then climbed out of the truck. Before closing the door, he looked at Erichson and said, "I hope it's not real soon." Then he closed the door.

Erichson drove down the road back towards town and pulled off onto the shoulder. After making a number of notes in a pad he kept in his corduroy sport coat, he drove off. He knew exactly with whom he would have his next interview.

Keegan O'Connor had been in his study for the customary three hours, and was standing at the Mr. Coffee in Grace's office measuring coffee grounds by the time she burst into the office at nine, filled with the excitement of gossipy news.

"Guess what?" she exclaimed as she hung her coat.

Keegan turned on the coffee, leaned against the countertop with arms folded and said, "The rapture has taken place, and only you and I remain on earth. A dream come true!"

"You *have* been at sea too long!" Grace said as she took her seat and swiveled to face Keegan. "Eddie Conger, he's the husband of the young woman, Sarah, you met with the other day, well Eddie was..."

The phone rang.

"Hold that thought," Grace said to Keegan, "you won't believe when I tell you." She answered the phone, "Grace's (she smiled and winked at Keegan) United Methodist Church, good morning."

Keegan waited, feeling a little titillated by Grace's enthusiasm. He listened as her voice became immediately serious and very business-like. "Yes...Oh, how dreadful...Yes, I'm sure he will...Hold on just a moment, I'll put him on."

Ignoring the mute button, Grace held her palm over the mouthpiece of the handset and said to Keegan in hushed tones, "This is about what I was going to tell you. Eddie Conger was murdered last night. Shot to death in his cellar, I hear. This is Barbara Ross on the line, she has Sarah with her, and she wants to speak to you."

Keegan could feel his adrenaline kick in at the news. For a community full of firearms, hunters and target shooters, this was the first murder he knew of in town since long before he came – probably more than thirty years.

He reached for Grace's phone and she waved him off saying, "You'd better take this in your study. I'll bring your coffee when it's ready."

Keegan went to his desk, and as he reached for his phone he realized that he did not know, from what Grace had just said, whether he had Barbara or Sarah on the other end of the line. "Hello, Keegan here."

"Hi, Keegan. I'm so thankful I found you in."

"Hi, Barb." Keegan was relieved to hear Barbara's familiar and calm voice. "From what little Grace filled me in on, it sounds like you folks have had an eventful night."

"You have no idea," Barbara's voice was calm, but it was also tired and worried. "We've been up most of the night, or at least it feels like we have."

"How is Sarah bearing up under the shock?" Keegan asked. He leaned back into his chair.

"She's sleeping now," said Barb. "I think Doctor Shapiro gave her something to calm her nerves last night. It seemed to really take effect around midnight, and she's still sleeping pretty soundly."

"I'm glad for that small blessing," Keegan said. "How are you doing? This has got to be tough on your family."

There was a brief silence, then, "We're OK. It's such a shock. A murder in the neighborhood! Who would do such a thing? We're a little cramped for space, but we'll manage. I'm worried about Sarah and the kids. Could you come over to see them? Maybe at lunch time? She'll be up by then, and will have had time to freshen up. I've kept my kids home from school to keep Sarah's children occupied. And the dog is keeping track of all of them."

Keegan felt the instant pang of guilt he always felt when he had to choose between two pressing obligations. He wanted very much to keep his standing date with Eileen for lunch, to be with her while she was feeling so miserable, and while life seemed so tentative. But Sarah didn't ask to have her husband murdered, and her children certainly didn't deserve to be fatherless so early in life. "Sure, Barb," Keegan said, "I'll stop by at noon."

"Thanks, Keeg," Barb sounded somewhat relieved. "I'll see you then."

Keegan leaned forward and hung up the phone. Grace came into the study bearing a cup of steaming coffee, and on a plate from the kitchen reading GRACE UNITED METHODIST CHURCH around the perimeter and the denomination's cross and flame emblazoned in the center, rode a large piece of her homemade Jewish Coffeecake.

This had become, by all means, a favorite treat of Keegan's that Grace started him on shortly after his arrival in Fort George. Eileen said that Grace single-handedly added ten pounds to him over the last three years. When first introduced to the cake, he asked her what made it Jewish. Grace had said she'd no idea; it was simply the name on her recipe card. Maybe it was the cream cheese.

Looking up at Grace with a smile spreading over this face, Keegan asked, "How did you know to bring this in today?"

"Just a feeling. It sounds like you'll be stopping by Barbara's today?"

"Yeah, lunch at noon."

"Then you leave here by ten-thirty to be with Eileen for a bit." Grace turned to head back into her office. She stopped at the threshold, turned to Keegan and said, "Understand?"

"Yes, mother."

Chief Erichson was seated in the living room of Daniel Callahan's new chalet on Indian Camp Hollow Road. The spacious house sat on a huge lot that caused Erichson to think the union president business must be very good.

Callahan sat on the edge of his sofa. Several times through the morning's questioning he shifted his weight as if about to stand, but didn't. Callahan's eyes seemed never to leave Erichson. The stare felt unnaturally steady.

"So, Mr. Callahan," Chief Erichson said, "you're telling me that you are personally aware of nothing unusual last night at Congers' place, before Mrs. Conger came out of the house screaming. You heard nothing out of the ordinary. You saw nothing out of the ordinary, and you did nothing out of the ordinary – other than your picketing."

"Yeah, yeah, that's about it," Callahan said, nodding.

"You're lying to me, Mr. Callahan." The chief stared at Callahan's eyes, giving as good as he got. "Why would you want to lie to me?"

"I ain't ly…"

"Please, Mr. Callahan," the chief said raising his hand as if to stop traffic, "don't compound the transgression."

Erichson removed a note pad from an inside pocket of his corduroy sport coat, thumbed through a few pages, closed the cover and returned it to his pocket.

"I've met with some of the men present last night," Erichson said, "and some remember you sneaking around back of the Conger place. You understand how that interests me, can't you?"

Callahan shot to his feet, the chief felt all of the muscles in his body respond with tension expecting to defend against something, but Callahan seemed to think better of his posture and sat back down again.

"Why those lying sons-of…"

"Mr. Callahan, please. Stop the theatrics!" Erichson said. "Just tell me what you were doing around the back of Conger's house."

Callahan pulled a pack of Basics brand cigarettes out of his shirt pocket and lit one. He tossed the pack on the coffee table in front of him and took two puffs.

"I had a little score to settle with Eddie Conger, is all," Callahan finally said.

"And did you decide to settle your score with Mr. Conger with a deer slug through his head?"

"Jesus! No! Is that how he got it? Damn! Shee-it." This time Callahan did get up. He bent over to roll ashes off his cigarette into the tray on the coffee table, then wandered over to his living room window and stared out for a moment.

Erichson wasn't sure if Callahan's response was genuinely shocked or if he protested too much. Remaining in his seated position with legs crossed, he watched and waited for Callahan to settle down.

"Shee-it!" Callahan said again, shaking his head. He returned to the sofa, almost sat, then did.

"How did you even the score, Mr. Callahan?"

"Glass, man. Glass is all. Car for car, we was even. But I had a broken nose, and I decided something of his had to be broken." Callahan leaned over the coffee table and rotated more ashes off into the tray. "I found a two by four lying in back of the garage and knocked out all the glass I could find on the back of the guy's house. I swear, that's it. Just the damn glass!" He drew deeply on the cigarette.

"Then what?" asked the chief.

"Then nothing. I went back out front, when that shit-for-brains Mickey saw me coming out and made a big deal of it. I'll get him for telling you, and…"

"You'll get nobody. You're in enough trouble, don't you think?"

"Yeah, sure," said Callahan.

"Tell me about Erik Brookhough."

"What about him? He's one of my boys. He was there picketing with the rest of us."

"One of your boys?"

"Yeah, well, he's been mouthin' off some lately, but he's one of my union boys. What about him?"

"He was also seen moving to the back of the Conger home by others. I thought you might tell me what you boys were up to."

"I never saw him back there. In fact, now that you bring him up, I never saw him again from the time I went back there and busted some glass. When I came back out front I joined the guys, popped a beer, and the next thing I know Eddie's wife is out front screamin' at us, callin' us murderers and all kinds of shit. Then you show up, sirens blaring and," Callahan shrugged, "here we are."

Convinced he had heard all he was about to, Chief Erichson wrapped up his interview. "You keep where I can get easy hold of you, Mr. Callahan," Erichson said, "If you want to leave town to buy shoes at the Dexter outlet in Glens Falls, or number two pencils in Ticonderoga, you ask me for permission."

The Ross house was one of the old mill houses that lined both sides of Benedict Street. In the mill's heyday, it provided elegant housing for its middle and upper management. In many respects the houses were precursors of post war development housing utilizing four basic floor plans; but each house was set differently on its lot and used unique siding, window and door treatments, all of which combined to provide enough visual variation so as to avoid the look of tract housing.

About thirty years ago, the mill decided to get out of the real estate business, and sold the houses to their current residents. As the homes changed hands, and endured varying degrees of care, some, like the Ross', maintained their stately appeal while others fell into disrepair.

Halloween decorations, had there been any, were gone and the porch stood decorated with bundled corn stalks standing sentry to the front door. A small table inside the French doors was bedecked with a cornucopia display of various squash and Indian corn. A grapevine wreath, with waxed fall colored leaves inserted, hung on the front door.

As Keegan waited a step down from the landing level, he was greeted by Barbara at the French doors of the expansive glassed-in front porch of her home. The family dog bounded out the front door, shouldered by Barbara, and leapt at Keegan hitting him square in the chest with her front paws nearly knocking him over. The dog headed on down the street towards some neighborhood kids playing with a ball.

"Ohmygod, Keegan, I'm so sorry," Barbara said, rushing down the porch stairs to assist him. "Are you hurt? That damn dog." Barbara brushed at Keegan's coat "She did the same thing to Sarah not long ago. Knocked her right down. Are you okay?"

"I'm fine, Barb. Just a little surprised." He sucked in a little wind, and gestured for Barbara to lead the way. "You say the dog pounced on Sarah the same way?"

"It must have been nearly a week ago. I'm surprised she didn't bruise more than she did." Barb moved up the porch stairs "Come on in." They moved inside the porch and Barbara turned to Keegan and held her hand up to stop him.

"Thanks for coming, Keegan," she said, "can we talk here, a little out of the cold, for a moment?"

"Sure, Barb." He took off his hat and coat. "How's Sarah doing?"

"Okay, I guess," Barbara said as she took Keegan's hat and coat and folded the coat over her arm. "She moves between being teary eyed, and calming down. We've heard nothing from the police, and we're not sure about anything regarding Eddie's body, or who did it, or anything. Her whole life seems very much up in the air. Her kids play with mine. Then after a while they will notice their mother in tears and sometimes cry with her. Then they'll be distracted by play again."

"Pretty normal behavior for a family whose husband and father has been ripped away, stolen from them." Keegan motioned towards the living room and said, "Let's go in."

Barbara led the way off the porch and into the front parlor through the interior entrance way. Sarah, dressed in a sweatshirt and jeans, looked up to see Keegan, and immediately stood to greet him.

"Oh, thank you for coming," Sarah managed, then broke into sobs.

Keegan stood in the middle of the Ross parlor with Sarah's arms wrapped around him, and her face sobbing into his sweater vest. He held her about the shoulders and looked at Barbara, hoping for a little help in soothing Sarah.

Barbara draped Keegan's coat over an occasional chair in the parlor closest to the entrance way and went to Keegan and Sarah. She placed her left hand on Sarah's arm and stroked Sarah's hair with the other hand. She cooed soothing affirmations to Sarah and guided her and Keegan to the sofa to sit.

As Sarah began to quiet, Barbara offered to make tea, and left for the kitchen at the back of the house.

Keegan managed to set Sarah upright by the shoulders and said, "I am very sorry about Eddie's death."

"You're very kind for coming," Sarah said. She dabbed at her eyes, then looked at Keegan and said, "Even my own father hasn't contacted me." The last comment brought a new welling in her eyes, but she seemed to fight it back with an angry set to her jaw.

Keegan had little use for the oh-so-very-righteous Reverend Weakley, but he found it difficult to believe the man would be so intentionally insensitive towards his daughter.

"Sarah," Keegan said "I don't know all of what you went through last night, or even this morning, but is it possible your father doesn't know what's happened?"

"That's hard to believe, Pastor. Eddie's in the paper and on the radio. Everybody must know by now." There was an edge to her voice. "His whole flock must have phoned him by now."

Barbara came back into the parlor with a tray of finger sandwiches and napkins. "You can start on these while you wait for the tea." She placed the tray on the coffee table in front of the sofa and said, "The kettle's on. The tea will be ready shortly." She sat in a chair close by.

Keegan nodded thanks to Barbara and said to Sarah, "I understand you're pretty much up in the air about Eddie's remains, and what kinds of preparations you can make for his funeral, about when you can return home, and the like. If you would like, I'd be happy to make some of those phone calls to see if I can find out any information for you."

Sarah had sat back into the sofa and had begun to stare off into space as Keegan spoke. The shock and fatigue of the events were obvious. She sat silent for a while. Her eyes were red and puffy. Keegan noticed that she was wearing none of the makeup she wore in his study. She looked fresher, aside from the puffy eyes, almost healthier. No teenage perfume was in the air.

"I do need to learn these things, don't I?" she said.

"Yes," Keegan said, "If not now, then soon. I can look into some of this, and then get back to you."

The kettle in the kitchen whistled its beckoning call, and Barbara rose to answer.

Sarah shifted herself in the sofa, drawing her legs up along side of her on the cushions to face Keegan.

"Pastor, I'd like you to do Eddie's funeral," she said.

"I would have thought sure that you'd have your father do the service." Keegan's head was cocked at her suggestion. "He might be hurt if you have me do it."

"You don't do funerals for people not a part of your flock?" she asked.

"That's not it at all," Keegan said. "It's simply that I'm not sure you would be comfortable with the kind of funeral service a Methodist pastor would conduct. Not to mention, I think it could cause some serious hard feelings between you and your father. Maybe it would be better if I only attended as a member of the community, or friend of the family." He hoped she would not pursue this further.

"No," she said. "I don't think I care what my daddy thinks. Besides, he didn't like Eddie very much anyway." She folded her arms and looked over at the sandwiches. After a brief moment she looked back over at Keegan and continued, "He'd only want to send him to hell anyway. I want you to do the funeral."

Barbara returned with tea, and Keegan was glad for the distraction. He searched his mind for a good excuse not to do the funeral. He was sure his presence would create a hellish exchange with Weakley. As he accepted tea, the conversation around him turned briefly to tasty sandwiches and low fat mayonnaise. His mental search ended when Sarah brought the conversation back to him and the funeral.

"Will you do the service, Pastor?"

Keegan looked at Sarah, then at Barbara, then back to Sarah, and with a voice that sounded more defeated than pastoral he said, "It's against my better judgment … but, I'll do the service."

Sarah quickly put her tea on the coffee table, leaned over to Keegan with her knees buried in the cushions, put her arms around his neck, and kissed him on the cheek. "Thank you, Pastor; I knew you would take care of me."

Keegan noticed a raised eyebrow from Barbara Ross.

Sarah retreated, picked up her tea, and added a cookie to her saucer before sitting back into her place with legs drawn up under her.

Keegan cleared his throat then asked, "Which of the two funeral homes in town do you expect to use, Sarah? I'll start with a call there."

"Daddy used Forest and Turnbull when Mommy died twenty years ago. Maybe I should have them take care of Eddie." She raised the teacup to her lips, took a sip, replaced the cup on its saucer and nodded. "I'll have them do Eddie."

"I'm sure Mr. Forest will do a fine job. I'll give him a call when I return to my study." Keegan hitched to the edge of his seat and continued, "Before I leave, let's have a word of prayer together." When finished he asked, "Does anything else come to mind before I go?"

Both Sarah and Barbara shook their heads in the negative and Keegan rose to his feet.

"I think it best I contact your father to let him know of the arrangements," Keegan said as he extended his hand to shake Sarah's. "If you should want to change your mind about anything after speaking to your father, please feel free to do so. I only wish to be supportive."

Sarah shook his hand, closed her eyes squeezing out waiting tears, and nodded gratitude.

Barbara moved to the occasional chair where she had laid Keegan's hat and coat. She picked them up, and not relinquishing them, she said, "I'll see you to the door, Keegan."

They walked out onto the porch where Barbara turned to face Keegan and said, "Well, you've certainly made a friend."

"Yes, I guess so." Keegan couldn't decide from Barbara's tone of voice whether she was making fun of him or reproving him."

"Thanks for coming, Keegan." Barbara helped him on with his coat then handed him his hat and said, "I know it was very much appreciated. Really, by both of us."

"Glad I can help," Keegan said, not altogether sure he was. He adjusted his coat. "I don't mind telling you I feel a little apprehensive about dealing with her father. I don't think he's going to take this very well."

Keegan opened the door and paused. He turned to Barbara and asked, "By the way, have you mentioned any of what you know about Sarah's and Eddie's relationship, the abuse, to Chief Erichson?"

"No, not yet," Barbara said. She stood by the door with folded arms. "Do you think I should?"

"I'm not sure," Keegan said and scratched at his beard. "All things considered, it's probably best for him to have too much information, even irrelevant information, rather than not enough." With a final tug at the chinstrap, he added, "Yeah, tell him."

Keegan decided to drive to the Forest and Turnbull Funeral Home rather than call. By the time he finished with Forest and dropped by to see Weakley, he was pretty sure he'd be wasted for the day.

He pulled up in front of Forest and Turnbull (Turnbull had been dead for more than two decades, but old man Forest kept the name on the business out of respect for his late partner) and let himself into the business office.

John Forest, seated at his desk, looked at least as old as Moses, and possibly even as old as God. When he stood erect, his six foot four inch frame imposed upon you irrespective of his age. He wore his thinning hair combed straight back, and sported a waxed and turned up handlebar mustache – an affectation grown once he joined The Racing City Chorus, a fifty-voice barbershop ensemble down in Saratoga Springs. The three piece charcoal grey suit completed the look for this community pillar.

John looked up from his desk and smiled broadly, exposing a mouthful of his own teeth beneath the handlebar. He rose with hand extended, and suddenly a look of concern spread across his face.

"My God, Keegan, nothing has happened to Eileen, has it?"

"She's not ready for the grim reaper, or you, John." The two men shook hands.

"Thank God," John said, and he landed hard in his chair. "Well then, what brings you my way?" John closed the folder of papers he was working on and put them off to one side of the desk. Keegan liked the way the old man managed to make him feel as if he were the only person on the planet. It was old Forest's style. He managed to make everyone feel like the focus of the universe.

"I've just come from seeing Sarah Conger," Keegan said.

"Bad business, that. I hope they get the s.o.b."

"To be sure," Keegan said. "Sarah Conger wants you to make funeral arrangements for Eddie. Apparently you buried her mother twenty years ago, or so."

"Yeah I remember that." John Forest leaned back in his desk chair and began to play with the end of his mustache. "Her mom was the Reverend Weakley's wife. Which leads me to ask how you got involved in this?"

"I wonder the same thing, John," Keegan said with a shake of his head. "Suffice it to say, I'm in, like it or not, and so are you."

John pulled out a funeral arrangement form from the desk and began to write Eddie Conger's name at the top. Then, noticing that Keegan was still standing in his office, he pointed to a chair next to the desk and said, "Sit, lad, sit." He scribbled briefly and added, "Where is the deceased now, Keegan?"

"I suspect he's in the hospital morgue." Keegan sat and crossed his legs. "I would also suspect Eli Shapiro has been doing an autopsy, so you'll have to contact him about getting the body released to you. I'm sure you know a great deal more about that end than I do."

"Yes and no, Keegan," John said looking up from his work. "Over all of the years I've been in business in this community, more than fifty years, I could count the number of murders on one hand and have plenty of fingers unaccounted for."

"That's just as well," Keegan said as he stood up. "I'll leave this in your capable hands. Call me when you expect to meet with Sarah and I'll try to be there. She's staying with the Ross family on Benedict. Just now, I'm off to see Bill Weakley."

"Very well, Keegan." John rose to extend his hand and added, "Good luck with him, lad. He's an odd one."

Keegan pulled his car up to the curb in front of Bill Weakley's parsonage. As he got out of the car and made his way up the sidewalk to the front door, he hoped Weakley would not be home. He rang the doorbell. Weakley opened the door. Keegan's heart sank.

"Hello, Bill," Keegan said.

"You may call me Pastor Weakley," came the stony faced response.

Keegan fought back his impulse to excoriate the under-educated layman who called himself a member of the clergy. Instead, he took a deep breath and tried again. "Bill, I..."

"I said you..."

Keegan held up his hand to silence Weakley and continued, "You may not have seen the morning paper or been listening to the radio, so I came to be sure you knew that your son-in-law was murdered last night."

Weakley stared at Keegan with an expressionless face. Finally he asked "Is Sarah all right?"

"Shaken, certainly. I believe she may be upset with you. She believes you probably know and have neglected to see her."

"Then you've seen her," Weakley said as if he had a bad taste in his mouth.

"I have." Keegan was becoming irritated over being forced to have this conversation on the steps of the Lighthouse parsonage, but reminded himself that he really didn't want to be there in the first place. "I'd like to suggest that she needs her family now. She needs you."

"I don't need a Godless heathen like you telling me what my little girl needs." Weakley's expression changed from stony indifference to the narrowed eyes and set jaw of loathsome anger.

"Then you'll love this news." Keegan could feel his anger slip its mooring. He took one step up to gain eye level to Weakley and said, "Until I hear otherwise from Mrs. Sarah Conger, I will officiate over the funeral of her husband, Mr. Edward Conger. And you, sir, should you wish to consult with me regarding Mrs. Conger, may do so only if you are prepared to speak to me civilly." With that, Keegan made an about face, descended the stairs, and headed directly to his car.

"You sheep stealing demon of Satan!" Weakley called after him, shouting into the street, "I'll see you in hell! The wrath of God will visit upon..."

Keegan slammed the car door, cutting off Weakley's tirade. The Intrepid started immediately. Keegan backed into the Weakley driveway and pulled out with his front tires spinning out some of the driveway gravel.

As he drove home to Eileen and an afternoon Manhattan, he decided he would call the chair of the church trustees and let her know that he would not be in attendance at the evening meeting. Dealing with Weakley and Conger was about all he was going to be up to for the next couple of days.

Doctor Eli Shapiro opened the door between his office and the waiting room and called in Chief Erichson. The two men exchanged handshakes, pleasantries about the weather and a good hunting season and sat across from each other over the good doctor's desk.

116

The office had an intimate feel about it with family photos and a mounted three foot Northern Pike on the walls. An examining table waited by the far wall with a Norman Rockwell print hanging over it of a little boy probing his dog with a stethoscope.

"So," Erichson said, making the transition from pleasantries to business, "What have you got for me on the Conger case?"

"It's really pretty basic," Eli said and handed the Chief a thin file folder. "You probably have it all figured on your own."

Erichson scanned the written report in silence then closed the folder and said, "But you'll give me the benefit of your expertise, won't you, doctor?"

"When haven't I?" Eli quipped. He leaned back in his chair and put his feet up on the corner of his desk, crossed at the ankles. With hands behind his head he instructed, "Based upon the brain matter and blood pattern on the foundation wall to Mr. Conger's left, he was seated at his work bench, and sitting upright. At the moment of his murder, he was facing forward."

"Murder?" the Chief interrupted. "No possibility of suicide?"

"None," said Eli. "No powder burns or residue about the wound. His hands were covered with it, but the man was reloading his own deer hunting ammo, so that's to be expected." Eli could see that Erichson was making a few notes on the cover of the folder, so he waited for the Chief to finish.

"Okay, go on."

"Let's see," said Eli as he tried to remember where he left off. "Oh yeah, at the moment of murder he was facing forward. The point of entry was immediately behind the right temple. The exit was the whole left side of his head, which makes much of the rest of what I have to say a guess."

"How's that, Doc?" Erichson's eyebrows pinched.

"With so much of the skull blown out, it becomes difficult to determine the direction from which the projectile came. A definitive entrance and exit hole, one that almost certainly would have been made from a fully, or even partially, jacketed slug, would have provided two holes in the skull. Between those two holes a slug path may be drawn which, when extrapolated, can estimate the point from which the shot was taken."

"You can't do that this time?"

"Not very well. This slug had only a gas check – to protect the bottom of the slug from the exploding gasses in the cartridge. It was also made of a much softer alloy than commercial ammunition. Once this slug hit flesh and bone, it mushroomed to nearly four times its starting diameter. It built up so much pressure inside Eddie Conger's skull that it literally exploded out the left side of his head."

"In other words, the exit wound was so big, that you can't make an accurate assessment about where the shot came from?"

"That's about it. I'll give you my best guess," Eli said with a shrug, "but that's all it is, a guess."

"Let's have it."

"Based upon where Conger was sitting, and the blood pattern on the wall, my best guess is that he was shot anywhere from the area that encompasses the third step from the bottom of the cellar staircase to a spot maybe as much as five feet in front of the staircase. That includes the open cellar window."

"Yeah," said the Chief, "how about that window. Why do you think it was open on such a cool evening?"

"Ventilation. The kerosene heater was going. Eddie didn't want to die of asphyxiation."

"Poor bastard," Erichson said, shaking his head. "Go ahead and finish up."

"Finally, the slug could have been fired as close as fifteen feet, which would be stepping into the cellar a small way. Other than a bit of final conjecture, that's about it."

"Well, let's have the conjecture too," said Erichson, "I know you love to do this to me."

"You're so right, my friend. Here it is. Since he was facing forward at the time of impact, I surmise that, one, he did not hear the intruder, or two, the intruder did not represent a threat to Mr. Conger. And since there was a racket outside, and your report indicates that the tumbler was running on the work bench, either could be true."

"Thanks, you're a big help."

"All in a day's, and night's, work," Eli said. He brought his feet down and sat upright in his chair. Reaching into the pencil drawer of the desk he said, "One final tidbit." He held out one of Eddie's deer slayers. "I took this from the murder scene and compared it with the slug that killed Eddie."

"And?" the Chief pressed.

"And," said Eli, "Mr. Conger was killed with one of his own reloads."

Keegan managed to get his coat and hat hung in the entrance way closet before MaryKay came out to greet him.

"Hi, Keeg," she said, "I'm glad you got home early."

"Why?" This sounded like trouble to Keegan. "What's up?"

"I learned this afternoon that my sister in Allentown, you know, the one I love so much," she rolled her eyes to emphasize her sarcasm, "well, she's fallen and broken a hip." She clicked her tongue in disapproval and continued, "Sooo, that means I'll be heading to Pennsylvania to help her out for a while. Like her or not she's the only sister I've got." She reached into the closet and pulled out her jacket.

"Of course," she continued to prattle on, "if the roles were reversed I could whistle Dixie waiting for her to show up." She threw the jacket over her shoulders and said, "Gotta go. I won't be leaving until Monday. She doesn't need me in the hospital. But you might want to plan on looking in on Eileen throughout the day." She reached up and gave Keegan a peck on the cheek and finished with, "I'm awful sorry about leaving you in the middle of this." She opened the front door, stepped out onto the porch, and turned back to Keegan, "Sometimes family can be a real pain in the ass, can't they?" She turned and left.

Keegan stood in the entrance way and took a few moments to process all of what MaryKay had just said before heading on into the house and looking in on Eileen. He found her out on the back deck in the late afternoon sun. She was reading a book.

"Hello, Mrs. O'Connor," he said.

"Hello, Reverend." She looked up and over her shoulder at Keegan.

"How ya feeling?"

"Nearly as terrible as yesterday." Eileen closed her book and got up to come into the house. "It's getting a little chilly out there." As she got to Keegan she gave him a hello kiss and asked, "How was your day?"

He swatted her fanny as she passed by him and walked towards the living room. He said, "I'm about to make a double Manhattan. Would you like anything?"

"Hmm," she intoned, "That kind of a day, eh? Nothing for me, thanks. The chemo, you know."

Keegan mixed his drink, brought it into the living room and sat in the recliner next to Eileen. He took a sip.

"Tell me about it," she said and looked over at him.

"Nothing significant." He closed his eyes to rest them and hoped Eileen would not press. He did not want to unload on her. He wanted her energies concentrated on healing from the cancer.

"Keegan, please. Tell me."

He turned his head and opened his eyes to look at his wife. "No big deal, really. I don't want to trouble you with some of the pettiness that makes up my day. It was simply a frustrating kind of day, or at least it ended that way."

"Keegan, please don't shut me out." Eileen twisted in her seat to face Keegan and leaned on the chair arm closest to him. "Right now, being cooped up and feeling so miserable, you and MaryKay are my only links to the world. Talk to me the way you always have. Let me live now ... just in case I can't..." Her eyes welled up and tears wetted her cheeks, "in case I don't beat this."

Keegan got out of his seat, knelt next to Eileen, embraced her hard, and they cried in each other's arms.

Art Erichson unlocked his back door, stepped into his kitchen and closed the door with the back of his left foot. He draped his jacket over the back of a kitchen chair and noticed the answering machine blinking at him. He pushed the play back button and heard an automated sales pitch for vinyl siding and vinyl clad replacement windows, and a second message that got his heart pumping.

"Chief Erichson," the disembodied voice said, "this is Mickey Miles. Uh, I thought of something you, umm, ought to know. Anyway, give me a call, and we'll talk. Okay?"

NOVEMBER 7th
FRIDAY

Chief Erichson decided to give Mickey Miles a break and leave him in peace on the picket line. As arranged over the phone at six-thirty that morning the Chief stood at quarter to four in the afternoon rapping on Mickey's front door.

Mickey swung the door wide. "Hello, Chief. Come on in." Mickey stepped aside and let the Chief in. Erichson walked to the center of the living room and turned to watch Mickey close the door and return.

"Would ya like a beer, or uh, maybe coffee?" asked Mickey.

"No thanks, Mickey," Erichson said, waving Mickey off. "Just tell me what it is you think I ought to know."

Mickey pulled a pack of Lucky Strikes out of his work shirt pocket, yanked one, offered the pack to the Chief who refused, returned the pack and pulled out a Zippo and lit the butt. He took the long drag that a practiced and addicted smoker takes for that initial nicotine hit, held his breath momentarily, then exhaled out the corner of his mouth, blowing the smoke away from Erichson.

Erichson waited patiently for the passing of this ritual, knowing it was the usual prelude to some real or imagined betrayal.

"Ready?" Erichson said, gently prodding.

"Yeah, I think so," Mickey said and turned to go sit in an overstuffed chair that a cat had mistaken for a scratching post. The Chief responded by sitting on the sofa, next to an over-indulged expanse of cat who blinked sleepy annoyance at the Chief's disturbing its slumber.

Mickey took one more deep drag, brushed the ash off the end of his cigarette into the beanbag ash tray on the arm of the chair and said, "This may not be anything, anything at all Chief."

"Maybe not, Mickey," the Chief said, trying to sound relaxed in an effort to put Mickey at ease. "But let me be the judge of that. Anything you can tell me may be of help."

"Yeah, well, that's what I thought." Mickey rolled the cigarette between his fingers. "Eddie Conger had one close friend that I know of, Bucky Dwyer."

"Bucky?" Art asked and pulled out his note pad.

"Yeah. I think Larry is his real name," Mickey said, "but I've heard him called Bucky. I'd see them at The Stallions from time to time, and I think they were hunting buddies."

Mickey took a drag, and Art made notes.

"Anyway, it occurred to me that if anybody would know if Eddie Conger was getting into it with someone, he might be the guy." Mickey inhaled long on the butt, put it out in the tray half unsmoked, and pulled out the pack as he exhaled. He looked up at the Chief and said, "I saw on TV years ago that the last half of a butt is the worst half for ya." He hung another on his lip, lighted it with two short puffs, and rolled over on one hip to slip the Zippo back into his pocket. "I'm trying to cut back. Damn things'll kill me."

"They may very well," the Chief said as he sat forward on the edge of the sofa cushion. "Is that it?" Erichson didn't think he masked the disappointment in his voice very well, and he silently cursed himself for his lack of tact.

"Well, yeah. I thought I was bein' helpful."

"You are," said the Chief. "I mean, is there anything more you can think of that might be of help? Anything you can add about this Bucky or Mr. Conger?" He hoped he may have redeemed the insult.

"No, that's about it, Chief. I hope it leads to something."

Chief Erichson stood, unconsciously brushed cat hair off his trousers and thanked Mickey for this help and assured him of the Chief's future gratitude should Mickey recall any further information.

Once Erichson got outside and headed towards the Blazer, he could hear the police radio calling him. He opened the vehicle door and reached in to grab the mike and respond.

"Erichson here."

"Chief, this is Smith. Are you alone? I've got the ballistics report for you."

"Yeah, go ahead." Erichson sidled in on the seat and closed the cruiser door.

"The slug that killed Eddie mushroomed too much to tell for certain what gun shot it. Best guess from the lab is the Conger Mossberg that we

122

sent along with the slug. That rifle has been discharged, and there were fragments of foam rubber around the muzzle that match the pillow on the cellar floor."

"Pretty much as we suspected."

"Right, Chief. One last thing. The Mossberg was wiped pretty clean. A smudged palm print, and one fairly clear fingerprint. Maybe enough for a clear identification."

"Run the prints," Erichson said. He started the Blazer's motor. "As for the murder weapon, slug match or no, it seems pretty conclusive." He dropped the transmission into gear. "A cabinet full of guns with his prints all over them, except for his deer rifle during hunting season. Anything else?"

"No sir," crackled Smith's voice. "That about does it."

"Good work. Erichson out."

At about four-thirty Keegan walked into the Forest and Turnbull Funeral Home and was greeted by one of the men that John Forest hired to assist at funerals to park cars, help little old ladies get up and down the front steps, and move the body from the prep-room into a casket and out into the chapel.

"Good afternoon, Reverend O'Connor." The gent who met him was a member of Grace Methodist. He took Keegan's coat and hat and whispered a little too loud for Keegan's comfort, "Wait until you get in there." He nodded towards the chapel. "These Lighthouse people are a piece of work." The old man winked at Keegan and left to hang his belongings in the cloak room.

Before Keegan could move through the entrance hall and pass by the double doors into the chapel, John Forest popped his head out of his side office and called Keegan in.

"Hi, Keegan," John said, extending his hand, "glad you came in."

"Just trying to get a feel for who Eddie Conger was from those who visit tonight," Keegan said, accepting the hand shake.

"You've never had a Lighthouse funeral before, Keegan. No cause to." John signaled for Keegan to sit, and John took his place at his desk. "So you're in for a real experience."

"How's that John?" Keegan sat and crossed his legs.

"They don't do weeping and wailing, Keeg. They do singing and dancing, shouting and fainting." John had a broad smile on his face, and looked as if he was about to watch a great practical joke played on Keegan.

"Well," said Keegan, 'I guess I'll just muddle through."

"That you will lad, that you will." John kept his smile and seemed almost to want to break out in a chuckle as he stood to usher Keegan towards the office door. Before opening the door for Keegan, John paused and said, "Expect the unexpected, roll with the circumstances, don't let it throw you off your pace and you'll do fine. This evening will be a crash course of what you may expect tomorrow at the funeral." He opened the door, patted Keegan on the back with a "Go get 'em" and closed the door.

Keegan was sure he heard a little light laughter in the office behind him. He approached the double doors to the chapel and paused there with his hand on the doorknob. He was conscious of his quickened heartbeat. He took a deep breath and opened the door. He stepped through the double doors into the chapel and stayed at the back of the room as he looked about to get his bearings.

The canned organ music usually piped through the funeral home's PA was missing. Instead a young woman played guitar and sang praise songs off to one side at the front of the room. Others casually joined her. They all seemed to wear placid angelic faces with Mona Lisa smiles. A half dozen others swayed, even danced, to the music with arms outstretched overhead and faces turned upward, entranced. Throughout the room people were in prayer. One woman near the back of the room spoke in tongues as she stood. The man seated next to her seemed to be interpreting the unfamiliar sounds with a flair for King James English. Another man knelt at the closed casket and bobbed back and forth like an Orthodox Jew at the Jerusalem Wailing Wall. Keegan listened to the chapel cacophony. There was something about this unfamiliar mix of sights and sounds that seemed right and appropriate. It was an expression of hope in the presence of death. It certainly wasn't a sedate Methodist wake, but the event had its own integrity.

Keegan spotted Sarah near the front of the chapel seated near the guitar player. She sang with the others. From where he stood, he could see she wore a black knit top with a single strand of pearls. Her hair was pulled back into a scrunchie, and hung gracefully down her back. He left the safety of the back wall and made his way towards her through the crowded room, which he estimated contained nearly the entire Lighthouse congregation. As he neared the front of the room he could hear the man kneeling at the casket praying for the redemption of Eddie's soul, "a known and terrible sinner."

Keegan rounded to the front of the room and caught Sarah's eye. She rose full of smiles and quickly threw her arms around Keegan's neck and hugged him.

"Thank you so much for coming, Pastor Keegan!" she said.

"Of course, I'm pleased to be here." He was surprised to feel his face flush.

"Come, sit next to me for a while." Sarah took Keegan by the arm and dew him towards the front row of chairs. She sat and pulled Keegan into the chair next to her and wrapped both of her arms around his. She immediately returned to singing lowly and leaned her head on Keegan's shoulder. Her scent had changed. Gone was the teenage fragrance. She wore something much more subtle. Gone too, was the heavy makeup.

Keegan felt a pang of guilt run through his belly, and images of Eileen at home crossed the view of his mind's eye. But he also enjoyed this woman's reliance upon him. With his free hand, he patted one of hers, and sat back to listen to the singing.

"Hi, Chief. This is a surprise."

The late twenties to thirty-ish man answering the door had one of the most pronounced overbites Chief Erichson had ever seen. "Mr. Lawrence Dwyer?"

"That's me," said the young man with an unassuming easy way about himself. He obviously recognized the Chief although Erichson was sure they had never met. One of the many benefits of living in a small community. "Come on in, and take a load off." The Chief stepped into the living room and turned to extend a hand. Larry shook it and pointed to an overstuffed chair in the small and tidy living room. "You caught me just before I left for Eddie's wake."

When Erichson sat he was within view of the dining room beyond, where he observed two young boys busily playing with a Lionel train. The track entwined about the legs of the dining room table, and from the sounds of their play, the chairs had been designated as houses and businesses in their imaginary town.

Larry sat on the arm of the sofa across from the Chief and asked, "Would you like some coffee, or maybe tea?"

"You know," said the Chief, "a cup of tea sounds good. I'd like that." Arthur Erichson took a liking to this young man. He seemed genuine and open, like someone you'd call a friend.

"Marty," Larry called out to the kitchen, "would you put the kettle on for tea?"

"Larry, you don't have time for tea," a woman's voice called back, "you have to get to the funeral home."

Larry went over to the arch separating the living room from the dining room and called out once again, "It's not for me, hon, it's for the police chief."

"Oh." Her response sounded startled.

Erichson heard the clank of the kettle followed by running water and then the dull clunk of the full kettle set upon the stove.

Larry returned to the arm of the sofa, consciously or unconsciously indicating he was in a bit of a hurry.

"I won't keep you long," the Chief said. "As I'm sure you suspect, this is in reference to Eddie Conger."

"I figured that," Larry said as his wife appeared in the archway.

"Good evening, Chief Erichson," she said.

Arthur stood to greet the stocky young woman.

"The tea's on," she continued. "Can I interest you in fresh baked brownies? They're warm out of the oven."

"Well..." Art's mouth began an instant watering and against his better judgment he said, "Yes, that sounds wonderful." Then, remembering the purpose of his trip, he returned his attention to Larry and said, "I understand that you and Eddie Conger were pretty close friends. Is that right?"

"It sure is...uh...was, Chief. We hunted, fished. We tried to get the families together some, but that didn't work out."

"Why was that?" The Chief pulled out his pad and opened it to the next available page.

Larry looked over his shoulder at the empty archway, then back to Art. "Truthfully, the women didn't get along. Marty thought Sarah was a little snooty. Putting on airs. On top of that Marty got real frosted when Sarah started telling her Roman Catholics were hell bound for following the whore of Babylon or something." He made the hushed sound of an explosion and raised his hands in the sign of a mushroom cloud. "And let me tell you, don't ever say anything against the church or the Pope in front of my wife. She's one of those life long Catholics that..."

"Thanks, Larry," the Chief said. "I get the picture. What can you tell me about Eddie?"

Marty came into the living room with a TV tray full of brownies and tea, and a second tray folded and tucked under her arm. Larry rose to take the second tray and set it up in front of the Chief. Marty placed a mug of tea in front of him and held out the plate of brownies. Pleasantries were exchanged around the trays.

"Sorry, but back to business. You were telling me about Eddie," Erichson said.

"Yeah, that's right." Larry sipped his tea. "Eddie was a good guy. Me and him have been friends for a long time. He was kinda like the older brother I never had."

"It sounds like you two were pretty close."

"Yeah." Larry paused a moment and stirred his tea again. "I can't believe he's gone."

"I'm sure," said Art. "Murder rips people from their loved ones." He allowed Larry to think a moment and sipped at his tea. "Please, go on. Anything you can tell me may be helpful."

"Eddie was about the only guy who would sometimes stick up for me. I'd get an awful razzin' about my teeth. People callin' me Bucky and all. Eddie would get them to lay off."

Erichson thought he noticed a glisten in Larry's eyes. He let the situation rest for a moment and glanced about the room. His eyes rested on a framed photo on top of the TV of Larry and Eddie holding a trophy deer between them. Art got up and walked to the TV and picked up the picture.

"An eight pointer" Erichson said. "Nice buck. When did you bag it?

"Last year," Larry said as he got up to join the Chief. "Eddie was real proud because he got it with one of his own reloads. I'll show you."

Larry left the Chief at the TV and went into the dining room. He unlocked the bottom drawer to a small gun cabinet and pulled out a box of rifle cartridges. After closing and locking the drawer, he returned to the Chief and handed them to him.

"You're pretty careful," Erichson said, pointing to the cabinet.

Larry glanced back at the cabinet and then to the Chief, "Like the NRA says, gun safety is no accident. I keep the place pretty child proof."

The Chief opened the box of shells. Of the twenty spaces available, eight were filled with bright and shiny reloaded casings. He pulled one out and examined it. It was identical to those found on Eddie's work bench.

"Eddie called them his deer slayers. He was real proud of them." Larry seemed to smile with a bit of pride himself.

"I can imagine," said the Chief, replacing the cartridge. "Was he in the habit of selling these do you know?"

"Oh no. Eddie didn't sell any of these," Larry said. "They were like his secret formula. Kind of like my wife refusing to share her brownie recipe.

He gave some away, like to me and his father-in-law, but he didn't sell any."

The Chief handed the box of shells back to Larry and asked, "Have you used all twelve of the missing rounds?"

"Oh no," Larry said. He took the box and returned to the cabinet. "I've used two this season. Clean misses, too." He unlocked the cabinet and replaced the box and locked the cabinet again. "I hated to waste the rounds. The other ten I gave to Dan Callahan. He and Eddie weren't getting along, and I knew Callahan hunted, so I made a small gift of them to him and told him they were from Eddie." Larry returned to the living room and finished, "Kinda like a peace offering. It didn't work."

"It didn't work?" the Chief asked, hoping to learn something new.

"Naw," said Larry returning to the sofa and his brownie. He took a bite, and washed it down with some tea then continued, "They still got into a ruckus at The Stallions, and there were some rumors that Callahan torched Eddie's truck, and then there's that business of picketing his house on the night he was killed. I'd say it didn't work." He finished his tea.

Chief Erichson went back to the tray by his chair and picked up his note pad. "Does anything else come to mind you think might be helpful?"

"Well, there's the business of Eddie's boy."

"What's that?"

Larry put his tea and brownie down and scooted to the end of his seat and leaned forward. "Apparently, Eddie's boy William ain't his. He's Callahan's."

"Did Eddie tell you this?" Erichson asked.

"Naw," Larry said, and he relaxed into his sofa. "It's rumor. I guess when Eddie and Callahan were into it on the picket line, some of the guys overheard Eddie tell Callahan to stay away from Sarah. And there was some claim about William being Callahan's kid. It's kinda mixed up. You know how rumors are."

"Yes, I do" the Chief said. "But sometimes they're just the right mix." Erichson wrote quickly in his pad. "Anything else?"

"Not off hand. Not about Eddie."

"About someone else?"

"Talking about Callahan just reminded me that one of his thugs, a guy called Brow, is starting his own campaign for Union president."

"How does this enter into this?" asked Erichson as he scribbled notes.

"It's just that Brow was at The Stallions the night Eddie rearranged Callahan's nose and I hear he was at Eddie's the night he was killed and talking about doing something that would take Callahan out of the running for president. Just more rumor from the picket lines."

"That's all very helpful," Erichson said. He extended his hand again and said, "I'll get out of your way and let you get off to the wake."

John Forest announced the closing of visiting hours and the assembled revelers began to come forward to pay their last respects to Eddie and wish Sarah well.

She stood to greet her friends and congregants and dragged Keegan to stand at her side. To each well-wisher she introduced Keegan as her pastor. The reaction was universally surprised though respectful.

Nearly two dozen people stood on line waiting to say good-bye. Near the end of the line was Daniel Callahan. He wore a dress shirt open at the neck by two buttons. A gold chain hung around his neck. His jacket was leather. He wore silver-tipped cowboy boots.

When Callahan made his way to Sarah, he placed his hands on her shoulders and leaned in close to her ear and whispered. Keegan noticed that as he turned to leave, his right hand casually moved from her shoulder and brushed by her breast in a caressing motion. Keegan also noticed she didn't react.

NOVEMBER 8TH
SATURDAY

Keegan arrived at Forest and Turnbull's by nine-fifteen in the morning. He exchanged customary greetings with the gents dressed in black or gray who stood at the curb and at the front door of the mortuary, who parked and kept track of the order of cars for the funeral procession, who hung coats, offered tissues to the teary eyed, then drank coffee in the back room while the funeral service took place until it was time once again to look grim-faced, usher everyone out, settle the body deeper into the casket, close the lid and head off to the cemetery for the decedent's eternal dirt nap.

As he entered the chapel room, the scene looked frozen in time from the evening before, with a possible change of clothes for some.

Keegan walked to the front of the room and greeted Sarah. She was dressed in a simple navy shift. The pearls made a repeat appearance. Her makeup and scent were light. He stood in front of her as she sat in the front row and bowing to speak quietly in her ear he asked, "How are you holding up?"

She said nothing, but smiled the smile of the bereaved when they are too spent to respond in any other way. She looked to her two children seated on either side of her and squeezed their hands, then she put her arms around them to hug them into herself.

To Sarah's right, one seat beyond her son William, Barbara Ross sat in her supporting role. Keegan moved to shake her hand; and as she rose to greet him she took his hand and pulled him in closer to whisper, "I'm so glad you're taking care of this for her, Keegan. Her father has been impossible."

Embarrassed for Sarah, thinking she may have overheard and maybe even embarrassed for Barbara over her unusual lack of tact, he mouthed a "thanks" and put his index finger to his lips.

Keegan returned to Sarah and squatted at her knees and asked, "Has anything more occurred to you for inclusion in this morning's service since we spoke last night?"

With her arms still about her children, Sarah smiled wanly and said, "No, Pastor...whatever you say I know will be very reassuring."

"Very well," said Keegan, "we'll begin in a few minutes." He got up and walked to the back of the room and through the double doors out into the receiving hall. The young lady who had been playing the guitar the night before as well as this morning was finishing up with, "*Jesus is all the world to me, I want no better friend; I trust him now, I'll trust him when Life's fleeting days shall end.*"

Keegan slipped into John Forest's office where the funeral director had made it a practice to have a cleared desk and a glass of water waiting for clergy to center themselves for the service while the last of the well-wishers arrived for the funeral. Here, Keegan would review the notes he had made the night before, and wait undisturbed until John came to get him.

After a short while a knock came at the door, and John poked his head in to say, "We're ready when you are, Pastor."

There were certain unspoken and unwritten rites that Keegan had come to expect at funerals. Each mortician had his or her own peculiar choreography at the beginning and end of the funeral service. Where John was concerned, he expected the pastor to follow him into the chapel. The pastor would stop at a place from which he or she would address the congregation. John would bring the portable lectern from its waiting place off to the side of the chapel, and put it in front of the pastor, turning on the podium light. Then John would leave the room signaling that the pastor was now in charge. Keegan had always interpreted this gesture to mean, *if you don't like the service, take it up with the pastor.*

The beginning ritual took place with practiced precision. Even the young guitar player recognized the signal to stop singing and to move off to the side.

With the memorization wrought from too many funerals Keegan began the service with the opening United Methodist liturgy. The crowd before him was decidedly unfamiliar with ritual in any form other than the rite of spontaneity, and his cues for liturgical responses went unheeded. Sarah looked up to him with what appeared to be the inculcated look of the enraptured. Some of those gathered wore the screwed up faces or blank stares of the lost and confused. Others prayed silently with closed eyes and uplifted faces and hands. Still others stared into their black flappy Bibles moving their lips to inaudible holy words. A few deigned to gaze upon Keegan with a look that told him they had decided before arriving that this Methodist had no message of hope for them.

Barbara Ross alone had responded to some of the familiar cues, but her lone voice made her self conscious; and after looking around herself at the unfamiliar gathering, she too grew silent and unresponsive. In a brief moment of consternation Keegan thought he would be sure to *thank* her for her support. Then, mentally berating himself for not realizing that the crowd would be ill prepared for Methodist liturgy, he closed his service book and said, "Brothers and sisters, I did not have the privilege of knowing Eddie Conger in this life. From what I heard last night during the visiting hours, I will count that as my loss."

Sarah, still engaged, closed her eyes and with an alluring smile nodded approval.

"It would be a mistake," Keegan continued, "for me to try to eulogize a man I did not know. I would not do him justice and you would know I was a fraud."

A man who had folded his arms and bowed his head as if to snooze looked up, furrowed his brow and squinted like he was examining Keegan.

"The stories of this man's life, the important stories, are your stories," Keegan said. "The stories you shared last night, later today over lunch or dinner, or possibly now, these are the stories that allow Eddie to live on in the here and now with us while God takes care of the hereafter."

Keegan paused long enough to gaze over the congregation and make eye contact with those with whom he seemed to be connecting. Looking at each in turn he said, "I would like to invite those of you who have a remembrance of Eddie to please share that with us now. A loving memory, a funny occurrence, some anecdote that represents Eddie to you."

Keegan had tried this at a number of ol' time Methodist funerals and had been met with the stony silence of very sober ol' time Methodists. He had been told by a few that such informal ways were not appreciated. But the response from the Lighthouse bunch was quite different.

The man who had prayed at the casket the evening before mentioned that he appreciated Eddie's robust voice at the Christmas Eve hymn sings and closed with "May the Lord be forgiving of brother Eddie's backsliding and receive him into the heavenly kingdom anyway."

This was followed by numerous "Amens."

A woman remembered Eddie had changed a flat tire for her in a parking lot. Another woman, surrounded by a flock of dirty looking children, stood and said, "Mr. Conger knew my husban' was on a toot, an' when he gotta deer, he brung it ta my cabin and tolt me it was fer me and mine. He was a good man. God rest his soul." She said her last four words with careful precision as if saying the words properly would somehow make it so.

As each person stood to say their piece, Keegan scanned the congregation to see where others had their hands up to be recognized like school children waiting with the correct answer. As he looked over the faces, his eyes fell on Chief Art Erichson. When their eyes locked, the Chief nodded acknowledgment, then glanced down into his lap. He was making notes. At first Keegan was angry at this intrusion of the secular into the holy, but then decided that the Chief's presence mattered little so long as it did not disrupt the proceedings.

After several more people witnessed to their general good feelings and good wishes for the immortal soul of Eddie Conger, there was a short lull in volunteers. Keegan waited a moment just in case there was a reticent person who needed to suck in a breath of courage before speaking up. Hearing none, Keegan opened the service book searching for that portion of the liturgy that closed the service before making his own closing remarks.

As he lifted his head to speak, he saw the Reverend Weakley striding down the center aisle. Weakley leaned forward as he strode, as if walking on the decks of a ship under way against a mighty wind. His fists were clenched and swinging with each stride. His eyebrows were pinched and his eyes were the narrow slit of a man focusing on his target and ready for combat. He stopped short of Keegan near the front of the room and turned to face the crowd and stretched out his arms.

"I call upon God Almighty," Weakley shouted, "to commit the immortal soul of Edward Conger to eternal damnation in the fiery depths of unholy hell!"

Sarah turned in her seat, obviously startled by her father's voice.

"That's quite enough!" Keegan called out from the lectern.

Weakley shot a quick glance first at Keegan and then at his daughter before continuing to address the gathering, "This man beat and bruised his wife. He abused his children..."

Keegan called back for John Forest to come in.

"...and the death he was dealt was nothing more..." Weakley droned on.

John Forest entered and stopped at the double doors. He glanced about the room, and looked as if he were a man caught in an earthquake and was unsure of the whereabouts of the exits.

"...than the manifestation of the wrath of God upon the unholy," extolled Pastor Weakley.

John Forest called to the gents dressed in black or gray, who drank coffee in the back room, to give him a hand.

Keegan noticed out of the corner of his eye that Chief Erichson was writing feverishly.

Sarah was facing front, bent over in her seat sobbing into her hands. Her children held onto her in a futile attempt to console her. Barbara Ross had moved to kneel in front of Sarah and embrace them all as if to protect them from the storm of hell-fire.

"This devil the Methodists call a pastor has been consorting with my daughter," railed Weakley.

Two gray clad coffee drinkers appeared at the double doors of the chapel.

"With all the wiles of Satan himself," continued Weakley, "this man leads Sarah into the ways of darkness!"

At the direction of mortician Forest, the two men who appeared at the doors came forward to Pastor Weakley and grasped him by the arms. As the distraught pastor of The Good News Apostolic Lighthouse was escorted out, he called back, "You who listen to the words of this deceiver will share Eddie Conger's eternal fate, a fate condemned to the fires of hell at the judgment seat of the Almighty!"

Finally the double doors to the receiving hall closed, and further sounds were muffled into obscurity. The chapel congregation murmured to itself.

Keegan moved to the knot of people that was Sarah, Barbara, and children, and offered Sarah his handkerchief. He stood with one hand on Barbara's shoulder and the other hand on Sarah's, feeling powerless to regain control of the circumstance.

After Sarah quieted some, Keegan bent down and whispered, "I'll draw the service to a close if you're ready."

Without looking up, she nodded approval.

Keegan went back to the podium, and with hands raised said, "Brothers and sisters, we regret that Pastor Weakley felt compelled to vent his anger upon you all. We hope that you will pray for him during this distressing time that God will work in him a healing of his spirit, and that God will work in us a healing of any ill will we might know as a result of the disruption. Let us pause for a moment of silent prayer." The gathering grew quiet. Keegan lowered his arms. A scattering of whispered prayers floated through the room.

"Our brother Eddie was a hunter," Keegan said when he decided the crowd was sufficiently attentive. "He loved the woods God created, and he loved the chase of the hunt." Keegan paused, and the crowd once again focused upon the reason for their gathering.

"Esau, son of Isaac, and brother of Jacob, was also a hunter. He was also the favorite of his father because Esau provided savory meat for the family's meals." Keegan looked to the woman with the dirty brood and said, "Not unlike Esau, Eddie provided a deer for the family that honored his memory a few moments ago." The woman smiled at Keegan and nodded vigorously.

"While I cannot witness to Eddie's saintliness," this remark of Keegan's elicited several chuckles, "I can testify to my belief that God uses us all to work out his purposes in this world; and that all of us, carpenter, homemaker, grocery clerk, ... hunter, have a role to play in the kingdom of God."

Keegan brought the service to a close with prayer which served as a cue to John Forest to perform his final rite. The tall and stately mortician moved to the front of the chapel and put the podium back in its place of silent vigilance as Keegan went to Sarah.

"Would you like to be escorted out first," Keegan asked "or would you prefer to wait until the others exit?"

She looked up at him and with the eyes of a whipped puppy dog pleaded, "Oh, Pastor, please get me out of here."

Forest stood in the center aisle and announced, "The funeral service for Edward Conger is now concluded. Any who wish to pay their final respects to the deceased or the family may come forward and..." John Forest continued with his ritual as Keegan stepped out of the choreography. He took Sarah by the arm and encouraged her to her feet, and signaled to Barbara Ross to follow. He escorted Sarah through the double doors and asked one of the black suits to take Sarah to her car. Barbara followed behind with the children in tow. Keegan then took a spot near the double doors to greet people as they left and to mentally catch his breath.

At John Forest's direction the crowd exited. Respectfully quiet whispers exchanged reactions to Pastor Weakley's performance. An occasional hand shook Keegan's and the owner's voice acknowledged, "Nice service, Pastor."

Chief Erichson passed by and with a wink said, "You're good under pressure, Reverend. We'll talk."

Valley View Cemetery was a pleasant place as far as Keegan was concerned. Its rolling hills, well kept grounds, and tree lined access roads gave the impression of being on a proud estate. The century old oaks with their brown and dead leaves refusing to give in to fall watched over the funeral crowd. The hemlock forest that stood at the back of the cemetery hiding the creek singing below moved majestically in the wind they blocked from the procession.

One by one, as the assembly stepped up to the grave site, John Forest handed them a flower to be placed atop the highly polished casket as a final farewell gesture. Keegan said the familiar words of committal and the pine casket was lowered into the concrete vault that waited below.

Sarah, assisted by John Forest, paused a moment, seemed to offer a silent prayer, and dropped her flower. Looking into the grave, she said in a voice only loud enough for those closest to hear, "Till death us do part, Eddie." Still assisted by John, she walked off towards the waiting car as Keegan watched. At the edge of the dispersing crowd he noticed a man chewing a cigar who seemed almost out of place. Not far from him, Chief Erichson stood making notes.

With nearly everyone in their cars, held in place by the hearse blocking the access road, John Forest called the six burly pallbearers to the roadside near the hearse to prepare for the final ritual of a Forest and Turnbull funeral.

"All right, you gents, line up along the roadside here," John said, waving his hand through the air drawing an imaginary line. Keegan always tried to avoid this part of the event by slipping into the passenger seat of the hearse. "Stand at attention," instructed John Forest, "with your right hand over your heart as the cars drive by. And for heaven's sake, look pious!"

NOVEMBER 9TH
SUNDAY

"Let there be peace on earth, and let it begin with me." The hymn ended and Keegan rose to the pulpit. Looking over the congregation he discovered that Sarah, her children, and Barbara Ross had entered near the back of the church while the congregation sang. The good Reverend Weakley will be after my hide for sure, Keegan thought, when he finds out his daughter and grandchildren are worshipping in the Methodist church.

He had not anticipated the new widow in his congregation when preparing the morning's message about community violence relative to the mill strike. But Keegan had long ago come to the conclusion that God worked towards God's end irrespective of what Keegan thought to be appropriate.

He launched into his sermon and elicited agreement from the congregation that violence, as a general concept, was not a good thing. While his examples were distant, such as Washington or even as close as Schenectady with increasing drug trafficking the congregation nodded concurrence. But when Keegan brought the issue home to roost concerning the violence on the picket line and recent murder and associating those acts with faithlessness, he managed to rile some union sentiments. Keegan knew he had everyone's attention because there were no candy wrappers being unwound. No one cleared a throat or blew a nose. There was only silence. Near the end of his sermon, after calling acts of violence the very embodiment of evil, one of the men who had been sitting with clenched jaw now unfolded his arms that had attempted to cover his ample belly and got up, side stepped over the others warming up the pew, and walked out.

When the worship hour concluded, Keegan stood at the back of the sanctuary to greet the congregants. On her way out, Grace shook Keegan's hand and said with her usual good humor, "You weren't out to make any friends today, were you?"

"Not my job," Keegan said and smiled.

Nearly everyone else left saying little other than "g'mornin'" or "bye now." Not one offered even the most perfunctory "good sermon, Reverend." Score one point for prophetic ministry, he thought. I'd better go home, call the bishop, and tell her to expect some angry calls seeking my replacement.

As people filed out, he noticed Barbara Ross and her charges, Sarah and children, hanging back. They worked themselves into line with only a handful of the ladies-of-the-blue-hair-society behind them.

When Barbara and Sarah made their way to Keegan, Sarah reached out and hugged him. Her scent was still subtle. The embrace was too long, and the full body press seemed to be conveying too much of the wrong kind of emotion. In his peripheral vision Keegan could see old lady Batchelder whisper behind a gloved hand into the ear of Miss Graham who returned the favor.

Sarah broke off her embrace and said, "Thank you so much Pastor, for all you did yesterday. I don't know how we would have gotten through my daddy's outburst without you."

Before he could reply, Sarah left him, with children in tow, and stepped out into the main hall leading to the rest of the facility. Barbara stepped up to Keegan and said, "See me at coffee hour. I'll have one ready for you." Then she too was gone.

Old lady Batchelder gripped Keegan's hand in one of hers, and patted the back of his with her other hand. With the face of sublime inquisition she asked, "And how is your poor sick *wife*, Pastor?"

"Seriously ill," Keegan responded, turning her hand over and proceeding to pat the back of it with his free hand to signal he got the message. "Thank you for asking." She withdrew.

The sanctuary emptied, and after dropping off his robe in the study, he headed for the fellowship hall and coffee.

Barbara met him at the entrance to the hall with a mug of coffee extended, "Here you go, Keeg."

He took a sip then said, "Thanks, the caffeine will do me good."

As he started to step further into the hall, Barbara blocked his path. "Let me speak to you here, away from the others."

"Okay, shoot."

"Keeg, I'm worried about Sarah."

"How so?"

"Her reaction to her husband's murder doesn't feel right," Barbara said. She nodded her head in Sarah's direction and added, "Look at her."

Across the fellowship hall Sarah was close to the table with the coffee and desserts that were spread out. Eight or ten women and a couple of men had gathered around her, serving her coffee and cookies, offering condolences and otherwise attempting to be supportive. Sarah was holding court. Her face was light and smiling. She tossed her hair from one side to the other as she turned to address first one person and the next.

Keegan returned his attention to Barbara and said, "It may only be her religious training. She's been taught that when the faithful die, they go on to their reward, and the deceased is better off – even to be envied. To be remorseful is to be selfish."

Barbara screwed up her face and said, "So I was selfish when I grieved the death of my brother when he was killed by a crack-head driver?"

"From Sarah's perspective, possibly," said Keegan. "I, on the other hand, would say you were simply being genuine. Anger at the crack-head, anger over your brother's untimely death, and sorrow over your own sense of loss were perfectly normal feelings. Certainly we have hope in the afterlife, but we also acknowledge our losses in the here and now. Even Jesus wept at the loss of his dear friend, Lazarus."

"So why doesn't Sarah?" Barbara asked as she shifted her weight from one hip to the other.

"From my perspective," Keegan answered, "it's a matter of religious denial. She's denying her feelings in order to conform to a set of religious prerequisites."

"So this is okay?" Barbara drew her eyebrows up and together in a confused expression.

"I don't know about okay. Let's say it works for some. It may for her. If it doesn't, she'll need you more than ever to help put her life together when all of this sinks in. Frankly, it also makes me wonder what other mental or emotional accommodations have been made, or can be made, in order to preserve her religious precepts."

Arthur Erichson knocked on the front door sash. He decided that late afternoon was a respectful enough time to go calling on the Reverend Weakley. He stood on the front porch of the small parsonage next to the Lighthouse church. The door rested slightly ajar. The porch floor boards were denuded of paint and those closest to the end had the damp feathered edges of rot. One near the front door bore a stress crack, and the Chief was careful not to step on it. He made a mental note to avoid it on his way out of the house.

Weakley opened the front door of the house and left the storm door closed. He made no motion to open it. The two men stood looking at one another.

The Chief broke the silence. "Your door was opened. You should keep it locked."

"No need," said Pastor Weakley, "I fear no evil. The Lord's rod and staff comfort me."

Oh brother, the Chief thought. He said, "May I come in?"

"No."

"Why not?" Erichson asked with a cocked eyebrow.

"It's the Lord's day. We are called to keep it holy. Have you no respect for that?"

"Yes, I do, Pastor," Erichson said, raising his voice to be heard through the storm door, "But I also expect the Lord would want us to catch the man who broke his commandment not to kill. It could be said I am about holy business." Maybe all those years in Sunday School at the First Church of Albany had paid off after all, he thought.

Weakley stood silent for a moment longer.

"Pastor. Please," Erichson prodded.

Weakley pushed open the storm door and stood aside as the Chief entered the house. Weakley pointed to the chair next to a desk by the front window and Erichson sat down.

"Thank you, Pastor," the Chief said. "This won't take long."

Weakley remained silent as he sat facing the Chief with legs crossed and arms folded.

The Chief pulled out his note pad from the corduroy jacket, clicked his pen, and said, "You seemed pretty distraught yesterday at the funeral, Pastor. Is there something you think I ought to know?"

Weakley stared at Erichson and said in peevish strained measured tones, "If I knew anything I thought you needed, I would have called you."

"You want to tell me why you decided to interrupt Reverend O'Connor's service yesterday?"

Weakley clenched his jaw, relaxed it and said, "I have nothing to say about that sheep stealing mealy mouthed meddling Methodist."

The Chief decided that pursuing that line would only antagonize Weakley and he'd get nowhere. He made a mental note to press that hot button at a later date. Changing topics he said, "I understand that you and your son-in-law used to go hunting from time to time."

140

"Yes."

"Did you go often?"

"Often enough."

"How often was that?"

"Not very."

Erichson closed his eyes and subtly shook his head from side to side. "Come on, Pastor, can we be a little more cooperative here? Enough of the one syllable answers."

"What would you have me say?" Weakley unfolded his arms and put them on the arms of the chair.

"Just fill in around the edges of your answers, okay?" The Chief waited a moment, and Weakley nodded something that looked like agreement. "Fine, now how often did you and your son-in-law go hunting?"

"Usually a half dozen times during the deer season," Weakley answered. "Maybe birding once or twice in the fall, but he didn't much like that. It took too much skill."

"You don't sound as if you liked your son-in-law very much," said Erichson. He crossed his legs and tried to look as relaxed as he could, hoping to encourage Weakley to do the same.

"He was a sinner," Pastor Weakley said, "I tried to spend time with him in order to bring him to the Lord."

Erichson wrote as he considered his next question. "Yesterday you condemned Eddie for abusing your daughter. How long had that been going on?"

"I don't know," Weakley said. He clasped his hands in his lap and for the first time looked away from Erichson. "I only became aware of it recently."

"How so?"

"My daughter told me," Weakley said, and returning his gaze to the Chief added, "and she showed me her bruises."

"That must have infuriated you." Erichson watched Weakley carefully.

"It did." Weakley stared at Erichson expressionless.

"What did you do?"

"Prayed."

"And ...?"

"I confronted him one morning when we were hunting."

"You confront a man about abusing his wife while he's got a deer rifle in his hands?" Erichson's voice rose and betrayed his incredulity.

"I had nothing to fear," Pastor Weakley said, "the Lord was with me. The Lord is always with me."

"How did Eddie respond?"

"He denied everything. Said he and Sarah had fought and that it got out of hand, but that he did not beat her." Weakley got out of his chair and stepped to the front window and looked out towards the street. His arms hung at his sides and his fists were balled up. "I *saw* her bruises."

Not wanting to give Weakley a moment to catch up with himself, Erichson pressed him. "Then what happened?"

"Very little." Weakley looked over this shoulder at the Chief. His jaw was still set with anger, but his voice was controlled. He said, "The situation was tense enough that I left the woods and came home."

Erichson jotted notes, and Weakley returned to his chair. In the time it took Weakley to cross the room, the angry set to his jaw had been replaced by a face that looked drawn and gray. Erichson noticed for the first time that Weakley's eyes were deep set and wore dark circles. The Chief hoped the good Pastor might let something slip if pressed further while so obviously fatigued.

"Your son-in-law reloaded his own ammunition for hunting," Erichson said. "Do you know anything about that?"

The question restored Weakley to alertness. He sat straightened in his chair and said "I knew he reloaded, yes. But I don't pretend to know anything about it. What little I do know about guns and hunting I learned from Eddie as I was trying to get closer to him to win him for the Lord."

"Did Eddie ever give you any of his reloads?" the Chief asked.

"Yes. A box not long ago, as a matter of fact." Weakley opened a desk drawer and pulled out a cartridge box and placed it on the corner of the desk nearest to Erichson. "Why is it, Chief," Weakley said staring at Erichson, "that I suspect you already knew that?"

"Maybe so," the Chief said, and reached for the box of shells. He opened the box end, slid out the tray of rounds and saw six empty spaces. "There are only fourteen rounds here, Pastor. Where are the others?"

"In my jacket pocket," Weakley said as he rose from his chair and crossed to a closet near the front door. He pulled out a coat in hunter orange and rummaged through the right hand side pocket. He pulled out his hand, walked back to the desk and spilled out four more cartridges.

Erichson picked them up and put them into the empty slots in the box, leaving two empty places. He looked back up at Weakley who stood by watching.

"I shot at a running buck in the woods the day I confronted Eddie," Weakley said.

"Did you get it?"

"No. I missed. My mind wasn't on the hunt."

"Hmm," the Chief intoned and made a note. He stood and said, "I'd like to see your rifle, Pastor."

Weakley draped the hunter orange coat over the desk chair, returned to the entrance closet and pulled out a Remington rifle and handed it to the Chief who had followed him.

Erichson brought the piece up to his nose and sniffed the receiver end. He then removed the bolt, held the rifle to the light from the front door and peered down the barrel. Replacing the bolt, he returned the rifle to Weakley. "You keep it very clean, don't you?"

"Eddie taught me to clean it after each use," Weakley said as he took the rifle and returned it to the closet. "He even insisted I run an oil soaked patch through it if all I had done was to carry it out in the dampness. Never put a rifle away dirty, he always used to say."

"One final question Pastor," Erichson said. "It's the question we ask all people involved with a murder. Where were you when Eddie was killed?"

"It had been my intention to speak with Eddie about eight that night." Weakley jammed his hands into his pants pockets. "But I was detained by Clarence Berkley. I found him drunk on the front steps of the church again. I brought him to the parsonage, into the study where we were until about nine o'clock. When he began to come around, I took him to the Stewart's Shop to pump him full of coffee. Then I took him home to his sister."

Erichson held out his hand to Weakley and said, "I appreciate your cooperation, Pastor. I'll leave you now to the rest of your day."

Weakley took the Chief's hand and shook it saying, "May God bless your efforts."

The football teams met in silent holocaust on the twenty-eight yard line. With the play over, Gillette razors flashed across the screen of the muted idiot box, and Keegan returned his gaze to the book in his lap. Eileen was reading the latest Carla Neggers effort in the chair next to Keegan.

"Heads up, guy!" Eileen said. "The Dallas Cowgirls are doing their T and A routine."

Keegan looked up at the screen over the top of his reading glasses and said, "Uh-huh. Very nice. Verrry nice."

"Don't get too excited pal," Eileen said. "That's the closest you're going to get to a set of boobs for a long time."

Keegan looked over at his wife. Her lips smiled at him, but her eyes glistened with wetness. He held out his hand for hers and said, "I have everything I need sitting in the chair next to me."

"Good answer," she said, squeezing his hand and beating back tears. She retrieved her hand and turned back to her novel.

Keegan killed the TV with the remote, kicked up the footrest on his La-Z-Boy, turned his Stephen King novel face down on his belly and reclined back in the chair with laced fingers behind his head.

He had his eyes closed for only a moment when he heard Eileen say, "You've been awfully quiet since you got home from church. Anything going on?"

"Sarah Conger showed up at worship with Barbara Ross," he said from behind closed eyes. "I expect I'll be hearing from the petulant Pastor Weakley."

"How does Sarah seem to be holding up?"

"Actually, that's kind of interesting," Keegan said as he brought his chair back to an upright position. "She's a bit of a study on denial. So much so that Barbara thought that there might be something wrong."

"There probably is," Eileen said, turning on her psychologist voice. "If it persists, denial can be very injurious."

"Yes Doctor," Keegan gibed, "but for now I think it's simply a harmless coping mechanism fostered by her brand of religion. And if it helps her cope with the murder of her husband, then more power to her."

Eileen folded her book and turned in her chair to face Keegan. "How about her children? What's happening there?"

"She and the kids are staying with Barbara. I expect they're as good as can be expected. They all face the long haul of putting their lives back together. I suspect that Sarah will be looking for work soon. Eddie was the lone bread winner."

Eileen had that off-in-the-distance look she got when she was processing some tidbit of information that Keegan had unwittingly dropped into the conversation and had mistaken as a mere nothing. She straightened around in her chair and opened her book but did not read. She removed her reading glasses and sucked on an ear stem as she gazed out the front window onto the street. Keegan knew better than to recline. There would soon follow a question or series of questions for him to answer. He turned over the thriller and began to read while he waited.

"What did Barbara tell you?" Eileen asked, "What did you see at church that makes you describe her behavior as denial?"

Keegan rested his book in his lap and described for Eileen the hug at worship, the disapproval of the blue-haired-society – about which Eileen acknowledged feigned thankfulness for their watchful eyes – the gaiety and gesticulated conversation Sarah held in the fellowship hall, her easy laughter, and the preponderance of god-talk.

"My only real concern," Keegan finished, "is if the framework of the denial begins to break down. If Barbara continues to bring her to our church and she's exposed to a different set of theological precepts, the realities of life and death as we see them could be devastating."

The distant look reappeared. Eileen again chewed on the ear-stem of her glasses and Keegan returned to his novel while awaiting the next question or observation.

"She doesn't have much family in the area, does she?" asked Eileen.

"Other than her father, none I'm aware of," Keegan said without looking up.

"Hmm," intoned Eileen. "I have a suggestion, tell me what you think." Eileen raised herself up and leaned over the arm of her chair closer to Keegan as if to share a confidence. "MaryKay will be leaving town tomorrow. And while I can still fend for myself, it can get pretty lonely around here by myself. And another episode of Oprah will send me screaming down the street pulling out what little hair the chemo hasn't already shed for me."

"Actually," said Keegan through a smirk he was not attempting to hide well, "I'd pay to see that!"

"Shut up." She didn't smile. Keegan listened. "I think I can still be pretty good company. And Sarah could maybe use another friend. But more importantly, maybe she needs to feel useful and occupied. I, on the other hand, could listen for some of those signs of denial, and maybe help her engage reality in a less traumatic way. She would be my one, sole, client and," Eileen extended her arms as if prepared to take a bow on stage, "Sarah would be the beneficiary of all my expertise."

"Hmm." He returned to his book to annoy Eileen.

Out of the corner of his eye, he could see her hanging over the chair arm waiting for a response.

"Well?" she insisted.

Keegan rested the book again, looked at Eileen and said, "Weren't you the one warning me about holy wars?"

"I know," Eileen answered. "But it could be good for her." She sat back into her chair, and as she twisted she winced in pain and cried out.

"What's happening?" asked Keegan, dropping the footrest on his recliner and moving to the edge of his seat.

"Pain," Eileen said, "post surgical maybe. Maybe something else."

"Do you want me to get you something for it?" Keegan asked.

Relaxing in her seat, Eileen said, "No, not until we speak to the doctor. I don't know what I can mix with the chemo."

She settled into her chair and rested a moment. Seeing her relax, Keegan sat back into his chair and opened the novel once again. He started to read the same paragraph for the fifth or sixth time when Eileen broke the silence.

"It would be good for me to have a little company and to put my mind to work. To focus on someone else."

"I don't know," said Keegan. "I have some misgivings about this." He stared at the paragraph but did not see.

"Will you at least ask her if she's interested in being a paid companion for a while?"

"*If* I speak to her again, and *if* it seems appropriate to the conversation, I'll explore the possibilities."

NOVEMBER 10TH
MONDAY

Keegan had been up and reading for a couple of hours when he heard Eileen stirring in the bedroom overhead. With that cue, he prepared her a bacon and eggs breakfast with English muffins, jam, coffee, and juice.

He knew she wouldn't eat all of it, but he also knew they had to fight the tendency towards extreme weight loss as a result of the chemotherapy. With a beginning weight of one hundred twenty-five pounds on her five and one half foot frame, Eileen didn't have much room to move before she entered a dangerously low body weight. Only half way through her treatments and she was already down by twenty pounds.

Before putting on the eggs, he ran upstairs to see if she was ready to come to the dining room. Entering their bedroom he saw her pulling on a turtleneck sweater. As her head popped through the top, her face bore the same wince of pain he had seen the night before. "Is it worse?"

"No," she said with a sigh, "but it is persistent." She sat on the edge of the bed and already looked exhausted.

Keegan sat next to her and gave her a hug. "Do you feel up to coming downstairs, or shall I bring you breakfast in bed?"

"Breakfast? Yuch!"

"Downstairs it is." Keegan stood, took Eileen by the hands and brought her to her feet and led the way into the dining room and seated her. "Culinary delights momentarily," he said and headed for the kitchen.

"Keeg," Eileen called after him, "I really don't think I want any..."

"Your choice," he said, popping his head back into the dining room, "eat graciously or have me sit on your chest and force feed you."

"Okay, okay. I'd forgotten you were so mean in the morning. I like you better in your study at this hour."

Eileen picked up the newspaper from the table as Keegan brought her coffee. As she opened the paper her face flinched in pain one more time.

Keegan returned to the kitchen and came back to Eileen with the phone. "Call Eli's exchange," he said, "leave a message for him to call. You're going in today to see about that pain."

With Eileen settled for the morning and an appointment with Eli Shapiro scheduled for late afternoon, Keegan decided to look in on the Conger family.

As he turned onto Benedict Street, Keegan pulled up at the Ross residence, where he had last visited Sarah, without thinking. Realizing what he had done, he started to back out then thought better of it – Barbara could possibly be able to clue him in on what's happening before he saw Sarah. He parked the car and went to the door.

Barbara greeted Keegan on the porch with genuine pleasure. The family dog barked a greeting as Barb led Keegan into the living room where her two boys were playing with Sarah's boy and girl. She said to the children, "You four go play upstairs for a while please; the Reverend O'Connor and I would like to speak privately."

The children headed up the stairs to one of the bedrooms. Taking several steps at a time, the dog shouldered past the children and greeted them on the second floor landing.

Barbara sat on the edge of her sofa and Keegan sat across from her on a matching love seat.

"I'm glad you dropped by," she said.

"I gathered that by your dismissing the kids," Keegan said, sitting back and crossing his legs.

"You're here about Sarah, right?"

"Well, I did think you might be able to tell me how she's doing before I stop in on her."

"Oh, Keegan," Barbara sounded almost frantic as she rolled her eyes, "she's a wreck. Yesterday after dinner, the children went outside to play before it got dark, and my husband Wayne went into the office. Sarah and I were alone. We sat here in the living room quietly reading when suddenly she started sobbing. She couldn't stop. She started blaming herself for Eddie's death. She said she had killed him with her demands for money and a better house. She's convinced that one of the union toughs killed him for crossing the picket line. She said Eddie only crossed the line to satisfy her. My God, Keegan, she wailed so loud I thought for sure the neighbors would hear her. I was so scared for her I almost called the rescue squad to take her to the hospital to calm her down."

"Good grief, Barbara," Keegan said, "you had one hell of an afternoon."

"All I could think to do was to hold her and rock her," Barbara said, "right there on the love seat. She held onto me and cried her eyes out. Finally, after nearly an hour, she let up and fell asleep on my shoulder as we sat there. I didn't move from her side for another hour."

Keegan shook his head and said, "I'm sorry you had to go through that. But, I'm sure you've been a real blessing to your friend."

"Well, thanks for the vote of confidence," Barbara said. "The truth of the matter is, it's wearing me out. I really want to get back to my own routine." She sat further back into her own seat away from the edge. She sighed, then added, "In time, I suppose." Then, suddenly energized, she said, "Speaking of blessings," and she folded her arms as if disgusted, "that minister father of hers ought to be taken out and shot before he can be of any further *blessing* to his daughter!"

"Oh?" Keegan perked up at that.

"Sarah tried calling him at least a half dozen times yesterday," Barbara said, "and that self-righteous son-of-a…"

"Barbara!" Keegan chided. Red actually rose up Barbara's neck and flushed her cheeks a bit.

"Sorry," she said, "it's just that he made me so angry."

"I understand, I'm only trying to yank your chain. I shouldn't have interrupted. Go on."

"The man hung up on his daughter every time." Barbara unfolded her arms and pounded the arm of the sofa and let loose with an angry "Huhh!" She added, "Only once did he actually speak to her; on the second or third call. He told her to seek advice from the false Methodist prophet. Imagine that! The man won't even see his own daughter after she's lost her husband!" Barbara refolded her arms and gripped herself tighter, widened her eyes, grit her teeth and let out another "Huhh!"

"Let's not start any holy wars, Barbara," Keegan said. "Is Sarah upstairs? Maybe I should see her."

"No," Barbara said and relaxed some. Her face softened. "She insisted on going back to her house to see what kind of a mess was left behind."

"You let her go alone?"

"She insisted. She was much better this morning, and I know that Chief Erichson and the constables cleaned up the cellar for her. After a few threats and some bribes, I managed to get Wayne and a couple of men from church to paint the cellar walls and floor on Saturday while

Sarah and the children were busy with the funeral and reception." A look of satisfaction came over her face and she added, "It's amazing how much cooperation you can get from men when their wives threaten a little domestic strike of their own."

"You've done well by your friend, Barbara. Someday, if not already, she'll appreciate it."

Barbara blushed again, which surprised Keegan. He'd not seen that side of Barbara before.

"She needs a pastor, Keegan. She needs you."

Sarah answered Keegan's knock with tears in her eyes, but they weren't bloodshot, and her breath was not hitching. She smiled wanly, brought Keegan into the living room, and they sat across from one another.

She popped up as if startled and said, "Oh, would you like something to drink? Or maybe something to eat. Lordy, there's enough food left over from the funeral to feed a family for a month."

"No, nothing," said Keegan, "please, relax. I only dropped by to see how you and the children were doing."

"I think we're all right." She said. Keegan noticed she seemed more comfortable looking at his face and didn't avert her eyes to the floor as she used to. "Barbara said she would take care of the children for a couple of days to let me settle all of the legal things and let life calm down. She's been so wonderful. I didn't realize what a good friend she was."

Keegan nodded agreement.

"Most everything here at the house is in pretty good order," Sarah observed. She stood and moved towards the kitchen, waved at the cellar door and said, "Someone even painted the cellar for me and replaced all the broken glass." Turning to face Keegan she ended with, "I don't even know who to thank." She no sooner finished speaking when the first tears rolled down her cheek. Her face began to contort in bereaved anguish; she covered her face with her hands and started to sob.

Keegan rose to cross the room and place a fresh handkerchief in Sarah's hands and led her back to her seat. They sat together for some time as she let the tears of grief, anger, estrangement and uncertainty flow. Keegan knew there wasn't a thing he could do or say to stem the tide. He let the tears roll. He hated tears.

Through hitching breath and snuffling Sarah managed to say, "I'm sorry for this display."

"It's all a part of it," Keegan assured her.

"I feel so confused." She sat up and tried to dry her eyes and cheeks, but the tears kept coming. "I don't really know what to do next. I thought I might see my next step here. Maybe figure things out. But I only feel more lost."

"It's a little soon after the storm," said Keegan, "to find your bearings and get under way. Maybe what you need is a little time in port to rest and plot your course."

Sarah scowled and shook her head gently. "We've always considered that kind of thing in other religions to show a lack of faith in God. We've always been taught that we should rejoice at another's death and their victory, and to go on with our lives as if nothing happened. Like the hymn, *we shall go rejoicing.*"

Keegan took a deep breath, more to control a twinge of anger at the expressed attitude than for air, and said, "We consider a mourning time as nothing more than acknowledging our own sense of loss; that new emptiness we experience at the death of a loved one. It could even be considered a way of honoring the dead."

Sarah responded almost defensively, "But Jesus said 'Let the dead bury the dead'."

"So he did," said Keegan "but he also took time out to weep over the death of his close friend Lazarus." Keegan softened his voice and continued, "I think if Jesus took time out to grieve, that it's okay for us to do the same."

Sarah sat in silence.

After a bit Keegan asked "Do you have family or friends you can stay with for a week or so?"

"Barbara has been very good to me, and has taken the kids off my hands for a while, but I don't want to impose any more than I have to."

Keegan could hear Eileen's proposition echoing through his mind. He tried to suppress it. He wasn't altogether sure he wanted to get so involved in Sarah's life when his own was getting complicated enough. Fully involved with his own internal debate he was vaguely aware of Sarah prattling on about getting the kids back in school, wondering if Eddie's company pension and Social Security benefits would be enough to get by on, or if she'd have to look for work soon. Finally, Eileen won the mental argument.

"Let me make an offer," started Keegan, "and I want you to feel free to turn it down." PLEASE turn it down, he thought.

Sarah looked directly at him with the anticipation of a faithful retriever waiting to chase the Frisbee. He was aware of two conflicting emotions. He wanted to embrace Sarah and protect her from the torments of life. He also wanted to run screaming down the street as if the Devil himself were in pursuit.

"As you may already know, my wife Eileen has had cancer surgery and is currently undergoing chemotherapy. Some days she is quite ill. Most days she feels very weak. A close friend of hers, who has been good enough to spend most mornings with her for company, has to be away for a few weeks. If you would be willing…"

"Yes, of course I will," Sarah said, almost shouting.

Keegan was startled by her enthusiasm and protested, "But I've not yet asked…"

"You want me to stay with your wife mornings," Sarah said, cutting him off again. "Yes, I'd like that. You've been so helpful, it would be a wonderful way for me to repay your kindness."

"I don't want you to feel obligated," Keegan said. "Really, I don't." He had a sinking feeling and cursed himself for not being more insistent in his mental argument with Eileen. "By the same token it would give you a place away from your home, a little peace while Barbara cares for your children, and Eileen is good company. She listens well, if you care to talk with her about some of what you're feeling." Thinking he could turn the offer into more of a business relation Keegan added, "We know you're concerned about finances, and while we can't pay much we'd certainly compensate you for…"

"Pay? I wouldn't!" Sarah said. "I couldn't! Let this be my gift to you."

"It only seems right that we…"

"It's a perfect idea," exclaimed Sarah in her schoolgirl way. "It will feel like heaven." She leaned into Keegan and gave him a quick embrace. "When should I come? Now?"

"No, not now." Keegan felt dizzy. "I'll ask Eileen to call you this evening after supper to arrange a first meeting. Will you be at Barbara's?"

"You won't call?"

"I think it would be better if you made your arrangements with Eileen, start to get to know her over the phone. I'll have her call."

"Okay," Sarah said. "I'll be at the Ross' tonight."

"Very good," said Keegan as he stood. "It sounds like a date in the making." As soon as he said the word *date* he regretted it. He moved towards the door and added what he hoped would be a course correction. "I'm sure you two will learn to like each other very much."

"I'm sure we will," Sarah said and opened the door for Keegan. "Thanks so much for stopping by." Then in the open doorway Sarah put both arms around Keegan's neck and gave him the same long hug he had grown to expect.

Eileen understood Eli had practiced medicine in the Fort George area his entire career, and while not a native, he had been accepted by the locals because of his immediate adoption of their easy ways and because of his genuine care and concern. The man even made house calls! In the examining room Eli finished taking blood from Eileen, placed a gauze pad inside her elbow and folded her arm.

"I should have the results of your blood tests by Wednesday, Eileen," he said.

"How does the rest of me check out, Doctor?"

"You're losing too much weight." He sat on the end of his desk facing Eileen, who remained sitting on the examining table. He folded his arms, then moved his right hand to frame his chin. "Before you leave I'll give you a list of high caloric food supplements that may help. Other than that, you're healing nicely from the surgery. The report from the oncologist is unremarkable."

"What about the pain I described to you?" Eileen asked.

From where he sat Eli spread his arms out wide and said, "Do this."

Eileen spread her arms as wide as she could, dropping the gauze pad from the inside of her elbow. She stopped when the muscle pain in her chest caused too much pain. "This is as far as I go."

"Okay. Put your arms down," Eli said. He moved to the table next to Eileen and put a band-aid on her arm. "The fact that you've moved your arms that far is remarkable. I don't think you have anything to worry about where your post surgical healing is concerned."

"But that's not the pain that worries me," said Eileen. Holding her hand over an area near the top of her stomach and slightly to the right she said, "It's the stitch in my side that concerns me."

Eli issued the response that irritates most patients and intoned, "Hmmm." He moved towards Eileen and said, "Lie back down on the table." He began to probe Eileen's side where she had indicated discomfort and said, "Tell me if I hurt you."

On his second prod Eileen called "OW."

"Hmm."

"Hmm, what?" insisted Eileen.

"Hmm, we won't know until I get the results of your blood test. Your liver is taking a beating with the chemo and it may be telling you about it." He returned to his desk, sat on the corner, and jotted a note in her chart. "You can sit up."

Eileen sat up and swung her legs back over the side of the table. "That's it?"

"For now, yes. Other than that, go home and take care of yourself, and EAT."

"Yes, Doctor," Eileen said with a sarcastic lilt. She rolled her sleeves down and buttoned the cuffs. "Is there anything I can take for the pain, if it gets bothersome?"

"You can take an aspirin now and again," Eli said as he made an additional note in Eileen's file, "but not more often that necessary. Put up with a little pain. It won't hurt you."

"Very funny, Eli," Eileen said. "So, I can take an aspirin or a little Tylenol when I—"

"GOOD GOD, NO, Eileen." Eli's response was so vehement that Eileen's heart jumped. "Didn't your oncologist tell you about that?"

"What? I guess not."

"A little aspirin, okay," Eli said. "But acetaminophen is absolutely out!"

Eileen was feeling a little bewildered at Eli's reaction to what she thought was a pretty normal question. "What's the problem with acetaminophen?"

"Wait a minute," Eli said as he crossed the examining room and called out, "Keegan, come in here please." Eli waited at the door until Keegan entered the room and then closed the door. Keegan stood by Eileen and carried deep furrows in his brow that told Eileen he was worried.

Eli returned to the corner of his desk. With folded arms, he said, "I want you both to hear this little lesson in medicine, so listen up. Under no circumstances should Eileen use acetaminophen, or any other pain reliever containing acetaminophen while she's on chemotherapy. A little aspirin when necessary is okay. But acetaminophen is out. Understand?"

Eileen nodded. Keegan looked from her to Eli and said, "You make this sound pretty serious."

"You're damn right I do," Eli said. "That particular pain killer could put Eileen out of her pain permanently. Acetaminophen is toxic to chemo patients!"

"You're kidding! How? Why?" asked Keegan.

"Acetaminophen relies upon an enzyme produced by your liver to break it down into its component parts that then serve to block pain," Eli said. "Chemotherapy wreaks havoc on the patient's liver – nearly killing it. What's left of the liver isn't enough to produce the appropriate enzyme to break down the drug. And when it's not broken down, acetaminophen is toxic. For the chemo patient, acetaminophen in high enough or persistent doses, is lethal."

NOVEMBER 11TH
TUESDAY

The Ross household had just settled down from the first flurry of wake-up-and-get-started activity. William and Becky had been the first to move through the morning bathroom routine before the Ross boys were up. Barbara had the four children at the table eating breakfast when Wayne came downstairs fully dressed but half asleep.

"You're wearing one gray sock and one black sock, honey," she said to Wayne.

He sat down with the children, sipped at the coffee Barbara had poured and then looked down at his feet under the table. "Close enough" he said, and poured a bowl full of raisin bran. "I have a matching pair upstairs."

The phone rang. Barbara answered it. Wayne doused his cereal with skim milk and Becky pushed away from the table to run upstairs. Wayne sipped at his coffee again, the eldest Ross boy downed an eight ounce glass of OJ and reported with a mighty belch. He looked proud and William giggled. Wayne unfurled the newspaper to the sports section, no doubt to check upon the Dallas Cowboys, and spooned in some raisin bran – the breakfast of regular guys, he would quip. Barbara hung up the phone.

"Who was that at this hour of the morning?" Wayne managed around a mouthful of cereal.

"Sarah," Barbara said. "She wants me to come over this morning to help her sort clothes."

"Hmm." He turned a page.

"She must be getting ready to give Eddie's clothes away." She poured herself a cup of coffee and sat at the table next to Wayne. "That's probably a good sign, don't you think?"

155

"Hm? Yeah, sure." He sipped.

"Anyway, I told her I'd come over after I got my five kids off."

"That's nice, hon." He turned the page again. "You know, the company stock went up an eighth yesterday."

Sarah greeted Barbara at the back door.

"I got here as soon as I got everyone on their way," Barbara said.

"Follow me," Sarah said. "I'm so glad you could come." She headed through the kitchen and up the staircase to the bedrooms.

"You sounded like you were fired up to sort through Eddie's things – like you were ready now and the next minute would be too late."

"Oh, it's not Eddie's things I want to go through," Sarah said moving down the hall and into her room. "I took all of his things to the church thrift ship yesterday."

As the two women stood in the bedroom, Barbara could see that half of the double closet was completely barren.

"Well," Barbara shrugged, "what did you need me for?"

"To sort *my* clothes, silly." Sarah moved to the closet and hugged a gathering of clothes hangers and apparel and withdrew them from the closet and plopped them on the bed. "I need you to tell me what Methodists wear."

"Excuse me?"

"I want to look like a Methodist."

Barbara sat on the edge of the bed and held the sides of her head. "Hold on, Sarah. What's this all about? What do you mean you want to look like a Methodist?"

"I'm going to be helping Pastor Keegan," Sarah said and sat beside Barbara, "and his poor sick wife. And I want to look just right. If I'm going to be a fixture in the Methodist parsonage I need to look the part. And these," she flipped up the sleeve of a knit dress, "simply won't do."

"What's this about helping Eileen?"

"Pastor asked if I would be her helper, a companion, for a few days. While he goes about his ministry. He's truly a dedicated man, isn't he?"

"Isn't he." Barbara raised an eyebrow.

"Anyway," Sarah stood to face her closet, "that's why I asked you to help. Today's my first day, and I want to be sure I please Kee..., uh, Pastor and Eileen." She turned to Barbara. "So, what do I keep and what do I throw out?"

"I'm still a little lost," said Barbara shaking her head. "I don't think I understand what you want. I'm not sure what a Methodist *looks* like."

"When I've been in your church," Sarah said and sat beside Barbara again, "everyone looks so, so expensive. Sophisticated. The people in my church all look like a bunch of hicks. All that flannel and denim."

"Ah, well, you weren't looking close enough." Barbara leaned back on her elbows. "There's plenty of flannel and denim. Sure there's plenty of people who dress well, but that's not a function of being Methodist. It's what people feel comfortable in. Come to think about it, it's more a function of age. Older people seem to dress more for church. Younger people dress for the weekend."

"Maybe so," Sarah said and stood again as if to brush aside everything Barbara had said, "but I'm due for a change. A step up."

Eileen had returned to her recliner and Keegan had finished the lunch dishes when the doorbell rang. He dried his hands as he crossed the dining room and the entrance way then slung the towel over his shoulder and opened the front door.

"Hi, Pastor Keegan," Sarah said with a cheerful voice. She was dressed in black slacks and a bright blue three-season nylon jacket. She wore a fleece hair band over her ears.

"Hello, Sarah, its good of you to come." Keegan stepped aside and waved Sarah in.

"Oh, I'm happy to help." Sarah stepped through the door and glanced about as she removed the hair band and stuffed it in her jacket pocket. "This is an elegant house, Pastor."

"That's nice of you to say. Here, let me take your things." Sarah removed her jacket and handed it to Keegan as he spoke. "Eileen's really done quite a bit with it. It had been neglected by both the church and the previous parsonage family, so she's refinished some of the woodwork and papered nearly every room in the house. She's made it feel like a home. Come on in."

Keegan led the way from the entrance way down the short hall to the dining room and adjoining living room where Eileen was seated. Bringing Sarah closer to Eileen, Keegan made introductions.

"I'm really delighted you agreed to our offer," Eileen said, extending her hand. "It will be a great comfort to me, and will relieve Keegan of some of the worry over me while he tries to tend the parish."

"I'm glad to help," Sarah said accepting Eileen's hand. "Like I told Pastor, it's nice to be able to repay him for some of the help he's given me."

"Keeg," Eileen said, "show Sarah around the house so she'll feel more comfortable about her surroundings."

"This way," Keegan said, pointing the way towards the kitchen, "We'll begin in the place where Eileen concocts most of her sins."

The tour concluded as Keegan closed the door to the bedroom he used as a home study.

"That does it," Keegan said. He led the way down the upstairs hall towards the front stairs and back down into the entrance way. Sarah followed along, sometimes fingering a wall hanging or running her hand along the textured wallpaper. "You've seen the whole place from stem to stern. Any questions?"

"Oh, no," she said. "I'm sure I'll be very happy here."

They returned to the living room where Eileen was reading. She looked up as they entered and said, "How was the tour?"

"I believe we're ship shape," Keegan said. "I'll head for church and let you two ladies get to know each other a little better."

"Women, Keegan," Eileen said.

"Huh?"

Sarah sat on the hassock near Eileen.

"Women," Eileen repeated. "We don't want to be referred to as ladies any longer, we're women."

"Please. Spare me, Eileen." Keegan felt some irritation over Eileen's timing of her feminism. He went to the hall closet and got his hat and coat.

"I think it's important to be a lady," he heard Sarah say. "Particularly as a pastor's wife, you must find yourself setting many examples for the ladies of the church."

"Thank you for that enlightened perspective, Sarah," Keegan said upon reentering the living room. "On that high note, I shall entrust you to one another's care."

NOVEMBER 12TH
WEDNESDAY

Eileen sat across the table from Keegan. Her size eight clothes hung on her like sacks. She wore a bright blue silk scarf tied over her head to hide the loss of hair. She was never without a scarf. Her face was drawn and immutable dark circles had formed around her eyes.

"You've hardly touched your breakfast." Keegan coaxed.

"You can't cook," Eileen cracked with a smile.

Thank God for her smile and wise-ass remarks, Keegan thought. He couldn't think of a come back. "Would you like me to fix something else? A milkshake?"

"I'd only lose it before I got it all down," she said.

"Eileen, please, you've got to try to keep your strength." When he allowed himself to think about it he worried he might be losing her.

"Keegan," she snapped and waved him off. "Not now. Maybe later. Maybe I'll manage one of Sarah's milkshakes. It stayed down yesterday."

"All right, hon," Keegan said. He was afraid he was wearing his worried face but couldn't help it: Eileen didn't seem to notice or care. He sipped at his coffee and decided to change the topic. "You were fast asleep when I got back from taking Sarah home last evening. How did your first day go with her?"

"She's a lovely girl, Keegan."

"I thought you were women," Keegan said.

"Sarah is a girl at heart," Eileen continued. She straightened up, and her speech sounded more energized. "After you introduced us and left for the church yesterday, we got acquainted and managed a good deal of small talk."

"Did she talk about Eddie or her father?"

159

"No, she seemed to want to avoid both topics altogether. Maybe today." Eileen pushed the egg on her plate around with her fork, then slipped a morsel in her mouth and swallowed. "She's very eager to please. She insisted upon doing some housework. Then she made me the most delicious milkshake I think I've ever had. She said she'd make an even better one today when she returned with some of her own ingredients." She sipped at her coffee.

"It sounds like you've made a new friend," Keegan said after knocking back his orange juice.

"I think so, Keeg." She placed her elbow on the edge of the table and rested her chin on her palm. "We haven't quite clicked, but then, the circumstances are somewhat contrived."

"She said she would come by about quarter to nine. It's nearly eight thirty now. Why don't you head off to church and leave me alone to greet her. I'm weak, not a complete invalid. I'll be fine."

"Are you sure? Maybe I should clear the table."

"It may be better if you're gone. Sarah is very conscious of your being the pastor. I think if you're out of the way, she may relax. Maybe she'll stop seeing me as the pastor's wife, and see me first as Eileen Letterman."

"As you wish." Keegan mopped off his mouth with his napkin and stood. He brushed toast crumbs out of his chinstrap beard and went over to Eileen and kissed her. "I'll call in an hour or so," he said and left the room.

Eileen pulled the newspaper closer to herself and started to read the front page. Without looking up she said, "Good luck at the Crusades."

"Good morning, Keeg," Grace said as he entered her office from the hall. He went directly to the coffee pot and Grace continued, "There are two phone messages on your desk – one from Chief Erichson." Keegan prepared his coffee as she prattled on. "The parish seems to be holding its own – no crises, no funerals, no calls for weddings or baptisms, the treasurer says we're current on our bills, the heating and plumbing works so far today, and Pastor Weakley is waiting for you in your study."

Keegan, who was moving towards his study, stopped dead, looked at Grace and mouthed, *Weakley*?

Grace nodded yes.

Keegan responded with a shrug and mouthed, *Why*?

Grace shrugged back and whispered, "He insisted on waiting for you when I told him you weren't in yet."

He cocked an eyebrow and went for the closed door between the adjoining offices. As Keegan crossed the threshold into the study, Weakley stood up from the straight back chair facing Keegan's desk.

"Pastor O'Connor," Weakley began immediately, "I wish to speak to you about..."

"Good morning, Bill," said Keegan as if Weakley had not yet begun, "please sit down." As Keegan took his place at the desk, he set his coffee mug by the intercom and stabbed at the open key as he passed his hand over it. As he sat, Keegan noticed an angry look pass over Weakley's face. Keegan wasn't sure if it was because he had cut Weakley off or called him by his first name when he knew Weakley preferred to be addressed as pastor. It didn't matter; he liked having Weakley on the defensive.

Weakley sat and offered a reluctant "Good morning."

"Now then, Bill, what's on your mind?" Keegan asked, beginning the conversation anew on his own terms.

"I'm here about my daughter." Weakley sat bolt upright and gripped the arms of his chair. "I'm here to learn what your intentions may be."

"Excuse me?" Keegan said. "My intentions?"

"You know precisely what I mean. You're attempting to steal this girl away from the paths of righteousness."

Keegan rocked back in his chair and said, "Bill, your daughter doesn't need you to be her pastor just now. She needs you to be her father."

"How dare you presume to tell me how to relate to my little girl?" Weakley jumped to his feet and clenched his fists at his sides.

"Bill, I'm only suggesting..."

"No!" shouted Weakley. "You do not suggest to me, you devil of Satan! Like a wolf you creep into the Lord's sheep pen and steal those whom he calls by name." Weakley stepped up against the front of Keegan's desk and leaned over the top of it, bracing himself on his balled up fists. "I suspect you of indecencies behind closed doors with my little girl. And I charge you before God with condemning her soul to hell." Weakley spun on his heels and headed for the hall door. There he stopped and added, "May the wrath of God fall upon you." He swung open the door and left.

Dramatic exits must run in the family, Keegan thought as he got up to cross the room and close the door. As he returned to his desk, Grace appeared at the adjoining door and leaned against the jamb.

"Interesting way to begin your morning," she said.

"I guess. I could do without any more excitement," Keegan said as he returned to his desk.

"No such luck," Grace said. "You can toss the phone message from Chief Erichson." She stood erect and gestured to someone in her office to come in. "The Chief stopped by to see you just as Pastor Weakley was making his exit." The Chief appeared at the doorway and entered with hand extended to greet Keegan. "Reverend O'Connor," Erichson greeted.

"Please, just call me Keegan." He stood to receive the Chief. The two men shook hands, and at Keegan's direction the Chief took the chair that Weakley had only moments before vacated.

The Chief looked directly at Keegan and said, "It sounded as though you two had a great deal to talk about, Reverend."

"His family's been through a great deal," Keegan said with his hands folded atop the desk. "We all react to grief and guilt differently."

"Interesting word choice, guilt."

"Hm?" Keegan questioned, unsure what the chief meant. "I only meant that at times of death we confront the self recrimination that comes from remembering all of the things we left undone or unsaid with regards to the deceased."

"Yes," said the Chief, "or possibly the things we wish were left unsaid or undone."

"Exactly," agreed Keegan. "In any event, what brings you by, Chief?"

"Things," said the Chief drawing out the word, "that probably would have been better left unsaid or undone."

"You'll have to be a little more straightforward, Chief," Keegan said, "I'm not real good at picking up subtleties." He sipped at his coffee, then offered, "Would you like a cup?"

"I won't be here that long thanks," Erichson said. He brought out his note pad and pen, and with them in his lap he asked, "I understand Reverend, that you've been seeing quite a bit of Sarah Conger."

"That happens when you prepare for a funeral," Keegan said, nonplussed by the question.

"And before?" asked Erichson.

Keegan remained propped on his elbows with his hands clasped in front of him on the desk. "A couple of days before Eddie's murder Sarah made an appointment to see me through the recommendation of one of her friends, Barbara Ross. Barbara is our Sunday School Superintendent."

"Did she keep her appointment?"

"Yes. A week ago Monday."

"What did she see you about?"

"There's a problem there, Chief. I really can't divulge the content of that conversation."

"You realize," said the Chief, "that is not a privilege recognized for Protestant clergy." He shifted his weight in the chair and crossed his legs.

"I understand," Keegan said. He leaned back in his chair. "But you must understand that if this confidence is breached, then the rest of my parish has no reason to entrust me with their secrets. The secrets that keep them from God."

"How far will you work with me, Reverend?"

"I'll tell you what I believe is a part of public knowledge. Maybe even public suspicion if I think it will be of help. No more."

"That's taking a lot on yourself, Reverend. It might hang you."

"Crucifixion has been an occupational hazard for a long time."

"Hm." The Chief changed the crossing of his legs. "What do you think you can tell me about Ms. Conger's visit?"

"There was some trouble in the marriage." Keegan leaned back over his desk.

"What kind of trouble?"

"I can tell you it seemed like the usual sort of problems that come to a mill town during a strike – not enough money and too much booze."

"Anything else?"

"Probable abuse. That's an observation anyone with eyes could have made. She came in here pretty bruised up one afternoon and exhibited a lot of the symptoms of an abused wife."

The Chief took a few moments to scribble on his pad. Keegan nursed his coffee.

"What kinds of symptoms?" the Chief asked.

"Nervous. Very time conscious. A felt need to return home to prepare lunch for her husband."

After jotting a few more notes, Erichson looked up at Keegan and said, "You're not going to like my next question Reverend, but it's got to be asked."

Keegan hadn't been crazy about the questioning thus far, but his curiosity was piqued and he sat back in his seat, almost bracing himself.

"Are you romantically involved with Sarah Conger?" Erichson asked.

Keegan was flooded with emotion. He was embarrassed by the question and instantly wished the intercom were not on. His surprise flustered him and he couldn't formulate a response in his mind. His eyes widened and he lifted his arms in a shrug. Then he thought he probably looked the guilty fool. Then his mind turned to Weakley. That was it! "Weakley told you that, didn't he? That son-of-a..."

"Please just answer the question," insisted Erichson.

"No!" Keegan said more loudly than he intended. "The woman has experienced a tragedy. She has no responsive family. She's turned to me for pastoral care; and my wife and I are trying to be helpful. In fact, Sarah Conger should be with my wife this minute. That's the long and the short of it."

"Sorry, Reverend," Erichson said as he folded his pad and returned it to his coat pocket, "it had to be explored." He got up and extended his hand. "You've got more trouble than Pastor Weakley talking about you, Reverend. The town's got a few wags. And one of those wags has added together one former sailor turned preacher with a sickly wife, to a pretty new widow, and come up with a twosome."

"Gossip is the sharing of small lies by smaller minds Chief," Keegan said, accepting the policeman's hand.

"Maybe so, Reverend, but I have to follow up every hint of a lead." The Chief headed for the hall door then stopped to turn back to Keegan. "By the way. Do you do much hunting?"

"Not in years. Why do you ask?" Keegan remained standing behind his desk.

"What did you use?"

"An old Winchester .30 -.30." Keegan decided he liked this line of questioning even less than the last.

"Kind of light weight, don't you think?"

"It serves the purpose. Besides, if it's not inside of seventy-five yards I let it pass. I'm not that good a shot."

"Now, Reverend," the Chief said, "a man with your military background needn't be modest about marksmanship."

"What's this about? Are you implying I may be a suspect?"

"Can you tell me why we found your fingerprints on the murder weapon in the Conger house?" the Chief asked, and leaned on the door sill.

"I paid a visit to their home. Eddie showed me his gun collection and handed me a deer rifle. That was the only firearm I touched." Keegan could feel himself break out in a sweat. He couldn't believe he was under suspicion.

"Well, Reverend, you managed to handle the murder weapon and leave the only readable set of prints. So rumor would have me believe you might have motive. And your prints would indicate at least some opportunity. With your military background and familiarity with firearms, I'd say it could have been you." The Chief opened the door then added, "We'll talk more later."

The Chief made his exit and Keegan plunked back down in his seat. With his head in his hands, he began to think now would be a good time for a three month family leave. His head was splitting. He reached into his suit coat pocket, pulled out a small Tylenol bottle, popped the top and shook out two, then three tablets. Keegan snapped the tablets into his mouth, took a mouthful of tepid coffee and swallowed hard. He noticed his pocket vial was nearly empty again and made a mental note to drop by the pharmacy.

By mid morning Eileen was having trouble keeping her eyes open. The TV was on and someone was bed-hopping on one of the soaps. Sarah, with her legs drawn up under her and looking through a copy of *Newsweek*, had roosted in Keegan's chair.

Eileen looked over at Sarah and said "I'm sorry to be such poor company this morning, Sarah, but I believe I'll go lie down for a bit."

"You look kind of peaked." Sarah put the magazine down and got up. "I'll run up with you."

The two women went upstairs to Eileen and Keegan's bedroom. Eileen moved to the bed to stretch out. Sarah took the comforter from the foot of the bed and placed it over Eileen. She then took Eileen's bathrobe that had also been draped over the end of the bed and asked "Where should I hang this?"

"Don't bother, Sarah," Eileen said sleepily.

"It's no bother," Sarah said and headed for the closet. She opened the closet door and pushed clothes to the side looking for a coat hanger. "Oh, Eileen, this is beautiful!"

Eileen looked over towards Sarah and saw that she held up a black décolleté cocktail dress. She sat up and looked at the dress as Sarah held it up to herself. Eileen remembered admiring herself in the dress.

"It's a show stopper, Sarah," Eileen responded. Only three months before she had crammed herself into a *Wonderbra* and worn that dress bursting with cleavage to the new bishop's reception in Albany. Keegan's eyes had popped at the sight of her and the two of them had delighted in causing a small stir at an otherwise colorless and mind numbing affair. She felt a pang of grief come over her as she considered that she would never again wear such a dress.

"It looks like it would fit you," Eileen added. Sarah looked at herself in the full length mirror on the inside of the closet door, and twirled from side to side. "Why don't you take it? You'll look great in it."

"Oh, I couldn't," Sarah said without taking her eyes off herself. "It's much too nice. I could never repay you."

"Nonsense. Your willingness to keep me company is more than payment enough," said Eileen. Hoping to make light of the situation, Eileen said "Besides, I no longer have what that dress begs to show off."

"It's so...so naughty. I don't know where I'd wear it," Sarah said turning to Eileen. "My daddy will have a fit if he sees me in this." An impish smile broke out over her face and she added, "But only if he *sees* me in this." Sarah moved to the side of Eileen's bed and sat upon the edge. She put her arms around Eileen's neck and hugged her, saying, "Thank you for this, and for sharing your husband with me." Sarah immediately got up and moved toward the bedroom door and as she left said, "I've got to go see how I look in this. You have a good rest."

Eileen rested back on the bed and pulled the comforter up over her shoulders. Thank you for sharing your husband, she thought. Maybe so, but my operator's permit hasn't expired ... yet. She closed her eyes and drifted into a fitful sleep.

With the troubling results of Eileen Letterman's blood work in front of him, Eli phoned her. It was answered on the second ring.

"Hello, Eileen?" Eli greeted.

"No, I'm sorry, Eileen is unavailable. Who is this?"

"This is Doctor Shapiro," he said, "It's quite important that I speak to Eileen. Uh, with whom am I speaking?" Eli ran the fingers of his right hand through his full head of grey hair and stopped at the crown and scratched there before raking the back of his neck with his fingernails.

"This is a friend of the family," said the disembodied female voice on the other end of the line. "If you'll leave a message I'll be sure to pass it along and have her call you when she finishes her nap."

It was a familiar voice, but Eli couldn't quite place it. He knew the recent federal law prohibited him from leaving a message with a stranger but he didn't like being put off and he very much wanted the information to be in Eileen's hands as soon as possible. If this person is in the house looking after Eileen, then she must be trustworthy, Eli reasoned. "Very well," he said, "please tell Ms. Letterman that the results of her blood work are in." He wanted to say Eileen's liver functions were extremely low, much worse than normal, but didn't feel free to say that much to the young voice. "I'm postponing her next chemo treatment. Do you have that?"

"Yes. I've written it all down," said the young voice.

"Oh, and remind her," Eli said, wanting to be sure to emphasize his earlier warning, "to avoid all acetaminophen. That drug would be fatal."

Eileen was awakened by the sounds of a tray sliding onto the night stand next to the bed. From behind closed eyes and through the lifting fog of sleep she could hear Sarah's gentle and soothing voice say, "Eileen. Eileen, it's time you try to eat something."

Eileen opened her eyes to see Sarah's smile shine down on her, and magnificent cleavage pout from the black cocktail dress taunting her. She managed a sleepy "Thanks" and propped herself up on one elbow. "You really didn't have to do this, Sarah," Eileen protested.

"I know," Sarah responded, still flashing her smile, "but I wanted to. I made you another milkshake to go with your sandwich. You seemed to enjoy it so much yesterday."

"I did." Eileen sat up and put her pillow behind her back and rested against the headboard. "It was much better than that Ensure supplement Eli had me try."

"This will be even better," Sarah insisted. She seemed eager for Eileen to try the shake. "I made it with unsweetened cocoa, chocolate ice cream, a touch of vanilla and malt. I also used a little nutmeg, and cinnamon. Go on, try it."

"It sounds delightful." Eileen sipped at the milkshake and was treated to a chocolate taste so rich that it bore a bitterness to the aftertaste. The vanilla and spices added more to the aroma than to the palate. The intensity of the flavor broke through the deadening effects of the chemo treatments and made Eileen want to drink it simply because it was the first thing that had taste, let alone actually tasting good. "Hmm," Eileen hummed with closed eyes, "You're right, this is even better than yesterday's." She drank deeply. Her stomach roiled, but Eileen swallowed hard several times, determined to keep the delight down.

Sarah sat on the edge of the bed as Eileen drank the shake. "You make that dress look gorgeous," Eileen said.

Sarah ran her hands over the skirt of the dress and said, "After I tried it on, I couldn't bear to take it off. It's the most beautiful dress I've ever owned. It's so ... grown up." She took her eyes off the dress and returned them to Eileen and said, "Maybe I should take it off."

"Not on my account Sarah, it's your dress now. You wear it any time you like." Eileen took a bite of sandwich and forced herself to chew.

Sarah moved to a wooden rocking chair just beyond the nightstand and said, "Doctor Shapiro called while you were napping."

"What did he have to say?" Eileen forced herself to swallow.

"Something about your blood test being back. And he wants to postpone your next treatment." Sarah smiled.

"Hmm," Eileen said, "I'm surprised to hear that. Did he say anything else?"

"He said he'd like you to call back." Sarah stood and said, "I'll put in a call now if you like?"

"Yes, that would be a good idea," Eileen said, and she drew on her milk shake. Sarah picked up the phone from the nightstand and dialed Eli's number. After she heard the ringing, she handed the phone to Eileen. As Eileen conversed first with the receptionist and then the doctor, Sarah left the room for a bit then returned.

"Everything okay?" Sarah asked as she sat on the edge of the bed again.

"Not great news, but we'll manage." Eileen didn't want to say more, so she bit again into her sandwich to fill her mouth and end further conversation for the moment. The taste of the sandwich brought on a wave of nausea she could not control. She dropped the sandwich to the floor as she grabbed for the wastebasket that waited by the nightstand and vomited.

Sarah rushed to her side, and like a mother doting over a helpless child, she held Eileen's forehead and supported her ribs as Eileen convulsed and heaved herself empty. Sarah cooed *poor-dears* and *god-bless-you* until Eileen quieted and needed only to spit and blow the sour taste and smell from her mouth and nose.

Sarah ran to the bathroom and returned with a glass of water and a warm washcloth. Eileen washed out her mouth and spit into the basket.

"Maybe the shake was too rich," Sarah said, handing Eileen the warm washcloth. "I shouldn't have made it so rich, you poor thing."

"Please, Sarah," Eileen managed, "don't change the milkshake. They taste so good. It was simply too much all at once." She wiped her face with the cloth and added, "We'll try again later."

Sarah picked up the basket and carried it into the bathroom, and Eileen could hear her empty it into the toilet and rinse the basket in the tub.

By the time Sarah returned to the bedroom Eileen had swung her legs over the side of the bed and was wiping off splattered vomit from her blouse and slacks.

"Sometimes life is more trouble than it's worth," Eileen muttered.

"Don't you ever say that," Sarah said and threw down the basket. She grabbed Eileen by the shoulders and gave her a jarring. She stared into Eileen's eyes and in a voice that reminded Eileen of one of the nuns in her elementary Catholic school said, "You don't know how lucky you are – sick or not."

Eileen realized that Sarah had taken her grumblings seriously and tried to protest, but Sarah would hear none of it.

"You live in a fine home," Sarah continued, "you have an education and your own career." Sarah began to pace the room. "You're married to a man who has community respect. A man who loves you, and is gentle with you. Your children must be grown enough to be away, so you have him all to yourself." Sarah turned to face Eileen and with the look of a fundamentalist preacher condemning all within earshot to an eternity in hell she finished with, "Don't you talk of dying."

Eileen was amazed by Sarah's fury. Her own remark seemed too innocent to generate such a response. With what she felt sure was a look of confusion, she said the only thing that came to mind, "We couldn't have children."

Sarah's face changed instantly from that of Jonathan Edwards preaching *Sinner in the Palm of an Angry God* to one of complete pity. "I'm … I'm so sorry, I had no idea that…"

"No. Please, Sarah." Eileen, surprised not only by her own private exposure, but now by the almost overwhelming and unwelcome pity of the other said, "I don't want your sympathy. That's an old issue for both Keegan and me. Resolved and put to bed long ago."

"I spoke out of turn," said Sarah. "Such a tragedy." She sat alongside Eileen and put one arm over Eileen's shoulder. "You and Pastor Keegan would have made such good parents, such good and loving…"

"Stop it!" Eileen said. She was feeling more anger towards Sarah than she wanted to. "I don't need to revisit that earlier grief at this point in my life." Eileen started to get to her feet when a stabbing pain inside her ribs brought her back down on the bed.

Sarah moved to embrace Eileen again but Eileen waved her off and tried for her feet again. Making it, she started across the room.

"If you'll excuse me," Eileen said as she walked slowly across the room, "I'll clean up in the bathroom and change my clothes. Maybe it would be best if you waited downstairs and we'll begin again on a fresh note." She exited the room.

From the hall Eileen could hear a faint, "Yes, ma'am," from what sounded like a shamed Sarah.

Keegan got home around three-thirty in the afternoon. He found Eileen and Sarah spending the cold and blustery day in the living room talking amicably and making fun of one of the afternoon soaps. Eileen was sucking on a large chocolate milkshake and Sarah, clad in a cocktail dress, had a cup of tea with the bag still in the cup. As he entered the room he was greeted with a duet of "Hellos."

He bent low to kiss Eileen.

"You sit here," Sarah said and got up from Keegan's usual place. "I'll get you a cup of tea. Eileen told me you always have tea." She put her own cup on the end table near Keegan's chair and left for the kitchen with Keegan watching after her.

"A-hem," coughed Eileen. Keegan looked to her as he sat down. She whispered, "You may look, but I'll break your arm if you touch."

Keegan feigned shock at the suggestion.

Eileen smiled at his antics, and while making a breaking gesture with her hands she whispered, "Always remember."

Keegan leaned over the arm of his chair and Eileen mimicked him and the two met for a gentle kiss. With the kettle beginning to sing in the background, Keegan asked in a low voice, "How has the day gone?"

"Pretty good, actually. We hit a rough spot around lunch time, but ironed it out over the afternoon and I think we've enjoyed each other's company."

Sarah came back into the room and placed Keegan's tea next to her own on the end table. As she lingered over the tea stirring in the sugar, Keegan found himself enjoying the view. An "A-hem" came from Eileen's direction and he could feel a slight flush come over him. He picked up the mug and tried to hide his face behind it as he sipped. Sarah took her tea to a seat on the sofa nearest Eileen and sat with her legs curled under her.

The two women resumed their chat and mocking remarks about *General Hospital*. Keegan was glad for the peace and a little time to regain his natural color without attention being drawn to it.

The soap ended at four. The women had finished their drinks and Keegan's was nearly drained. A lull in their conversation occurred and Keegan broke in.

"Has Eli called with the blood test results?"

"Yes," said Eileen. "It doesn't sound good."

"Why? What did he tell you?" Keegan could feel his face draw up into a picture of concern. He damned himself for it because he didn't want to lend further apprehension to Eileen's worries.

"Mainly," said Eileen, and she heaved a sigh, "that the liver functions are way below what is usually expected under chemo. So he's postponed my next treatment and once again admonished me to avoid acetaminophen because of the liver."

"Is there anything else we should be doing or trying?" Keegan asked. He wanted to add that this sounded very serious, but kept his own counsel.

"He didn't indicate anything. He just said I was to relax, force myself to eat, and let my body recover from the treatments. He'd consult with the oncologist about altering the treatments for the future. Otherwise, just sit tight."

"Easier said than done," Keegan said.

Eileen shifted her weight, pulled the remote control out from her seat cushion and clicked the TV off. The three sat in silence for a moment. Sarah moved to place her mug on the coffee table in front of her, and that brought Keegan around to the present.

"Is it about time I take Sarah home?" Keegan said. "It's kind of a nasty afternoon for a walk."

"Oh, what a shame," Eileen responded, "we've been having such a good time." The change in topic seemed to rally Eileen around.

"I'm really glad you said that, Eileen," Sarah said as she unfolded her legs and placed her hands in her lap. She took a deep breath, and sharing her gaze between Keegan and Eileen she went on, "I'd like to ask a big favor."

"Sure, ask it," Eileen said.

Keegan, already distracted by the morning's interviews with Weakley and Erichson, was not so sure he was ready for a favor to be asked of him.

"With Billy and Becky at Barbara's for the week," Sarah said, "my house is really empty. I don't like being there alone at night." She concentrated her gaze on Eileen. "And I know this is asking a lot, but could I spend a night or two with you folks?"

"Sure. No problem." Keegan was so relieved that the request didn't require any special effort on his part that he blurted out his agreement before looking at Eileen. He added, "I'll run you home and you can pick up some clothes." Then he looked over at Eileen.

Eileen, looking at Keegan with one raised eyebrow, didn't appear to be in complete agreement. She returned her eyes to Sarah and said, "That will be fine, Sarah. Time away from home might do you good."

"Wonderful!" Sarah clapped her hands together. "Thank you both, so much." She moved to Eileen and kissed her on the cheek, and did the same with Keegan, then moved toward the entrance hall. "I'll get my jacket and be ready."

In Sarah's absence Eileen glared at Keegan, and he responded with a shrug. He wasn't altogether sure why Eileen was upset, but he was sure he would hear about it later. In the meantime, his headache had not subsided any. He reached for the tablet bottle in his suit coat pocket and moved to the kitchen for water and downed two acetaminophen tablets before shuttling Sarah home for her belongings.

Keegan pulled up in front of the Conger house. He got out and moved to the passenger side of the car and let Sarah out.

"You're such a gentleman," Sarah said as she swung her legs out of the car and accepted Keegan's assisting hand.

"Just doin' what my mama taught me," Keegan responded. "Treat a woman like a lady, she always used to say."

The two walked up the sidewalk to the front porch and paused as Sarah unlocked her door. "Would you like to come in out of the cold while I collect a few things?"

"No, thanks," said Keegan. "It would be best for me to wait in the car."

"Please," said Sarah. She looked up at Keegan with a little girl pout. "It will make me feel bad thinking of you waiting outside in the cold while I pack a few things."

"Well, all right," Keegan said. His stomach tightened and told him this was not a good move.

"Great," she said. And the two entered the house and Keegan closed the door.

"Would you like a cup of tea while you wait?" she asked. She removed her jacket and tossed it onto the sofa. "I can have some ready in no time."

"No, thanks," Keegan said. He was feeling uncomfortable and remained standing in the middle of the living room with his hands behind his back rocking on his feet. "I'll wait here while you get ready."

"Okay, I'll be right down." Sarah ran up the stairs to the bedroom and Keegan could hear a succession of opening and closing closet doors and dresser drawers.

Keegan paced about the room. He knew being inside the Conger home alone with Sarah would add fuel to Chief Erichson's fire of suspicion. And now that he had time to think, he realized how stupid it was to allow Sarah to stay with Eileen and him for a couple of nights. He wanted out and wanted out soon. He moved to the foot of the stairs.

"Will you be much longer?" Keegan called.

"I'll be right with you," came Sarah's reply.

Keegan returned to the living room and began his pacing. He stopped at an overstuffed chair where needlework was stashed beside it on the floor. On the end table next to the chair were a couple of women's magazine – *Ladies' Home Journal* and *Cosmo*. Next to the magazines lay half a dozen books. Keegan sat and picked up the top volume. *The Wife Abuse Syndrome* was the first. The second was Alan Dershowitz' book, *The Abuse Excuse*. At least she was trying to better understand her situation, he thought, and take steps to rectify the problem. Good for her.

He heard footfalls descend the staircase and he got up to greet Sarah across the room near the front door.

"Ready?" he asked.

"Yup," she said and handed him the front door key. "Would you lock the door? I'll carry my own bag."

"Sure," Keegan said. He opened the door and Sarah stepped out onto the porch. She turned to face him and put her bag down while Keegan closed and locked the door. With that done, he faced Sarah and returned her key.

Sarah ignored the key and looked into Keegan's eyes and said, "You have been so kind to me. I've never known such love in a man." She stepped into Keegan, placed both arms around his neck and kissed him deeply.

Keegan first reacted with an embrace and immediately felt guilty over enjoying this young woman's affection, however inappropriate it was. Gently he took hold of her forearms and brought them to her side as he broke off the kiss. "Sarah, you're very flattering. And you're very welcome to our help, but your affection makes me very uncomfortable."

"Silly," she said and stepped back and arched both eyebrows with the look of surprise. She patted him once on the chest and added, "I'm only saying thanks the best way I know how." She bent over to pick up her bag and headed off towards the car.

Keegan followed along behind. Whew, he thought, if that's thanks, I wonder what her idea of passion is like? He drew the collar of his overcoat up around his neck to guard against the evening chill and wind. The tree-lined street was nearly barren of leaves. Some of the lawns had been raked and their leaves bagged and ready for the town to pick them up and carry off to be mulched. The leaves in a neighbor's orange pumpkin bag across the street had settled since Halloween, affording the lawn decoration the sunken caved-in look of a rotted jack-o-lantern.

Keegan opened the door of the car and Sarah slid in with her overnight bag. He moved his gaze up along the street as he crossed around the front of the car to the driver's side. The autumn light was growing dim. A group of four or five children were playing hide and seek two houses down. Beyond them an old man was erecting a shrub protector to shield the hedges from the winter snows. Across the street Keegan noticed a

Blazer parked at the curb about four doors down. Chief Erichson was sitting in the town's cruiser.

Sarah ran upstairs to settle into the O'Connor guest room. Eileen and Keegan took their places side by side in the living room.

"Now that you've brought her home like a lost puppy dog, what do you think of Sarah?" Eileen asked in a low and confidential tone.

"There's a certain edge to your voice."

"Just answer the question."

"She's a sweet kid," Keegan said. The King novel was in his lap but as yet unopened.

"Who's thinking of her as a child now?"

"Yeah, okay."

"What else?"

"She's a young woman overwhelmed by the circumstances of life. She's trying to regain her compass bearings."

"Anything else?"

"Hmm," intoned Keegan, "I don't think so. That about covers it."

"What about affection?" inquired Eileen.

"She seems to crave it," Keegan observed.

"And you're providing it," Eileen's voice turned a bit raspy in her whisper.

Keegan cocked both his head and an eyebrow.

"I think you're becoming infatuated with this sweet young thing," Eileen insisted.

"Oh, give me a break." Keegan thumped open his novel and stared into it without seeing the page.

"Keegan," Eileen rasped, and touched his arm, "look at me."

He did.

"I'm sick. I feel like hell. I look like hell. But I'm not brain dead. I can see. I see her falling for you, and I can see your approving looks at her."

Keegan could see Eileen's eyes well up with tears.

"I don't even know if you're aware of it. But it hurts. It hurts more than this damn cancer." Her tears spilled and wet her cheeks.

Keegan put his book on the table next to him, pulled out his handkerchief, blotted Eileen's cheeks dry, then placed it in her hand.

"She's a pretty woman, Eileen," he said, "no different than the eye popping bikini clad 38D's you've pointed out to me on the beach at Hilton Head. It's just that this particular eye popper has turned to us for help."

He reached over to touch Eileen's cheek. She took his hand and held it. He asked, "Will you be okay with this?"

"I don't think I am, Keeg," Eileen said. "I believe there's more to this than you realize."

NOVEMBER 13TH
THURSDAY

Eileen was feeling more miserable than she believed anyone could and still be alive. She could hear Keegan's morning routine in the hall bathroom. Breakfast smells were wafting upstairs from the kitchen. She couldn't quite make out the odor, but then she hadn't been able to smell much of anything lately – and what she did smell she didn't like. It sounded as though Sarah were singing downstairs.

She threw the covers off and swung her legs around to the edge of the bed. Her side cramped in pain at the motion and she caught herself from crying out. I won't let Keegan hear me, she thought, he has enough on his mind.

Eileen stood and moved to her bureau and leaned on it while she gazed into the mirror at herself. Her face was drawn. The circles under her eyes had darkened. The skin on her body, once tight and pink, had begun to hang loose and take on a sallow appearance. You look like a mortuary student's first assignment, she thought. She pulled open a bureau drawer and rummaged for a head scarf. I need one that goes with jaundice. She smirked at her own gallows humor, then thought, damn, that's not funny. She pulled out a brilliant yellow scarf, tied it about her head and hoped that people would assume it was the scarf that was causing the yellow cast to her skin.

Keegan returned to the bedroom. "You're up," he said. He came to Eileen and kissed her. "How are you feeling this morning?"

"Not well," she said. Eileen sat on the edge of the bed and added, "But you know I go through hell for a few days after the chemo."

176

"It's been better than a week," Keegan said and sat beside her to hold her hands. "You've usually come out of this by now with the past treatments."

"It'll pass," she assured Keegan and squeezed his hand. "Maybe it's just the pain in my side that's fatiguing me so. It kept me up a good part of last night."

"Why didn't you wake me?" Keegan was wearing his worried expression and Eileen loved him for it.

"There wasn't anything you could do, Keeg. If I thought you could, I would have disturbed you."

"How about now? Do you need anything?"

"I think I'd like an aspirin. Maybe on an empty stomach it will get to the pain sooner."

Keegan squeezed her hand and left. He returned with the aspirin bottle and a glass of water, and handed them to her.

"After you take this," Keegan said, "you will eat some breakfast. Your stomach shouldn't stay empty. Particularly with aspirin."

"Yes, doctor," Eileen said with a sarcastic tone. She popped out two aspirin into her hand. After considering her pain level and Keegan's unwanted advice about an empty stomach, she placed one tablet on her tongue and returned the other to the bottle. After swallowing water, she put the glass on the nightstand next to an empty milkshake glass from the night before.

"Maybe I shouldn't have drunk that shake so late last night," she said.

"Why do you say that?" Keegan asked from in front of the bureau mirror where he tied a plaid tie around his neck.

"Indigestion, I suppose."

Keegan returned to the bedside and asked, "Do you want to stay up here for a while? I'll bring breakfast up to you."

"And leave you alone with the damsel in distress?" Eileen got to her feet. "I don't think so." She moved towards the door.

"Humph," responded Keegan. He followed Eileen out of the bedroom and down the stairs into the dining room.

Eileen suddenly felt like she was a guest in her own home. The dining room was brightly lit. The table was formally set with water glasses, juice glasses, dinner plates, cups and saucers instead of their usual mugs, linen napkins in napkin rings, and fresh flowers. The newspaper was unfolded and next to Keegan's place setting. Sarah, looking like an ad for *Irish Spring* soap, was dressed in a full length green satin robe and pouring coffee. "Good morning," she lilted.

Eileen stood at the entrance to the dining room and no words came to mind.

Keegan stepped up behind her and said simply, "Wow."

"Please sit," Sarah said and waved them in. "Breakfast is ready. Blueberry pancakes. Sorry I had to use frozen blueberries. We have honey or maple syrup, fresh squeezed orange juice, and coffee with a dash of vanilla flavoring." She spun around and disappeared into the kitchen.

Eileen took her usual place, still speechless.

Keegan sat down, sipped at the coffee, and let loose with an all too contented and annoying "Ahhh."

Sarah returned with a platter full of pancakes with steam and aroma rising. As she placed the platter on the table she said, "Be careful, the platter's been in the oven to keep everything warm. Dig in."

Sarah stood looking over the handiwork. Eileen noticed the youthful, lean and firm figure beneath the flimsy fabric of Sarah's robe.

"This is all quite overwhelming," Eileen finally said.

"Oh, it's nothing, just my way of saying thanks," Sarah said. "I'll go get more coffee."

"That's a lovely robe," Eileen said before Sarah could get away. "What color do you call that?"

"This?" Sarah paused before the kitchen door and looked over her shoulder at Eileen. "This is called hunter green." She started for the kitchen again.

"I'll bet," muttered Eileen.

Sarah stopped, "What was that?"

"I'll get … one," Eileen said aloud. "It's so lovely, I'll get one, is what I said."

"Oh," said Sarah. "It might not do you justice. The color, I mean." And she was gone.

Keegan seemed oblivious to the exchange between Sarah and Eileen and ate pancakes with humming and contented sounds that broke Eileen's heart with each utterance.

After breakfast, Eileen forced herself to follow Keegan to the door as he set out for the church. After she kissed him, she said, "Please come home early today."

About an hour after her noontime milkshake, Eileen took to her bed. Sleep, at least, masked the near constant ache in her side. When the phone on the nightstand awoke her, she answered it only to hear Sarah already receiving the call.

"Mrs. O'Connor?" a young female voice asked.

"Yes," answered Sarah.

Eileen instantly filled with anger. The nerve of this interloper!

"I'd like to make arrangements with Reverend O'Connor for a wedding next July?" queried the voice.

"I'm sorry," answered Sarah, "the pastor is not here just now. But you can reach him at the church number."

Maybe, considered Eileen, it was simply easier to field the question than to try to make explanations.

"Thank you, I'll try the office," said the young voice and hung up.

Eileen put the receiver down gently. After all, she thought, Sarah's been nothing but helpful. If I were feeling better, I probably wouldn't even think about this. She put her head back on the pillow and drifted off into a fitful sleep and dreamt of drowning in a sea of green.

"Keegan, Chief Erichson is here to see you." Grace stepped back from the doorway adjoining her office with Keegan's study and the Chief walked through. Grace closed the door behind them.

"What can I do for you, Chief?" Keegan asked, offering a seat by his desk. Arthur Erichson took the seat, crossed his legs and placed his hat upon his knee. Keegan, feeling on guard, sat upright with his elbows resting on the arms of his chair.

"Well, sir," said Erichson, pulling on his clean shaven chin, "from what I got a look at last night on the Conger porch, I'd say that you and the new widow have more than a pastoral relationship. To my mind, that seems to confirm the rumors I described in our earlier conversation. Some might even say there's evidence of motive."

Keegan's face screwed up and he said, "I don't think I like this, Chief."

"No reason you should, Reverend," said Erichson. "Maybe you'd like to tell me about it."

"I think I'd rather hear more from you first. It doesn't seem likely you'd come here to tell me about seeing two silhouettes on the shades."

"Okay, Reverend. Here's what I see." Erichson said, switching his legs over, "I see a man with twenty years service in the United States Navy. I checked to learn that you scored *expert* with the M-15, then the M-16 while a Marine Corpsman in the Navy. Something most preachers probably can't say for themselves. You've been married some time, but now your wife is seriously ill, and word around town is that she's probably not going to make it. Not long ago, you started to *counsel* Mrs. Conger."

Keegan was absolutely sure he did not like the way Erichson said counsel.

"Not long after," continued the Chief, "Mrs. Conger's husband is *expertly* shot through the right temple and instantly killed. Less than a week after the victim becomes daisy fertilizer, I witness you lip lockin' the new widow, which verifies widely circulated rumors about town. All of this, and fingerprints. Now, if you were in my shoes, what kinds of conclusions would you draw from that?"

"Do you prefer to make accusations, or would you like to hear an explanation?" Damn, he thought, that sounded too defensive – but who wouldn't be? Keegan started to shift his weight in his seat then stopped, not wanting to appear as if he were squirming. Inside, he was squirming like hell.

"Please, go right ahead," said Erichson, "I'd love to hear something convincing." He pulled out a note pad and pen and prepared to write.

"Sarah Conger is a very vulnerable and needy woman who does not always know how to appropriately express her appreciation." Keegan rocked back in his chair. "I think I can say without revealing any confidences that her background has kept her immature, and hugs and kisses have been her way to navigate around a strict father, and possibly an abusive husband.

The Chief scribbled in his note pad. He looked up at Keegan, stared at him for a time, then asked, "Are you a rescuer?"

"Excuse me?"

"A rescuer. You know, a person who feels compelled to bail other people out of their troubles. I hear clergy are often the rescuing type."

"A little out of your area of expertise, aren't you, Chief?" Keegan said, trying to control a smile. He feared it escaped looking like a smirk.

"We police types take our fair share of Psychology 101."

"Hm," Keegan intoned. "In any event, twenty years in the Navy is enough to cure anyone of being a rescuer. I prefer to think of myself as someone who equips people with tools to take their own action and get on with life. I don't want to rescue them. And I don't want them dependent upon me, in case you've also heard that clergy tend toward co-dependency."

The Chief scribbled. Without looking up he asked, "Reverend, where were you at about eight o'clock on the evening of Wednesday, November fifth?"

Keegan sat upright and in his most formal voice said, "I left a town board meeting about eight. You can check that with Father Fish. I came directly here, to my study, to wrap up some of the material left over from that meeting and got home by nine o'clock. I remember getting home in time to tape a TV program my wife usually likes to watch."

"Is that it? Any witnesses?"

"No. At least not until I got home. My neighbor can verify that."

"Did you see anyone else after leaving Father Fish and before arriving home who can verify your whereabouts?"

"No," said Keegan. He realized that somehow he had become a prime suspect. "I remember that a little after eight-thirty someone knocked at the church door. I looked out the window and saw a small figure, but couldn't tell who it was. By the time I answered the door, they were gone."

"Man or a woman?"

"I couldn't tell. Possibly a small man, or a medium sized woman."

Eileen sat in the living room alternating between reading and nodding off when a knock came at the front door. Sarah excused herself to go answer it.

Sarah opened the door and said, "What are you doing here?"

From beyond the dining room and down the entrance hall Eileen could hear a good part of the conversation.

"Hey, lover," a male voice said, "is that any way to greet the father of your firstborn?"

Eileen decided she had to see this. She got out of her chair and crossed the room to a straight backed occasional chair that allowed her to catch glimpses of the hallway action reflected in the dining room mirror over the sideboard.

Sarah glanced over her shoulder, then back at her guest and said in forced hushed tones, "Danny, you shouldn't be here. What if someone sees?" Nodding her head back towards the dining room she added, "What if she hears?"

"What's with the brush off? Who cares?" The man was medium build. He wore work clothes, but they were clean. They didn't have the look of being in the mill all day.

"I care," said Sarah, sounding insistent, "I don't want you here. You'll ruin..." Eileen couldn't catch what Sarah's voice had trailed off on.

"Come on Sarah, Eddie's out of the way. Maybe you're ready for a real man."

The man stepped forward and grabbed Sarah and kissed her hard. Sarah seemed to struggle, but Eileen couldn't tell if it was a sincere effort, or a tease.

The kiss broke off. Eileen was unsure who brought it to an end. Sarah rasped a few more words at the man and pushed him towards the door. She said something about wanting security, status and love. He seemed to be unconcerned with what Sarah wanted and treated it all like a game. Before leaving, he turned quickly and grabbed Sarah by the fanny and added a fast kiss. Eileen returned to her easy chair and heard Sarah close the front door and sigh.

When Sarah returned to the living room and sat, Eileen asked, "Who was that?"

"Oh, an old high school friend," Sarah said, flipping through a *Ladies' Home Journal*. "One I'd just as soon not see right now." Then she looked up at Eileen and said, "Say, isn't it time for your afternoon shake? We need to try to keep your strength up."

The nightstand clock glowed its low Martian green light announcing eleven-thirty-nine. Eileen rolled over onto her side to face Keegan. He lay on his back with his fingers laced across his belly, staring at the ceiling.

"So the Chief thinks you're a suspect, eh?" she asked.

"It seems to be one of his observations," Keegan said, fixing his stare at the ceiling. "I suppose bringing Sarah in with us doesn't help the appearance of guilt where he's concerned."

"It's hard for me to rest thinking I may be in bed with a cold-blooded murderer," Eileen said, putting her index finger to his temple and clicking her tongue.

"You're a big help, Eileen," he said, rolling his eyes over to her. "Go to sleep."

They rested in silence for a long while, and Eileen could still see Keegan blinking at the ceiling. The rhythm of his breath was nowhere near that of sleep.

"You look about as ready to sleep as I do," she said.

"Do you need something?" Keegan turned his head to face her. "Are you in pain?"

"No more than usual. I simply can't get Sarah off my mind."

Keegan rolled over and propped himself on his elbow. "Something in particular or general ruminations?"

"Very particular," Eileen answered. "Now it's time for my story. This afternoon a man paid a visit to Sarah."

"What did he want?"

Eileen watched Keegan's face as closely as she could by the light filtered into the room from the street lamp kitty-corner across the way.

"I'm not really sure," Eileen said. "Sarah kept him in the entrance way and kept her end of the conversation in whispers. I could still overhear most of it."

Keegan smirked and said, "Overhear? Or eavesdrop?"

"I simply have wonderful hearing!" Eileen was glad for his smile and for the opportunity to poke fun. "I didn't spend my youth blowing out my eardrums with headphones listing to *The Animals* sing *House of the Rising Sun*, or my early adulthood listening to a battleship roar. I overheard." She added a playful pout and rolled over onto her back. At once she regretted the immature girlish display but was surprised that she found the energy to play at all.

Keegan looked down on her and with smirk still in place he said, "You digress."

"Hmm," Eileen sounded. "Anyway, it seemed that what he had in mind was to play a little grab-ass, and I'm not altogether sure that Sarah didn't want him to."

"What do you mean by that?" he asked.

"He grabbed at her and kissed her and had his hands all over her. *And*," Eileen added with the corner of her mouth drawn, "she wasn't putting up much of a struggle. I don't know how she plays her sexual games, but she may even have been egging him on with a voice saying no, no, no, and eyes beckoning yes, yes, yes."

"I thought you feminists said no always meant NO."

"Yeah, well, the word hasn't got out to everyone yet," Eileen said.

Keegan lay back down and said, "It sounds like you're making a mountain out of a molehill."

"You haven't heard the best part yet," Eileen said in a voice even more hushed than before.

Keegan looked over at her and wore a pinched brow.

Feeling too tired to roll over, Eileen turned her head towards Keegan and continued, "The man said something about being the father of her son, and Sarah didn't make any protest over his comment. Then he said she might be ready for a real man now that Eddie was out of the way."

"Out of the way?"

"Yes," Eileen said, "That's what he said. Do you think it could mean..."

"Did you pick up a name for this guy?" Keegan asked.

"Hmm," intoned Eileen, "I know she called him by name once. David? No ... Danny. She called him Danny. Does that mean anything to you?"

"I think so," said Keegan, returning his stare to the ceiling. "It was probably Dan Callahan. He's the union president, and general all around rabble rouser. At Eddie's wake, I'm pretty sure I saw him grab one of Sarah's breasts as he greeted her on the pretense of paying his respects."

Eileen fixed her gaze on Keegan through the dark. She watched him blink at the ceiling, maybe lost in thought. "What do you think it means?" she asked.

"I think it means that things always look worse in the dark," he said, turning toward her. "Let's see what the light of day brings." He leaned over and gave her a gentle kiss and returned to his position of interlaced fingers and repose. His eyes closed.

Eileen lay on her back and stared sleepless at the ceiling, unwilling to sleep, unwilling to return to her restless green sea and her helpless drowning.

NOVEMBER 14TH
FRIDAY

The more Keegan sat in his study thinking about his conversation with Eileen the night before, the more troubled he became. His impressions of Sarah as an oppressed victim of her religion, father, and husband – a helpless waif of a girl – were not jelling well with the take charge alluring woman he found in his home. She seemed capable, efficient, almost business-like around the house. Even her clothes seemed to have changed. Gone were the little-girl dresses, gone was the teenager scent, gone was the overdone makeup; and in their place lived a young woman dressed in modest length skirts or slacks and fitted blouses, gentle fragrances and little to no makeup. Her look reminded him of … of Eileen? Of course, that made sense. After all, Eileen has given her that cocktail dress. She had probably given her some other items as well; maybe even some fashion advice.

But there was still an incongruity between the personality of the girl at the wake, or at her home, and that of the take-charge woman that emerged nearly overnight.

Keegan heard Grace enter her office and he wandered out to her space where the two of them exchanged greetings and small talk.

Keegan poured himself a second mug of coffee from the pot he brewed when he first arrived. He then turned to Grace and asked, "How long have you known Sarah Conger?"

"Since before she saw the light of day from her mama's womb." Grace busied herself settling in at her desk.

"But how did you come to know her as a young girl? Certainly not through church."

"She and one of my girls were the same age," Grace said, dumping her purse in the bottom drawer of her desk and then turning on the computer. "Both of mine were only eleven months apart, so the three girls played together a good deal."

Keegan moved over to Grace's desk and sat on the corner. "Tell me about her. What are your impressions about her?"

Grace stopped what she was doing to look at Keegan. With a tilt to her head she asked, "What's up?"

"I'm not sure. Nothing probably. For now, educate me." Keegan sipped at his coffee.

Grace spoke of a little girl who spent as much time as she was allowed by her parents with Grace's daughters. The girls played in the woods in back of her home, whiled away hours with dolls or coloring books.

As the girls grew older there came a time when Sarah was not allowed to join in with some of the activities of Grace's daughters. Beach parties were out because Pastor Weakley felt they were nothing more than mating rituals with too much exposed skin.

"He might be right," Keegan said with a smirk. "At least that's what they were when I was a kid."

"Even so," Grace continued, "Halloween parties and trick-or-treat were forbidden because they were pagan. Christmas was too commercial, Easter wasn't taken seriously enough, and Saturday afternoon movies at the State Theater were of the devil." Grace shifted around in her seat to better face Keegan before continuing.

"As the girls became teenagers," she said, "other than Girl Scouts they had even less in common. Dating was out for Sarah. Her father was very protective. Makeup, jewelry, fashion were all signs of vanity, and the poor girl was sent off to school looking like a drab little mouse; to be made fun of by the rest of the kids. I think my girls were her only friends," Grace finished.

Keegan had managed to drain his mug and was back filling it for the third time as he asked Grace to tell him about the Girl Scouts.

"Not much to tell, really," Grace said. "Typical girl stuff of the period. Some camp outs including shrieks over spiders and frogs. Merit badges for sewing, baking, biking, marksmanship, swimming, hiking and the like. That's about it."

"Marksmanship?" Keegan quizzed.

"Most of the girls around here have daddies who hunt and fish," Grace said as she returned her look to Keegan. "Some of them wished they had sons, others just feel that their girls should be familiar with firearms. Both of my girls are good shots. It's just kind of natural around here."

"Are you telling me Weakley wanted a son, or wanted his daughter familiar with firearms?" Keegan asked.

"Oh, heavens," Grace said with a smirk. "Sarah just went off with my girls for the marksmanship merit badge. Weakley didn't know anything about it until it was all over. He about had a cow!"

"What about when the girls went off to college?" Keegan asked and returned to the corner of Grace's desk. "What happened to Sarah?"

"She went away, too," Grace said. She leaned back in her chair away from the desk and rested an elbow on the computer table behind her. "My girls went off to state colleges – one to Albany and one to Plattsburgh. Sarah went off to a church college out of state somewhere. But she wasn't gone long."

"How so?"

"I can't remember if she was gone for nearly a whole year or only for a semester. But she came home early, in the middle of one term, and married Eddie Conger a couple of weeks later." Grace shrugged her shoulders and added, "I didn't even know they had dated, much less been serious enough to get married."

Then Grace leaned forward again over her desk and with raised eyebrows said, "About six or seven months later little William arrived in this world. He was a seven and a half pound preemie, if you get my drift."

Breakfast had been cleared away, and Eileen had managed a restful nap during the mid-morning. Sarah had done a load of laundry and now the two women sat in the living room reading. Eileen was dressed in slacks and blouse, refusing to give in to the illness and be clad only in nightgown and robe. Sarah was in blue jeans and flannel shirt, and had her legs drawn up alongside of herself on the sofa.

Eileen was pleased that Sarah's dress had become more casual and comfortable. She also decided that she had not done what she had planned where Sarah was concerned. Her own fatigue, and even her own jealousy, had prevented her from trying to be of help to this young widow. Feeling a little more rested, and willing to give Sarah the benefit of the doubt, she decided to try.

"Sarah," Eileen began, "I need to say thanks for your gracious help these last few days."

Sarah put her magazine flat in her lap. "You're more than welcome, Eileen," Sarah said and smiled. "You and Keegan have been so good to me, letting me stay with you for a few days and all. It's been good to be away from the house."

"We've not talked much about the house, or Eddie, or the night he died," Eileen said. "Sometimes when we grieve, it's helpful to talk with someone about what we're feeling. If you would like to talk about it I'd like to listen. Maybe return to you some of the kindness you've shown me."

"Thank you," Sarah said slowly, "but when I think about it I feel so many emotions I don't know where to begin."

Eileen found her opening, and in her best professional voice she said, "Why don't you tell me about the kinds of emotions you're feeling."

"There are so many things I feel," Sarah said. She stared off into space and twirled her hair around her index finger for a moment. Then she returned her gaze to Eileen. "It's so confusing."

"Tell me about one or two."

"There's hurt, the emptiness you feel when someone dies. And I worry a lot about the kids growing up without a father. But the two strongest things I feel are scared and angry."

"What are you scared about?" Eileen said and nodded understanding.

"What's going to happen to me?" Sarah said, her eyes welling up. "I'm scared about what's going to happen to me."

It occurred to Eileen that this was the first time she had seen Sarah near tears.

"Will I be able to keep the house?" Sarah continued. "I don't know how much insurance we had. I don't even know *if* we had insurance. If I go to work, will I still be an adequate mother? You know, my father says only greedy women, or women who hate men, go to work and leave their children. What will happen to my children?" Sarah's tears began to flow.

Eileen let Sarah cry for a while without interrupting. She felt angry with Pastor Weakley for having imposed such narrow views on his daughter. No wonder she was confused. The tears were probably a result of that confusion and internal conflict. After a few moments Sarah began to collect herself.

"When I get the most scared," Sarah said, "I start to get mad." She pounded the arm of the sofa and startled Eileen. The change in Sarah from grief to intense anger was remarkable.

"What do you feel angry about?" asked Eileen.

"I'm mad at Eddie for dying. I know that's silly."

"Not at all, it's quite normal," reassured Eileen.

"I feel like he's abandoned the children and me. It's like he's off hunting or fishing for the weekend, and left me with the kids, to clean the house and pay the bills. Only this time he's not coming back and that really pisses me off!" Sarah flashed a sheepish look at Eileen and added, "Sorry, I shouldn't have said that."

"I've heard it before. Go ahead."

"I get mad at my father." Sarah brought her legs around in front of her and put her feet on the floor. She leaned forward and rested her elbows on her knees and held her head. "Daddy tried to get along with Eddie. But he was always trying to convert him, bring him to church, pointing out his sinful ways – his drinking and going away a lot of weekends during hunting and fishing seasons, and missing church. Daddy was always telling Eddie he was going to burn in hell."

A long silence followed. Then Eileen said, "How did all of this make you feel?"

"Embarrassed." Sarah's shoulders slumped. "Eddie would tell me about it and I would feel embarrassed about my father. It felt like Daddy was humiliating me in front of my husband, and the Bible tells a child to honor her father and a wife to obey her husband. Being humiliated didn't make any of that easier. You obey Pastor Keegan, right?"

"No," Eileen said. "I don't obey. We discuss and agree upon solutions. But I..."

"But the Bible says..."

"Sarah, please," Eileen said and shook her head, "you'd better have that discussion with Keegan. He's the resident theologian. I'm the psychologist. I can understand your religious principles without sharing them. Okay?"

Sarah nodded consent.

"You felt as though your father humiliated you in front of your husband," Eileen urged. "Go on."

"Then, sometimes on Sunday," Sarah said with an intensifying voice, "Daddy would make up some story to illustrate a point in his sermon, and I would know that story was about Eddie and me. And I'm pretty sure that nearly everyone in church knew it was about Eddie and me."

"So, you not only felt as though your father humiliated you to your husband, but that he humiliated both you and your husband in front of the whole congregation."

Sarah's fists were clenched, a darkness came over her face and she growled, "I hate him." Almost immediately she looked up at Eileen and said, "I shouldn't have said that, I, I don't hate him. You can't hate your father, he's God's emissary to the household."

"It's okay to express feelings, Sarah," Eileen said and raised her hands in a calming motion trying to soothe Sarah. "It's best if you can own your feelings, then you can get behind them to quiet the fears and dispel the anger. If you don't acknowledge the anger, you can't resolve it. It's okay."

Sarah flashed a quick and pathetic smile, then hung her head, staring at the floor between her feet.

Eileen waited.

Sarah looked up at her and said, "I think I'd like a cup of tea. Would you like some?"

Eileen agreed, and Sarah made herself busy in the kitchen. Eileen surmised that Sarah was taking a breather from giving a hard look at her situation for the first time. When Sarah returned with the tea and a couple of Oreo cookies for each of them, she took Keegan's chair closer to Eileen. Eileen felt this was a good sign, signaling an increase in the level of trust Sarah had in her.

After the two settled in again Eileen urged Sarah on, "What else makes you angry?"

"The strikers," said Sarah with nearly the same tone of anger she had used to describe her father. It was as if a valve had opened and the anger spilled out. "My Eddie had to cross the picket line to go to work and put up with their yelling and shouting and name calling. And then they came to my house! Damn them!" Sarah slammed her mug of tea on the coffee table, spilling some. She got up and moved over to the fireplace and braced herself on the mantle. Staring off to a side window she whispered, "May they burn in hell."

Eileen decided to press her luck and asked, "The man who was here yesterday, is he a striker?"

"Yes!" Sarah snapped and turned an icy glare on Eileen. "And damn him too, Danny Callahan! He's part of the reason my Eddie's dead." Sarah left the mantle and paced slowly about the room. "Him and his union." She screwed up her face and spit the word union out as if she had bitten into a fall apple only to get a mouthful of worm.

"Didn't you say yesterday he was an old high school friend that had come to see you?"

"Yes," Sarah said and stopped her pacing to look at Eileen. "He *was* an old high school friend." She began her pacing again. "He's no friend now." She returned to the sofa and sat, once again resting her elbows on her knees and holding her head. "I wonder if he didn't kill Eddie, or have him killed by one of his union thugs."

"That's a pretty serious charge," observed Eileen, "have you mentioned anything to Chief Erichson?"

Sarah sat up and looked at Eileen and said sternly, "I shouted it at the top of my lungs when he drove up that night. I shouted it at all the strikers who were in my front hard. I shouted it so God himself could hear me!"

Sarah turned quickly away from Eileen and sat back in the sofa with arms folded, facing the fireplace.

She looked to be sulking to Eileen. Eileen sipped at her tea and let Sarah collect her thoughts. She felt she had learned more about her house guest in the last thirty or forty minutes than she had over the last couple of days of observation and small talk.

After a long silence, and after Sarah's body seemed to relax some, Eileen said, "Why don't you tell me about that night? It might help if you tell me how you discovered Eddie."

Sarah didn't move her stare from the cold and silent fireplace. The muscles in her arms tensed and drew closer around her ribs. Then, speaking as if a disinterested bystander, she began to tell the evening's story.

"Eddie and I were supposed to have a discussion about what was troubling us when he got home. Naturally, he didn't get home before I had to leave for choir practice. I knew that would piss him off; it always did when he got home and knew I was at church instead of waiting on him. While at choir, someone – who came late – said they saw strikers picketing my house and shouting for Eddie to come out. I got scared and decided I'd better go see what was happening. So I left church and went home. When I got to the back yard, our lot abuts the church property, I could see that all of the windows of my back porch were broken. There was glass all over the inside of my porch – everywhere!" She grabbed the sides of her head and held still for a moment. Eileen remained silent, letting Sarah collect herself.

"I was really frightened," Sarah said when she was ready. She clasped her hands in front of herself. "If Eddie had seen that he'd have gone wild! The whole place was dark. There weren't any lights on anywhere. When I stepped into the kitchen, I felt around for the light switch. For whatever reason, I remember smelling cigar smoke and thinking Eddie was some kind of fool if he was smoking around his reloading. I found the switch and turned the lights on. As soon as I turned on the lights, I could hear the pickets outside get louder, shouting their nasty stuff. Then I noticed I could hear Eddie's brass tumbler in the cellar." She stood and began pacing again. "I shouted downstairs, but he didn't answer." She stabbed at the air and said, "I tried turning the cellar light on, but it must have blown out and Eddie hadn't replaced the bulb yet. So I picked my way down the stairs until I saw Eddie sprawled out on his reloading bench, kind of like he was taking a nap."

Sarah returned to the sofa and hid her face in her hands. She did not cry, but remained silent for a long while. "I called, but he didn't answer."

She looked up at Eileen. "When I got closer, I could see the blood, and the brains, and, and ... the blood. I ran upstairs and called the police and the ambulance. While I waited, all I could hear were the strikers shooting off their big mouths, and so I went out on my porch and started yelling at them. The demons!"

Eileen was struck by the fact that Sarah seemed to tell her story as if rehearsed. Her cadence never faltered. Her pauses seemed timed for effect. Her tone never changed. The tale seemed so ... so staged – as if she had told it a hundred times and was now bored with it.

After a short pause Sarah turned her face towards Eileen and said, "And that's how Sarah learned she was a widow." The smile that followed seemed unnatural and out of place to Eileen.

"Maybe we've talked enough on the topic for the time being," Eileen said. Then raising her cup she added, "How about more tea?"

Sarah's expression softened and the nature of the smile changed and had a more pathetic quality. "Okay," she said, "I'll heat up the kettle. It shouldn't take long. I have to put the laundry away, would you like to come upstairs and we'll talk up there while I do that?"

Eileen agreed and Sarah went out into the kitchen to turn the kettle on.

Eileen was sure it was due to her fatigue, but she felt nearly overwhelmed by Sarah's internal conflicts. She leaned her head back against the chair and closed her eyes for a brief rest.

When Sarah returned, the two walked upstairs to the bedroom. No sooner did they make it to the chair in the bedroom when the kettle began to sing its readiness. Sarah disappeared and immediately came back with more tea and two more Oreo cookies each. She left again and returned with two stacks of folded laundry.

As Sarah lifted various laundered items that belonged to Keegan, Eileen motioned to the appropriate shirt, sock, undershirt and shorts drawers. As Sarah began to put Eileen's clothes away, she opened the drawer for her slip and paused. Sarah put the slip on top of the bureau and removed from the drawer a satin and lace thong bodysuit. Sarah held it up to examine it – underwired demi cups, lace-up front, garter straps.

Holding the garment out in front of her as if it might bite, she turned to Eileen and said, "How do you explain this?"

Eileen wasn't sure how Sarah meant the question, but decided to interpret the tone of voice as a friendly jibe. "Do I need to explain it?"

"Is this appropriate for a pastor's wife?" Sarah asked in the same ambiguous tone.

"If Keegan has been less than attentive," Eileen said, "I sometimes find he needs a little distraction from his work." Introspectively she added, "It'll take more than that to help me distract Keeg in the future."

Sarah crumpled the bodysuit, jammed it back into the drawer and said, "I think that's disgusting for a pastor's wife. I won't... wouldn't wear it." She put Eileen's blouses in their drawer quickly and slammed the drawer, catching a blouse collar in the process. A sweater she simply tossed on the bed, and stockings were slipped into the same drawer as the bodysuit without hardly opening it.

Eileen watched in silence. She thought this an interesting and conflicted reaction from someone who just the other day gratefully accepted a sexy cocktail dress and wore it for the afternoon. Then it dawned on her that Sarah had not asked where any of Eileen's clothes went. She knew! She must have gone through Eileen's drawers earlier and seen everything before. She knew where everything belonged! The bodysuit routine was an act! Who is this woman?

Sarah slammed the last bureau drawer, turned to Eileen and said, "I'm ready to go downstairs. Do you want to come or stay?"

"You go ahead," Eileen said. She decided to let things cool awhile. "I'll finish my tea here and follow you down later." The morning's session had exhausted her, and the pain in her side had intensified over the last hour. She thought she might even lie down.

"Fine," said Sarah and she started to leave. Stopping at the bedroom door she turned to say, "It's nearly noon. I'll make lunch." She left waiting for no reply.

After about thirty minutes Eileen made her way downstairs. As she approached the living room Sarah called from the kitchen, "Come to the dining room. I have lunch ready."

Eileen went to the table and Sarah set a tall chocolate milkshake in front of her. Sarah sat across from Eileen with a tuna sandwich and a glass of milk. Eileen watched as Sarah bit into the sandwich and chewed with deliberate strokes. Eileen sucked on the straw and savored the bittersweet taste.

After a moment Eileen said, "It's unfortunate that things got a little intense upstairs."

Sarah bit her sandwich and chewed.

Hoping to uncover some of the roots of Sarah's emotional conflicts, Eileen decided she would gently press her to explore some the feelings expressed in the bedroom. Eileen waited until she saw Sarah swallow, then asked, "Is there anything more you'd like to say about it?"

"You want to talk about it? You want to know who else makes me angry?" snapped Sarah. "Okay. You do, that's who."

"Do you want to tell me why?" Eileen had not expected this, although now that it had happened she supposed she should have seen it coming.

"All right," Sarah said slowly, staring into Eileen's eyes. Her stare made Eileen feel almost threatened. Eileen tried to mask whatever might be showing on her face by lifting her milkshake and taking a long draw on the straw.

"Your questions this morning make me angry," Sarah said. "We were getting along pretty well, but now I feel like you're peering at me under a microscope."

"Sarah, I'm sorry, I didn't mean..."

"No. You asked for this, now listen," continued Sarah. "Your husband has been wonderful to me: loving, caring, and a perfect gentleman. But I feel as though you don't trust me, as if you think I'm an interloper." Her eyes filled with tears, but she blinked them back. "I try to be of help, to feed you, to make you more comfortable in your last ... but I'm met with suspicion and cutting remarks – like your snipe at my robe being hunter green."

"You're right, I'm sorry." Eileen was feeling suddenly defensive over Sarah's accusations. She had been suspicious. "I shouldn't have..." Eileen's words were rolled over by Sarah's monologue.

"And your self-pity makes me angry, too," Sarah said.

"Just what do you mean by self-pity?" The remark brought Eileen up short. Her defensiveness turned to anger and she could feel herself lose her composure. But it was as if Eileen had said nothing.

"You're sick," Sarah snapped. "So what? A lot of people get sick, but they don't sing the blues over it. They don't make their husbands pay the price. You don't seem to realize the many blessings you've had in this life. A loving and gentle man, a man who is important in the community, a man who's respected by everyone. And you get that too, just because you're married to him! But, I'm not sure you deserve it!" Sarah's hands slapped the table. "You say you don't obey him," Sarah went on. Her tirade seemed to have no end. "What finer man deserves to have a loving and supportive wife who will obey, who will model for the whole town what it means to be a good Christian wife and mother? Someone who keeps her own name? Or someone who will love him, care for him, stand by him, give him babies?"

"You little bitch!" Eileen exploded. "How dare you try to do this to me!" The pain in Eileen's side felt like a knife piercing her side. But her anger – no, her rage – allowed her to ignore the discomfort for the time being. All she wanted now, ALL she wanted was to hurt this temptress. "I expressed my innermost feelings to you to open myself to you, to offer friendship." Eileen's voice was rising along with her anger. "You respond by taking that and trying to use it to manipulate your way into our lives, into MY life! You behave like I'm all but dead and buried." Eileen stood and braced herself on the table. She could feel the blood pound in her head. "You've set your sights on my life and I won't let you have it. I'm not done living it yet! Now get out. Get out of my house this very instant!"

Sarah sat looking at Eileen in quiet defiance. Her arms folded and resting on the table in front of her she said, "Keegan has not asked me to leave. I think I'll stay until he tells me to leave."

Eileen felt her jaw clench and her grip around the milkshake glass tightened so, that her strength surprised her. She watched herself with dispassionate professional curiosity as if it were someone else who lifted the glass and cocked it by her ear, then let it fly with surprising force and accuracy for Sarah's head.

Sarah's face registered startled shock just before she ducked. The glass shattered across the wall behind her, splattering chocolate milkshake over the formal floral print wallpaper.

"Get out of my house!" Eileen screamed louder than she had ever heard herself before.

Sarah stood at her place and looked across to Eileen. With her eyes narrowed and brow furrowed, and with a low and steady voice she said, "Why won't you die?"

Eileen's chest heaved with her breathing. She returned Sarah's stare and with equally steady voice responded, "So you can't have my life, or my husband."

Sarah went to the hall closet, retrieved her jacket and left through the front door.

Eileen gripped her side, stumbled into the living room, and collapsed on the sofa. Her head was swimming and she began to slip into unconsciousness. Sleep? Faint? She wondered as she fell, fell, fell into the drowning depths of the green sea.

He opened the front door of his house and Chief Erichson was waiting for him.

"Daniel Callahan," Erichson said, "I have a warrant to search your premises for reloaded .308 ammo and any rifle that may discharge same."

"You can't just come bargin' in like…"

Erichson stepped through the front door, stiff arming Callahan to one side. Constable Dirkson trailed behind.

"Don't get in the way, Mr. Callahan," Erichson said, "It would be considered an obstruction of justice and I'd have to arrest you. Go sit down."

Callahan stepped aside, then apparently thought better of it and came around in front of Erichson.

"I haven't done nothin', you don't have a right..."

Erichson placed his palm on Callahan's chest and pushed as he stepped into Callahan moving him backwards towards the sofa. When Callahan's legs backed into the furniture, his rump landed in the seat. Erichson pointed his finger in Callahan's face and leaned over him.

"A search of Mr. Conger's locker at the mill," Erichson said, "revealed a hand written death threat. That note bears your fingerprints. We found a couple of beer cans on Mr. Conger's lawn that also have your finger prints. I imagine I'll find your finger prints in other places where they don't belong. Do you have any explanations?"

"It was just to scare him. The note was just to get him to stop bein' a scab." Sweat sprouted on Callahan's brow.

"How did you get the note into his locker?" the Chief pressed. As long as Callahan was talking, he was willing to listen.

"It wasn't hard. The lockers are a pain in the ass. Most guys disable the locks to make it easy to get in and out. Conger did the same. I just opened it and put the note in his lunch bag." Callahan squirmed in his seat. "It was just supposed to scare him, is all."

"Chief?" Dirkson came to Erichson's side.

"What is it?" Erichson answered.

"We've got a handful of Eddie Conger's reloads," Dirkson said, "and a .308 deer rifle."

"Election is coming up soon boys," Brow Brookhough said as he wiped beer foam from his mouth on his jacket sleeve and slapped the mug back on The Stallions Bar table. "Conger's dead and Callahan looks good for it." He took a cigar from his jacket pocket, removed it from its tin sleeve, snipped off the end and lit it. "Over the next week, beginning Monday, we gotta start making noise about Callahan taking the union down into the sewer with him as he's looking guilty as hell over this Conger thing."

"I dunno, Brow, I think the guys are pretty spooked by Conger's murder." Mickey played with his mug on the table. "I think the less said about it, the better."

"Yeah, me too," chimed in Stretch.

"I didn't ask you idiots to think. This is my campaign, and you're doing what I tell ya. Starting Monday you two guys make noise about Callahan looking good for this murder, remind guys about Conger's kid being Callahan's, the bad blood over the last couple of weeks, the truck fire, all that stuff."

"But maybe Dan didn't do it," Stretch said.

"I don't give a damn who did it," Brow growled at the two. We're gonna make like Callahan did it and I'm going to be the new Union President."

Keegan found it impossible to concentrate on the worship service he was preparing. Eileen's observations of the night before, and his own conflicting impressions of Sarah plagued his mind. He wondered how he would find out what went on at the Lighthouse Church that might help him get a better understanding of Sarah, and the events of the night of the murder. It's certain Weakley won't tell me anything that would help. He'd love to see me accused of his son-in-law's murder.

Grace broke through his ruminations when she called from her office, "Keegan, will you have the worship bulletin ready for me to type and copy this afternoon?"

The secretary, he thought, the secretary at the Lighthouse Church, if they had one, would know. "I'm not sure," Keegan answered, "if I don't have it ready, I'll take care of it myself."

"Not on your life," Grace called back. "I'll be blamed for all of your typos. I'm leaving for lunch, you leave it on my desk and I'll come in early tomorrow to run it off." The lights in Grace's office blinked out and Keegan heard a door close and footfalls pass down the corridor.

Keegan pulled the hymnal over to try to select the week's hymns. Someone will complain about the hymn selection. Someone always does, he thought. I should let the organist select ... The organist! The organist at the Lighthouse, she'd know what was going on! Who's the organist?

The outside door to fellowship hall slammed shut. Keegan spun around in his chair and ran to his window and opened it. "Grace!" he shouted.

Grace stopped in her tracks on the sidewalk and looked through the overgrown shrubs in the direction of his voice. "Yes?"

"Who's the organist?"

She put her hands on her hips in the way women do when they want to call you a foolish child but don't and said, "You know very well who our organist is, Keegan O'Connor."

"Yes, yes," Keegan responded, exasperated with his own lack of clarity, "I mean, who's the organist over at the Lighthouse?"

"Oh," said Grace, "that's Leona Thomas, and she plays the piano. They don't have an organ over at the Lighthouse. Everybody knows that." And she left.

Keegan looked up the Thomas' address in the phone book, found it on Roger's Rock Road, and headed out to pay a visit.

Leona Thomas answered the door before Keegan was finished knocking on it. "Yes?" she said.

Keegan introduced himself then said, "I hope you'll forgive the intrusion, but I'm trying to piece together the events of the evening of November fifth, when Eddie Conger was murdered. I believe it will aid me in helping Sarah Conger cope with the tragedy."

"Sarah Conger already has a pastor." Leona Thomas's voice matched the mid-November chill.

"I understand," he said, "and I have no designs on Pastor Weakley's sheep." He decided to remove his cap for effect and try a little lingo of the religious right. "But I thought maybe you'd be willing to help your very troubled sister in Christ. You'd extend to her your right hand of fellowship in her time of need, wouldn't you?"

"Of course, Pastor Keegan," she said. Her face softened and her voice sounded more inviting when she added, "But I wouldn't want Pastor Weakley to think I was helping a Methodist convert his daughter." She stood aside and motioned for Keegan to enter.

"I understand your reservation," Keegan said as he stepped inside to a small and neat living room. On a coffee table too big for the room, in front of a love seat, rested a pulpit sized Bible. Up against the far wall was a very old Wurlitzer upright piano that reminded him of the one that sat in his piano teacher's house in Schenectady when he was a child taking lessons. "Thank you for being so gracious to a fellow pilgrim." After having said the last, he wondered if he might have laid it on a bit thick in his attempt to speak their language.

"Please have a seat, Pastor. How may I help our sister Sarah?"

Keegan sat in a rocking chair close to the front door while Leona Thomas sat on the piano bench. "I don't have a specific request," Keegan said, "I was hoping you could simply tell me the story of that night, and I might hear something that would help. Would you do that?"

"Hmm," she intoned, crossing her legs and shifting her considerable bulk on the bench, causing it to creak a plaintive protest. She folded her arms, rested them on her bosom and stared at the wall over Keegan's head. "Let me think," she said. "That was the night I arrived about on time, and Pastor Weakley about bit my head off."

"Oh?" Keegan said.

"He was in a terrible anxious mood," Leona said. She looked to be settling in for some gossip. "Anyway, I remember Sarah coming in to practice late with Miss Berkley. I remember because I gave them both a stern look for disturbing the others. I have a hard and fast rule about starting choir practice on time, and Pastor's daughter or not you're expected to be there. And that goes for old Miss Berkley, too. It doesn't matter to the lord if you're eighty-two or not, he..."

"I'm sure the Lord is quite a disciplinarian," broke in Keegan, "but maybe we could return to the topic."

Leona returned both feet to the floor and wiggled back and forth on the bench as if to work herself into the hard wood. "Hmph, well, as I was saying, Sarah came in late. She flummoxed her choir music, dropped papers, sang off key, and was generally useless to us or to God for the night."

Then Leona Thomas put her hands on her hips and leaned forward to say, "Then, as if the evening hadn't gone poorly enough already, in comes waltzing Jean Fremont, and she's all abuzz about pickets in front of the Conger house – you know that Eddie Conger was a scab, don't you – well anyway Jean starts telling what she saw, and no amount of dirty looks from me was going to settle her down. So, I had to just let her run her course and hope that there would still be time for me to rehearse the choir. Do you have any idea how difficult it is to rehearse a choir with all that commotion going on, well I'll tell you..."

"Please, Mrs. Thomas, tell me about Sarah." The woman's pace was making Keegan dizzy.

"Well," said Leona Thomas, settling back into her arms-across-bosom posture, "She was pretty upset by the news. It's only understandable. After all, can you imagine what it must be like having a bunch of rowdies picketing your house? Sarah stayed a little while longer, but her singing didn't improve any. She must have realized that herself, because after a bit she just got up and left. She didn't say good-bye, or excuse me, or anything. Just up and left. Well, I suppose we can excuse her being impolite under the circumstances, with her husband dead and all. Although, she didn't know he was dead at the time, did she? Nooo. She was simply impolite because she was. Isn't it awful how people have become so impolite these days, why I think it's terrible, terrible I say, when you consider..."

"Mrs. Thomas, about Sarah?" Keegan expected to be labeled impolite himself by the time Mrs. Thomas began reporting this conversation. "Are you aware of anything else that she may have said or done that evening that might help me understand?"

Leona Thomas got that far-off look in her eyes as she looked over Keegan's head. "No ... no, nothing comes to mind. After she left, that's all there was to it until I read in the papers about the murder. Wasn't that just awful? Talk about being impolite. Imagine coming into a man's home and killing him. Impolite? My God that's impolite!"

Keegan got up and walked towards the door. Leona Thomas followed along, continuing her running commentary on the godlessness of the community. When he got to the door he turned around and offered his hand to thank the Lighthouse piano player when he thought to ask, "You said Pastor Weakley was agitated that evening. Do you know why?"

"He said he was going to be off at some business or other, probably old man Berkley who was drunk on the steps by the time Sarah left choir rehearsal."

"Old man Berkley?"

"Miss Berkley, you know, the woman that came in late with Sarah. Her worthless brother was drunk again that night, and sitting on the church steps for all the world to see. I think he does that just to embarrass Miss Berkley. And the way that old woman takes care of her brother. She keeps him at her house near the end of this road, out by Roger's Rock on the lake. Poor old woman, all the way out there all alone, with only a drunk for company. Anyway, Pastor Weakley sometimes sits up all night with him trying to sober him up and lead him to the Lord. I'm sure that man is a constant disappointment to both Pastor and to the Almighty. Why, I think that man's been a drunk all of his life. Satan got hold of him early on, Pastor, you know how Satan does that to a man, well I suspect he got hold of old man Berkley long ago when..."

"Thank you, Mrs. Thomas," Keegan said as he bent over to take the woman's hand from her hip and pump it a few times. "You've been most helpful. I shouldn't take up any more of your time," he continued without taking a breath and moving out of the door. "I'm sure you've got some practicing to do for the Lord, and I better be about his business as well. He continued to talk as he made his way down the walk towards his car, "You know what they say about idle time and the devil's workshop, well I'd better be off now, so long, and thanks again." When Keegan got to his car, he immediately started the engine and backed out of the driveway, fearful the woman would begin to relate some other bit of irrelevant trivia and follow after him.

200

Since Leona Thomas said that the Berkley duo lived out by Roger's Rock, Keegan decided to run out to the end of the road to see if he could find them.

About a tenth of a mile before the road ended, Keegan found the Berkley mailbox. It stood rusted and cocked to one side with its door hung slack-jaw open. At the end of a dirt driveway, mostly grown over, were the remnants of a once proud lake home. The house had been battered bare of paint by the storms that came out of the south up the lake. Keegan pulled into the drive. Split gray clapboards hung from rusted nails. The yard had gone to seed years before. Were it not for the 1965 Ford Fairlane sitting in the back yard, one would assume it was an abandoned property.

The man who greeted Keegan at the door looked to be a weathered man in his seventies. The veins in his nose glowed the telltale neon of a problem drinker. Keegan introduced himself and was surprised when the man said, "Come in. Always glad to meet another man of the cloth. Name's Clarence."

Clarence led the way from the back door into the kitchen. He called up a set of stairs, "Phoebe! Phoebe! We've got a guest! Come on down and meet one of your kind!" He turned back to Keegan and said, "Set yourself down, preacher. It's long past lunch time, but I haven't et yet. Like a sandwich?"

Keegan, still standing just inside the door, took an instant liking to the old man. His stomach grumbled at the suggestion of food and he accepted the offer.

"Good," the old man said, "go on and set yourself at the table there, I'll getcha something." Clarence rummaged through the fridge and the kitchen cabinets.

Keegan could hear halting footfalls on the second floor. As those footfalls made their way down the stairs, Clarence returned to the table with a loaf of bread, a package of Oscar Mayer mystery meat, mustard, a sandwich plate and table knife. He spread them out over the table and said, "There ya go, preacher, use what ya need. I'll join you in a minute, mother nature calls." Clarence left the kitchen and moved down a short hall to the first door on the left. Keegan began to make himself a sandwich.

An ancient woman entered the kitchen from the stairs and stood at the bottom stair looking at Keegan. He stood to greet her and said, "Hello, I'm..."

"Oh, I know who you are, Pastor O'Connor." She waved him down and said, "Sit, sit." She moved towards the table and said, "The town's much too small for me not to know who you are." As she sat down and looked over the table setting, she clicked her tongue and remarked, "I see Clarence has been his usual gracious self." She stood again and offered, "Shall I at least make a pot of coffee, or brew you a cup of tea?"

At that, Clarence flushed the toilet, opened the door down the hall and called out to the kitchen as he walked towards them, "The only brew a man's interested in, is in the fridge." Standing at the fridge Clarence asked, "Ya want a beer, preacher?"

"Sure, that sounds like a fine idea." Keegan decided the old man was trying to shock his clergy sensitivities. He winked at Phoebe to his left, and turned his head to greet Clarence on his right and said, "But none of that light stuff."

Clarence brought his head up and raised both eyebrows. "Well, I'll be damned..."

"You probably will be," Phoebe said.

"... a real man for a preacher," Clarence finished. He pulled two beer cans from the fridge and plunked them on the kitchen table. "Nothing fancy, preacher, just a Bud."

"A Bud will do fine, thanks." Keegan popped the top and offered the can up, to which Clarence responded by sideswiping it with his own can in a casual toast.

Clarence seated himself, looked over at Phoebe and while nodding at Keegan said, "Keep this one, Sis, he's okay."

"He's not ours to keep, you old drunk, he's the Methodist pastor in town."

"Pity," Clarence said, knocking back his beer. Looking at Keegan, he said, "I thought you Methodists were a no dancin', no gamblin', no drinkin', no-damn-fun-at-all sort."

Tabling his own beer after washing down a bit of sandwich Keegan said, "Traditionally, that's us. But some of us were not always Methodist and we bring some of our sinful ways with us. Which brings me to the reason for my visit."

Clarence's countenance fell dramatically and he said, "Damn. Another one come to save my soul. Well, have at it preacher, better men than you have tried."

Keegan brushed some crumbs from his beard and said, "My purpose is a little different from that."

Clarence brightened.

"If you're willing, I'd like to discuss the evening of November fifth when Eddie Conger was murdered."

Phoebe, who by now had brewed herself a cup of tea and had returned to the table asked, "What's your interest in this, Pastor?"

"Sarah has turned to us for support," Keegan said, fixing his gaze on the old woman. "We're trying to help her, not interfere with the Lighthouse congregation."

"It must be difficult," Phoebe said as she stirred her tea, "to go to your pastor for help when he's also your father." She tapped her spoon on the rim of her cup as if she'd made a decision and said, "I'm glad she's found spiritual guidance in this time of trouble. We'll help any way we can."

Clarence clunked his can on the table and said, "I won't tell you a thing." He leaned over in Keegan's direction and smiled. "I was completely drunk. Don't remember a thing. Want another beer, preacher?"

"No thanks," said Keegan, one's my limit."

"Something you should learn," Phoebe said to her brother.

"Maybe," Keegan said to Phoebe, "you'd begin by telling me anything at all you can remember about that night."

Phoebe sipped her tea then said, "Sarah and I arrived together a few minutes late for choir practice that night. The queen bee, that's Leona Thomas our pianist, made sure we knew she didn't appreciate our tardiness. Screw her."

Keegan was startled by Phoebe's last comment, and an expression of surprise must have blushed over his face because Phoebe said, "Sorry about that. Too many years living alone with a coarse-talking drunk."

Clarence grunted and popped open his second beer.

"Sarah seemed distracted all evening," Phoebe continued. "She had a serious case of the dropsy's. First her hymnal hit the floor, then her sheet music, then she spilled her purse out. She was a wreck. I suppose the strike had her on edge – it does most of us."

"Not me," Clarence quipped and knocked back his beer.

"Pay no attention to him," Phoebe said and touched Keegan's hand. "It only encourages his nonsense." She withdrew her hand and continued, "Jean Fremont came into practice nearly an hour late filled with the news that picketers were marching outside Sarah's house. In no time, rehearsal was shot as everyone was listening to Jean tell what she saw. Leona was so angry she about popped. It was kind of funny to watch. But poor Sarah was so distressed by the news that she left shortly. As a matter of fact, when she left the building, I could see Clarence here sitting on the church steps drunk as usual."

"So she tells me," Clarence added with a grin spreading across his ruddy face. His eyes were taking on the heavy look of a drunk's returning buzz.

Keegan turned to Clarence, hoping it wasn't too late to ask him some questions. "What do you remember, Clarence? Or when do you begin to remember that evening?"

"Want another beer, preacher?" Clarence started to get up but Keegan grabbed his arm.

"No," said Keegan, "and I wish you wouldn't until we finish talking. I need what little of your sobriety is left."

"Whoa!" exclaimed Clarence, "That feels like I was hit by a truck!" He sat back down, looked at Keegan and said, "Okay, preacher. Since you can shoot straight, so can I. I don't remember when I left home that night. I probably started drinking about eleven or noon, like today. I'm a little late getting started today, I've got some catchin' up to do. I was no doubt too drunk to eat supper, and didn't care. I don't remember leaving home, and I don't remember sitting on the church steps; but then, I never remember sitting on the church steps and my Sis here says that's where I end up a lot. I don't remember when Pastor Weakley came and got me, and I don't remember when we got to the Stewart's Ice Cream Shop." He stopped, raised his fist to his sternum, beat his chest three or four times and let loose with a mighty belch. "Ah, that's better. Room for another beer."

Keegan glared at the old man and said nothing.

"No, eh?" Clarence said. "Okay. I do remember coming around at Stewart's about ten o'clock or so. Weakley, God love the man, he keeps trying to reform this ol' drunk with the Almighty, coffee and donuts. He filled me with so much coffee I pissed the bed that night. Weakley can be a pain in my ass from time to time. Anyway, he brought me home about eleven or so – Sis would know better about that. I went to bed and didn't wake up 'til nine or ten the next morning when Sis told me the radio said the Conger boy had been killed. End of story."

"So," Keegan said and shrugged, "you're telling me that from sometime after noon, maybe one or two, to about ten that night, you remember nothing?"

"Yup."

"No conversations? No faces come to mind? No sensation about where you were or with whom you might have been?"

Clarence scratched at his head and ran his hand down the back of his neck. "Well," he said, "sometime before Stewart's, I remember being warm and cozy. All snuggled up. Like someone was tuckin' me in a couch or a bed for a nap. But, that's about all."

Keegan thanked his host and hostess for lunch and conversation and made his excuses for leaving. Both of the Berkleys escorted him to the kitchen door. As Keegan stepped out, the old man called, "Hey preacher."

Keegan stopped at his car door and turned around.

"Drop by again," Clarence said, "we'll pop another."

"Thanks," said Keegan, "I may just do that." He slipped into the car, started the engine, waved to the old siblings, and backed out of the drive.

It was after two in the afternoon, and Keegan knew Eileen would be looking for him soon. As he drove back into the village along Roger's Rock Road he came up on The Lighthouse Church. Keegan suddenly had a strong impulse to pull over across the street from the church and park.

The sign in front of the church was inexpertly hand painted, and announced *Sunday School 9 AM; Divine Worship 11 AM Sunday; Prayer Meeting 7 PM Sunday; Pastor William Weakley, Shepherd.* The building needed paint and repairs, but no more than most white clapboard Methodist churches. The house to the left of the church also had a sign, obviously painted by the same hand as the church sign. It read *Church parsonage, ALL WELCOME.* I'll bet I'm not, thought Keegan.

He got out of the car and walked over to the front stairs of the church. He didn't know what he was looking for, but felt compelled to examine them. He climbed the steps and tried the front door. It was locked. He stepped down one level and sat on the top landing. What am I looking for? he wondered.

He leaned against the hand railing and wondered how long Clarence had sat there on November fifth. Then it occurred to him that from where he was seated, the doors of the church would hit him when opened. No one from inside would be able to see him because he'd be behind the door, squished up against the hand rail. He scooted away from the door and down a stair and sat there. At this place he would not be hit, and when the door swung open, those inside would be able to see someone sitting on the steps.

Keegan looked around and saw nothing remarkable. You could see the entire street looking south towards Amherst Avenue and the village. He had essentially the same view looking north – the whole street and all of the houses for a hundred yards or so.

From this vantage point, Keegan noticed that he could see the front door of the parsonage, but the side door near the back of the house was out of view. Movement at the front window attracted his eye and Keegan saw Bill Weakley watching him through the parsonage front window. Even from this distance, Weakley's anger showed on his face. In the words of a neat old lady, screw him.

He got up and moved to the yard between the church and the parsonage. He expected Weakley to come flying out of the house to chase him off with some scriptural threats of hellfire and damnation, but nothing happened.

As he moved to the back of the church, the back of the Conger home came into view through a tangle of weeds and brush. A well-beaten path between the properties existed. Keegan followed it.

The path opened up into the Conger backyard. He was facing the backside of the house and a single stall garage. The windows of the porch had been replaced and someone had slapped some fresh white paint on some of the clapboards. The paint didn't match, and something was bleeding through the fresh coat. It looked like spray painted graffiti. Probably something left by the strikers, or some kids after the fact. As he moved closer, he could make out some of the nearly foot-tall letters, then all of the letters: *BURN IN HELL.* It struck Keegan as an odd thing for the strikers to write about a scab. Not kids.

Keegan made his way around the house. First he went down the side between the house and garage, then around front past the porch, and back down the other side. There was little to notice other than the fact that the foundation windows all had neat little curtains that were drawn shut. All except the curtains on the last window he passed at the rear of the house. Keegan stopped at the window, removed a glove and dropped it on the ground, and placed his knee on it so he could get down and peer into the cellar window. From here he could get a clear line of sight of Eddie's workbench. Anybody could have killed him from here, Keegan thought. But, they would have had to break or open the window first. With his nose close to the ground he caught a whiff of an old stale cigar butt. He found a squashed butt with a Macanudo label. He picked it up to scrutinize it.

"I'll take that," a voice stated from behind Keegan, startling him so that he nearly dropped the butt.

Chief Erichson held out a plastic baggie and indicated that Keegan was to drop the cigar butt into it.

"Are you looking for me?" Keegan asked.

"Nope. I found you."

Keegan stood and brushed himself off. He furrowed his brow and asked, "What for?"

"Oh, I always find it interesting to see the Methodist minister in town wandering around the Apostolic church. And then I find it even more interesting that you seem to be visiting the Conger house on Benedict Street by way of Roger's Rock Road. Wouldn't you find that interesting if you were me?"

"Maybe so, Chief," Keegan responded, "but you're steering a course for the wrong port. Navigate by the lighthouse." He left the Chief, returned to his car, and headed home.

On the way home, Keegan decided to stop by the Stewart's shop on the off chance that someone might have seen Clarence. He pulled into the lot and walked into the convenience store. He sat on one of the low-backed stools at the counter and waited for the girl behind the counter to finish ringing out another customer.

"What would you like?" she asked. Her name tag read SALLY and bore a small ribbon proclaiming EMPLOYEE OF THE MONTH.

"I think coffee would hit the spot, Sally," Keegan said.

She went off and returned with a large brown mug, a spoon, a napkin, and a fresh pot of java. She placed everything before Keegan with practiced time saving moves and poured his coffee.

"Excuse me, Sally," Keegan started, "but you didn't happen to work the night of the murder, did you?"

"Oh, wasn't that gawd-awful?" she said and covered her mouth over the horror of it. "The police scanner on the counter had the whole store talking about it that night."

"So you were working that night?" Keegan took a long sip of the steamy coffee. He could feel it brace his weary body. Another customer entered and sat two stools down from Keegan.

"Just a minute," Sally said, "I'll be right back." She left to serve the other who requested coffee and a Danish, then came back to finish her conversation with Keegan.

"Do you know who Pastor Weakley is?" Keegan asked.

"Oh sure," she said. She stood holding the coffee pot. "He's the Lighthouse preacher. A nice man, but a little scary. All those Bible tracts."

"Bible tracts?"

"He leaves a different one on the counter every time he's in."

"Do you remember whether or not Pastor Weakley was in here on the night of the murder?" Keegan drained his mug and Sally filled it again immediately.

She put the pot on the counter and screwed up her face in thought. "Yeah, come to think of it. He brought the drunk in that night too. He brings the same drunk in here from time to time to try to sober him up. It doesn't seem to work."

"About what time would you say he got in?" Keegan took another long drink from the mug. Sally moved to warm it, but Keegan covered the mug with his hand signaling enough.

"I'd say it was around nine, or a little after. It was just before Mr. Forest came in with some of the men from the funeral home after calling hours. I remember that 'cause I remember thinking how ironic it was to have a bunch of funeral guys in here getting coffee just as we were hearing about another funeral needing doin'."

Erichson saw Keegan pull away from the curb as he made his way towards the cruiser from between the Lighthouse Church and the parsonage. After he got in he pulled the cigar stub from his pocket and looked at it through the plastic bag. He tossed it on the seat next to him, started the Blazer and sped off. Inside of five minutes he was cruising the picket line at the mill, looking for Mickey Miles. Spying his target, he pulled over and waved Mickey to the car. As Mickey approached the cruiser the chief powered the passenger window down.

"Chief, what's up?" asked Mickey after leaning on the window sill with his elbows and peering into the cruiser.

"Just a quick question, Mickey."

"Yeah, sure."

"On the night Conger was murdered. Did any of the guys smoke cigars?"

"Oh, sure, Chief. Brow smokes some fancy ten dollar cigar. He thinks it makes him look like a union president."

"Have you seen him today?"

"I saw him earlier, about noon. He was making noise about needing a new union president, how we needed someone who could lead, not poke another man's wife, and how he was the right one for the job. Union president, that is, not the poking part. I haven't seen him for the last couple of hours or so."

"Thanks, Mickey. You've been helpful." The chief dropped the cruiser into gear and headed back to the village.

When Keegan got home at ten minutes after three he found Eileen in the living room, curled up on the sofa, in tears. He knelt by her side and asked what the problem was.

"Sarah and I had a real blow-out," Eileen said, wiping her eyes with the handkerchief Keegan handed her. "I was gently questioning her, or at least I thought I was, about the night of Eddie's murder. I thought I could help her deal with some of her feelings."

Keegan sat on the floor. "I take it she didn't respond well to your questions."

"Actually, things went pretty well for the first half hour or so," Eileen said and sniffed. "But later on, when the conversation turned to you, she turned into a shrew, an evil tempered shrew! Do you realize that woman wants my life? MY life! And she wants you to go along with it."

Keegan looked at his wife and with a smirk asked, "Do you think you might have gotten a touch of the green-eyed monster with your last chemo treatment?"

Eileen sat up, reached over and grabbed her husband's shirt collar, leaned into his face and said, "That woman is waiting for me to die."

NOVEMBER 15TH
SATURDAY

Keegan awoke to the sounds of Eileen vomiting in the bathroom down the hall. He rolled over and reached for his glasses on the nightstand and slipped them on so he could make out the time on the radio alarm. Seven-twelve. He rolled onto his back and listened to the blood throb in his ears as last night's headache crept up the back of his neck and over the top to his frontal lobe. That third Manhattan before bed had not been a good idea.

Eileen appeared in the bedroom door, steadying herself on the jamb. "Keegan," she said, "help me to bed. I think I may fall."

Keegan threw the covers off and leaped out of bed to Eileen's side. Taking her by the elbow, and with his other arm around her waist, he led her to the bed and gently eased her down.

"I'm calling Eli," he said, "you should be recovering from the effects of the chemo by now."

"You'll only get the exchange," she said. She grimaced as she swung her legs up. "Eli's not in yet. It's too early."

"I'll ask the answering service to call him at home as soon as possible. He needs to see you." Keegan picked up the bedroom phone and made his call while watching Eileen.

Her eyes were more jaundiced, she was still losing weight. She was getting weaker and vomiting more often. Keegan finished speaking with the exchange and was assured the doctor would be notified as soon as possible. He hung up and sat on the edge of the bed and reached out to caress Eileen's head. Her scarf was gone, and Keegan realized that it was the first time Eileen had permitted herself to be seen without her head covered. She was ebbing to a new low.

"The doctor will call. I'll go fix us some breakfast," Keegan said as he rose to his feet.

"Don't bother for me," she said, "unless you want to be changing the bed clothes."

"I'll chance it. You need to eat."

As Keegan prepared a breakfast he hoped would break through his wife's nausea, his mind sailed between concern for Eileen and his curiosity about Sarah and her conversation with Eileen the day before. He wondered how it all fit, or if it fit at all.

The coffee started to drip and Keegan had the bacon frying. He recalled that Sarah was pretty badly bruised when he first met her and wondered if she could have killed her husband? He turned the bacon and grease spattered on his hands.

"Ow! Damn!" He put the lid back on the frying pan. Did Sarah think her life was threatened, he wondered. Or the lives of her children? Could she have killed out of self defense?

Keegan pulled the pan off the burner, placed the bacon on paper towels to soak up the grease, and drained the pan grease into an empty milk carton on the counter. What about the books on the end table? Insights? He popped two frozen waffles in the toaster and cracked three eggs in the frying pan. Surely Chief Erichson has thought of all of this.

He scrambled the eggs in the pan. Yeah, the Chief has thought of this and rejected it. He thinks I did it!

The waffles popped up. He placed one on each plate, then scooped out about one egg's worth of scramble for Eileen and two for himself. He poured honey over his waffle and placed the plate along with two cups of coffee on a tray to take upstairs. Moving to the fridge, Keegan opened the freezer, removed the chocolate ice cream, and placed a big scoop of Breyer's in the middle of Eileen's waffle.

When Keegan returned to the bedroom, he found Eileen propped up against the headboard sound asleep. He placed the tray on the nightstand next to her and gently touched her as he called her name. She jerked awake, opened her eyes and smiled at him. "I guess I dozed off."

"I guess so. Breakfast is ready." He put the bed tray they kept in the room over Eileen's lap and placed her breakfast in front of her.

She looked at the tray and back to Keegan. "Waffle a la mode?"

"Thought I'd try a little something different," he said, feeling a little like a child hoping to please mom on mother's day with fledgling culinary skills.

Eileen shook her head, lifted her fork, and as she examined the melting mound on her waffle said with a wan smile, "It actually appeals to me," and she began to eat.

211

The two ate their meals in silence. With something on his stomach, Keegan decided to get the Tylenol from his sport coat pocket to kill the headache. He dropped the last two from the small bottle into his hand and downed them with the last of his coffee. He went to the bathroom medicine cabinet to replenish the pocket bottle from the larger container. He emptied the last four tablets into the smaller bottle and tossed the larger container into the wastebasket, making a mental note to stop by the pharmacy to pick up a fresh supply on the way home.

While Keegan was in the bathroom preparing for the day, the phone rang and he heard Eileen answer it. When he returned to the bedroom he asked who had called.

"Eli," Eileen said. "He questioned me over the phone. He said he'd stop by between eleven this morning and one in the afternoon."

"Good," said Keegan, sitting on the edge of his side of the bed to tie his shoes. "How are you if I go to the office and work on my sermon for a couple of hours?"

"I'll be fine," said Eileen, "but I think I'm going to stay up here for a while. I didn't sleep well last night, and I want to nap some." She settled in under the covers and added, "Will you come home before Eli gets here? I'd like you to hear whatever he has to say."

"Certainly." Keegan looked around to his wife and saw for the first time ever, a hint of fear in her eyes. "Of course, I'll be here." They looked lovingly at one another for a moment and Keegan asked, "Are you sure it's okay for me to leave you? I can stay until after Eli comes."

"No, go ahead, Keeg," she said, "depending on what Eli says, I may not want to let you go this afternoon."

Keegan leaned over to kiss her and whispered, "I love you."

"I know," she whispered, and closed her eyes.

Keegan cleared the tray away and headed downstairs for the kitchen and out for the church. With hat and coat on, he walked out the front door and closed it behind him. He heard the lock fall into place and stopped.

Damn, he thought, if Eli gets here before I do, he won't be able to get in. Keegan unlocked the door and went back into the house to the kitchen. On scrap paper he wrote a note, peeled off a strip of tape from a roll in the drawer, returned to the front door and hung it in the window. The note read, ELI – COME ON IN. Keegan set the door bolt open, closed the door behind him and walked to the church.

Eileen had been in and out of a light sleep most of the morning when she thought she heard the front door open and close. The radio alarm read ten-fifty.

"Eli?" she called from her bed. "I'm upstairs!"

There was no answer. She waited a moment and then heard kitchen noises.

"Keegan?" She waited. "Keegan," she called again. "Is that you?"

The noises stopped and she heard footfalls go to the back staircase that led from the kitchen to the back end of the upstairs hall. The staircase door opened, and a voice called up, "Eileen! It's me, Sarah! I've come with a peace offering. I'll be up in a minute!"

Sarah? Why did she come? Eileen reached for the phone and dialed Keegan's church study. It rang once, then twice, then three times and four. "Hi. You've reached Grace United Methodist Church..."

Eileen tried to interrupt, "Keegan, Sarah's here, come home."

"... where no one is available to take your call just now," continued Keegan's voice on the recorded message. "If you'd leave a..." Eileen hung up.

She dialed Eli's number. While she waited for someone to answer she wondered what she would say. Eli, come quick, I'm afraid of Sarah? Why am I afraid? The receptionist answered the phone, "Doctor Shapiro's office."

"Is Eli available, this is Eileen Letterman."

"I'm sorry," said the voice, "the doctor is making house calls. Shall I ask him to call you when he returns?"

From the kitchen, the sound of the blender whirred and stopped.

"Please page him on his beeper." Eileen's mind buzzed with excuses. She settled on, "I'm feeling much worse than when I called this morning. Tell him I need him. Now."

The sound of the blender roared once again.

"I'll see what I can do, Ms. Letterman," the receptionist said. "Will that be all?"

"Yes." Eileen knew the voice had little or no intention of paging Eli. "Please hurry. It's urgent." She hung up and believed that the receptionist would do nothing.

Sarah appeared in the bedroom door. "I behaved badly yesterday," she said. She was dressed in slacks and turtleneck sweater, and stood holding the same tray upon which Keegan had brought her breakfast. "I wanted to make amends." Sarah stepped into the room and placed the tray on the bed in front of Eileen.

On the tray sat a large frosty chocolate milkshake and a large slice of chocolate layer cake with thick dark chocolate frosting. The aroma of the desserts made Eileen's mouth water. It seemed only the heavy sweet flavor of the chocolate managed to break through the dulling effect of the chemo treatments on her sense of taste. But, amends?

Eileen looked up at Sarah and asked, "How did you get in?"

"Oh, the door was open. A note said to come on in, so I did," Sarah said as she sat at the foot of the bed.

Eileen looked over the tray and returned her gaze to Sarah and said, "This is all very thoughtful, but I don't think what happened yesterday can be fixed with cake and a milkshake."

"I know," Sarah said with a downward look and a slight pout. "Maybe you'll give me another chance." She looked up at Eileen's face with anguished eyes. "I'm so sorry for what I said. I couldn't sleep last night. I know how much you like my shakes, and I thought maybe we could begin again."

Sarah wore such a pathetic look that Eileen found herself forgiving the hurtful remarks of the day before.

"Apology accepted," Eileen said, "but you join me. Go get yourself a piece of cake and tea, and we'll begin again."

Sarah smiled at Eileen's acceptance and left for the kitchen. Eileen picked up the fork and dipped into the rich looking chocolate cake.

The week's sermon was not forming well for Keegan. His mind was too distracted to concentrate on *Blessed Are Those Who Mourn*, his topic for the week. He pushed himself away from his desk and moved out into Grace's office where he had a pot of coffee on. As he poured his fourth for the morning the wall clock chimed eleven bells.

"Damn," Keegan said, looking up at the clock and spilling coffee over his wrist. "I should be home by now."

He put the pot and cup down, turned the Mr. Coffee off and went back into his study to grab his hat and coat. If I'm lucky, he thought, Eli will be his usual late self and I'll have time to drop by the pharmacy on my way home.

Keegan headed north on Lake George Avenue, then west up Amherst to the pharmacy across the street from Saint Ann's rectory. He breezed into the shop, picked up a box of Band-Aids and a five hundred count bottle of acetaminophen tablets and brought them to the counter.

"Howdy do, Rev?" greeted Dale, the pharmacist at that location for more than fifty years.

"Fine, Dale, and yourself?" responded Keegan.

"Oh fine, thanks," Dale said as he rang up the Band-Aids. He picked up the large plastic bottle of acetaminophen and said, "You can put these back, Rev, you don't need 'em."

Keegan screwed up his face at Dale and asked, "What makes you say that?"

"Sarah Conger was waiting for me this morning on the sidewalk to open up," Dale said, leaning on his cash register. "By the way, that's awful nice of you folks taking care of her, with Ms. Letterman so ill and all. I hope her pain is better. Oh, yeah, that's why Sarah was here. She said your missus was in pain and needed quite a bit of Tylenol to help her cope. I sold her the same five hundred count generic stuff..."

Eileen! Acetaminophen! Pain in her side! LIVER pain! My God! Keegan ran down the aisles of the pharmacy leaving Dale in mid-sentence, "... you got here. It's a real money saver. Hey, what about your Band-Aids?"

Keegan ran up Amherst Avenue to Flintlock and headed south towards his home and Eileen. Please, dear God, let it only be Eileen. Don't let Sarah be there, he prayed. As he passed people on the sidewalk they looked at him as if a madman had just passed them by. His coat tails drifted behind him, and he was heedless to the fact that his hat fell off his head. It was only a quarter mile, three-eighths at the most. But Keegan had not been all that fond of calisthenics. With a tenth of a mile to go, he was straining for breath. His heart was pounding from exertion, or adrenaline, or both. As his home came into view he found his feet hitting the pavement harder and faster until he burst through his front door yelling "Eileen!"

There was no answer.

He raced into the living room. No Eileen. He screamed her name again and heard only silence. He went into the kitchen and saw the blender on the counter. Next to it stood an open five hundred count bottle of acetaminophen. White powder was on the counter top. Keegan wet his finger and touched the powder, then lifted it to his tongue hoping for the sweetness of sugar. It was bitter. He pulled out a tablet from the bottle and tasted it. The same!

"Eileen!" he screamed and pulled open the door to the back staircase and raced up the stairs to the bedroom.

There he found Eileen stretched out on the bed and Sarah standing over her. Sarah looked over at Keegan. She wore a smile reminiscent of the one she wore at Eddie's wake.

"Doesn't she look peaceful?" Sarah said. "She's at rest now."

Keegan pushed Sarah aside and picked up Eileen's wrist and searched for a pulse. He could feel none. He put his ear to Eileen's chest. He could hear a heartbeat, faint, thready and irregular. Her breathing was shallow.

He jumped over the bed to the nightstand on his side and picked up the phone.

"What are you doing, Keegan?" asked Sarah. Her look was confused, somewhere between concern or worry and pouting.

Keegan focused on the phone and dialed 911.

"What are you doing, my love?" Sarah insisted, moving closer. The pout was coming through.

Dispatch answered. Sarah moved out of Keegan's view.

"This is an emergency!" Keegan shouted into the phone. "Send an ambulance to seventy-seven..."

The phone went dead. Keegan turned to see Sarah holding the phone cord freshly ripped out of the wall.

"She's at rest now, dear," Sarah said as if instructing a child. "You need to let her go. It's our time to be together now."

"You poor sick bitch," Keegan said with a mixture of contempt and pity. He couldn't believe what he was hearing. He ran down the hall and down the stairs back into the kitchen where he dialed 911 and successfully called for help.

Keegan ran back up the stairs to the bedroom and found Sarah holding his pillow over Eileen's face. He ran to Sarah, grabbed her by the arm and flung her across the room. Eileen was blue. He put his ear to her chest once again and heard nothing.

"You've killed her!" Keegan pulled the pillow out from under Eileen's head. Then he balled his fists over her sternum and began to administer CPR.

Sarah stood off to the side as if a panicked child who had witnessed a terrible accident.

"Keegan, you've got to stop," Sarah pleaded. "Let her go! She wants to die. She wants you to have a whole woman for the rest of your life!"

The bed didn't offer enough resistance to Keegan's efforts at massaging Eileen's heart. He pulled her lifeless body to the floor and began to pump her chest. He stopped, knelt by her head and, holding her nostrils, breathed into her lungs. "Live, Eileen, live!"

"You're mine now!" Sarah screamed. "She's dead, it's my turn!"

Keegan looked up at Sarah as he pumped Eileen's chest, wanting to keep an eye out for her.

"Let me love you," she shouted. "You deserve a woman who will stand by you. A woman who will obey her husband." She cupped her breasts with her hands and called, "A woman who can smother you in affection and love, a woman who can give you babies and feed them with mother's milk."

Keegan blew into Eileen's lungs.

"You've - got - to - stop!" Sarah shrieked and shoved him with such force that he flew off Eileen and slammed into the nightstand. His scalp tore open on the corner of the stand and he began to bleed down the side of his face.

"Oh my God, I'm sorry!" screamed Sarah. She held her hands over her mouth in horror. "I didn't mean to hurt you, Eddie!" She moved to Keegan's side and tried to daub at his wound with facial tissue.

Keegan put his hand squarely in the center of Sarah's chest. "Get away from me," he growled and pushed as hard as he could. From her crouching position over him she flew backwards and smashed into the wall, cracking the plaster and bringing down a framed photo of the Ticonderoga waterfalls.

Keegan returned to administering CPR on Eileen. "I'm not ready for you to leave me, Eileen. I love you! Come back!"

"I love you too," Sarah cooed from where she landed. She got to her feet and stood nearer to Keegan.

"You come any closer to my wife," Keegan managed through clenched jaws, "and I'll kill you where you stand."

"You still want her back?" Sarah stamped her foot and repeated, "*You want her back?*" As she stood looking down on Keegan and his dead wife, perplexity grew over the face and slowly turned to a new rage. "You could have me! Me! And you want her?"

Keegan blew more oxygen into Eileen's lungs. He moved his eyes in the direction where Sarah had been standing and she was missing. He immediately looked up and saw her standing over him with a table lamp held high overhead on its downward arch toward his head. Instinctively his left arm went up as the lamp came crashing over it. A shard of ceramic tore through his shirtsleeve and gashed his wrist, slicing tissue and veins.

Sarah's eyes grew wide at the sight of the blood, and she stopped long enough to cry, "Eddie, I'm soo sorrryyy."

The pause was all Keegan needed. He got first to one knee, then to one foot as he reached for Sarah's neck with his bleeding left hand. With his hand clenched firmly around her throat, Keegan drew back with his right fist and let fly for a direct hit on Sarah's jaw. He could hear the snap of her jaw bone and saw a trickle of blood flow from her mouth as she crumpled unconscious to the bedroom floor.

Before Sarah hit the deck, Keegan had retrieved a t-shirt from the chest of drawers and wrapped it tightly around his wrist to slow his own bleeding. Then he knelt beside Eileen and continued to massage her heart and fill her lungs with air.

"Live, Eileen," Keegan called. "Please dear God, let her live!"

He heard a groan from behind and looked over at Sarah. She lay where he left her, unconscious, but experiencing pain. Not enough, he thought. He worked Eileen's chest.

"Rescue squad!" came a shout from the downstairs entrance way. "Where are you?"

"We're upstairs!" Keegan shouted.

He heard the loud clatter and clunking of squad members dragging their equipment up the stairs. The first volunteer entered the bedroom wearing the Adirondack uniform of blue jeans and flannel shirt. He looked at Eileen wearing a blood soaked top, receiving CPR from a man with a blood soaked t-shirt wrapped around his wrist, and a woman with a blood stained neck lying on the floor unconscious.

"Shit," he said, "we're in a hell of a mess here, ain't we?" He snapped on latex gloves and a face mask. He put his hand on Keegan's shoulder and said, "Let me take over, pal."

"The blood's mine," Keegan said as he got out of the way.

The first squad member began to pump Eileen's chest, a second attended her with a hand squeezed respirator. The first called to a third squad member, an extraordinarily fat man, only then reaching the room. "Look after this guy," the first said, "he's bleedin' like a son-of-a-bitch. And check out the other woman. It looks like she's bleeding at the neck."

"She's not bleeding," shouted Keegan. "That's my blood too. I hit her. I think I broke her jaw."

The fat man moved amazingly quickly to Sarah and checked her over. "Just like he said," he called out to the room. He moved back to his first aid supply case, opened it, struggled into latex gloves, and put on a face mask and safety glasses before unwrapping Keegan's wrist and allowing the blood soaked t-shirt to fall to the floor.

"Damn, you're lucky. No arterial damage, but serious vascular damage." He immediately applied pressure with one hand while he yanked gauze pads and adhesive tape and applied them single-handedly with competent expertise.

"How's my wife?" Keegan called. Keegan never took his eyes off Eileen.

They ignored Keegan's question and went about their jobs. The man with the respirator listened for a heartbeat with his stethoscope. "She's back," he said to the first. "Thready. I think we can transport."

The fat man finished taping Keegan's wrist and said to Keegan, "What's with her?" He nodded in Sarah's direction.

"She tried to kill my wife." Keegan said, glancing over at Sarah then returning his stare to Eileen. He added, "Call the Chief. I think she murdered her husband."

Eileen lay unconscious. She was intubated and her breathing, regulated by automatic respirator, was steady, full, and strong. I.V.'s were attempting to flush her system of the acetaminophen overdose she had ingested over the last week

Keegan sat in the vinyl covered excuse for an easy chair in Eileen's intensive care unit in Fort George's community hospital. His head throbbed from the nightstand injury. He wore six stitches in his scalp. His wrist was sutured, bandaged, and held in a sling. It throbbed. The emotional numbness he felt blocked the pain. He prayed as hard as he had ever prayed before.

From what seemed a great distance away, Keegan heard his name being called. He turned his eyes from the stillness of his wife, in the direction of the voice, and saw Eli standing there.

Eli pulled over a folding chair and sat knee to knee with Keegan. "I can't tell you much," he said. "The lab tests aren't complete, but she's in serious shape."

"Will she," Keegan's throat cracked with dryness and he swallowed, trying to lubricate it. "Will she live?"

"I don't know." Eli stared into Keegan's eyes and Keegan could see tears well up in them. Eli shook his head, "I don't know. Maybe not."

Keegan faced Eileen and fought back his own tears. He looked back to Eli and asked, "When will you know?"

"Twenty-four, maybe forty-eight hours."

Keegan nodded.

"I expect you'll want to stay the night?"

"If I can," answered Keegan.

"I'll arrange for a cot," Eli said as he stood up and put the folding chair back up against the wall where he found it. He stopped at Keegan's side and said, "Chief Erichson is in the waiting room. He says he'd like to see you if you're up to it."

Keegan nodded consent and got up to follow Eli out of the ICU and into the waiting room. The Chief rose to greet Keegan and shake his hand. As the two men sat, Eli excused himself and returned to the ICU.

"I won't keep you long, Reverend," said Erichson, "but I need for you to give me a complete statement about what happened. Not now, but later tonight or tomorrow."

"Sure, Chief," Keegan said. "For now, the thumbnail sketch is this: it looks like she was trying to kill Eileen with acetaminophen. And when that didn't work to her satisfaction, Sarah smothered her. That's when I found her and broke her jaw in the struggle to get her off my wife."

"Yeah," Erichson said, "that's pretty much how the rescue squad figured it."

"What's Sarah telling you?" Keegan asked. He expected to hear almost anything.

"Difficult to say, Reverend," the Chief said as he stood to go. "It's kind of hard to make out what she's saying with her jaw wired shut. What she did say was pretty disjointed and crazy. Doc Shapiro gave her a sedative so she wouldn't damage herself more, and she hasn't said anything since." He put his hat on and extended his hand to Keegan, who received it. "I've got Constable Dirkson on her door. Her father's been in visiting with her. When Eli gives the okay, we'll question her more thoroughly until we can sort things out. Call me when you're ready to give me your statement."

Keegan agreed and the Chief left. Keegan returned to his wife's hospital room and prepared to spend the evening and night in prayer.

"Daddy," Sarah whispered, "Jesus will forgive me, won't he?" She lay in her hospital bed. The room light was dimmed. There was a terrible throb in her jaw. She could not open it or move it from side to side. She felt the roughness of wires on the insides of her cheeks. There was a stinging pain in her left forearm where an I.V. delivered its trickle. Her father sat in a chair at her bedside and bent over her in prayer. The glossolalia flowed from his lips. Sarah understood none of the holy speech but drew comfort from listening to the tongues of angels.

"Daddy," Sarah said, "even though I wasn't married any more, Keegan was. We couldn't be together yet." She felt tears roll down her cheeks. Her father did not look up. He prayed his ecstatic prayers. "I couldn't let Keegan divorce Eileen; I didn't want him to burn in hell for me." She

snuffled. "And Jesus forgave the murderer on the cross next to him, didn't he Daddy? Won't Jesus forgive me?"
Her father prayed on.

NOVEMBER 16TH
SUNDAY

Keegan was awakened by the gentle nudging of the morning duty nurse coming on shift. Coming out of the fog of disquieted sleep upon the vinyl not-so-easy chair, he looked hazily at the nurse leaning over him and asked, "How is she?" Grogginess gave way to adrenaline as he sat upright, expecting some bad news.

"There's no change, Reverend O'Connor." The nurse kept her firm hand on his left shoulder, preventing him from jerking it around and possibly injuring himself, and she spoke with a voice barely above a whisper. "I thought you'd like a chance to go home and freshen up while we give Ms. Letterman her meds, change her I.V. and bathe her."

"What time is it?" he asked.

"About seven-thirty."

"Thanks," he said, "I'll do that." As Keegan rolled out of the chair and carefully straightened his arms and legs, stretching out the night's kinks, he wondered to himself why he had not taken advantage of the cot Eli had arranged.

The ambulance ride of the previous afternoon had left him without transportation. He left the hospital and made his way home on foot. The crisp Adirondack air of the gray November morning chilled him and brought him to full alertness by the end of his twenty minute walk.

Keegan climbed the steps to his front porch, put his key into the lock but found the door already unlocked, and his note to Eli still in the door window. He realized that in the rush to the hospital no one thought to lock up the parsonage. He closed the door behind him, tossed his keys on the marble topped table in the entrance way and ran up the stairs for the bedroom.

As he stepped into the bedroom, he was shocked by the undisturbed scene of the struggle. The bed was rumpled, furniture was strewn about, and the broken lamp lay on the floor. His blood stained the bedclothes, the floor, and the corner of the nightstand as well as trailing across the floor to the bureau. He stood in the middle of the floor for a moment shaking his head and feeling a little sick.

He moved to the bed, and with his right hand pulled the bedspread over the rumpled and stained bedclothes so he would not have to look at them. With the side of his shoe he pushed broken lamp shards out of the way so as not to step on them with his bare feet.

Keegan then pulled fresh clothes from his closet and bureau and laid them out on the bed. He eased his left arm out of the sling, stripped down and headed down the hall for the bathroom.

After finishing his shower he returned to the bedroom and began dressing. The feel of fresh clothes seemed reassuring. Nothing like a shower and shave to get a man in sailing trim. Once dressed, he sat on the edge of the bed to tie his shoes.

Near the bedroom door, Keegan heard two loud clicks. He looked towards the sound and saw William Weakley standing in the doorway. Two more loud clicks sounded as Weakley slammed the bolt of a deer rifle forward and locked it home. Weakley held the rifle steady, aimed at Keegan's chest.

"What's going on?" Keegan said. His mind raced, considering ways out. He could either dive for the window and a two story drop, or go through Weakley. Neither seemed likely.

"He took my little girl and led her astray." Weakley stepped into the room by two paces and stood fast. His eyes were wide, and the tone of his voice was that of a sawdust trail preacher at a tent meeting. "He led my innocent little girl into the ways of iniquity and despair. He brought my little girl to the brink of losing her soul to the evil of this world!"

"Who are you talking about, Weakley?" Keegan asked. He hoped that talk might calm Weakley down. Maybe a pastoral train of thought would change his attitude. Weakley took one more step into the room. With Weakley's last step, Keegan began to see a place for his own move. Come on, Weakley, he thought, just a few more steps.

"The Lord Jesus Christ said," preached Weakley, "'But whosoever shall offend one of these little ones which believe in me, it were better for him that a millstone were hanged about his neck, and that he were drowned in the depth of the sea.' Matthew, chapter eighteen, verse six."

"Tell me, Pastor," coaxed Keegan as he tensed every muscle he could command, "have you hung a millstone about someone's neck? Have you exacted some revenge on behalf of the Lord?"

"You understand!" Weakley shouted. His face brightened with delight. "This is wonderful. Then you'll understand why I have to kill you as well." He took one step closer.

"Kill me as well?" Keegan said. He slowly drew his legs in closer to get them under his weight. Keep coming, he hoped. "Have you killed before, Pastor?"

"Eddie offended the faith of my little girl," Weakley preached. "Eddie was leading my little girl away from the path of righteousness and into the ways of hellfire and damnation."

"How did Eddie manage to do this?" Keegan asked. Come on Weakley. A little closer.

"My little girl was considering divorce. I had to save her from that act of damnation."

"So, you killed Eddie?" Keegan thought he was as well positioned to spring as he could be.

"I prayed to God to show me how to place Eddie in his eternal and caring hands, and how to protect my little girl." Weakley squinted at Keegan over the rifle barrel. "And the Lord answered my prayer. He showed me the way."

"What about 'thou shalt not kill'?" Keegan asked.

"Jesus forgave the murderer who hanged with him," Weakley said. He sounded as if her were instructing a dolt. "I'm sure that killer did not have salvation as the motive for his crime." Weakley smiled the smile of the crazed. "Surely Jesus will forgive my little indiscretion."

"Indiscretion?" Keegan said. "You call two murders an indiscretion? You idiot!" Keegan instantly regretted the last.

"God called upon me to vanquish this evil from the earth. He had to be killed." Weakley went grim-faced and his voice lowered as he said, "I thought you understood. But what could a Methodist understand about answering the call of the Lord Almighty? You're little more than a pagan yourself. What could you understand about God calling your name late at night commanding you to do his bidding? Nothing, that's what, nothing!"

"Tell me, Pastor Weakley," Keegan said. He hoped he could regain some calm after his last slip. "How did you manage to do this deed of God? Maybe I can learn from you."

"You'll learn nothing of the ways of God from me," Weakley said with his maniacal grin returning. "You're not capable of learning the ways of

God. But I'll tell you what God had me do. It will give you something to mull over during your eternity in hell."

Keegan tried to put his most attentive face on and concentrated as hard as he could on Weakley's next step.

"I took two of Eddie's reloads with me and my own rifle. It seemed most fitting a killer of souls be done in by his own handiwork. When I entered the house that night I could hear the brass tumbler in the cellar. Strikers were shouting outside. I thought it even more fitting that he be condemned to hell by his own instrument of torment. I knew the noise would cover my footsteps, so I went into the living room and got his own prized rifle and loaded it." As Weakley spoke he lowered the rifle to a more restful position.

"But the presence of the strikers worried me. What if they heard the shot? So, from Eddie's sofa, I took a throw pillow. I went out into the kitchen and got a roll of duct tape I knew Eddie kept in the pantry. I taped the pillow to the muzzle of the rifle. Then I crept down the dimly lit cellar stairs. He never heard a thing. The strikers were shouting outside, the tumbler rattled on, and God allowed me to enter undetected." At this last comment Weakley looked adoringly towards the ceiling.

"A great calm came over me as I stood at the bottom of the stairs and took steady aim for Eddie's head. The gun discharged with an amazing puff of foam rubber." He giggled as he gestured with one hand to demonstrate a puff of debris.

"The pillow fell to the floor," Weakley continued. "Eddie slumped over as if to take a nap. It was remarkably easy. With God's work done, I went to the kitchen, used the hand towel to wipe my prints from the gun, replaced it in the cabinet, retrieved my own and went home to continue to care for Clarence. The devil and whiskey have a hold on Clarence, you know." With the story finished, he shouldered the rifle.

Weakley didn't move and Keegan began to worry he might not come in range for a lunge at the rifle barrel. He had to keep him talking, draw him in somehow.

"Isn't killing another man prohibited by the commandments of the Lord Almighty?" Keegan asked. "How can you square this murder with God?"

"Of course, you fool!" shouted Weakley, "unless, unless the commandment is annulled by the demands of Jesus Christ who said that all laws are summed up by a love of God and a love of neighbor. And Jesus demands that those who would lead the little ones astray, like my little girl, should die. The most loving thing I can do for one who would act contrary to the will of the Lord would be to end their miserable self-destructive lives!"

"But Jesus admonished you," Keegan said, "to tie a millstone around the offender's neck, not use a rifle." He hoped an appeal to Weakley's literal understanding of scripture might be the way to distract him.

"You really are a fool, aren't you?" said Weakley as he took one half step forward and pointed the rifle at Keegan's head. "Or you think I am. I know, and you know, Jesus spoke metaphorically about the millstone."

Oh, fine, thought Keegan, a fundamentalist who sees metaphor when he needs one. "Are you sure that Jesus didn't speak metaphorically about death?" Keegan tried.

"You are the Devil, aren't you?" shouted Weakley, taking a step back and dropping the rifle to his waist, as if in horror and astonishment.

"I'm no devil," Keegan said. His heart sank with Weakley's step back. Keegan decided he needed to shrink the space between them and slowly rose to his feet. With arms spread in a gesture of reception, he added, "I'm a simple pastor like you."

"NOT LIKE ME!" Weakley's jaw locked and his eyes narrowed. "YOU LED MY LITTLE GIRL ASTRAY. FOR THAT YOU HAVE TO DIE." Weakley once again raised the rifle from his waist to his shoulder and placed his cheek on the stock plate.

"What if you're wrong?" Keegan asked. He took a half step forward.

"STAY WHERE YOU ARE!" shouted Weakley.

"What if God doesn't want another killing?" persisted Keegan. "What if God never wanted the first?"

"I'm not wrong," seethed Weakley. "But if I am, and if I burn in hell over Eddie, killing you to save my little girl's soul won't condemn me further." As he sighted with his right eye and squinted his left he added, "I'll give you the privilege of praying for forgiveness before I exact God's retribution upon one who has offended His holy will."

"Since I am in the presence of one of God's avenging angels," Keegan said, attempting one last effort at diverting Weakley's attention, "would the angel pray with me that I might know the forgiveness of God?"

"Jesus said," Weakley responded and smiled at Keegan, "'Behold I sent you forth as sheep in the midst of wolves: be ye therefore wise as serpents,' that's Matthew chapter sixteen, verse ten. You can't trick me. Pray alone if you know how."

"You didn't finish the verse, Pastor," Keegan said. "Go ahead, finish the verse. How does the Lord Jesus finish his sentence?"

Weakley stood silent and became more stony-faced.

"I'll tell you how Jesus finishes," Keegan said, deciding that goading Weakley could do little additional harm, "Jesus said, 'be harmless as doves.' Get it, Weakley? Harmless as doves! And the quote comes from

Matthew chapter ten, verse sixteen, you illiterate pompous ass. If you're going to quote scripture, at least get it right!"

Keegan could see Weakley grip the rifle tighter against his shoulder and begin to pull back on the trigger.

"Prepare to burn in hell," Weakley whispered.

As Keegan prepared to let the muscles of his legs spring in his last ditch effort to pounce on Weakley, a voice in the hall shouted, "FREEZE, WEAKLEY!"

Weakley started to glance over his left shoulder at the voice. Keegan sprung at him, deflecting the barrel of the rifle upward and out with his left forearm. The action tore open stitches and Keegan's wrist began bleeding. Moving towards the surprised Weakley, Keegan turned his back into him, gripped the top of the barrel with his right hand and jabbed his left elbow into Weakley's face. As Weakley went back from the impact, his finger closed around the trigger and the rifle discharged.

Weakley lost his balance and fell to the floor, bleeding from his nose. Chief Erichson was on him in an instant, rolling him over and handcuffing the pastor of the Good News Apostolic Lighthouse.

"Where in hell did you come from?" asked Keegan, standing in the middle of the room holding Weakley's rifle in one hand and bleeding from the other.

"Just down the street," Erichson said, hauling Weakley to his feet. "Dirkson and I have been on you and Weakley all night."

"In that case, what the hell took you so long?"

"Had to be sure," said the Chief. "Until I heard everything he had to say, I wasn't altogether sure it might not have been you that murdered Eddie, and might have been doing your wife in."

"Oh great," said Keegan.

"Come on, Reverend," Erichson said, "I'll get you back to the hospital to have you put back together again, and tell you the rest of the story."

The Chief sat with Keegan in the hospital emergency room explaining the morning's events while the attending physician patched up Keegan.

"So how long had you people been following Weakley?" asked Keegan.

"Only since last night," Erichson said. "But you're another story."

"*I'm* another story?" The physician finished with Keegan and excused himself. Keegan looked at the doctor's handiwork and slipped his arm into a new sling.

"You have to understand, Reverend, you began to look pretty suspicious to me," Erichson said, "so I decided to press some of your buttons to see if I could get you to do something to incriminate yourself. That's when I paid you those visits at your office and led you to believe you were a prime suspect."

"Follow me," Keegan said and slid off the examining table and headed for the ER door. "I'm heading for my wife's room." Erichson followed along. Keegan asked, "Did I respond well to your button pushing?"

"Beautifully," said Erichson. "You started snooping around in places that had not occurred to me. You questioned different people than I questioned. And after you talked to them, I interviewed them."

"I hope that was helpful."

"Very," said Erichson, "It helped me think more in religion terms instead of the mill strike, although Callahan and Brookhough both interested me. I began to think more about that *Burn in Hell* graffiti on the back of the Conger house. It seemed less likely that kind of scrawl would be linked to the strike. The more I stuck with you, the more I figured it was either Weakley who killed the Conger lad, or it was you, making it look like Weakley killed him. After Dirkson reported that he overheard Sarah Conger tell her father that the attempt on Eileen was to enable you and her to get together, we were pretty sure you were our man, and that you'd manipulated the new young widow."

The pair rounded a bend in the corridor and moved out of the emergency area towards the critical care units.

"Dirkson," the Chief continued, "also heard Weakley mutter something about bringing the wrath of God down upon you."

"So that's when you were convinced I was innocent?" Keegan adjusted his sling as they entered the I.C.U. waiting area.

"No," said Erichson. "It just meant Weakley thought you were guilty of something – maybe of killing his son-in-law, or maybe of having an affair with his daughter."

Keegan looked at Erichson and said, "You just didn't want to let go of me, did you?"

"Couldn't, Reverend," Erichson said with a smirk. "I don't like thinking this way, but one suspect is as good as another. And both of mine were clergy. I figured, come hell or high water, I was going to piss God off with an arrest of one of his boys."

"When were you convinced I was innocent?" Keegan sat in one of the waiting room chair.

"I assigned Dirkson to follow Weakley and keep me posted." Erichson sat alongside Keegan and crossed his legs. "Weakley went from the hospital to his house, left immediately with a long bundle and headed directly to your house. According to Dirkson, he waltzed right through the open front door into the dark house and never came out. The next morning you showed up for a shower and a change of clothes. That's when Dirkson and I met up outside your place. There was no doubt something was coming to a head.

Dirkson and I made our way into your place through the front door and stood in the entrance way for a few moments. We heard the usual shower noises and were about to lose interest when we heard voices. We crept up the stairs to listen in, and once we heard everything we thought we needed to convict him and clear you, we moved in. Just in time, I might add."

"Damn near too late, if you ask me," Keegan said and rose to his feet. "Just the same, I'm glad you were there when you were." He extended his hand and Erichson rose to take it. "I'll head in to see Eileen now. Thanks, Chief."

"I hope she pulls through," Erichson said.

Keegan entered Eileen's room. The respirator filled her lungs. The heart monitor indicated an erratic rhythm. A nurse adjusted an I.V. Eli sat in a chair next to her bed.

"Will she make it?" Keegan asked.

"I don't know," responded Eli. His eyes were wet.

NOVEMBER 17TH
MONDAY

After lunch, delivered via one fresh I.V., Eileen was beginning to feel a little better. She had vague remembrances of slipping in and out of consciousness the day before and recalled at least once coming to and experiencing extreme relief at realizing she was alive. Sometime late Sunday she had been extubated.

Keegan sat squirming in the vinyl covered easy chair in the corner of the hospital room while Eli finished examining Eileen.

"Well young lady," Eli said as he put her wrist back on the bed, "you're on your way back to the land of the living. Your color is coming around and your pulse and blood pressure are normal." He picked up the chart from the corner of her bed where he had placed it upon entering and scribbled.

"We're still waiting for the results of this morning's blood work," Eli continued as he put the chart down and folded his arms. "You're not out of the woods. That acetaminophen is serious business; a number of people have died by accidental overdose with that stuff. And then we've got to get back to work on your cancer."

"So, Eli," Eileen said with the best smirk she could manage, "are you trying to cheer me up or what?"

"Sorry Eileen." Eli turned sheepish and unfolded his arms to slip his hands into his pockets. "I guess I'll sum up by saying its all guarded good news for now." He patted her foot through the sheets and added, "I'll leave you two alone and come back when the results are in." He left.

Eileen looked over at Keegan who was rising out of his chair. "Come over here and give me a kiss."

Keegan sat on the edge of her bed, bent over Eileen and they kissed long and hard.

"Well," Eileen said, "I'm still in the dark about what happened. Fill me in."

"Where shall I begin?"

Eileen furrowed her brow in thought then said, "The last thing I remember is feeling faint after I ate some cake and had some chocolate shake that Sarah made."

Keegan took Eileen's hand in his own, settled in on the edge of her bed, and began the story from where he entered the parsonage calling Eileen's name, and ending with the report Chief Erichson had given him.

Eileen squeezed his hand and asked, "Is that the whole story?"

"The long and the short of it," he said. "I'll embellish it next week."

Eileen drew Keegan's hand up to her neck and held out her other I.V. entangled arm.

Keegan responded by wrapping her in his free arm, and they embraced the embrace of lifelong lovers.

"Till death us do part," Keegan whispered.

Eileen pulled back and looked into his eyes and said, "I can be very patient."

Printed in the United States
49146LVS00004B/19-120